Christ...
CARRINGTON'S

Alexandra Brown is the author of the Carrington's series; set in a department store in the pretty seaside town of Mulberry-on-Sea, it follows the life, loves and laughs of sales assistant, Georgie Hart.

Alexandra is the former City Girl columnist for *The London Paper* and has written for a range of publications including *YOU Magazine*, *Cosmopolitan* and *Elle*. When she isn't writing, Alexandra likes to indulge her online shopping addiction while watching trashy TV and tweeting way too much. She lives near Brighton, on the South Coast of England, with her husband, daughter and a very shiny black Labrador puppy.

Follow Alexandra on Twitter: @alexbrownbooks

Also by Alexandra Brown

Cupcakes at Carrington's

Ebook-only novella

Me and Mr Carrington

Christmas at
CARRINGTON'S
Alexandra Brown

HARPER

Harper
An imprint of HarperCollins*Publishers*
77–85 Fulham Palace Road,
Hammersmith, London W6 8JB

www.harpercollins.co.uk

A Paperback Original 2013
1

A catalogue record for this book
is available from the British Library

ISBN: 978-0-00-748825-4

Set in Brika by FMG using Atomik ePublisher from Easypress

Printed and bound in Great Britain by
Clays Ltd, St Ives plc

MIX
Paper from
responsible sources

FSC C007454

FSC™ is a non-profit international organisation established to promote
the responsible management of the world's forests. Products carrying the
FSC label are independently certified to assure consumers that they come
from forests that are managed to meet the social, economic and
ecological needs of present and future generations,
and other controlled sources.

Find out more about HarperCollins and the environment at
www.harpercollins.co.uk/green

Acknowledgements

Firstly, and most importantly, a big, massive, HUGE thank you to everyone who read *Cupcakes At Carrington's*, and has taken the time to contact me with kind comments or to put a lovely review on Amazon. It means the world to me. It spurs me on and makes it all worthwhile.

Kate Bradley for keeping me calm, making me laugh and for being everything I hoped for in an editor. Kimberley, Penny, Claire, Jaime, Liz, Martha and all at HarperCollins for their support, talent and expertise.

My agent, Tim Bates, for telling me what's normal and for giving me back my writing mojo.

Olly Bates, for kindly sharing her delicious chocolate-orange cupcake recipe. Truly scrumptious x

Kimberley Chambers, Elizabeth Haynes, Belinda Jones and Sasha Wagstaff – your generosity is so very much appreciated.

Caroline Smailes for being a brilliant writing buddy; your patience astounds me and the Poundland chat STILL won't leave me alone. Not that I'm bothered, of course x

Lisa Hilton for testing the recipes and spurring me on from the start.

Jadzia Kopiel, for everything; you're the wisest woman I know.

My lovely, supportive father-in-law, Dr Brown, for sharing the memories of his family's department store, Brown's in Newtonards. I hope I've captured a whiff of the memory.

Yeeman To, for being a fantastic sales assistant and telling me all about it; your generosity is very much appreciated and any exaggerations or fabrications are totally down to me. Thalia Harding for telling me about Harrods.

Denyse King, for generously sharing some of her midwifery expertise.

QT for showing me love and light every day and for patting my arm when the going gets tough, even if you are convinced that mummies don't write books ... only bunny rabbits do! I love you sweetheart with all my heart xoxoxo. Oh gawd, I'm going to cry. AGAIN.

My husband Paul, aka Cheeks, for holding the fort and bringing me cake and cups of tea ... you are my happy-ever-after.

And you, lovely reader, for taking the time to read this book, I really hope you enjoy it, and I'd love to chat if you do, so please find me via Twitter @alexbrownbooks, Facebook.com/alexandrabrownauthor or at my pretty new website www.alexandrabrown.co.uk

For Dusty and Monty,
together again

Prologue

I never used to believe in lust at first sight. You know, the kind where your tummy tingles and your heart soars so high it feels as if it might just burst right out of your chest, cartoon style, and do a deliriously euphoric freeform dance around the room? But I certainly do now. Oh yes, because that's exactly how I felt the very first time I clapped eyes on Tom. And he's going to be here, right outside the door to my flat in approximately five minutes. I literally *can not wait*. I truly think he might be the one. I hope so. Now, that really would be pretty special indeed.

The doorbell buzzes, sending my pulse into overdrive. He's here. And on time – previous boyfriends could certainly learn a thing or two about timekeeping from him. I practically tear down the hallway to press the intercom before pausing to inhale hard through my nose and exhale even harder, keen to create a modicum of breeziness.

'Hello,' I breathe, in what I hope is a sophisticated, nonchalant-sounding voice, à la Angelina Jolie, or someone equally poised. I can't imagine she ever legged it down her hallway gushing to let Brad in. Oh no no no.

1

'It's me,' Tom says. *Mmm, familiar. And I like it.* For a nanosecond I contemplate asking 'Who?', to create an airy, elusive aura, but quickly decide against it. It's not my style to play games, even if the relationship is brand new and we're both still learning how to 'be' with each other. Besides, I don't want him thinking I'm some kind of a milly with a stack of men on the go.

'Hi Tom.' I glance at the screen and smile on seeing him attempt to smooth his tangle of thick dark curls. With his velvety brown eyes and year-round Mediterranean real tan, he's utterly delicious and, to be honest, I never in my wildest dreams thought I stood a chance. He has the kind of looks and background that could bag him a supermodel, but without any trace of arrogance or sense of entitlement that the beautiful people sometimes have. And occasionally I have to pinch myself ... that he wants me, ordinary Georgie Hart from Mulberry-On-Sea, a size 14 on a good day, with a brunette bob that often does a spectacular impression of a pair of floppy spaniel ears, especially if I don't use my giant sleep-in Velcro rollers for a bit of extra bouf.

'Georgie, can you come downstairs please?'

'Sure,' I reply, wondering what he's up to as I reach for my coat. We had planned to snuggle up and watch a film. I have popcorn and Häagen-Dazs.

'Change of plan. It's a surprise. Quick, you must come down right now.' His voice is full of boyish excitement and I love this side of him – the stark contrast to his usual

2

serious, business-like demeanour at work. Tom works at Carrington's too, the department store where I run the Women's Accessories section. In fact, he owns the store; he's the managing director, the majority shareholder, so we have to be discreet. Not that the other staff mind – quite the opposite, in fact, they all really like him – but still, nobody wants to see the boss indulging in a PDA in the workplace. I'm sure it's not the done thing for people in his position. An 'emerging captain of industry', as one *FT* reporter recently crowned him.

After grabbing my key and pulling the door closed behind me, I bomb down the stairs and arrive in the little foyer area. Tom is leaning casually against the row of mailboxes with an extremely cheeky-looking smile on his beautiful face. *Mm-mmm, dreamy.* He'd be perfect starring in one of those rom-com films. I tiptoe up to give him a kiss and he circles my waist before pulling me in close to his left hip and treating me to a burst of his delicious chocolatey scent. I'm just about to press my tingling body against his when he takes a quick step backwards.

'Oops, careful. Don't want to squash this little dude.' He winks.

'Little dude?' I crease my forehead.

'That's right. Mr Cheeks.' Tom gives me one of his 'butter-wouldn't-melt' looks.

'Mr Cheeks?' I repeat, my eyes flicking towards Tom's jacket. And, oh my God. He pulls the zip down and a tiny black fluffy head pops out.

'Georgie, meet Mr Cheeks, named on account of him being very cheeky.'

'A kitten! You have a kitten.' Wow. How cute is that? Not only is he an incredibly sexy man with a fantastic sense of humour, but he loves animals too ... he's practically perfect. 'How come you never said?' I ask, giving Mr Cheeks a stroke. 'And why have you brought him with you?'

'Err, well, he's not actually my kitten.' Tom gives me a sheepish look.

'Who does he belong to, then?'

'You?' His mouth twitches into a smile as he lifts one eyebrow.

'Don't be silly. You can't buy me a kitten,' I say, incredulously. I've never had a pet of my own before.

'Of course I can. I can do whatever I like,' he jokes, treating me to a huge grin. 'Isn't he sweet?' And he lifts Mr Cheeks out of his jacket and snuggles him in the crook of his elbow.

'Aw, poor thing, he's trembling all over.'

'And is it any wonder?' Sighing, Tom shakes his head. He looks really concerned.

'What do you mean?'

'Come on, let's go upstairs and I'll tell you all about it.'

It turns out that Mr Cheeks is a stray. He arrived at Tom's back door in the middle of the night, meowing and whimpering, trembling all over and covered in mud. Tom took him in and hand-fed him cooked chopped chicken before bathing him and letting him sleep on his bed.

'So, you'll let Mr Cheeks stay then?' We're sitting side-by-side on my sofa with the kitten still snuggled in the crook of Tom's elbow. Mr Cheeks is really timid and seems to have latched on to Tom like a security blanket. Tom turns to me and tenderly pushes a stray chunk of hair out of my eyes, making my face tingle.

'*Weell* ... he is too cute for words.' I hesitate momentarily. 'But I can't, really I can't. He'll be here on his own all day while I'm at work.'

'I'm sure he'll get used to it ... I bet he'll be out swaggering around the neighbourhood, or whatever it is cats do all day, in no time. Or I'd be happy to pay for a cat-sitter if he starts to pine through loneliness,' Tom suggests, entwining his fingers around mine.

'Don't be daft. Why don't you keep him yourself? He seems to have really taken to you ... '

'I'd love to, but my house just isn't practical, not with my canvases and paint everywhere, and he's already clawed through the Venice waterway.'

'Ooops,' I say, remembering the exquisite picture. Tom had just started painting it the first time I went to his house, and it's truly magnificent. He has a real gift, even if he does nonchalantly dismiss it as '*Just something I do to relax.*'

'And you know how often I'm away from home, travelling to meet suppliers and up to board meetings in

London. It really wouldn't be fair. Anyway, I think he'd much sooner snuggle up to you of an evening – just like me.' Tom grins as he puts an arm around my shoulders and gently pulls me in close before kissing the bridge of my nose.

'Stop it,' I tease, pressing my palm against his firm chest. 'I know what you're doing.'

'*Whaaaat?*' Tom replies, trying to sound and look all innocent. 'It's the truth, isn't it Mr Cheeks?' And he takes the kitten's little paws and places them on my arm. 'Aw, look at his little face. Those soulful green eyes. And he has nobody. He's just an orphan. And, ahh, *looooook* … ' Tom pauses as the kitten leans his tiny chin on my arm. 'See, he absolutely adores you already,' Tom beams, after giving Mr Cheeks a quick proud-dad glance for his perfect timing.

'No he doesn't,' I smile. 'He adores you.'

'Hmm, I'm not so sure. Hang on a minute.' Tom lifts the kitten up to his ear and pretends to listen to him talking. 'What's that, little fella?' he asks Mr Cheeks before turning back to face me. 'He says I should kiss you and that will make you take him in.'

'Oh did he?' I try not to laugh.

'Yep.' Tom places Mr Cheeks down on the rug before lifting my chin and pushing me back on the sofa. But he doesn't kiss me. Instead, he lifts my hands up over my head, secures them under a cushion and then tickles me all over until I can bear it no longer.

'*Stooooop*. Please,' I gasp, now desperate to feel his lips on mine. Having his face in such close proximity is divine, but such a massive tease, especially when I can't move to touch him.

Eventually, I manage to wriggle my arms out from under the cushion and slip them around Tom's back instead.

'So you'll let him live with you then?' Tom props himself up on one elbow so he's lying next to me now, and does puppy-dog eyes. 'I'll cover all his expenses. Vet bills, vaccines, food, etc.,' he pleads, and I can't help thinking how incredible he is. Kind, funny, and he seems to really care about this stray kitten — which, let's face it, he could have just ignored, as I'm sure lots of men would have done after being woken up in the middle of the night. But not Tom, he was giving the scrawny, bedraggled cat a bath at 4 a.m.! That's proper tenderness right there ...

'OK, on one condition.' I shake my head in surrender.

'Anything. I couldn't bear to leave him at an animal shelter. Not now. Not after everything he's been through, and he's already used to a certain living standard too. It would be too cruel for words. We could share him. And then at least I'd know he was safe when I'm away on business.' Tom tickles me again.

'OK. Don't milk it,' I say, trying to catch my breath as I push his hand away.

'Ha! Nice pun. I like it.' I give him a blank look. 'Cat.

Milk lovers.' He winks. 'Oh never mind,' he adds, smiling cheekily. 'So, what's the condition?'

'That you do everything Mr Cheeks tells you to,' I say, trying to keep a serious face.

'Hmmm, OK,' Tom replies slowly and suggestively, circling his index finger over the back of my hand. I lean towards Mr Cheeks, pretending to listen to him speak.

'He says the first thing you must do is kiss me.' And Tom does. My tummy flips over and over as I roll onto my side and melt into his arms, and I honestly don't think I've ever felt this happy. Not ever. And now we have a kitten in common. A bona fide joint responsibility, and everyone knows what that means ... I wonder if it's too soon to say the L word?

1

Eight shopping weeks until Christmas

It's Monday evening in Mulberry-On-Sea and, by the size of Sam's smile, it's obvious she has some exciting news to share. I close the front door to my flat behind her and she practically skips on into the shoebox-sized lounge, closely followed by a gust of crisp, wintery-cold air. Taking her swingy faux-fur cape, I bundle it onto a radiator to keep warm.

'It's blooming perishing out there.' Sam whips off her gloves and rubs her hands together before pulling an exaggerated freezing face. 'And with only fifty-four days until Christmas Day – well, I bet it snows. Just imagine, a proper, gloriously glistening white Christmas, now wouldn't that be magical?'

'Sure would,' I say, handing her the latest edition of *I Heart TV* magazine. Sam loves all those soaps and reality shows. Me too. And there's a special sneak preview feature inside, of what's on over Christmas. I was perusing the wine aisle in Tesco when she texted me to get her a copy.

'Thanks Georgie.' She grins and takes the magazine.

'It'll be like our very own giant snow globe. We could even go ice-skating. Mandy, who works at the town hall, came in the other day for a chocolate orange cupcake with banoffee coffee and said they're building a rink in the market square in the centre of town. Apparently there's going to be real reindeers and stalls selling hot chocolate with huge dollops of squirty cream dusted with cinnamon and mini-marshmallows, and, well, she didn't actually go into that much detail, but you know what I mean ... they're bound to, aren't they? And roasted chestnuts and all those handcrafted Christmassy gifts that have no use *what-so-ever*, but we still love them anyway.' She pauses to catch her breath, her natural blonde corkscrew curls bouncing around her shoulders. 'In fact, I'm going to see about getting a stall. I could sell mugs of steaming mulled wine and sticky sausage sandwiches, and what about slabs of fruity Christmas cake stacked high with velvety melt-in-the-mouth marzipan icing? Mm-mmm. Yes, everyone loves cake!'

Sam owns Cupcakes At Carrington's, the café concession on the fifth floor of Carrington's department store, and is a real foodie. She's also privy to all kinds of tantalising gossip gleaned from her loyal customers, office workers from the firms around the market square in the centre of town, staff from the hotels down along the seafront, and just about everyone who lives or works within a ten-mile radius. When Felicity Ashbeck-Smyth, one of Carrington's regular customers and owner of

Mulberry-On-Sea's very own temple of holistic enlight-enment, was caught with a cannabis plant in her yoga studio, Sam was the first to know. And Sam's café really is the best place in Mulberry if you fancy a legendary afternoon tea. Cupcakes and scones piled high with strawberry jam and clotted cream mingled with the cutest little artisan bread rolls crammed with locally sourced ham and delicious homemade chutney. You just can't beat it after a hard day's shopping at Carrington's, *the store with more*, as our strapline says.

'Never mind the squirty cream. I want to hear your news.' I steer her towards the sofa before flopping down on a beanbag nearby.

'Ohmigod. I can't believe I've been here for a whole five minutes and still not told you, I'm practically bursting. I found out last night, but wanted to say face to face. Georgie, you will die when I tell you.' Sam leans over to clutch my arm.

'Come on then.' I nod, encouragingly.

'OK, after three, because you know I've fantasised about this moment for so long that I'm not even sure I can actually say the words out loud, just in case I'm dreaming.

'For crying out loud. Will you please tell me?' I laugh, now absolutely desperate to hear her news.

'Right, deep breath. One two three ... I'm pregnant!' she screams, clapping her hands together up under her chin. Pure bliss radiates around her like an aura as I take in the news.

'Oh Sam, that's fantastic, I'm so happy for you. Come here.' After hauling myself out of the beanbag, I reach across to give her an enormous hug. Sam has wanted to be part of a big family for as long as I've known her, and that must be fifteen years, at least. We used to go to the same boarding school, before I got kicked out after Dad gambled away everything we had. He sold secrets from the trade floor of the bank where he worked and ended up in prison for five and a half years, but that's a whole other story.

Sam and I shared a bedroom, and she'd lie awake at night wondering about her mum, Christy, an interior designer who ran off to LA with a famous rock star client when Sam was only five years old. She was devastated, and even though Sam hasn't mentioned her for years now, I think she still struggles to understand why Christy left, but then who can blame her? Christy literally did a moonlight flit. There at bedtime and gone by breakfast.

'Congratulations! And to Nathan too, I bet he's delighted,' I say, making a mental note to bomb up to Childrenswear on the fourth floor, first thing tomorrow morning when I get into work. Poppy, the sales assistant up there, said they had a delivery last week of the cutest little bunny romper suits she'd ever seen. They even have big floppy ears on the hood and a detachable fluffy rabbit tail for the bottom. I'll get the pink and blue, to cover both eventualities. But what if Sam goes gender-neutral like Belinda? She's another regular customer and her son and daughter are always dressed in identical green or yellow smock shirts with baggy knee-length shorts – a stand against commercial gender stereotyping, apparently. Hmmm, maybe I should get the lemon romper suit too, just in case.

'Georgie, you know Nathan cried. Big tumbling man tears, he's so happy,' Sam says.

'Of course he is, he adores you, and now you're going to be a proper gorgeous little family. It's the best news ever. Can I tell Dad?' I ask, knowing how fond she is of him. Sam's wonderful dad, Alfie Palmer, the charismatic and incredibly wealthy owner of Palmer Estates, one of the biggest estate agencies in the country, died earlier this year, leaving his millions to Sam; it meant no expense was spared on their extremely emotional wedding on a picturesque hillside overlooking Lake Como. But it wasn't the same as Alfie actually being there, so my dad stepped in to do the honours and I felt so proud of him. Nathan's parents live in Italy, so it was the perfect location for them to marry in before travelling around Europe for the summer, followed by a magical second honeymoon in New York and Hawaii last month.

'Of course you can. Although it's probably best to wait a bit. It's very early days.'

'So when is the baby due?'

'I'm not entirely sure. In about eight months' time?' she laughs, making big wide eyes and waving her hands in the air.

'Aw, so he or she could be a honeymoon baby then.' I quickly count the weeks off in my head.

'Sure could be. And ohmigod, Georgie, you've just given me a brainwave.'

'I have?' I ask cautiously. You never know with Sam and her madcap ideas sometimes.

'Of course, if it's a girl we can call her Honey ... *sooo* romantic.' I let out a little sigh of relief, pleased that Manhattan or Honolulu aren't in the running as suitable baby monikers. 'Or, no wait. Hold on!' Sam clutches my arm as she thinks for a second before announcing, '*Honey Moon Taylor!* How perfect is that?' she beams, stretching her hand up and wide in a semi-circle above her head, as if visualising the words emblazoned in flashing lights across a billboard. My mind boggles. Sam is a real queen of hearts, a matchmaker, a true romantic, but I've never seen her like this before, so animated with baby love. And we've never really talked about having babies before, I'm not that interested, to be honest, unlike her.

'Very,' I say, secretly wondering if Nathan would go for it. He's a maritime lawyer, loaded and solid; he strikes me as a more traditional-name-type guy. 'I'm absolutely made up for you both and this calls for a proper celebration. Dinner and fizz somewhere posh. Orange juice for you obvs.' I laugh.

'I can't tell you how happy that makes me feel.' Sam beams. 'No more Jägerbombs for me,' she shrugs. 'We could try out that new restaurant down by the marina, the swanky one that's opened up to cater for the visiting glamouratti arriving on their yachts.'

'Good idea, but in the meantime these will have to do.' I pull open a box of mince pies and offer them to her. Sam takes three. I give her a look.

'*Whaat?*'

'I didn't say a word,' I smile as she crams one of the pies into her mouth.

'One for me and one for the baby,' she explains, in between bites.

'And that one?' I point to the pie still clutched in her left hand.

'Could be twins.' Sam winks and collapses back into the sofa. 'Nathan's dad is a twin and you know what they say about twins running in families. God, I'd actually *love* to have twins. Double sweetness.'

Laughing and shaking my head, I flick the television on and help myself to another mince pie.

'Sooo, talking of romance, how are things going with Tom?' Sam makes big eyes and gives me a hopeful grin.

'*Weell* ... ' I hesitate, unsure if I'm ready to share the exquisite details of his practically perfect taut chest, or his delicious chocolatey scent. Or the way he tilts his head to one side and smiles in an endearingly attentive way when I talk, or the way my thighs tingle when he gives me a cheeky surreptitious wink from across the shop floor.

'Oooh, carry on. No need to be coy,' Sam says, giving

me a gentle nudge in the ribs with her foot. 'How was your date last night?'

'Oh Sam, it was perfect as always. He's so funny. And such a gentleman. Turned up with treats for Mr Cheeks and a little box of Belgian truffles for me. We went out for tapas and chatted all evening, taking a romantic stroll along the moonlit beach – his idea, and he even carried my heels after I changed into flats to make it over the pebbles before we cuddled up by the pier, then back here an—'

'Cor! Tell me more.'

'We talked. Just work stuff, you know, his plans for the store, how he wants to rekindle the glory from its heyday, make Carrington's magnificent again, maybe open more shops in other locations, that kind of thing,' I say, keeping the rest to myself. How worried he is about pulling it off while trying to ignore the whispers and speculation in the business world over his acumen. He's only twenty-nine, two years older than me. And Sam is my best friend, we usually tell each other everything. And Tom didn't say any of this was a secret, but still, I guess he assumed he doesn't need to. Anyway, I'm flattered that he trusts me, and I don't want to do anything to break his trust.

'Hmmm, is that all? But I want to hear about the sex. I know he's been away for work, but your long distance flirtation has been going on for long enough now. You've had Mr Cheeks for well over a month and, like I said before, a shared pet is *huge*. Practically living together. Tell me you at least had a snog.' Sam eyes me eagerly.

'Of course,' I grin, relishing the exquisite memory of his lips firm on mine and his fingers entwined in my hair as he pulled open my blouse, pushed up my skirt and swung me across the kitchen table. It was amazing. Like something out of a film, and I feel breathless just thinking about it.

'Did you get naked?'

'Mmmm.' I smile. Last night was our first time, well ... first, second and third times, to be fair. A glorious hat-trick medley of kitchen table, up against the wall in my hall, followed by an incredible bedroom finale, each time more thrilling than the last. Then we stayed up nearly all night, chatting and laughing together, swapping cringeworthy stories from our respective teenage years with a bit of truth or dare thrown in. But I'm not ready to share the details with Sam. I want to savour the memory to myself for just a little longer. I fantasised about sleeping with Tom from the very moment I clapped eyes on him, when he turned up in the staff canteen on his first day at work. Of course, I didn't know he was actually Tom Carrington then; he went undercover, pretended he was just another sales assistant. All part of his plan to assess the store from the ground floor as it were, before buying it from his aunt Camille, whose grandfather was the original Mr Harry Carrington, aka Dirty Harry, on account of his philandering ways with the showgirls from the old music hall on Lovelace Road. Tom has assured me, though, that Dirty Harry's antics are not a genetic familial trait, which is a big relief.

'Skin on skin?' Sam probes.

'Stop it,' I laugh.

'Did he stay the night?'

'No. Well, yes, kind of, but he had to leave in the early hours, said he had a Skype meeting first thing with a foreign supplier and needed some much overdue sleep.'

'So how many times have you actually seen him now?'

'Well, we've had three or four proper dates, but with him away so much, up to London for meetings or overseas sourcing new stock lines, you know how keen he is to be really hands-on in the business, we haven't had that many opportunities to see as much of each other as we'd like.'

'*Sooo!* Georgie, these days you can have sex on a first date if you want to. That's what the suffragettes did for us. They gave us that choice. If you want sex then have it. I do,' Sam says, winking before making a serious face, and I contemplate telling her everything. 'And let's face it, Tom is not only extremely charming, funny, kind to animals,' she pauses to glance at Mr Cheeks who is ensconced on a cushion purring contently, 'he's F-I-T. Grab hold of him with both hands ... one on each—' If only she knew.

'Bum cheek,' we yell in unison before cracking up. 'Yes, yes I know. You don't have to remind me,' I wheeze, the memory of his beautifully firm bottom beneath his tight white Calvin's making my cheeks flush.

Settling down, I flick on the TV and search through the channels.

'Stop! Go back a bit,' Sam yells, kicking her shoes off and tucking her feet up under her legs. I press the remote control and swig a mouthful of wine before polishing off the rest of a mince pie. I think about retrieving another box from the freezer. Tesco are flogging them as part of a special run-up to Christmas promotion – buy one, get two free. I have eighteen boxes. 'There, that's it. Let's watch this.'

'What is it?'

'Ahh, you know, you must have seen it before. It's that new series – undercover programme with what's-her-name.' I give her a blank look. 'Kelly Cooper. She's totally bonkers and sorts out flagging companies and stuff with her madcap, brilliantly unorthodox ideas. It's on every week until Christmas.'

'Oh right,' I say, helping myself to the last mince pie. The adverts finish and an older woman with wild orange Medusa curls and funky green geek glasses is talking directly to the camera in a stage-whisper voice, and she looks just like Ronald McDonald. She's wearing a swirly patterned Westwood playsuit and a curly plastic earpiece, and keeps glancing at a computer surveillance screen.

'Oooh, here she goes!' Sam is suddenly glued to the screen. I neck another mouthful of wine and start flicking through the *I Heart TV* mag, wondering if it's still too early to set up my Christmas Sky+ viewing schedule.

'What's she doing?' I ask, glancing up as the camera pans to a younger woman in a car park pulling on a big floppy hat and shades.

'She's getting ready to go to wherever they're filming. It's always a secret until they arrive inside, makes it more thrilling and authentic. Last season's show was called *Kelly Cooper Come Onboard* and it was on an Italian cruise ship stuffed full of lush sailors. Swoon.' Sam makes dreamy eyes.

'Cor! I like the sound of that.'

'It was amazing. I've got the whole series in box set. I'll lend it to you. Anyway, first off she'll be seeing if the business is up to scratch. It never is. That's the whole point of the show. And then she helps them get their act together. Come up with new ideas to increase revenue, that kind of thing. Oh God, I love this programme.' Sam is practically hyperventilating now. 'That's Zara, her glamorous assistant. She's actually her daughter in real life,' she adds, all matter-of-factly.

'But it is real life,' I say, feeling confused and wondering how I completely managed to miss watching this programme before now. I'm usually right there when it comes to a decent reality show.

'Hmmm, guess so ... anyway, she's the one who goes undercover, hence the hat and shades, Kelly is way too vibrant and recognisable.' *That's one way of putting it*. I resist the urge to smirk while Sam does the whole fan-girl thing. 'And that guy is the cameraman, he's there to capture Zara's experiences, with a secret hidden camera, obviously. Don't want to alert the staff, so they put on an act; it would ruin everything if they were on best behaviour. That's just boring. And don't be fooled by Kelly – she may appear all jolly and fun at first, but underneath she's ruthless, a total ballbuster when it comes to promoting her TV shows and whipping businesses into shape. She really tells it like it is and doesn't take any prisoners. In her last series, she made them sack five people.'

'What for?' I ask, instantly feeling sorry for the ones that lost their jobs.

'I'm not sure, just read something about it in one of those celebrity gossip magazines. Sniggering when she was talking, most likely. Wouldn't surprise me. That's what she's like,' Sam says.

My mobile rings and, on seeing it's Eddie, my other best friend and Tom's personal assistant (well, boy assistant or BA for short), I press to answer.

'Get your tellybox on *right now!*' he shrieks, totally bypassing the introductions bit and almost perforating my eardrum in the process.

'OK, calm down, it's already on. Where's the drama?'

'Dollface. You will not believe this. Gird your ladyballs. S-C-R-E-A-M.'

'What are you going on about? Eddie, have you been at the booze cabinet?' I laugh.

'Oh darling, *purlease* with the vulgarity ... now is not the time to make me out to be some kind of lush. Now, will you just shut up and watch.'

Doing as I'm told, I stare at the screen. And freeze – motionless like the gold statue that stands on a box outside Mulberry-On-Sea station. I'd know that cherry-wood panelling anywhere.

I can hear my own blood pumping. The camera zooms to a woman browsing through the Women's Accessories department, and I know I'm not mistaken. Sam flings herself upright but doesn't utter a word. She knows it too. It's Carrington's. *My Carrington's!*

It's the actual department store where I work and I feel clammy with fear. I want to throw up. A rivulet of sweat snakes a path all the way down my back. Sam jumps up. I toss the magazine down on the sofa and Sam clutches my free hand. We stand together in silence. Our jaws hang open as Kelly's secret camera, which must be secreted inside Zara's hat, glides around the gloriously decadent Art Deco store before coming to a halt up near the key winter merchandise. And right next to the very display podium that I set up a few weeks ago.

Annie, one of the sales assistants who works with me, comes into view. She's lounging nonchalantly behind the counter with her back to the camera and *oh my God* ... she's texting on her mobile, totally oblivious to the woman who is now swinging a gorgeous, caramel-coloured, Billy-the-goatskin or whatever, £900 Anya

Hindmarch tote on her shoulder while admiring the view in the long mirror. The very mirror I had installed specifically to entice customers to try on the bags. Because every decent sales assistant knows: *those who try it, buy it*.

Zara glances in Annie's direction, and then raises a perfectly groomed HD eyebrow at the camera guy, as if deliberately drawing the viewer's attention to the fact that she's being ignored. Now the camera is panning towards the window display and *oh my actual God*. I want to die! Right now, in my shoebox lounge with a lump of partially chewed mince pie trapped inside my gullet. My arse is only gyrating around to that Beyoncé tune, 'Single Ladies'. I'm even wagging my left hand in the air and pointing to my ring finger. And I swear they've put a wide angle on the shot. I know my bum is big, but it ain't *that* flipping big.

'Boom boom, peng ting! Yo go *girlfrieeend* ... get jiggy with it and all that. You are magnificent,' Eddie bellows, like he's some sort of badass gangsta boy, and I think I might actually faint. With his voice shrieking in my ear and my wiggling bottom on the screen it's like a total sensory overload. And my phone hand seems to have gripped itself into a spasm, so now I have the gnarled fist of an ancient old husk of a woman too, which will probably wither from inactivity and render me a cripple by the age of twenty-eight. *Grreat*. Big bum and club fist – not an attractive look. What on earth was I thinking?

I'm usually so efficient at approaching customers, we

both are. Annie and I always wait a few seconds, nobody wants to be pounced on the very minute they show an interest in the merch. OK, so we might send the odd text message when the shop floor is quiet, that's why we keep our mobiles on silent in our pockets – we're not supposed to, but everyone does. But we never ignore the customers. No, not ever!

'This is so fucking *ma-jor*. You're going to be a dramality star.' Eddie sounds like he's about to holler himself into a hernia, he's that elated for me.

'A *whaat?*' I shout, fear and humiliation making my voice sound shrill.

'You know … *dramality*. Real but made up. You're going to be famous. You are going to be a celebrity and, let's face it, that's what everyone wants to be these days,' he sniffs, as if he's the authority on popular culture all of a sudden. 'You're going to be on that jungle programme, baring your teeth like a baboon when your cheeks peel back to your ears as you're dropped from a helicopter into the Australian bush. You're going to have your wardrobe critiqued in *Now* magazine. You're going to win a BAFTA. Oh darling, I always knew you were a true star.' He pauses momentarily and actually sounds genuinely emotional. 'You're going to feature in the *Daily Mail* sidebar of shame. You're going to make a mint from doing your own fitness DVD. You're going to have your own fake tan product range. *Sweet Jesus* … you might even get your own TV show!' Eddie pauses to suck in a massive gasp of air before he's off again. 'I wonder if I'll get to be in the show too. You must ask that delicious man of yours. In fact, call him. *Right now!* Tell him how much I adore Kelly. Been a fan for years, darling. Oh hang on angel.' There's a muffled silence for a second, and then I hear Eddie shouting out to his boyfriend, Ciaran. 'Is my best suit back from the dry cleaners?' More silence follows. '*Whaat?* Never mind watching *Top Gear* on your iPad mini. Check it! Check the wardrobe right now. I need the suit for work tomorrow. It's vital.' Eddie huffs. 'Honestly, that boy has no sense of urgency. This is my moment. And I'm going to need representation. A manager! I'm going to call that blonde woman. Claire off the telly. That's right. The one who represents Pete.'

'Pete?' I mutter, racking my brains. I've never heard Eddie mention having a famous friend called Pete.

'Yes, Pete! As in *Peter Andre?*' Eddie says in a stagey voice, like he's his best friend forever and I'm the only person on the whole planet who doesn't know it.

'Don't you think you're being a bit hasty?' I venture, having already decided I'm having no part of this. And how come Tom never mentioned it? I'm going to call him ... but not to get him to ask Kelly to include Eddie. No. To tell him that he's bang out of order and it's probably illegal anyway. They can't just rock up at Carrington's and start randomly filming Annie and me. What about our privacy? It's stalking! That's what it is. And what about our human rights? I'll phone up that court in The Hague; they're bound to know if I have the right to go to work without worrying about my backside being plastered across the TV screen of every blooming home in the country. The whole world, in fact! If you count all those ex-pat satellite viewers in places like the Costa del Sol. And not forgetting hotels and laptops. These days you can be anywhere and still get your favourite TV channels. Oh God.

Now the initial shock is starting to wear off, I'm devastated. And really hurt if I'm totally honest. I feel like a fool. A fool for thinking that Tom trusted me. Obviously not enough to share this monumental revelation, and it can't have happened overnight. He must have been 'in talks', as he likes to say, with the TV channel for absolutely ages, but he didn't even think to utter a word about it. And like a fool I fell for his smouldering looks and fun-loving attitude. And I took in Mr Cheeks for him. I even read up on Renaissance art just so I could appear cultured and educated, show an interest in his passion for painting. It just goes to show that you can't trust anyone these days. And those big hardback arty books don't come cheap either.

I glance back at the screen in time to hear Kelly talking directly into the camera.

'Seems these shop girls are more interested in having a good time than serving *you*.' And to emphasise her point, she sticks her index finger out, just like Lord Kitchener in that wartime poster. All she needs is the leather queen moustache.

'*Awks!*' Eddie sniggers like a smartarse, making me wish I could reach inside the phone to slap him.

'Stop it.'

'Oh, I'm sorry, sweetcheeks, really I am. Ignore her. It's probably all for the cameras. You know how these TV personalities like to mix things up a bit. Honestly, it's not that bad. Quite exciting, in fact ... just think, you're going to be an actual star – nothing less than you deserve, of course,' he states. 'The camera obviously loves you, petal, and one day you'll look back and laugh too. Promise. It's just the shock of the surprise, that's all. I'm your best friend, and as such it's my job to tell you if you look ridic ... but you don't, you honestly don't. Quite the opposite. Sassy and magnificent.' I ignore him.

'But how dare she?'

Something isn't right, because we never neglect customers. I don't understand how they've managed to make it look as though we do. Sam squeezes my free hand tightly and gives me a reassuring but tentative grin. 'And who says, "shop girls" anyway, these days? Talk about old-fashioned!'

'Don't worry, lover, I bet you know much more than she does about retail sales. Just focus on the fabulous perks that are going to be surging your way,' Eddie says. 'Yep. It's move over *TOWIE* and *Made In Chelsea* and Hello *Carringtonnnnn's!*' he sings, like he's about to star in the next West End musical theatre smash hit.

Well, we'll see about that.

'I have to go,' I say in a trance-like state to end the call, and I drop my phone down onto the carpet. I really thought Tom and I had something. Something really special. I had even started to think he might be the real deal. Everyone says you just know when you meet your one, and that's exactly how I felt right from the very first moment I saw him. I was standing by the help-yourself salad bar in the staff canteen with my cheeks flushing and my mouth actually hanging open. He's the quintessential tall dark gorgeous guy. Kind. Especially to animals. Calm. Impeccably mannered. Generous. Intelligent. Artistic. Gentle. Sometimes cheeky. Fantastic in bed. But how wrong was I? If he doesn't even trust me enough to mention something as epic as Carrington's starring in a reality TV show, then what does that say about our relationship? He obviously doesn't feel the same way. And I'm so glad I held back on mentioning the L word. I grab my phone back up and punch out his number. I can't wait to hear what he has to say for himself.

2

I'm on the bus making my way to work and I'm still devastated. After Kelly's show last night, I spent the rest of the evening going over and over the sequence of events for the last month or so, until a trickle of realisation dawned in the early hours of this morning. The film footage was doctored! Edited to look as if Annie ignored Zara, the customer, when in actual fact she hadn't. It's the only explanation. Especially as we only had one of those Anya bags in stock and I distinctly remember Annie's elation when she sold it. *To Zara*. Must have been.

Annie was whooping about adding the commission from the sale to her savings so she'd have nearly enough money to get the Flo Rida tatt removed from the spot just above her left boob. She'd had it done in a moment of madness on a *crazeee* hen weekend along the coast in Brighton, after hooking up with a guy called Vince who had gold teeth and seriously intricate sleeve tattoos. She's regretted it ever since. I even remember saying she could have next Thursday off because it was the only appointment available at the laser clinic this side of Christmas. And we never normally allow it, not with

Thursdays being late-night shopping, especially as the run-up to Christmas is our busiest time of year.

But what I'm absolutely gutted about is that Tom must have allowed Kelly to fix the sequence of events. He must have known she was going to portray us like that ... Surely he would have investigated, done his 'due diligence', as I've heard him say, before putting Carrington's, the business Dirty Harry started over a hundred years ago, in this ridiculous position. We'll be a laughing stock. Well, I already am. I've had seventeen tweets this morning from people wondering if I've seen the YouTube clip of my bottom. Somebody posted it up with the title *Carrington's Christmas Cracker!* Like I'm some sort of novelty joke. I couldn't even bring myself to look, but apparently it's had three hundred and eighteen hits already. *Cringe.* Hardly viral, but that's not the point.

And what about our loyal customers? They won't like being filmed. Some of them have been coming to the store since childhood, just like I did. Mum used to bring me to Carrington's, before she passed away when I was thirteen years old. She had multiple sclerosis, which had worn her down so much that when she caught pneumonia she just couldn't fight any more, so I ended up in foster care because Dad was still in prison and my only other relative, Uncle Geoffrey, couldn't – or wouldn't – take me in. But before it all happened, Mum and I would shop and eat fairy cakes in the old-fashioned tearoom and be happy together. This was years before

Sam took over and turned it into a cosy café where the cakes are now cupcakes and a Victoria sandwich is a layer cake with elderberry infused jam and gold glitter frosting decorated with delicate edible butterflies made from hand-spun Valrhona chocolate. Those Saturdays and school holidays were probably the best times of my life, although, thinking about it, my hat trick with Tom does come a pretty good second ... hmmm, but putting that aside, it's as if all those glorious memories have been tarnished now.

Taking a deep breath and swallowing hard, I jump off at the bus stop beside the bandstand to look across the road and up at the Carrington's frontage. Even after all this time it still excites me. An impressive, powder-blue Edwardian building with intricate white cornicing around enormous arched windows housing this year's Christmas display – a real wooden sleigh, piled high with wrapped presents, pulled by four life-size reindeer figurines. They even have faux brown fur, enormous antlers and jingle bells nestling on crimson collars at their necks. Shimmery fake snow is scattered on the floor and all around the edges of the windows. The display lights create a magical, almost Narnia-esque image within the white colonnaded walkway of olde worlde streetlamps and pretty hanging baskets, bursting with seasonal purple cyclamen swaying gently in the wintery-cold breeze.

Set in a prime location in the centre of Mulberry-On-Sea,

Carrington's department store is a family firm spanning three generations, offering old-style elegance with a strong sense of tradition; that special something, where loyal customers are addressed by name and the staff are treated like personal friends. No matter what's going on in the outside world, you know that when you step inside Carrington's you're entering a bubble of sparkly optimism where nothing bad ever happens. Well, until last night, that is. Thanks to Tom and his new best friend 'Ronald McDonald', everything's changed in an instance. Carrington's is a tradition, a landmark synonymous with Mulberry-On-Sea, and not some gaudy sideshow that relishes making fools of people. And that's exactly what I'm going to tell him, and her, if I get the chance.

Pushing through the door of the staff entrance at the side of the building, I say hello to a couple of the Clarins concession girls and head towards the rickety old gilt-caged staff lift. I unwind my super-chunky long knitted scarf as I go – I made it myself from a kit that came free with a magazine, all part of me doing my bit for the austerity drive. I've made a few maxi dresses, too, and a pair of curtains, with Mum's old sewing machine, some patterns I found in amongst Dad's stuff and a bit of help from Iris in Haberdashery.

'Hello lovey.' It's Mrs Grace, Carrington's oldest employee. She used to run my department, Women's Accessories, before retiring at the grand old age of seventy-one, but after her husband spanked all their savings on his pigeons, she had to come back to work. So she now looks after the stockrooms on a part-time basis and, if I'm not mistaken, she's changed her lipstick to movie-star red. Her Garnier blonde hair, which is usually bouffed up into a big Aunty Bessie bun, is now styled into an elegant beehive with a super sparkly diamanté clip holding it all altogether. And she's smoothing down a smart, two-piece skirt suit instead of her usual hand-crocheted waistcoat and easy-fit trousers. 'Isn't it exciting?' she says, crinkling the corners of her eyes.

'Exciting?' I say, not quite sure what she means as I press the call button for the lift. My heart is thumping with anticipation of the showdown that's about to unfold with Tom. I wonder if he's bracing himself too. He must know I'm on the warpath. When he didn't answer his phone last night, I left a very terse voicemail followed by a text. Well, four to be exact. Just to be on the safe side. He needs to know how seriously upset I am.

'With the film crew being here, dear. Did you see the show last night?' she asks, and I nod. 'Such innovation, your Tom is very clever. My Stan would never have come up with such an idea, but then he's far too busy messing around with those filthy birds.'

I can't believe it. Mrs Grace is the last person I thought would approve of Tom's actions. She's not even keen on TV, much preferring her bingo. And being such a stalwart for tradition, a self-appointed protector of the Carrington's good old days, she really wasn't happy when we got a memo saying not to address customers as Sir or Madam any more. Tom said research showed it sounded old-fashioned, that some women get offended by it, it makes them feel old – and, as much as it pains me to say, given how I feel about him at this precise moment in time, I do think he had a very good point.

'Oh dear, what is it love? You don't look very happy. Here ... ' Mrs Grace snaps open her granny bag and pulls out a crumpled pink-and-white striped paper bag full of pick 'n' mix sweets. 'These will cheer you up.'

'Thanks,' I say, helping myself to a slightly fluffy foam banana. I take a bite and relish the sugary taste.

'Take two, one is never enough,' she chuckles, rustling the bag enticingly, so I take a green pear drop to be polite and pop it in my pocket. 'I thought you youngsters loved the telly. It's the only reason I voted in favour of doing the show.'

'*Voted?* What do you mean?' I ask, creasing my forehead and racking my brains as I try to work out what's going on. She's standing directly underneath one of the original 1920s Tiffany wall lamps, which is casting an eerie glow on her face, and I can't help thinking that it makes her look like one of those spooky old china dolls.

'At the special staff meeting in the canteen after work one night. Ooh, it must have been a good few weeks ago now, may even have been a few months. My memory's not so good these days,' she chuckles as the lift arrives and I crank the cage door back. We step inside and I pull the door closed before pressing the gold button.

'Was everyone at this meeting?' I must be going mad. I definitely wasn't invited to a meeting, and surely Sam and Eddie would have mentioned it last night if they already knew about the TV show. Fair enough, Sam might not have known, given that she's not technically a Carrington's employee – her café business leases the space. But anyway, if she knew, maybe overheard one of the other sales assistants talking over a coffee perhaps, then she would definitely have told me, there's no way she would have kept a secret this massive. No, Sam was as shocked as I was. She was actually speechless, and it takes a lot for that to happen to Sam. Eddie, on the other hand, may have held out on me, but then he is Tom's BA so I suppose he's kind of conflicted, a bit. On second thoughts, no! There's no way Eddie would have managed to contain himself for a nanosecond, let alone weeks or even months – he was way too excited about me becoming a star.

'Oh no, just the board and a handful of senior staff,' Mrs Grace continues. 'I was invited because I used to be a manager. Confidentiality they said. On a "need-to-know" basis only.' She pushes her granny bag into the crook of her elbow before making little quotes signs with her bony fingers. 'But between you and me, I think I was only invited as a courtesy, probably to get me on side so I didn't form a protest.' She narrows her eyes. 'Oldest trick in the book – get the potential troublemaker on board first.' She chuckles. 'We even had to sign a form to say we wouldn't blab any of the details as it would spoil the surprise element of the show. *Very* Hollywood and hush-hush, it was. They gave us free pizza,' she says, pronouncing it *peeeza*, 'although I didn't have any as all that cheese gives me heartburn something rotten.' Mrs Grace pauses to pat her chest. 'And they paid for a cab home. Kelly wasn't actually in the meeting, just the production team, but her glamorous assistant was and she's a real beauty up close. All milky skin and bee-sting lips.'

Incredible. So some of the staff were allowed to know beforehand, but not me – *girlfriend of the majority share-holder!* Tom obviously deemed I didn't 'need to know'. Why would he do that? And I'm a supervisor. What on earth is going on? This just makes it a billion times worse. And what was I thinking by sleeping with him? I knew I should have waited until I'd worked out what a sneaky snake he is. I even confided in him about my 'trust issues with men', as the social worker neatly noted in my file when I left the care system. But then, is it any wonder, when my own Dad forged my signature, lumbering me with a stack of massive loans he'd taken out in my name to fund his gambling debts? I know Dad and I are putting it all behind us now and he's doing his best to win back my trust – but still, Tom could have at least kept it in mind. And then there was Brett, my last serious boyfriend. We were together for three years, totally loved-up, or so I thought, until he dumped me for a tall, gloriously beautiful woman with super-big blonde hair. A total contrast to my average height, freckly complexion and flyaway brunette bob. I saw them together not long after the split, holding hands and laughing over an intimate joke as they sauntered along the towpath down by the canal.

By the time I've said goodbye to Mrs Grace and slammed through the door to the executive floor, I'm almost in tears. I stride down the corridor and into the anteroom outside Tom's office. Inhaling hard through my nose, I blow out through O-shaped lips and brace myself.

3

'Hey dollface. What's up?' Eddie sprints around from behind his desk before smoothing down an immaculately cut charcoal grey suit with a cornflower blue open-neck shirt. His blond hair has been styled into a ridiculously dapper side-parting do with lashings of gel.

'So what happened to your twist-cut chinos and espadrille combo then? Take it Ciaran found your best suit,' I snap, thinking: so much for solidarity in the face of adversity. Eddie's wasted no time in reinventing himself to look like a slick TV star.

'Oh, those old rags?' He waves an imperious hand in the air. I glare at him. 'Why are you being so sulky?'

'*Sulky?*' I huff, making big eyes. 'Wouldn't you be if your boyfriend had sold you out to some TV company without even bothering to mention it?'

'But you were amazing on screen,' he says, enthusiastically.

'Hmmm,' I mutter as Eddie gives me a hug. He ponders for a moment before changing the subject.

'Come and see my Pussy!'

And, suddenly, I feel as though I've slipped inside a parallel universe. Grabbing my hand, Eddie pulls me over to his desk and scoops up a fluffy white bichon frise from a Burberry print dog basket nestled underneath. Around the dog's neck is a pink crystal collar, and all four of its spindly little legs are sporting lime- green knitted legwarmers. 'She's channelling her Eighties workout vibe, aren't you Pussy?' he explains. I stare for a bit before managing to drag myself back to reality.

'Eddie! Are you *insane?* You can't bring a dog into the store. And what kind of name is *Pussy* for a dog anyway?' I say in an incredulous whisper-voice, while resisting the urge to pet the cute puppy that's now licking the back of my hand with her tiny pink velvety tongue.

'Of course I can, everyone has a furchild these days – they're an essential accessory. And isn't she a darling? Anyway, Kelly adores her and has already said she can be in the show,' he says, pursing his lips and stroking the dog's head. 'And I'll have you know that Pussy is a very apt name for a department store pet.'

'*Whaat?*'

'As in Mrs Slocombe's cat, she called it Pussy.'

'Who?'

'*Are You Being Served* … ring any bells?' he says, pulling an exasperated face.

'What are you going on about?'

'Oh never mind. Before your time, obvs. Although, of course, I only have an extremely vague memory of

39

catching a glimpse of it once as a newborn peering up from my cradle,' he quickly adds.

'But this is Carrington's. A department store, in case you'd forgotten. People don't bring pets to work. And besides, since when did you have a dog?' I ask, desperately trying to keep up with it all.

'From about seven o'clock this morning when I arrived at work,' he pauses, and a faint glimmer of shame darts across his face. Eddie never ever exerts himself by doing extra hours. 'I thought it best to put in an early appearance, what with everything going on ... Tom might need me,' he explains, fiddling with Pussy's collar to avoid eye contact. 'I rescued her. Poor thing,' he adds, kissing the top of Pussy's head before settling her back down in the basket.

'Rescued her?'

'That's right. From the Carrington's pet spa,' he says.

'Pet spa?'

'Yes! Angel, why do you keep repeating everything I say?' Eddie tilts his head to one side and pulls an exaggerated curious face.

'Hazard a guess. Maybe it's because ... *I have no bloody idea what you're going on about*,' I say, flinching as my voice jumps up several octaves. 'It's like I've stumbled into some weird dream sequence. A nightmare even.'

'Oh don't be so dramatic. I know you have a tendency to put two and two together and come up with five billion, but honestly darling ... ' He shrugs.

40

'Ha! You're a fine one to talk.'

'Shush. I'm a queen. It's my job.' Eddie does kissy lips and tweaks my cheek. 'Besides, it's your most adorable foible.'

'What do you mean? I don't have foibles.' I shake my head and pull a face.

'Yes you do.'

'No I don't.' Eddie puts his arm around my shoulders and gives them a quick squeeze.

'Oh, you look so indignant. But that's why I love you,' he says. I stick my tongue out and Eddie laughs. 'Anyway, where was I? Oh yes ... about the spa, apparently it was one of Kelly's genius ideas to boost revenue. That dingy hairdressing salon next door has been cleared out and transformed into Carrington's very own pet boudoir ... just like at Harrods.' He drops his arm and makes impressive eyes. 'There's an adorable doggy exercise area, cute wardrobe accessories section and even an assortment of puppies and kittens to actually buy. I took one look at Pussy and thought *enough!*' He flings up a palm. 'I couldn't bear to think of her cooped up in a pokey little cage all day long waiting for some *RHONY* wannabe with a penchant for baby-pink marabou puff mules to buy her and call her Viennetta or something equally ludicrous.' He clenches his jaw in horror and I raise an eyebrow. 'You should see it in there, the transformation is incredible; must have been like one of those interior design programmes where Melinda turns up with a flash

41

mob of decorators and practically does out a whole house in like ... *under three minutes,*' he gasps in a very stagey voice, having obviously elevated himself to first-name terms with all the celebrities now.

'Slight exaggeration.'

'*Whatevs!* But I'm surprised you didn't spot the difference on your way into work.'

'I guess I had other things on my mind,' I mutter, wondering how they managed the makeover in such record time. It was still a hairdresser's when I left work on Saturday evening. 'Look, I have to see Tom before this whole place goes nuts.'

Pulling my coat off and dumping my bag down on Eddie's desk, I step around the enormous silver and purple themed Christmas tree, narrowly missing the mountainous pile of fake wrapped presents underneath, and head towards Tom's office.

'But you can't go in there.' Eddie does a running bodyslam at the door before pinning a hand on each side of the frame.

'Try and stop me,' I say, attempting to fling him out of my way by prising free the fingers of his right hand. He quickly caves in and turns around to face me.

'Really. Georgie, please, you don't want to go in there. Trust me. Not like this. Calm down first. Here. Open.' Performing a spectacular pincer move, Eddie grabs my jaw between his thumb and index finger, and without thinking I open my mouth just as he squirts two puffs of Bach Flower Remedy onto my tongue. In a desperate attempt to get rid of the flowery perfume taste that's swirling around my mouth, I quickly retrieve Mrs Grace's pear drop from my pocket, shove it in my mouth and crunch it up furiously, almost biting my tongue in the process. 'Oh dear. Here ... ' And Eddie grabs up a canary yellow paper fan from his desk and starts batting it around in front of my face. 'For stress, sweetie. For stress.'

'Will you just stop it?' I say, pushing the fan away and almost choking as the remainder of the pear drop propels down my throat. I cough really hard. Eddie jumps behind me and slings his arms around my boobs

'Get off me,' I say, untangling myself from his clutch. 'What do you think you are doing?' I turn around to face him.

'Spoilsport!' He sticks his bottom lip out. 'I've been dying to do the Heimlich manoeuvre ever since I went on that course. There's just no fun in being a Carrington's designated first-aider if all I'm doing is dishing out plasters for boring old paper cuts.'

'Well I'm sorry to disappoint,' I say, straightening my uniform of V-neck black top, trousers and gold Carrington's name badge.

'Oh please don't make a fuss. It's *sooo* not a good vibe. And Kelly is adorable. I think you're going to love her.' I raise my eyebrows. *He must be having a laugh*. 'Yes, I took the liberty of tactfully mentioning the ... ' he pauses, does a furtive left-then-right look before mouthing, '"shop girl" comment. And you know what, she just threw her head back and roared. Actually roared with laughter. She didn't mean anything by it. She said it's all part of the show, set up purely to entertain the audience, and she knows that you're a fabulous sales person in real life,' he gushes, like some deluded groupie.

'Eddie, are you totally bonkers? That Ronald McDonald lookalike made a complete fool of Annie and me,' I bellow. 'And why does everyone keep on implying that the show isn't real life? We're real people with real lives working in a traditional department store. Get over it.' I let out a big puff of air before smoothing down my hair.

'Oooh. *Harsh*,' Eddie whispers into my face, giving me a daggers look.

'No. *Reality*. So stick that in your *dramality* pipe and smoke it,' I say, suddenly desperate for a cigarette, even though I gave up smoking years ago. I only ever had a few on a Saturday night out anyway, not what I'd class as being a proper smoker, but I could really *really* do with a full-tar Benson right now.

'OK. Calm down. Of course we are, but who wants to plod on with their real life when they can have a much more fabulous pretend one crammed full of staged spontaneity?' Eddie says, clapping his hands together. And I give up.

Pushing past him into Tom's office, I stop short and instantly want to die. Kelly is standing right in front of me with her Lord Kitchener pointy finger sticking out and a massive grin spread across her face. And I bet she's heard everything.

'Hi, I'm Ronald McDonald,' she says, immediately confirming my fear and not missing a beat. 'And *you* must be Georgie, the star of the show! *Oh oh oh, oh oh ohhhh …*' she sings, whipping up her other hand and flicking it backwards and forwards, just like Beyoncé does in the 'Single Ladies' video. I stare goggle-eyed and speechless as she then turns to the side, tilts her body forward slightly, bends her elbows and starts pumping her arms up and down, left then right, in sequence with her alternating legs.'

Cuckoo! And she must know the whole dance routine. Sam was right, this woman is an utter fruit loop. Her big curls are flailing around. I jump back, suddenly conscious that she could whip my eye out without a moment's notice if I'm not careful.

'Err, yes. Um, sorry about that,' I eventually manage to speak. 'I, err … came to see Tom.' I do a desperate scan of the room, but he's not here. Kelly throws her arms around me, almost winding me in the process, before pulling back to study me.

'*Chillaaax,*' she says, in a kind of 'far-out', dreamy voice on seeing my tense face. She makes a peace sign with her fingers to emphasise her point. *Whaaaat? Who even says that anyway?* I resist the sudden urge to roll on the floor in hysterics and swivel my eyes around the room again instead. 'You and I are going to be besties,' Kelly ploughs on. 'Calling me Ronald McDonald is hilarious and those Beyoncé moves of yours were TV gold. Priceless. But we'll need to get Millie to sort you out before we can actually turn you towards the camera,' she says, leaning in to scrutinise me while I wonder what's wrong with my face.

'Who's Millie?' I manage, desperately trying to get a grip.

'The hair and make-up girl, of course. Will you want hair extensions?' she fires. 'Oh you're bound to. Hang on.' Looking back over her shoulder, she bellows towards Tom's private bathroom. 'Zara, call Xavier at Hair Fairies in Mayfair and tell him to bring the Balmain bag. Now, where were we?' she turns back to face me.

'Look, I don't mean to be rude but where is Tom?' I say, backing away from her. I wasn't planning on having an audience when I confronted him.

'Getting styled,' she replies, as if it's the most obvious answer ever. 'Won't be long. Come and sit with me and we can talk about my new show. *Kelly Cooper Come Instore*. Has a certain ring to it, don't you think?' She flounces around flamboyantly before flinging herself down on one of Tom's leather sofas, kicking her pumps off and making a loud jangling noise when she swings her feet up onto a couple of raw silk Santa Claus motif cushions, which only last Friday were on display in Homeware. I know, because I helped Mrs Grace unpack them from their special cashmere dust bags. She said we were lucky to get them as Selfridges were still waiting, according to her friend's granddaughter who works up there. Kelly crosses her legs, setting off the jingle-jangle sound again. She must have at least ten of those silver bohemian ankle bracelets on each leg. Hmmm, on closer inspection, a slight exaggeration maybe, but there's definitely a lot.

'I'd rather stand, thanks.'

'Fair enough.' She grabs a copy of *OK!* magazine and starts thumbing through it. Silence follows. I check my watch and see that it's nearly eight thirty, opening time. I think of Annie. I hope she's made it into work. She called me last night in tears. She's mortified too. And convinced she's going to be sacked and have to go back to cleaning and looking after her numerous brothers, sisters, nieces and nephews all day long. Annie is a Traveller and the first girl in her family ever to have a paid job. She said she'll never get another one because jobs are like gold dust in these double-dip times. And people are reluctant to employ her when they find out that she lives on the Traveller site on the outskirts of Mulberry, so she's worried she'll end up with the Flo Rida tatt and the memory of Vince with the gold teeth for ever more. I make a mental note to tell Tom about that too. Maybe he can get her some flowers or something to apologise. He can't just go around upsetting the sales assistants. 'Ooh, will you look at them?' Kelly pipes up, and thrusts the magazine out to show me a pic of Kate and Wills. You know, you have a look of her about you.'

'Mmm, if I lose about two stone and hand out beer goggles to everyone who glances my way,' I say, reluctantly. I don't really want to get into a conversation with Kelly when there's no point. The sooner this is over, the better, and I can go back to my normal life. Once Tom sees sense he's bound to have second thoughts and send her on her way. Kelly snorts with laughter.

'Don't be daft ... oh you are so hilarious,' she chortles, eyeing me up and down. 'And never mind, soon all the designer brand managers will be bombarding you with goodies; there'll be red-carpet events and you'll be getting free makeovers left, right and centre. I even had a sailor from my last series who got free sponsorship for a whole year from one of those gourmet diet delivery services. He lost six stone and scooped ten grand for a nearly nude spread in some sleb mag.'

'*Really?*' I say, instantly hating myself for showing an interest, but I've always fancied the idea of having food cooked and delivered to my door. Most of the time I'm so tired when I get home from work after being on my feet all day that I can't be bothered to cook proper meals from scratch. And I wonder if Sam knows which sailor it was.

'Oh yes, you wait and see. Ahh, here he is ... ' Kelly's eyes swivel towards the door. But it isn't Tom coming in, it's Zara, and she's swinging the gorgeous caramel-coloured Anya bag in her left hand. *I bloody knew it*. And Mrs Grace was right. She's utterly stunning in real life. Oh God, even I'm doing it now. *This is real life.* I say it over and over as a mantra inside my head as a reminder. I'm convinced it's the only way to keep a lid on this totally surreal scenario. 'Where's that gorgeous man, Tom? There's somebody here to see him,' Kelly says, flashing me a smile.

'He won't be long.' Zara jumps up on the corner of Tom's mahogany desk and tosses her cascade of honey-hued big hair around for a bit. And I'm sure her eyes narrow when she glances in my direction.

'Nice bag.' I can't resist.

'Perk of the job,' she replies, giving the buttery soft leather a quick stroke before discarding the exquisite bag down on the floor next to a wire-mesh bin that's overflowing with rubbish. 'I can take a message if you like, save you hanging around. I'm guessing you need to dash back down below stairs, as it were, to dust your shelves or something,' she giggles superficially, giving me the once-over like I'm the hired help. I ignore her and study the pattern on the wallpaper instead, wondering what her problem is.

The door opens again and Tom appears.

'I'm so sorry to keep you waiting.' He flashes a polite smile around the room but there's a flicker of apprehension when he sees me. After jumping up, Kelly dashes towards him, flings an arm around his chest and gives him a big squeeze. 'Oooh, the things I could do to you,' she says in a saucy voice, nestling her face into his left pec before pushing up on tiptoes and planting a big kiss on his cheek. Tom coughs discreetly and adjusts his cufflinks.

Momentarily I waver, blown away by his looks, which literally take my breath away. His eyes are the darkest velvety brown and nestle in sumptuous eyelashes that make me want to lick them right here and now. The thick curly black hair – which only two nights ago was entwined in my fingers during our mammoth love-making session – is now slicked back, giving him the appearance of a gorgeous Hollywood heart-throb, or how I imagine a young Jon Hamm might look in a *Mad Men* prequel.

'Georgie. What are you doing up here?' He breaks free from Kelly's grasp and walks towards me, his delicious chocolatey scent teasing all around me.

'We need to talk.' I swallow hard.

'Sure,' he says, easily. 'You OK? It's not Mr Cheeks is it?' He looks directly into my eyes and creases his forehead slightly.

'No, he's fine. Err ... ' I glance towards Kelly who is still gazing up at him like some lovestruck fan-girl.

'Right. Of course. Would you mind if we have a minute?' he says, turning first to Zara and then to Kelly.

'Catch you later. I've got a session with my shaman in any case,' Zara sniffs airily. She bounces down from the desk, practically canters over to Tom, plants a big smoochy kiss on his lips and runs a finger down his lapel before tossing a look over her shoulder in my direction.

'And I mustn't miss my call from Isabella. Can't wait to hear all about Costa Rica.' Kelly blows Tom a kiss as she heads towards the door.

'Then please give her my love and say that I've been thinking about her a lot. I promise to take her to lunch very soon.'

I wait for them to leave and then close the door before I turn towards Tom.

'*Isabella?*' I say in an accusatory voice, and the very second the word comes out of my mouth I want to shove my fist inside and pull out my tongue. This wasn't what I had in mind at all when I was lying in bed last night planning out the scene in my head. And I'm not usually the jealous type.

'Yes. My mother. Kelly and she were at Cambridge together,' he states, and I swear his Downton accent (upstairs, naturally) just got a little stronger.

'Oh, I see. That's nice,' I reply, feeling relieved and trying to make it sound as if it's really no big deal, that in fact I was merely being polite. But I realise in an instance just how little I really know about him and his family, and I didn't have Kelly down as a Cambridge University type at all. I imagine them all to be very serious and intellectual – she seems far too wacky to me. And I bet they don't read *OK!* magazine at Cambridge, much preferring some ancient Latin parchment or whatever, requiring the handler to wear special white gloves just to unravel it because it's tied up with a big scarlet ribbon made from real human peasant hair dyed with their blood.

'So, what did you want to talk to me about?' he asks casually, taking a step forward and circling an arm around my waist. I jump back. 'Hey, what's the matter?' He sounds concerned.

'What do you think?'

'I'm not sure, but I can see that you're upset. What is it?' He looks puzzled, as if he genuinely has no idea why.

'*Upset?* That's putting it mildly. Did you get my messages?'

'Yes,' he replies. I stare, waiting for him to elaborate.

'And?' My forehead creases.

'Oh, when I say I got them, I meant just a few minutes ago. Haven't had time to listen properly or read the text messages yet, though,' he explains, picking up a pile of papers from his desk and flicking through them.

'I see,' I say tightly, wondering why he's being so indifferent. I clear my throat. He stops flicking and places the papers back on the desk.

'Is this about the filming?' he smiles.

'Oh, duh! Ten out of ten, genius.' I fold my arms, wishing I could be cool and calm like him, instead of borderline hysterical. Tom gives me a strange look, kind of a mixture of bafflement and disappointment, and one I haven't seen on him before.

'Georgie, why are you being like this? It's not like you.' He steps towards me again, hesitates, and places a hand on my arm instead.

'Are you wearing guyliner?' I ask, suddenly distracted.

'Err, I think so.' He shrugs his shoulders and grins. 'The production team insisted on trying out some looks for the opening credits ... hence the tux.' He opens his arms to show off the midnight blue dinner suit and crisp white shirt, making him look even more adorable than ever. 'They're going with a "Mr Carrington" image, whatever that means.' His smile widens as he raises a perfectly groomed eyebrow.

'That's nice for you,' I say, in my best breezy voice.

'Oh come on, don't be like this.'

'Like what?' I ask, wishing I didn't sound so much like a sulky teenager.

'So emotional.'

'Well I'm sorry if I have emotions, but why didn't you tell me about the filming? Warn me at least?'

'I couldn't.'

'Of course you could. You're the boss, you can do whatever you like.'

'It's not quite as ... simple as that.' He glances down at the carpet and my cheeks smart from the implication.

'Then why don't you explain it to me then?'

'Look, I didn't mean anything malicious by it, but I can't just ... do whatever I like, as you say. Yes, Aunt Camille sold her majority share to me, to keep the store in the family – and with a bit of luck and lots of hard work, we'll manage to turn it around and keep us all employed for many more years to come. But there's the board to consider.' I bite my bottom lip. 'That's what doing the show is all about; it's an incredible opportunity for Carrington's and we are really lucky to be given the series,' he says, as though he's learnt it off by heart from an official statement that somebody prepared earlier for him.

'So it had nothing to do with your mother and Kelly being friends from Cambridge then?'

'A little, but Kelly will transform the business and really put us back on the map. Help us fend off this terminal decline.'

'And make fools of us. Me in particular – did you actually see the show last night?'

'Not yet. I got caught up on a conference call with a foreign supplier,' he explains. And I secretly wonder if it might be a blessing in disguise. I'm not sure I want him seeing my embarrassing debut on the TV screen, despite what Eddie says – he's my friend so he's bound to be kind about it.

'Was it any good?' Tom smiles and raises his eyebrows enthusiastically.

'No, it blooming wasn't! It was embarrassing, and they set me up. Annie too. Did you know they were going to edit the film to make us look like totally incompetent and inefficient sales assistants?'

'I'm sure it wasn't that bad.' He frowns, and then quickly adds, 'They didn't show your faces, did they?'

'Like that makes a difference,' I say, resisting the urge to slap his beautiful cheek.

'Well, they wanted to originally, but I stopped it,' he says, looking pleased with himself. I smart from his indifference and obvious loyalty to Kelly and Zara over me.

'You could have at least warned me.'

'I couldn't. The board voted in favour of signing the NDA with the production company.' I give him a blank look, hating myself all over again for feeling so out of my depth. 'Non-disclosure agreement,' he says, tactfully. 'So you see, I couldn't tell you, even if I'd wanted to.'

'So you wanted to then?' I ask, my spirits lifting slightly at the prospect of redeeming something from this hideous situation.

'I know how much you love these reality TV programmes. It was meant to be a surprise,' he says, deftly avoiding my question. He looks away.

'A *surprise?* Tom, you humiliated me. You kept a secret and it's not the first time.' I bite my lip again.

'Hang on a minute. I thought you understood about that,' he says, his voice dropping and his eyes flashing.

'Oh, I understood plenty. That you didn't trust me enough to let me know you were Tom Carrington posing as just another sales assistant.'

'And is it any wonder when you react like this?' he says, running a hand through his hair.

'Like what?' I say, glaring at him.

'Practically hysterical.'

'Well, I'm sorry if I'm too hysterical for you now.' My heart is hammering inside my chest.

'That's not what I said.' Silence follows. Tom clears his throat and turns away from me. 'I can't deal with this now, not here.'

'But I still don't understand why you didn't tell me. We've been flirting for months, and now dating. I thought we had something, or did I get it completely wrong?'

'Don't be ridiculous.'

'So I'm ridiculous now?'

'Georgie, this is getting us nowhere.'

'I couldn't agree more.' An awkward silence follows.

'So what do we do now?' It's Tom who speaks first.

'I have no idea. Why don't you decide ... seeing as you're the one in charge,' I snap.

'Fine,' he retaliates, looking really fired up as he paces around the room, flicking his shirtsleeve back to check the time on his watch. 'If I'm upsetting you so much, then maybe we should just call it a day ... ' He comes to a halt in front of me and stands with his hands on his hips, as if daring me to challenge his decision.

'Good. I was thinking just the same thing,' I say, desperately trying to keep my voice steady. I don't want to split up. I want us to be together. Having fun. Falling in love. Just like other blissfully happy couples. But I do have some pride, and if he isn't as into me as I thought, which is glaringly obvious given that he's this quick to suggest we split up, then maybe it's for the best we end it before it goes any further.

'Look, we should talk about it ... ' he says, his voice softening as if he wants to let me down gently.

'Sorry, I don't have time.' Ha! I'm busy too.

'I'm sorry.' He glances away.

'Well so am I.'

It takes me less than three seconds to leave the room, my shoulders stiff and my back constricting with a whole raft of horrible emotions. I grab my bag and coat from Eddie's desk, and quickly brush him away as he stands to reach a concerned hand out to my arm.

'Hey Georgie! Hang on,' Eddie calls out, but I'm gone, tears stinging my eyes as I run along the corridor and back to the safety of the staff lift. I push the cage door back and step inside before slumping against the wall and crying my heart out. And not graceful lady tears like Meryl at an Oscar acceptance speech. Oh no, these are big gulping heaving sobs that I just know are going to make my face look like a swollen blotchy balloon in about an hour or so.

4

O ver! I say the word over and over inside my head as I huddle inside the cubicle. I'm in the staff loo and I can't stop crying. Angry tears. Sad tears. All mingled together.

'Hey, you OK in there?'

'Err. Who is it?' I ask hesitantly, quickly wiping the back of a hand across my cheeks.

'It's me. Annie.' I pull open the door and she hands me a wedge of tissues. 'What's up?'

'It's nothing.'

'Bullshit! Tell me or I'm going downstairs right now to mess up your merch,' she says, flinging one hand onto her hip and twiddling her nose stud with the other.

'You wouldn't dare.' I manage a watery smile.

'Try me. You know those cute gold stars and sparkly white snowman shapes you spent all last week scattering amongst the DKNY shelves to create the perfect Christmassy display?'

'*Nooo.*' My eyes widen. 'It took me ages to stencil them, spray-paint them, cut them out and then place them artfully amongst the winter collection … '

'Exactly.' Another silence follows as I ponder on what to say. Everyone knows that Tom and I had started dating, but still ... instinct tells me that I need to be professional about us splitting up. Besides, I refuse to be the stereotypical girl who has a fling with the boss, ends up getting burnt and her colleagues all rally round feeling sorry for her while slagging off the guy. Tom doesn't deserve that. He's gorgeous, my perfect man, or so I had thought. What's happened between us doesn't change all that. I stick a smile on my face and take a deep breath. 'It's the reality TV programme, isn't it?' Annie says, interrupting my thoughts.

'Well, kind of,' I say, feeling relieved. 'Anyway, how are you? I thought you were upset about it too,' I say, shifting the focus away from me.

'Me? Oh no.' She flaps her hand and pulls a face. 'Yeah, I was a bit hacked off when I saw myself on the telly, but after Amy, the HR manager, said I'm not getting sacked, so this bad boy is still out of here, I'm cool with it.' And she pulls down her top to circle an index finger around the Flo Rida tattoo.

'Err, good,' I say, feeling increasingly like the biggest party pooper going. First Eddie, then Mrs Grace and now Annie – they're all keen to do the show. But how do they know it won't backfire, just like that old airport reality show with easyJet? The bit I saw was just a load of customers complaining, so what's to say Kelly's programme won't do the same to us? They've already made out that the service in Women's Accessories is rubbish. If they do that throughout the whole store, it could seriously damage Carrington's reputation forever. Instead of restoring the shop to its former glory, Tom will have ruined everything by calling in favours from old family friends. Maybe those doubters in the business world are right after all, and he is out of his depth.

'Yep, and that's not all – guess what?' Her eyes widen. 'We're getting eighty pounds per episode on top of our usual wages. Well, the ones doing the show are ... Denise in Home Electricals is well jelz. But I told her, there's no glamour in washing machines.' She laughs.

'Is that right?'

'Sure is. Best news I've had in ages. And think of all the freebies, designer gear, goody bags, red-carpet invites, PR appearances – they all pay: big money, too! I'm thinking Sam Faiers – move over darling. I *can not* wait. Amy also said there's going to be a special end-of-series Christmas wrap party with all of Kelly's celebrity friends coming. And it's going to be filmed *live!* And apparently, she actually knows Will.I.Am! Can you imagine? *Faint!* I've wanted to get close to him for like ... *ever since he was on* The Voice.' She clutches my arm in glee. 'It's going to be epic.' Annie drops my arm to spread a hand in the air. 'Bet we'll get free VIP entrance to the Sugar Hut and everything now,' she says, full of happiness as she shakes her frosted hair extensions back. 'Anyway, better jog on, don't want you bollicking me when I'm late back from tea break.' She grins and nudges me gently with her elbow before leaving.

I peer in the mirror to examine my face and quickly perform a tissue repair job on my make-up, cursing myself for having already dropped off my handbag. We used to stash our bags under the counters, but when Tom took over, that all changed, so now we have to stow them in lockers in the staff room upstairs. For our own protection, he said. Shame he wasn't bothered about that last night when my backside was being broadcast to the whole nation.

I checked YouTube from my phone when I was on the bus earlier, and my views are up to nearly five hundred now. And some guy even DM'd me on Twitter asking if I fancied joining him and Pu, his new Thai ladyboy bride-to-be, for a threesome. Hideous. Tears sting in my eyes again. I can't believe Tom and I are over before we even really started.

After letting out a long, shaky breath, I help myself to a generous spritz of complimentary Cavalli. One of the perfume girls left a couple of bottles as an incentive for us to direct customers to her section, so she can flog more special Christmas gift sets with the matching body lotion. I dab my eyes again and think of Annie's excitement, Eddie's too, but I haven't changed my mind, they'll just have to film around me. Or put one of those blurry things over my face or something, like magazines do to Harper or Suri when they haven't got permission to show their pictures.

After leaving the Ladies, I make my way along the narrow, winding staff corridor that's like a time warp with its original 1920s faded floral wallpaper. I have to step around a couple of stock trollies piled high with flattened cardboard boxes, to push through the double security doors that lead out to the shop floor.

It's lit up like a giant Santa's grotto full of goodies.

This year's festive theme instore is Winter Wonderland. Fake snow covers the normally black, swirly patterned carpet, and sparkly white model seals nestle inside Perspex balls suspended from a twinkly, Arctic-inspired ceiling. All of the display podiums are crammed with festive present ideas, pyjama sets tied up with scarlet satin ribbons, gloriously fragrant Jo Malone candles, glittery woollen mittens, luxury lingerie in tissue-packed boxes and every kind of perfume and aftershave gift set you can imagine. There's even a pop-up shop selling Santa-shaped gingerbread men, striped candy canes and chocolate tree decorations covered in foil, hanging from lengths of gold thread.

The magnificent Art Deco marble pillars are swathed in garlands of holly and ivy, mingled with silver, spray-painted pine cones. And the air is filled with a warming, cinnamony-orange scent, pumped from a machine hidden underneath the enormous, ceiling-tall Norwegian Christmas tree that stands in the centre of the floor, in between the two original wooden escalators. Customers are laughing and joking as they touch the merch. Children are weaving in and out of their parents' legs, eager to get down to the basement to see Father Christmas in his grotto, and hand over their wish list full of presents.

My mood lifts instantly. It's really hard to suppress the swirl of excitement on glimpsing the glorious array of festive colours in such a buzzy atmosphere. The run-up to Christmas is my absolute favourite time of the year instore, and it's not like I haven't split up with a guy before – I have. So I'm sure I'll survive. I'll have to. I think of my freezer jammed with all those mince pies and make a mental note to pop into Masood's corner shop on my way home for a carton of custard and a soppy film. He always has a stack of DVDs to choose from and you really can't beat a mince pie or two with a warm custard drizzle. That will cheer me up a bit. I might even get ten Benson too while I'm at it.

Making my way over to my counter, the best one on the floor, right opposite the main customer entrance and next to the giant, floor-to-ceiling Christmas window display, I make a conscious effort to pull myself together and put on a brave face. It wouldn't do to crumble in front of a customer. I like to think of the shop floor as a stage to perform on where everything else must be left behind the scenes, upstairs in the staff canteen or in the sanctuary of my cosy flat. Besides, for all I know, Zara, Kelly – or worse still, Tom – could be spying on me via the CCTV. Maybe that's how they doctored the film footage of Annie, supposedly texting and ignoring Zara. Hmmm.

I sneak a look around and my pulse speeds up. There! I knew it. Right there on the wall above the Marc Jacobs stand, glaring directly at the counter, is what looks suspiciously like a camera to me. A small, black, domed piece of plastic, and it definitely wasn't there last week. I know, because I was up there with my feather duster. I make a mental note to climb back up the long ladder and strategically place a weekender bag right in front of it. That should block the view. I could even put one of the miniature Christmas trees on the very top shelf. That will definitely do the trick.

I'm crouched down behind my counter, sorting through a box full of old Olympic merch from last year – sequinned Union Jack clutches and sparkly London 2012 key rings, couldn't even shift it during a BOGOF campaign – when a guy, wearing denim board shorts and the biggest funky Afro I've ever seen, waves one of those huge grey fluffy microphones in my face. Next to him is an arty-looking woman wearing leopard-print skinnies with blush patent wedges and a floaty vest top. She's got a red leather folder pressed inside her crossed arms.

'Can I help you?' I say, shoving the box under the counter with my foot.

'Perfect!' The woman ignores me and whips out what looks like a paint chart from her folder, and holds it up near my shoulder.

'What are you doing?' I pull a face and push the chart away.

'This is her. The girl. The one Kelly wants heavily featured,' the woman says to the guy.

'*Hellooo*. I am here, you know,' I say, feeling irked at the mention of Kelly's name. It's her fault Tom and I have split up. Everything was wonderful before she came on the scene. I wave my hand in an attempt to get their attention.

'Oh, sorry. How do you feel about cerise?' the woman says, scrutinising me now.

'Cerise?' I repeat, thinking it's a bit random. 'Err, can't say I've given it much thought of late.'

'Or how about a rich chocolate or silky cream, with, wait for it – ' she does a massive, almost manic grin, and waves her hand around before glancing at the guy, who nods enthusiastically – 'a dash of delicate mint green? Oh yes, that would suit you far better. Bring out the gorgeous turquoise of your eyes.' She fiddles with the chart again. 'It's very important that we get the right palette for you.'

'Palette?' I say, conscious of sounding like a parrot now.

'For your clothes! Hence the light chart.' She gives the card a quick wave for emphasis. 'Sorry.' She puts the chart back inside the folder and stuffs it under her arm before pushing the pen into her messy ballerina bun for safekeeping. 'Hannah Lock. Production assistant.' She sticks a hand out to greet me and I notice her gorgeous French navy gel nails.

'Leo Aguda. Sound technician. Or Leo Afro, as they call me.' The guy with the microphone grins and raises a clenched fist for me to thump. Awkwardly, I duly oblige.

'Georgie Hart. Women's Accessories,' I say, sounding like a bit of a plum, but I'm not used to people announcing their name, surname and job description all in one go. 'And don't worry about a palette for me, I won't be needing one. Besides, I have a uniform,' I smile apologetically, having spotted a man with a little boy hovering near the Chloé display.

'Don't be silly. Kelly will want all of you sales assistants to be dressed in Carrington's clothes. How else can customers see what the store's merchandise will look like on them? She's already given Womenswear a makeover, replaced the entire stock with catwalk couture, all the latest fashions, instead of that dowdy, middle-of-the-road merch thing they had going on up there.' She rolls her eyes up towards the first floor while I wonder if I should mention that our regular customers obviously like the 'dowdy, middle-of-the-road look', as we've never had any complaints. 'And you might as well make the most of a free fabulous wardrobe opportunity,' she says, doing the manic grin again. 'You'll probably get to keep most of the clothes, and Kelly's already told the board about the new rule – Carrington's staff wear Carrington's clothes. End of.'

'I'm sorry, Hannah, but you'll have to excuse me. I have a customer to serve.' I gesture in the man's direction before heading over to greet him.

'Are you looking for a particular bag?' I ask, giving the guy a big smile. Out of the corner of my eye, I see Hannah nudge a little closer.

'Yes please. Something expensive for my wife. A Christmas present. Thought I'd get organised for a change,' he says in a lovely lilting Irish accent before ruffling the little boy's jet-black curly hair.

'Excuse me. Do you know where Father Christmas is?' The boy looks up at me, his big green eyes all sparkly with anticipation. 'I've got a list. Daddy said I can give it to him.'

'Well, I think he might be downstairs in his grotto.' I crouch down so I'm head height with the boy. 'And a list is a very good idea, how else will he know what you like best?' I smile. After studying my face for a bit, the boy flings his arms around my neck and gives me an enormous squeeze, practically winding me in the process. I pat his back tentatively, relishing the spontaneous moment of comfort.

'Hey, Declan, come on now.' I stand up and the man goes to scoop the boy up into his arms, but he's too quick and ducks behind the display. 'Sorry. My wife's just had a new baby and he's feeling a little bit left out,' the man whispers when the boy is out of earshot.

'Aw, would he like one of these little teddies?' I ask.

I take one of the fluffy white miniature bears down from the DKNY shelf and give it to the boy when he reappears. One of the brand managers brought in a batch for us to give away free with the purchase of every bag, but I'm sure they can spare one for a cute little boy.

'Thanks so much,' the guy says to me before turning to Declan and taking his hand. 'What do you say to the nice lady?'

'Thank you.' Declan giggles and snuggles into the bear, looking really chuffed before pushing it out towards me. 'He's called Nice Lady Bear.' The guy rolls his eyes and laughs, and I can't help laughing too.

'How much is this one?' The man quickly composes himself, and points to a gorgeous dusty pink, top handle Chloé bag with signature gold metalwork.

'Oh, good choice. This one is a limited edition; we only have two left and I can't guarantee delivery again this side of Christmas Day.'

'Is it a popular one, you know ... an It bag, or whatever they call them?' He pushes a hand through his hair as Declan simultaneously bounces Nice Lady Bear in his stomach.

'Oh yes, it was in *Elle* magazine last week.' I take the tag from the inside pocket and show it to him.

'Blimey, that's more than I paid for my first car.' He shakes his head and tweaks Declan's freckly nose.

'We have others if this one is a little more than you wanted to spend,' I say, discreetly. He hesitates for a moment before nodding decisively.

'I'll take it. Because she's worth it.' He shrugs.

'Shall we go over to my counter so I can gift-wrap it for you?' I smile.

After placing the bag in a soft white drawstring dust bag, and cocooning it in a puff of our signature powder-blue tissue, I tie it all up with an enormous navy satin ribbon and hand the guy his credit card back. I stow the bag in a giant gift box, sprinkle in a handful of silver snowflake confetti and close the lid, before carefully sliding it into one of our special Christmas-themed paper carrier bags. I twirl a length of red gingham ribbon around the handles.

'Thanks a million.' He takes the bag and hoists Declan up onto his shoulders.

Once they've headed off towards the escalator, Hannah darts in front of my face.

'Cor! Wish I had a husband like that – talk about thoughtful, and great with kids of course. And you are *soo gooood*. I can see why Kelly's earmarked you for a starring role. You're a natural sales woman, no coaching requirements for you!' she gushes, practically hyperventilating with sheer excitement. I stare at her, wondering if she's for real.

'That's because I *am* actually a sales woman. It's my job, in *real life*,' I say, stating the obvious.

'Yes, yes, of course you are, but well ... you know what I mean.' She does a little giggle. 'Now, Leo wants to check a few things with you and then we're good to roll. Friday afternoon, the quietest time in store I've been told, there'll be a short briefing, a run-through of the "scenario". Not too much, natch.' She giggles again. 'We want the show to be as authentic as possible.'

'But I'm not in the show,' I say, busying myself with updating my sales sheet.

'Of course you are. You're going to be a star,' she says, giving me a blank face, and quite clearly unable to comprehend my reluctance. She's obviously used to people begging for airtime.

'Nope, not me.' I put my sales sheet away and start stacking the ring trays on top of each other in preparation for giving the glass counter a good buffing over. I like everything to look pristine, as there's nothing worse than a messy point-of-sale area.

'But you have to be. Kelly wants you. And she always gets what she wants. She's the boss, she owns the production company, KCTV.'

'Well, not this time. And she doesn't own me. Anyway, it's not the law,' I say, probably a little too petulantly as I fold my arms to underline the point.

'It practically is.' Pursing her lips, Hannah grips the chart tighter and tries to stare me out.

'What do you mean?' I cave in first and glance at the floor before looking back at her face which is now a rhubarb-red colour.

'Check your employment contract. It's all covered in there. I'll be back.' And she marches off, closely followed by Leo, who has to do a gentle jog to keep up with her as he attempts to juggle the sound paraphernalia about his body at the same time.

5

So it's true. Hannah was right. I managed to hold out until my lunch break to check. And after waving off regular customers, Mr and Mrs Peabody, who never actually buy anything, they just like to come instore for a chat and to share pictures of their grandchildren who live in California, I'm in Amy's office with a copy of my employment contract on the desk in front of me.

'It's a wonderful opportunity for Carrington's,' Amy says, diplomatically. She's standing next to me, wearing a taupe Ted Baker trouser suit and pointing to sub-section nineteen, clause a hundred trillion, or whatever. It says Carrington's can use promotional material made within the store, read: FILM ME! And do what they like with it, or words to that effect. I stopped reading after a while. But it's right there on the back page, just above my signature, glaring like it's giving me the finger and yelling out 'hahahaha sucker!'

But who reads every single line of an employment contract? Not me, obviously. I was only fifteen when I got it and just thrilled to have a Saturday job paying me actual money to work in my favourite place. I still remember signing the contract, attempting a proper grown-up swirl with my new fountain pen. A gift from Alfie, he had sent it for my birthday. The pen came in a black velvet box, nestling inside on a bed of lilac satin, and I thought it was the best present I'd ever had. I glance again at my now girlish-looking signature. Georgina Hart. All twirly and written with a flourish. I even drew a little heart motif above my surname.

Getting the Saturday job was like a dream come true, somewhere I belonged. A welcome escape from my foster carer, Nanny Jean's house, and her bullying birth daughter, Kimberley. A year older than me, Kimberley would parade around the sitting room in a multitude of new outfits complete with mismatched accessories, bought from Topshop with a generous monthly allowance. I wanted the same. And if Nanny Jean wasn't going to be fair, then a Saturday job was the perfect solution. My own money. To do with what I liked. And Carrington's was a place where I could remember being with Mum. Kind of like a spiritual connection. Comforting. It was as if she was there standing right in front of me, oohing and ahhing as she admired a handbag spotted in a glossy magazine that she had flicked through whilst waiting to see her consultant at the hospital. I would be standing next to her, egging her on to buy it. Of course, I've learnt now that I don't have to be inside Carrington's to remember Mum – she's all around me, wherever I am – but still ... Carrington's on TV, broadcast to the whole world, potentially. Well, it changes everything. Everything I grew up with. It's as though it won't be my special place any more.

'So I have no choice then? And I can't have one of those blurry things to block out my face?' I say, cringing slightly. I feel foolish now after making such a fuss and being sniffy with Hannah, saying I wasn't doing it, when in actual fact I have no choice. I agreed to it, albeit without actually knowing. But there is an upside if I have to be part of the show – I guess a free new wardrobe, and the other perks that Annie was so excited about, aren't to be sniffed at.

'Not really. But if you're adamant about being excluded from this exciting initiative, then I could organise a transfer for you to another department. Home Electricals, for example?' she says, sounding corporate and robotic. 'They won't be featuring in *Kelly Cooper Come Instore*.' My heart sinks. Relegated to the basement. Like Annie said, there's no glamour down there – and, besides, I love working in Women's Accessories. 'Have a think about it. I'm sure I could find someone to cover for you with the amount of staff I've had in here already today, all of them begging to be in the show.'

'Oh right.'

'But I do understand if you're reluctant. The board were very specific that staff shouldn't be put under pressure to take part, if they really don't want to. We're not in the nature of forcing employees to do things against their will.'

'So why did they let Annie and me be portrayed as useless then?'

'Err, yes. Good point.' Her cheeks flush as she points an index finger in the air. 'And I'm very sorry about that. It won't happen again,' she says, giving me the impression that somebody more senior than her has asked this exact same question, and more than likely had a word with Kelly and KCTV. Well good! So they should. Carrington's prides itself on providing an exceptional service. Yes, sales have dwindled recently, but there's a recession on, so it's to be expected. And it's not as if we're the only shop suffering. And of course, a high-profile, prime-time TV show with a retail guru to help us turn things around will be good for business, but still, there's no need to make us look like complete Muppets.

'Definitely?' I say, an idea hatching inside my head.

'Yes, definitely. You have my word. You're very good at what you do, so it really would be a shame if we didn't show you off.' She tilts her head to the side and smiles sweetly.

'Hmm, well in that case, I suppose it might be OK,' I say, letting the idea grow some more. This could actually be an amazing opportunity to show the whole world how wonderful Carrington's is. How brilliant our customer service is. Coach-loads of tourists could come for special Christmas shopping sprees, just like they used to. Annie and I can show the viewers how we were misrepresented. I might even get a chance to prove that Annie didn't ignore Zara. In fact, Zara bought the creamy caramel Anya bag and was given a perfect customer service. Ha! See how *she* likes being set up.

'Great. See it as an opportunity. A chance to do your bit for Carrington's. We all know that business has dipped of late, and you really are one of our best sales supervisors. That's why you were chosen to be in the pilot.'

'*Really?*'

'Yes really.' She nods and smiles.

'So how will it work then?' I ask, feeling flattered.

'Well, my involvement was purely from a personnel perspective, but I've been told the show will be aired every Wednesday until Christmas. I think filming starts in a week or so and it will all be very spontaneous. You just turn up and get on with it, apparently.'

'I see. And I heard something about a live wrap party?'

'Yes, that's right, for KCTV and Carrington's staff, if they want to attend.'

'Even those that aren't part of the show?' I ask, figuring it's only fair if they are.

'Of course.'

'And what about the actual filming of the shows?'

'That will be on Sundays when the store is closed. Although Kelly has already suggested we revisit our opening times schedule. Sunday closing is archaic, she says.' And I'm sure I spot a fleeting look of weariness on Amy's face, making me wonder if Kelly has been giving her a hard time. But I guess it was inevitable – nowadays all of the big department stores are open on Sundays. 'KCTV did investigate filming every day, but their lawyers advised against it – apparently it's a legal minefield to film with so many members of the general public wandering around, and the board were worried about it putting our regular customers off from coming instore. You know how "traditional" some of them are.' And I certainly do. We nearly had a boycott on our hands when we tried to introduce an Ann Summers concession last year. Mrs Godfrey wrote a stern letter to the local trading stand-ards office stating that Rampant Rabbits had no place in Mulberry-On-Sea.

'But how will it work if there aren't any actual customers instore?'

'Oh, well, not all of the scenes will involve customers. Other parts of the retail operation will be featured on the show too. This initiative isn't just about KCTV helping us up our game, it's about opening our doors to viewers, potential new customers, and letting them see what goes on behind the scenes, as it were. Rather like a "docu-soap", I think was how one of the production team explained it to me.'

'Oh I see.' *A reality show, in other words.*

'Apparently KCTV are well renowned for their docu-mentary work and feel that our show could be an award contender,' she says, sounding as if she's been brainwashed.

'Wow.' I make big eyes.

'Yes, Kelly says everyone, the world over, is fascinated with department stores, so she wants to show people how other things work, such as supplier contact, stock control, merchandising and what goes on in the cash office – that kind of thing.' I think of Lauren, Doris and Suzanne who all work in the cash office, and wonder how they feel about being featured on *Kelly Cooper Come Instore*. 'Besides, they're not using real customers for the selling scenes,' Amy adds.

'Will they be pretend ones then?' I resist the urge to laugh out loud as I wonder how this is all going to work.

'That's right. KCTV are going to use actors for the actual customer interaction sequences,' she says, with a totally deadpan face. My smile quickly fades. 'They've already done a couple of trial runs this morning, and they were very successful apparently.'

'Trial runs?' They seem to have it all figured out. And I'm instantly reminded that this must have taken months to plan. I think of Tom again, keeping it a secret, and my heart sinks.

'That's right. I met one of the actors earlier, with his son – a really cute little boy with a gorgeous head of dark curls. He brought the boy along to make the performance seem more authentic. '

Whaat? Nooo, it can't be.

'Was the little boy called Declan by any chance?' I ask, mentally kicking myself for not having guessed that his dad was an actor.

'Oh yes, I think so, how do you know? Have you met him too?' Amy gives me a wide-eyed look.

'Err, yes. This morning. He bought a Chloé bag.' And there was me thinking reality TV shows were, in fact, *real*. I can't believe I didn't cotton on. I should have guessed, with their gorgeous accents and picture-perfect shopping scenario, like something straight out of a *Hallmark* film. And with Hannah practically breathing down my neck as I served the guy, and then pretending it was authentic with her 'wish I had a husband like that' comment. I make a mental note to scrutinise every customer more thoroughly in future. Just because I'm doing the show – under protest, *for the record* – doesn't mean Kelly can make a fool of me a second time. Besides, I'm only doing *Kelly Cooper Come Instore* to avoid having to flog boring washing machines downstairs, and because my swirly signatured fifteen-year-old self didn't know any better than to check for sneaky 'filming for worldwide TV broadcasting' clauses. I do a big, satisfying harrumph inside my head.

'Well, there you go. Nothing to it, just like any other day in Women's Accessories,' Amy says, attempting a bright smile that doesn't quite meet her eyes.

'I guess so.' I shrug. 'But it means losing a day off,' I add, wondering if anyone has thought about that – and it's not just me, all the staff have Sunday off. It might even be illegal to work six days per week. Ha! I don't remember seeing that covered anywhere in the contract.

'That's why all staff who choose to take part will be paid extra for their time, their normal salary plus an additional payment, and also benefit from other perks. Guest appearances, interviews ... Apparently it's not uncommon for the people who appear in Kelly's shows to go on and command considerable sums for doing all sorts of things – read bedtime stories to shoppers, I think was one suggestion, attend openings, magazine interviews; even appear on daytime TV, if they want to. And the board saw a whole stack of figures from KCTV showing how previous programmes boosted revenue for the businesses featured – by fifty per cent in some cases. So it really will be worth it, I'm sure, if Carrington's is revived and we all get to keep our jobs.'

'Wow. Fifty per cent! That's pretty impressive. It'll be like the boom days again.' Thinking back to that time, I remembered our sales figures were fantastic – Annie and I were almost doubling our salaries some months, with the amount of commission we made. And Carrington's could certainly do with a boost, the way sales had been flagging recently.

'Exactly. But you'll need to be here early, for make-up and stuff. They want to start shooting, as it were, at around 10 a.m. Is that OK for you?'

'Sure,' I say, thinking it will be worth losing my lazy Sunday mornings in bed and catching up on my Sky+ recordings to see Carrington's back on top. I couldn't bear it if the store went into a terminal decline and we all lost our jobs. And before Tom took over, that was a very real possibility. I can't even contemplate Carrington's going to the wall and having to close down. What would we do? We're like a big happy family that looks out for each other. Laughing and working together – with a bit of gossiping too, of course. Someone even did a tally once and worked out that there had been eleven Carrington's weddings over the years, where employees had married after meeting on the shop floor. Years ago, the staff actually used to board in the maze of rooms up in the attic and, during the Second World War, the underground tunnels, one of which meanders as far as Lovelace Street, a good mile away, were used as shelters during the blitz. The whole town, practically, took cover down there. Mrs Grace told me all about it. She remembers it clearly and she was only a little girl at the time. So, if Carrington's were to close, then it would be like ripping the heart out of Mulberry-On-Sea, and I don't think I could bear that. I decide to suck it up and get on with the show. I have to. For Carrington's.

And then it dawns on me, I'll need to add the *Kelly Cooper Come Instore* series to my recording schedule. The actual show that I'm going to be in – and, despite everything that's happened, a little shiver of excitement swirls through me. And hair extensions! I'm sure Kelly said something about hair extensions. I was so wound up this morning that I didn't really take it all in. I'm going to have big hair. I wonder if I'll get to have my teeth whitened too? Bound to! All the reality stars have perfect gleaming teeth. It's a basic. And maybe I'll get to go to film premières and stuff. Perhaps this won't be so bad after all.

'Well, thanks for explaining it all. Just wish I'd known before – maybe then it wouldn't have been such a massive shock, seeing myself on primetime TV like that, without any warning,' I explain, realising that I actually feel OK about it now. It was the shock, that's all. I panicked. If only Tom had told me, and sworn me to secrecy or something, not a single word would have passed my lips. And I could even have signed the NDA form too, and everything would still be perfect between us. I know how to keep a secret. I had plenty of practice when Dad was in prison – I hated people knowing and I even changed my surname to Mum's maiden name as a way of burying my past, but I'm over that now and refuse to make Dad my guilty secret any more. But as Sam said, the surprise element for the viewers would have been ruined. Well, they wouldn't have seen my jigging bottom, that's for sure. I would have made damn sure of it. I vow never to shake my booty ever again. Just in case there's a hidden camera lurking nearby.

'You're welcome to pop back any time if there's anything else you want to chat about,' she says, her voice softening now.

'Thank you.' I turn to leave.

'And Georgie?' she adds.

'Yes?' I stop and hold the door open with my foot. Amy hesitates and clears her throat.

'I know it's none of my business ... ' She pauses and fiddles with the sleeve of her jacket.

'Go on.' I smile encouragingly.

'Well, I just wanted to say that I know you and Tom were, err ... dating.' A blotchy rash appears on her neck. She's the first person up here on the executive floor to actually talk to me about our relationship ... well, if you can call it that now. 'Don't be too hard on him ... he really did want to tell you,' she adds.

'Oh?' My forehead creases and I motion for her to carry on.

'Yes, at first he was quite insistent on not signing the confidentiality agreement, and only caved in because the board were in danger of losing the show. He desperately wants Carrington's to benefit from the publicity, to turn the store around and secure the future for all of us.'

'I see.' She nods and I smile back. 'Thank you.'

On leaving Amy's office, I ponder on this insight as I make my way along the corridor. Maybe I was a little hasty in confronting Tom. I didn't exactly give him much time to explain, and maybe he was reluctant to sign the agreement because he really did want to tell me, but just couldn't, it was a business decision, nothing personal. Or maybe he genuinely did think it would be a wonderful surprise and that I'd love it, actually being in a reality TV show, instead of just lounging on the sofa necking wine and scoffing mince pies while watching one. I would probably have whooped for joy if I'd been shown in a positive light – after all, I love a good reality show as much as everyone else. And I guess we both just want the same thing at the end of the day: to make Carrington's glorious again.

I've got twenty minutes left of my lunch break so I decide to head to Tom's office, figuring everyone deserves a second chance. It was just an argument that got out of hand. A misunderstanding. People say stuff they don't really mean in the heat of the moment all the time. I know Sam 'dumped' Nathan at least three times in the run-up to their wedding. Bridezilla hormones, Sam called it, but, whatever it was, Nathan always forgave her, and Sam said that some of the best sex she ever had was after a bust-up. It got so passionate one time that she ended up with a row of little carpet burns all the way down her spine after they got carried away on the hall stairs.

My heart lifts at the prospect of making up with Tom. He could even stay over tonight and we could pick up from where we left off after our hat trick. I could wear my new black lacy Lejaby underwear – I treated myself when the range was on special offer in Lingerie. A warm sensation radiates through me as I run through the sizzling scene in my head. I might even be able to leave work a bit earlier. I'm sure Annie will cover for me, seeing as I covered for her three times last week. Then I can get the flat nice, change the bed linen, maybe light some candles and have a bubble bath before I get ready. It's going to be sensational. My heart soars and my cheeks pulse. *I can not wait.*

6

Eddie must be on his lunch break as his desk is empty when I arrive in the anteroom outside Tom's office. I can hear voices inside, so I knock on the door. No answer. I knock again. No answer. The voices stop. Silence follows. I've got my ear pressed to the door when it suddenly flings wide open and I end up doing a slapstick stumble over the threshold, even stepping completely out of my left New Look heel. How embarrassing. I quickly retrieve my shoe and wither a little inside.

'You just can't keep away, can you?' It's Zara. And I don't believe it. She's only got the dusty pink Chloé bag swinging jauntily in the crook of her elbow! It must be the one I sold this morning. Has to be. Unless it's a pure coincidence, which is highly unlikely as Carrington's is the only place around here to stock Chloé bags. Perhaps she already had the exact same one, I think, giving her the benefit of the doubt. Or maybe she bombed up to London at lightning speed after seeing her shaman, whatever one of those is. I make a mental note to Google it later.

'Excuse me?' I say, wishing I could say more, but seeing as she's the daughter of Tom's mother's friend, I quickly decide against antagonising her. If Tom and I are going to have a future together, then I'll need to get on with his friends. And I certainly don't want to upset his mother, Isabella Rossi, of the wealthy Italian Rossi dynasty, before I've even met her.

'Only joking,' she says, giving me a frosty smile that doesn't meet her eyes. 'What do you want?' she adds, rudely.

'Hello, I've come to see Tom.' I grin brightly, figuring I might as well make an effort to be friendly, even if she can't – kill them with kindness, that's what Mum used to tell me. I push a lock of hair behind my ear, and quickly smooth down my top.

'Well you'd better come in then.' She takes a minuscule step sideways, but keeps her free arm high on the door just above my head, so I have to duck down to enter the room, like a servile minion.

Inside, and Kelly is back on the sofa with her feet up and her eyes glued to a row of little TV monitors. There is stuff everywhere: clothes, shoes, and practically all of the cosmetic hall's stock, by the looks of it. Plastic crates of make-up cover every surface, mingled in with several empty bottles of champagne and plates of half-eaten sandwiches and crisps.

Kelly swings her feet down, making the now familiar jingle-jangly sound, and promptly steps on a giant can of Elnett super-hold hairspray, which she instantly boots out of the way. It rolls across the floor before clattering to a halt against the side of Tom's antique desk.

'Bloody junk. Is there no end to it all? *Milllleeeee*,' she hollers, and a few seconds later, a very striking and androgynous-looking woman who, I guess, is Millie the hair and make-up artist, comes tearing out of the bathroom. Her short dark hair is swept back to show off perfect dewy skin and shiny conker eyes. Freckles sprinkle her nose and cheekbones. She's dressed all in black apart from silver Converse trainers on her feet and a trio of primary-coloured Perspex bangles on her left wrist. Surprisingly, she doesn't appear to be wearing any make-up.

'Will you please quit yelling, Kel? I've got one hell of a hangover from all those Dirty Martinis you poured down my neck last night.' Millie pauses to clutch the right side of her head. 'So, what's up?' she adds, in a strong Geordie accent, before placing both hands on her hips, tilting her head to one side and grinning widely.

'When are we getting a proper space? I can't possibly be expected to work my magic in squalor like this.' Snorting loudly, Kelly sweeps a hand through the air to emphasise the perceived 'squalor' of Tom's office. I see she's changed her tune. What happened to the 'funky, sweetness and light, we'll be new besties forever' attitude she had going on this morning? And I see now what Sam means about not being fooled by her wacky exterior. I wouldn't want to get on the wrong side of her, that's for sure. Especially when she could insist I be sacked, just like the staff from her last series were.

'How should I know? I just do make-up. Last I heard, that guy on the executive floor ... ' Millie pauses to ponder. 'The preppy-looking one, could do ads for Ralph Lauren if he tanned up a bit. Works in customer relations or something.' Millie pauses again, momentarily deep in thought. 'James, that's it!' She clicks her fingers in the air, looking pleased at remembering his name. 'He knows someone who knows someone, so they're getting us suites at the Mulberry Grand Hotel. Not far from here. I've asked for a sea view,' she states in a blasé voice, before flinging a lid off a crate and rummaging through it.

I smile inwardly at the mention of James. We had a one-night stand once, ages ago; it was just before Valentine's Day – this was before Tom and I started going out together, obviously. It was very romantic, but James hadn't long split from his wife, Rebecca, after she dumped him for someone else and, well, it got complicated. Turned out he wasn't ready to have a new relationship – he was still in love with her. They're divorced now, and word on the shop floor is that he went on a date with Vicky a few weeks ago. She works in the Carrington's crèche and is very pretty and petite. Apparently, they were spotted in the Dog and Duck, the pub next to the cinema in the centre of town, and Vicky was all breezy and pretending to be uninterested, according to Emma, who works part-time in Stationery. But I'm pleased for him. We're just good friends now. He deserves to find his happy-ever-after.

'Well, if she's having a sea view, then so am I,' Zara says, before throwing a daggers look in Millie's direction, which she doesn't even notice. Millie is too busy reading the instructions on the back of an Illamasqua box of extra-length false eyelashes in intense blue. I can't help wondering who they are for? Oh God, not me I hope. *Nooo, surely not.* I'll look like a blow-up doll. And our regulars won't like it, that's for sure. I can just imagine Mrs Godfrey from the WI, all flaring and huffy, if I flutter long blue lashes while helping her to select a new rain bonnet. We tried to phase the bonnets out at one point, but the local WI had a word with Betty, our mumsy switchboard supervisor, who had a word with someone on the board, so the bonnets had to stay.

'Darling, you can have whatever you want,' Kelly says, sounding exasperated with her own daughter. Millie glances up from the crate, and on catching my eye she pulls a face before looking at Zara's back. So Millie has the cut of Zara then, I see.

'Well, in that case, I want to go to Paris.' Zara kicks the point of her left Loub against the cherry-wood panelling next to the fireplace.

'Oh not this again. Can't you just make do with more money instead?' Kelly sighs heavily and reaches for her handbag. 'Anyway, don't be ridiculous. You're needed here to help me with the show.'

'It's so unfair. How come everyone else gets to do the exotic bits while I'm stuck in this provincial dump that doesn't even have a wait list for Birkin's.' Zara jabs the panel again. I turn to look at Kelly, wondering what she'll come back with. It's like following the ball at Wimbledon.

'Sweetie, if you want another Birkin, then you only have to say and I'll put in a call to François. He owes me some merch, especially after all that product placement I did for him in my last series.' Kelly plucks a black credit card from her purse and waves it in Zara's direction to placate her. Zara ignores it.

My ears prick up at this revelation. Does this mean, then, that Annie and I will be selling Hermès bags? Oooh, I hope so. I wonder if this is one of Kelly's ideas to boost revenue for Carrington's and put us on a par with the famous department stores up in London. Or, better still, Annie and I could actually carry a Birkin bag in the show? They could film us arriving at work or something. You never know, we might even get to keep one, especially if it's been used and thereby can't be sold instore – now that would be amazing. And it would mean that I could dump the fake one I bought from a street seller in Marbs. Although, I can't see our regular customers forking out thousands for a handbag Who can afford to do that?

Or perhaps Kelly has ideas to attract new customers too, from out of town. Maybe down from London for a weekend, or how about a special exclusive event for the glamouratti from the boats moored up in Mulberry Marina. They all seem to be flocking here since the new casino opened, much to the annoyance of the local residence committee, I have to say. My neighbour, Frank, who does something on the parish council, ran a petition for well over a year and collected nearly nine hundred names. But anyway, I've seen some amazing super-yachts, and I've often wondered why we don't make more of this untapped flow of high-end customers. I'll talk to Tom about it, when we're alone. Could be my way of showing him that, actually, there are no hard feelings, and I'm keen for Kelly to work her magic and make Carrington's magnificent again. In just the same way he is. He could go back to confiding in me and it would become like our project, chatting and dissecting Kelly's progress together. You never know, KCTV may even do a second series. Tom did say that he'd been thinking about opening another store, perhaps, and what better way to drum up publicity than by involving the viewers – read, potential new customers – right from the start. I make a mental note to chat to Tom about this too.

Glancing at the wall clock, I see there's only five minutes left of my lunch break. I clear my throat.

'Oh, didn't see you there with all this junk in the way,' Kelly says, and I'm sure I detect a hint of frostiness in her voice. I wonder if Tom has had a go at her for making Annie and me look like fools. 'What can I do for you?'

'I've come to see Tom.' I smile.

'Oh he's gone. You just missed him,' Kelly replies, in a very airy voice.

'Ahh, that's right. Totes forgot,' Zara chips in, unconvincingly, as she gives me an up-and-down look before raising a sardonic eyebrow. *What is her problem?*

'Gone where? Do you know how long he'll be? I could come back later,' I say, deliberately keeping my voice light and breezy. I'm not giving Zara the satisfaction of seeing me rankled.

'To Paris, of course.'

'*Paris.*' The floor sways beneath me.

'Yep. To film the other half of the show. *The exciting bit,*' Zara adds, pointedly. 'The bit where the viewers will get to see him visiting high-end fashion houses – Paris, Milan, New York.' She counts off the cities on her fingers. 'Sourcing new stock lines, meeting suppliers, that kind of thing. And with a bit of luck I'll get to join him.'

I feel as though I'm suffocating. Tom has gone! Gone a trillion miles away, or it might as well be, seeing as we're over. How are we going to talk now? It just won't be the same on the phone; no – some things just have to be sorted out face to face. Silence follows.

'But he never said,' I manage, instantly hating myself for sounding all 'little girl lost'.

'Maybe he was too busy focusing on his priorities,' Zara offers, before inspecting her nails.

'It was very last-minute, to be fair. The flight was only booked this morning.' It's Millie, and she gives me a sympathetic smile.

'What's it to you, anyway?' Zara butts in, twiddling a diamond earring and flaring her nostrils.

'He's my ... ' I hesitate. What is he exactly? Before last night I thought he was my boyfriend, but now I have no idea. He never even mentioned Paris. I know he travels a lot, but since we started seeing each other he's made sure to tell me when he's going away. I'm stunned. How could I have got it so wrong? If he just wanted a good time, a casual fling, then why didn't he say so? Why did he come all the way to Italy to surprise me at Sam's wedding? Then appearing at my sun lounger wearing Daniel Craig-style trunks to show off his practically perfect body, teamed with an irresistibly cheeky grin. Why did he let me think we had a future? We had even chatted about spending Christmas together. I distinctly remember us laughing and saying how fab it would be to stay in one of those picturesque log cabins, with a roaring log fire, snuggled up together in red tartan blankets while sipping mugs of hot chocolate and looking out through frost-cornered windows as snow floats silently down from the sky. Just like in one of those soppy, old-fashioned Technicolor films, with Bing Crosby crooning in the background. It just doesn't add up. I feel so confused.

'Friend,' I finish lamely.

'And he's also the boss around here, so he doesn't have to answer to you.' It's Zara again. I give her a look. She throws me a sarcastic smile.

'Girls. Girls. Come on. Play nicely,' Kelly interrupts,

before putting her arm around Zara and giving her shoulder a rub. 'Honey, I can see why you're sweet on him, and who can blame you? He's *diviiiine*. Our very own Henry Cavill. Now, if I were ten years younger ... '

And the rest, I secretly think, feeling angry and hurt with Tom all over again. I can't keep up with this rollercoaster of emotions. One minute I want him so much it aches, and the next I'm left feeling devastated.

I take a deep breath, inwardly wishing my feelings for Tom weren't quite so obvious. I really wish I hadn't been so stubborn now. I should have swallowed my pride and agreed to talk later when it was more convenient. Instinctively, I pull my mobile from my pocket and quickly glance at the screen, willing him to have been in touch. To explain everything. Make it good again. But nothing. Just a text message from Dad, all in shouty capitals with no full stops, but at least he's trying. I bought him a mobile for his birthday a couple of months ago, and then he went on the silver-surfers' course at the community centre to master the art of communicating effectively in the electronic age. He's asking if I'll come for a late lunch on Sunday, says he has a bit of news to share.

I glance up and my face immediately freezes. Kelly is looking directly at Zara. She was talking to her, not me. No wonder Zara is being frosty: she fancies Tom and wants him all to herself. And it explains why she's so desperate to go to Paris. Probably thinks she'll seduce him up the Eiffel Tower or whatever. Flaming cheek! My heart sinks.

Well, if she thinks I give up that easily, then she's seriously mistaken. It's taken me a long time to meet Tom. OK, he's behaving a bit weirdly right now and, like Millie said, it was all very last-minute and I didn't exactly give him time to say he was about to board a flight to Paris before I ran out of his office. And it's early days and all couples have bumpy patches. But if Zara thinks she's going to steal him away from me with her supermodel looks and endless supply of designer handbags, then she's going to have a fight on her hands. If there's one thing I learnt during my time in foster care, it was that you have to stand up to the likes of Zara.

I turn on my heel, and for the second time today, I leave the room as quickly and quietly as I can. Only this time, Eddie isn't sitting outside to extend a consoling hand, and there aren't any tears. Just a stunned realisation, deep down, that it might really be over between Tom and me. No chance of us making up. And no matter how much of a brave face I try to put on things with my fighting talk and bluster, if Tom doesn't want to be with me, then, realistically, there isn't much I can do about it. I can't force him to want me. A shudder rattles right through me as a feeble sob catches in my throat.

7

The warm Christmassy smell of nutmeg and orange cocoons me like a comfort blanket as soon as I push open the door to Sam's café. Instantly, I feel myself calming down. Whenever I come in here, it's as though I've entered an oasis of calm, a stark contrast to the vibrant festive atmosphere just a few floors below.

I've just finished work and couldn't face being on the draughty damp bus and then sitting at home all alone with a mince pie and custard to keep me company. Not when I could have been wearing black lace underwear and having incredible sex with a man who, only yesterday, I seriously thought might be the one. My happy-ever-after. I swallow before biting down hard on my bottom lip.

'Hey, are you OK hun? You look frazzled.' Sam appears, wiping her hands on a candy-pink-striped apron as she comes around the counter towards me.

'Not really. You wouldn't believe the day I've had.' I pull a face and grip the strap of my handbag before hoisting it further onto my shoulder.

'Well, you grab a booth and I'll get us some cakes.

They always make things better.' She smiles and rubs my arm before heading off to the kitchen. Stacey, one of the waitresses, beckons me over to the best booth in the far corner, with full view of the café. Perfect for chatting and keeping an eye out to see who is coming or going.

'Thank you,' I say, flinging my bag down into one of the reclaimed train seats. Crimson red velvet, they're arranged in booths of four around low tables, with frilly shaded lamps that radiate a golden glow to create an authentic steam-train carriage feel. It's just like being in an old black-and-white film, or aboard the Orient Express, circa 1920, and very in keeping with the elegant Art Deco style of the nine-floor Carrington's building.

Sinking down into a seat, I study the rich burgundy flock wallpaper, counting the sequence of the pattern before it repeats all over again, and I can't help wondering if Kelly will want to rip it out and modernise everything. Install harsh strip lights and clinical tiled flooring, like some of the big chain stores up in London.

I've been thinking about things all afternoon in between serving seventeen customers. Mostly women, clutching paper lists as they try to get a head start with their Christmas shopping. I got so caught up in worrying about my wide-angled bottom being on TV that I didn't actually stop to think about the real impact for Carrington's of being in Kelly's show. She changes things! Improves businesses, supposedly. But what if her idea of improvement is dire? What will happen then?

Tom's not even here to keep an eye on her. I can't believe he's disappeared at a time like this. I just hope the board know what they're doing – surely Kelly will have to run big changes past them first?

Take the new pet spa next door – I bet she had to get authorisation to do that, she must have done. Well, if it comes to it, then I'm sure Tom's Aunt Camille will step in and put a stop to it. She has in the past, when things have got out of hand.

I pull my phone out of my bag and check again. Still nothing. And then I realise that I don't know how long the flight is. Tom might not even be there yet. He could be sipping champagne or having a deep-tissue massage in the business lounge, or whatever it is people do in there.

I'm contemplating sending him a text message, my finger is poised, when Sam appears and I realise that this really needs to be sorted out in person. Or at least in a proper telephone conversation. I resolve to call Tom later instead.

'There. Get your laughing gear around this,' Sam grins as she pushes a red velvet cupcake up to my lips. I manage a weak smile as I take the cake. After running my index finger over the buttercream icing, I pop it into my mouth. Mm-mmm. My favourite. 'So, tell me all about it,' she says, sitting down next to me and simultaneously sliding a three-tiered floral cake stand crammed with every cake imaginable onto the table. There is even a selection of macaroons – salted caramel, chocolate, pistachio, raspberry and vanilla. And Stacey appears with two enormous mugs of hot chocolate piled high with swirly peaks of marshmallow-topped cream. 'I've dropped a nip of brandy in yours. Thought you could do with it,' Sam says, giving me a cheeky wink as she takes a mug from Stacey and hands it to me.

'Thank you. Do I look that bad?'

I smile at Stacey as she places the other mug on the table, before heading back to the counter to serve a couple of old ladies who are nudging each other and chuckling naughtily as they point to two gooey chocolate éclairs inside the glass display cabinet.

'So, tell me all about it,' Sam says.

'I will. But first ... I want to give you this,' I pull the gift-wrapped parcel of three little Christmas-themed romper suits from my handbag. I called Poppy in Childrenswear, right after serving the fake customer and his son, and she had them waiting for me to collect on my way up here. She's included a really cute rattle too. It has reindeer bells and pictures of snowflakes on.

'Aw, thanks honey.' Sam shakes the parcel, making the bells jingle. 'Ooh, it sounds just like Christmas. Santa in his sleigh.' Her eyes light up. I smile. I'm really pleased I got it for her.

'So how are you feeling?' I ask, flitting my eyes downwards towards her stomach.

'Fine thanks. A bit tired, but to be expected I guess.' She rolls her eyes and grins.

'Well, just don't be overdoing it,' I say, pretending to be stern.

'You sound like Nathan's mum, Gloria. She's gone all mother hen since Nathan gave her the news this morning. We just couldn't wait, we're so excited. Anyway, she emailed me a link to some article she read about first trimester do's and don't's.' Sam laughs and shakes her curls back.

'It's nice that she cares though. I bet she's over the moon,' I say, remembering how Gloria was on the night of their wedding. She'd joined me on the veranda as I looked out across the lush green fields, bathed in the glow from an orange sunset, just to ask me to confirm again that Sam definitely wanted lots of babies. 'You can't be too careful these days with you girls leaving it later and later,' Gloria had said, her eyes all eager and sparkly as she clasped my hands in hers. And Sam isn't even thirty yet!

'It is, but ... ' Sam's voice trails off and she looks away.

'I know,' I say, reaching across the table to stroke her arm.

'Dad would have been so thrilled. And he'd have made a wonderful doting granddad. Probably have set up a trust fund and registered the baby for the best schools in the country by now,' Sam says, smiling wryly and giving her stomach a stroke.

'You can still do that,' I say gently, thinking of Sam's massive inheritance. She's a woman of considerable financial means and could certainly afford to take her pick of schools. 'If you want to, of course.'

'We'll see. But not boarding school. Even though I loved it, I'm not sure I could bear being away from my child. Not like ... ' Sam picks the side of her nail and I wonder if she's thinking about her mum. 'I've been pondering on whether or not I should try to contact my mother?' she adds, confirming my thoughts.

'Have you?' I ask softly, not really sure of what else to say. Sam has never mentioned this before.

'I don't know. Being pregnant has changed things in my head, made me curious to understand how she could just leave me. A little girl.'

'Oh Sam, she didn't leave you. She left your dad, Alfie.'

'Maybe. But then why didn't she ever call me from LA? Was it really too much trouble for her to pick up a phone to ask how I was?'

'Perhaps she just wasn't cut out to be a mum,' I say quietly, and immediately feel anxious, scared in case I've crossed an imaginary line. A short silence follows. 'I bet she thinks about you every day, though,' I quickly add. Sam shrugs. 'And you will be a fantastic mother. You're lovely and warm and caring, just like Alfie was.'

'Thank you.' Sam turns to face me. 'Anyway, I'm convinced there are twins in here,' she says to change the subject. After casting a quick glance around the café to make sure nobody is looking, she quickly loops her apron off over her head and pulls up her top before pushing out her tiny, size-six waist. 'Have you seen the size of me?'

'Don't be daft. Your tummy is still flat.'

'Hmmm. But not for much longer, and I intend on making the most of it.' She nudges me gently before taking a massive forkful of a very gooey-looking slice of chocolate cheesecake. 'Soo, tell me about your day,' she says, wiping crumbs from her lips. Sam is one of those people that really can eat whatever they want and stay slim. I imagine she'll have a tiny bump despite eating for two ... or even three.

'Oh Sam, it's the story of my life. Well "love life" to be precise. Tom and I are over before we really began,' I say, keeping my voice low so as not to be overheard.

'What do you mean, over?'

'Over! As in split up.'

'*Whaat?* I don't believe it. Just like that?' Sam makes wide eyes.

'Yep, just like that.'

Sam lets out a long whistle. I've told her everything. The NDA. Tom thinking I'd love the surprise of being in a reality show. Hannah and her colour chart. Zara snaffling two high-end designer bags for herself. Right down to her having the hots for Tom and practically chewing her own collar right through to escape Carrington's, just so she can sink her perfect veneers into him in Paris – the city of love, after all.

'So, let me get this straight – he suggested you call it a day and you agreed?' Sam says, raising an eyebrow as she scoops off a marshmallow and pops it into her mouth.

'That's right. Two can play at his game.'

'But hang on … you didn't actually want to split up?'

'Of course not,' I say, feebly.

'Hmm, and how do feel now?' she asks.

'Like I wish I'd never said the things I did.'

'So what are you going to do?'

'I don't know. Talk to him, I guess?'

'Good, because one of you has to be sensible. You can't just split up over nothing.'

'It's not nothing.'

'OK, he kept a secret, and not for the first time, granted – but still, it would be such a shame. You two are good together.' I manage a wry smile. 'I'm sure it'll be fine. You can sort this out. I promise.' Sam points to a generous slice of Battenberg on the top shelf of the cake stand and raises her eyebrows encouragingly. I waver before shaking my head.

'No, thank you. I'm stuffed.' I've already eaten my way though a red velvet cupcake and a delicious Christmas stollen slice smothered in dusty white icing sugar with an edible sprig of holly on top. I clutch my stomach.

'Why don't you just call him now and see if you can sort it out?' Sam tilts her head to one side. I hesitate.

'Because, I, well … '

'You want him to contact you?' she finishes for me, and I

nod. 'From what you've told me, you could have a wait – you know how "gentlemanly" he can be?' Sam does speech marks in the air and smiles. 'That year he spent at the exclusive polo school in Argentina certainly wasn't wasted. They turn out royalty too, you know.' She raises an eyebrow. 'So, my guess is he'll respect your decision, even if he didn't really want to split up and it was just all in the heat of the moment. If he's gone away thinking it's what you want, then ... '

'But what if Zara does go to Paris? You've seen how stunning she is. She makes Rosie Huntington-Whiteley look dowdy, for God's sake.'

'Georgie, have a bit more faith. You're gorgeous too. Plus Tom isn't like that. He's not going to jump straight into bed with Zara. She may well fancy him, but that doesn't mean the feeling is mutual. Besides, he'll probably be back soon, won't he? And then you two can talk properly?'

'I don't know.'

'Didn't you ask?'

'No, I just wanted to get out of his office as fast as I could,' I say, mulling over what she's said.

'Never mind. Eddie will know. Look, if it's really going to play on your mind, then let's stalk her.' Sam smiles mischievously as she licks cake crumbs from her fingertips.

'What do you mean?'

'Google her, of course. Knowledge is power and all that,' she laughs. 'Hold on.'

'Where are you going?'

103

'You'll see.'

Five minutes later, Sam returns with her iPad under her arm and sits down next to me.

'Right. Let's see what we can dish up on the handbag snatcher,' Sam sniffs, before flipping open the case and tapping the screen.

ZARA COOPER

'I'll start with that. Not sure if it's her real name, but there's bound to be something,' Sam says authoritatively and, a few seconds later, a list of entries appears on the screen. 'Ahh, here we go.' She clicks on a link titled *Zaramakesasplash* and we both start reading.

> *Stunning TV heiress had the sailors all of a lather when she treated them to a sneak preview of her super sexy new swimwear range …*

'Hmmm.' Sam stretches the screen to enlarge a picture of Zara in a cherry-red tasselled monokini that nicely accentuates her spectacular handspan waist and silicone missile boobs.

'She has her own swimwear range.' The words come out of my mouth but it's as if somebody else is saying them. My heart sinks. I can't compete with a swimwear model – the last time I dragged my boring black Speedo out of the cupboard it was covered in mildew.

'Well, I've never heard of it,' Sam snorts, and she should know: her vast array of bikinis, tankinis, wraps and Havaianas have their own sunshine-yellow-painted beachwear wardrobe installed in her summer season dressing room. Sam has two dressing rooms in her beach-front villa, one for Spring/Summer wear and the other for Autumn/Winter. 'Let's carry on. I saw that episode last season and she ends up skidding on a wet patch on the deck before practically cramming her face into the belly of a rotund man who was busy downing a very frothy lager. Hence the "lather" line. He spilt the whole pint over her.'

Sam scrolls through the entries before hesitating. Her finger hovers.

'What is it?' I ask on seeing her face.

'Err, nothing,' she mutters.

'Click it then.'

'Are you sure?'

'Yes. Just click it please.' And she does.

Saliva drains from my mouth. There, on the screen right in front of me, is a picture of Zara standing outside a nightclub, with her arms wrapped around Tom. Her lips are pressed on his. And the caption underneath says...

Childhood sweethearts destined for happy-ever-after ...

Tears sting in my eyes. A sickening heat prickles down my legs and arms leaving my hands feeling numb.

'That's enough.' Sam snaps the cover back on her iPad and swivels her face towards mine. 'Hey, don't cry,' she says gently, keeping her voice low and soothing. 'Why are you so upset? You said yourself that you'd only been on a few dates. It's not like you were sleeping together or anything, is it? You'll move on; you're only young and there are loads of fit men around. Tell you what, we'll go down to that bar by the marina one evening – there's bound to be a few good catches in there. Might even bag you a guy with a super-yacht, how thrilling would that be?' Sam nudges me with her elbow and I know she's just trying to cheer me up so I don't worry about being single again. After Brett, it took me nearly two years to get together with Tom. OK, I had the odd evening out with a few guys and then the one-night stand with James during that time too, but it's not the same as a proper boyfriend. I chew the inside of my cheek. Sam places the iPad on the table. Silence follows. And then she realises.

'Oh God, you *were* sleeping together, weren't you? Oh honey, come here.' Sam swings her arms around my shoulders and gives me an enormous hug, enveloping me in a heady mixture of Halston Woman perfume and vanilla frosting.

'I'm sorry.' I lean in to her for maximum comfort.

'What for?' She pulls back to see my face.

'For not telling you,' I say, running my index fingers under my eyes in a feeble attempt to keep my mascara intact.

'Don't be silly.'

'But we tell each other everything. It was only one night,' I sniff, unable to stem the tears any longer. I wipe the back of my hand across my cheek. 'I'm such a rubbish friend,' I add, feeling really sorry for myself. Sam places her hands on my arms.

'Now, listen. You are an amazing friend, and an amazing person, and if Tom doesn't realise when he's well off, then he's ... well, he's a mug, quite frankly.' Sam shakes her curls defiantly. 'I would call him an arse, a wanker even, but if you end up sorting it all out and marrying him or something, then you'll never forgive me. So for now, he's just a mug.' She grabs a napkin and hands it to me. 'A really crappy one. One that you get in Poundland or, worse still, one of those mugs that comes free with an Easter egg and practically melts your fingerprints right off because the china is so thin.' I attempt a watery smile.

'God, I'm sorry. I feel like such an idiot. I knew deep down that I was probably punching above my weight with Tom.' I pull a face.

'Will you stop it! You're my best friend and I love you, but I hate hearing you rubbish yourself like this. You're gorgeous, funny, kind – a bit bonkers sometimes, admittedly,' she shakes her head, 'but Tom is crazy about you. And I should know.'

'What do you mean?'

'Italy. Ring any bells? He couldn't wait to come and surprise you. He's besotted with you. I could hear it in

107

his voice, every time we spoke on the phone to go over the plans.'

'Well, he has a funny way of showing it,' I say, taking a massive slurp of hot chocolate and scalding the roof of my mouth in the process. I grab a slice of Battenberg and take a big bite to sooth the pain.

'He even said as much to Nathan ... how you're not like any other girl he's known.'

'I bet. Especially if they are all stunning like ... *Zaaara*. Even her name is flirty and glamorous-sounding.' I take another bite of the cake.

'Now that's enough,' Sam says. 'Will you please have a bit of faith? You're a grown, confident woman, so put a smile on your face, swallow your pride, find out what time it is in Paris and bloody call him. I'm not going to sit back while you throw a pity party for one.'

'I'm sorry,' I say in a feeble voice.

'And quit saying sorry.' She creases her forehead. 'Sorry,' she quickly adds, and we both crack up.

'Ha!' I'm the first to recover. 'I'm being silly, aren't I?' I pull a cartoon sad face to lighten the mood.

'A bit.' Sam holds up a thumb and index finger in front of my face as a measure. 'Look, life is too short. We both know that.' She squeezes my hand gently as the unspoken thought passes between us. I nod, remembering Mum, gone too soon, and now Alfie.

'Do you want Tom back?' she asks, looking serious now.

'Yes,' I say, relishing the feeling I get whenever I think

about him. I've never felt it so intensely and that has to mean something. Maybe he still is my one. And if there's a glimmer of a chance that he is, then I can't just give up. Some people search a lifetime looking for their one, so I should count myself lucky that he's here, right under my nose ... well, in Paris to be exact, if I really want to get picky about it.

'So go for what you want. Grab him with both hands—'

'One on each bum cheek.' I snort.

'Exactly. Don't let her steal him away from you. *Call him.*'

'OK. I will.' I swallow hard.

'Promise?'

'I promise. Now, can we please change the subject?'

'Yes,' Sam says, decisively. 'I'm going to have one of those 4D scans.'

'Fab.' I smile.

'It is.' Sam tries not to laugh again as we attempt a sensible conversation.

'Err, what is a 4D scan?'

'I have no idea. But Jenny – works in Greggs up by the station, you know, the one whose husband is in Afghanistan?' I nod. 'Well, she's pregnant as well and due a few months before me.'

'Ahh, that's nice,' I say, wondering how she managed it. Last time I bumped into Jenny on the bus, she said Tony was away on another tour.

'They got lucky during his last R&R,' Sam explains, as if reading my mind. 'Anyway, she gave me the number of a clinic over by the golf course that does a whole range of different scans, and they give you a DVD to take away. And if you sign up for the pay-per-view scheme, you can even go in and watch the baby whenever you like on their fifty-inch plasma screen. It's just like being at the cinema, she said. I'm so excited and I can't wait to see little Honey Moon Taylor making her debut. Wonder if she'll give me a wave,' Sam squeals, and I give her a big hug.

'Oh me too. When can you tell if it is actually a girl?' I ask.

'I'm not sure. But I just know there's a girl in here.' Sam rubs her tummy. 'At least there'd better be. I'm seeing gorgeous little dresses and Hello Kitty everywhere, not Bob the Builder and mountains of mud.' Sam rolls her eyes.

'And what about Nathan?'

'Ahh, he says any child is a gift and he just wants them to be happy and healthy. Me too, of course ... but a girl would be really nice,' she quickly adds.

'Hmm, well I hope little Honey has more luck than me with men,' I smile wryly.

'Oh, you'll be fine. Just call him.' Sam stands up and starts clearing the table. I help her carry the cake stand and mugs over to the counter. 'Let me know how it goes,' she says, pushing open the swing door to the kitchen with

110

her hip. I follow and place the mugs in the dishwasher, and the cake stand on the side, knowing how Sam likes them hand-washed instead.

'Will do.' I give her a quick kiss on the cheek. 'Oh, one last thing – do you know what a shaman is?'

'A *whaat?*' Sam shrugs and pulls a face. 'Can you eat it?'

'I don't think so,' I smile.

'Then I'm not interested. Why do you want to know?'

'Just something I heard earlier.'

'Is it important?'

'No!'

Waving, I push though the swing door and take a deep breath before leaving the café and heading towards the staff lift. I'm going to call into Masood's shop, and then ring Tom later because, it's like Sam said, I'm a grown, confident woman. I say it over and over as a mantra inside my head while doing my absolute best to ignore a raft of sabotaging thoughts about mince pies and custard with ten Benson thrown in, while Zara boards an aeroplane bound for Paris wearing the teeniest-tiniest string bikini she can find.

8

Seven shopping weeks until Christmas

It's Sunday morning and I'm admiring my gorgeous new big hair in the light-bulb-framed mirror and wondering if it might be just a bit over the top for a sales assistant. But Kelly insisted and who am I to argue? Besides, I secretly love my new hair extensions. I've gone from having a wispy brunette bob to mid-length luscious hair with caramel and honey highlights that swings back into place whenever I shake my head. I'm like something out of a L'Oréal advert. And I've had my teeth whitened, which was excruciating by the way, but sooo worth it as I now have a proper gleaming Hollywood smile.

Annie is sitting next to me and we're in the make-shift dressing room down in the basement, which has been adorned with paper chains and tinsel so it feels really Christmassy, especially when Michael Bublé starts singing 'It's Beginning to Look a Lot Like Christmas' on the radio. Kelly had an old stockroom cleared out and furnished with a row of chairs, mirrors and little changing cubicles. Every surface is crammed with cosmetics, packs of fashion tape, hair paraphernalia and continental breakfast platters, piled high with pastries and fruit, courtesy of Sam's café. An enormous clothes rail runs the length of the room, crammed with virtually all of Womenswear's stock, and an assortment of divine heels from Footwear. And I'm sure I spotted a pair of red lacquer-soled Louboutins nestling at the back – I sooo hope I get to wear them.

'See you later, Georgie,' Annie says, as Millie arrives to take her off somewhere.

'Yes, will do, and good luck,' I call out over my shoulder.

My mobile buzzes with the arrival of a text message. I quickly check the screen, hoping it's from Tom, but it isn't. I sag in disappointment on seeing that it's another message from Dad. Not that I don't like hearing from Dad, I do. I really do. Our relationship is great now and he's really getting the hang of texting; he wants to know if I prefer carrots, cauliflower cheese or both with my roast dinner later on. I still don't know the news he wants to share – he wouldn't say when we spoke on the phone yesterday, said it's best kept until he sees me – but it must be something important if he's actually cooking. It's not his forte. I tap out a reply and end it with a kiss followed by a heart icon – Dad will love it, inserting icons into a message is next on his agenda to master.

My finger hovers over the text message stream between Tom and me, and as I read the last four that I sent to him on Monday evening, right after seeing myself on TV, I cringe all over again. And like I have a trillion times – at least – since then, I ponder on sending him one last text.

After my chat with Sam in the café, I've tried calling Tom, several times in fact, but his number does an international ringing tone before going straight to voicemail, leaving me wondering if he's actually avoiding me on purpose. I'm reluctant to leave a voice message for fear of umming and ahhing or generally making a fool of myself by sounding desperate. I'm not sure I could bear it if he didn't call back. I decide to go ahead and text him instead. I've typed out:

Hi Tom hope you arrived safel

when Eddie appears, so I quickly delete it and shove the phone inside my pocket instead.

'*Heeeey sexy ladeeeee* ... ' Eddie sings, doing a lasso movement in the air and shaking his hips in proper gangnam style. Pussy is tucked under his free arm and she's wearing a Wonder Woman outfit complete with tiny red cape. I stroke her ear and she nuzzles into the palm of my hand as Eddie leans down to kiss my cheek.

'Thank you,' I say, doing a quick swing of my hair.

'Oooh, get you, very red carpet and swishy. Has Kelly forgotten that we're inside a department store located in a dull little seaside town?' he sniffs, giving Pussy a treat from a tiny plastic barrel attached to her lead.

'Maybe, but I'm not complaining.' I grin and turn back to face the mirror.

'Good. So no more tantrums about being a dramality star.' He squeezes my shoulder and smiles over my head in the mirror.

'Who, *me*?' I laugh, waving a hand in the air as if to shoo him away. 'And Mulberry-On-Sea isn't dull.' I pull a pretend indignant face. I love living here.

'Ha-ha. Well, it's hardly Hollywood now, is it?' Eddie quips. 'Anyway, what do you think of my look? Dapper and debonair, yes?' He does a twirl to show off another new suit. 'Ciaran reckons I look like Gary Barlow channelling lord of the manor at Glastonbury. In the VIP area, obvs – I don't do mud.' He curls his top lip.

'Hmm,' I nod. 'Well I can see why Ciaran thinks that. You look very suave in tweed, but are those green Hunter wellies really necessary?' Eddie pulls a face. 'Don't suppose you've heard from Tom yet?' I add, changing the subject.

'No sugar. Like I said when you asked me yesterday, and the day before, and the day before that, only emails – work-related ones. And no, I can't ask why he hasn't been in contact with you. More than my job's worth. He made it very clear after that time you asked me to find out about his favourite aftershave, right at the start when you wanted to get him a little present. He was very insistent on the importance of our relationship remaining professional. I'm his BA, not his GBF.' Eddie rolls his eyes. 'And y'all know how gloriously masterful and proper he can be,' he adds in an American accent as he flings the back of his left hand against his forehead like a lovestruck Southern belle in a back-and-white movie epic.

'Hmm. Well you must at least know when he's coming back. As his BA, won't you have booked the flight?' I say, giving my hair a quick pat.

'Oh no, KCTV take care of all that now. And with Tom away, I'm to be Kelly's go-to man while they're filming instore, so I'll be cutting back on my Carrington's work – Kelly needs me more.' He pauses to preen for a bit.

'I see.'

'He did mention that he was hoping to be back in a week or two, though.' My heart sinks at this news. I've really missed Tom and it's only been five days since I last saw him. I can't imagine another week, or possibly two, without him. 'But it depends – he's hoping to get his filming in the can, as it were up front. The plan is to then spread his scenes out over all of the weekly episodes, so the viewers think he's travelling for the duration of the series. I heard Kelly chatting about it to one of her flunkies.'

'Oh right.' But before I can probe him further, Zara appears by the clothes rail, wearing a brown peplum dress. Eddie swivels his head to follow my eye line.

'Ew, what's she come as? A pork pie!' he blurts out, before helping himself to a croissant. He pulls one claw off and stuffs it into his mouth.

'Eddie! Whisper voice, she might hear you,' I say, not wanting to antagonise her. She already hates me. The ghastly image from the internet, of her draped all over Tom, flashes inside my head, followed by an overwhelming sense of relief – at least she's still here and not in Paris! Small mercies, and all that, I suppose.

'Good,' he huffs, before giving Pussy a tiny bite of his croissant. 'That girl is driving me insane.'

'Why? What's she done?' I crease my forehead.

'What hasn't she done, more like? Parading around the executive floor with her Swarovski encrusted mobile welded to her ear while I do all the work running after Kelly and her entourage. Not that I mind, of course, Kelly is a proper ledge, but honestly – comes to something when her own daughter can't even be bothered to pick out a Christmas present for her. Had me calling all over the place in search of something suitable for a "mean old mare" – her words, not mine.'

'Ahh, such a shame,' I say, thinking how exciting it would be to be able to go Christmas shopping for Mum. She loved all the build-up, marking off the days on her kitchen calendar, and she always got teary on opening her present from me. I make a note to visit her grave soon; perhaps Dad and I could go together. I'd like that.

'Oh purlease, cry me a fucking river. That girl is up to something, I'm convinced of it.'

'What do you mean?'

'I mean, numerous international calls from the landline

in Tom's office. The bill arrived on Friday and it was nearly treble what it usually is. Flaming cheek, and it's not like she's so hard up for cash that she can't afford to pay for her own personal phone calls. Kelly gave her two thousand pounds the other day, in fifties. Just like that!' He clicks his fingers in the air. 'All because she wanted to pamper herself ahead of today's filming. Excuse me! But where do you know around here that charges money like that for a mani and pedi with a bit of a shoulder rub thrown in? Nowhere, that's where! I mean, what are they using? *Crushed diamond dust!*' Eddie flops down in the chair next to me. I try not to laugh at his indignation as he plonks Pussy on my lap and leans forward to inspect his teeth in the mirror.

'Uh-oh, here she comes.' Eddie elbows me and then jumps up and smoothes down his suit jacket.

'There you are! Eddie, sweetheart, I've been looking all over for you.' Zara flashes her perfect white veneers. 'What are you two talking about?' she adds, running a finger along the table in front of me.

'Oh, we were just saying how fabulous you look and how exciting today is going to be, weren't we Georgie?' Eddie kisses the air either side of Zara's head, which she reciprocates, while I cough as her flirty sweet Clive Christian perfume catches in my throat.

'Err, yes. That's right,' I say, recovering quickly and flashing big eyes in Eddie's direction when Zara isn't looking.

'Well, don't get too excited. We're going to be

focusing on highlighting your inadequacies today,' she says, inspecting her immaculately manicured nails and flashing me a look.

'Oh?' I stand up, so I'm operating from the same level as her, and hand Pussy back to Eddie.

'Yes. That's right. The board of directors asked KCTV to help you up your game, remember? So naturally we have to show the viewers that it needs upping in the first place, obviously. You're going to be dealing with a customer complaint.' Zara points at me. 'And you, darling,' she pauses to flutter her extra-long eyelashes at Eddie, 'well, you and the dog are going to be showing off the new pet spa.' She runs an index finger down Eddie's lapel.

'Fabulous. Kelly did mention it, hence the boots.' Eddie grins, twirling a welly-clad foot in the air. 'Can get very mucky in there with all that sluicing going on,' he adds, lowering his voice and pulling an exaggerated grimace. Zara does a tinkly laugh before shaking her big hair around for a bit while admiring herself in the mirror.

'OK, five minutes. Then can I have you all out on the shop floor?' someone shouts out, before I have a chance to quiz Zara for details. I can't imagine what the complaint is about; we don't get many disgruntled customers, other than the odd light-hearted comment from a local about the high-end bags being too expensive.

After doing more air kisses with Eddie, Zara sashays off with her mobile pressed up to her ear, and the first thing that pops into my head is – I wonder if it's Tom she's whispering to? I quickly shove the thought away and turn to face Eddie.

'*Whaaaat?*' he says, shrugging his shoulders and sticking his bottom lip out.

'Nothing.' I pull a face and roll my eyes.

'Honey-pie, I've got to keep her sweet. She could hold the key to my new career,' he says in a stagey voice, by way of explanation.

'Pardon?'

'As a dramality star, of course. I have to keep her on side. Besides, she actually knows Claire, Pete's manager, and if I play my cards right then she'll put a good word in for me. I'm convinced of it.'

'Well, five minutes ago you didn't trust her – talk about fickle,' I say, gratefully taking the Loubs from a wardrobe woman. I run an index finger over the buttery soft black leather. It takes me less than two seconds to kick off my New Look heels.

'And I still don't. But I'm not letting that stop me from lifting up a BAFTA at the telly awards next year. I've already rehearsed my speech,' he says, with a totally serious look on his face. My pulse quickens as I slip my feet inside the exquisite shoes and nod to confirm that they fit perfectly, and even if they didn't I'm not sure I'd admit it. I don't care if I end up crippled like a geisha – these shoes are *lush*. And they're staying on my feet.

After thanking the wardrobe woman profusely, I shake

off the black hairdresser's cape that I've been wearing to protect my clothes – a beautifully cut cream DVF trouser suit over a shimmery green butterfly-patterned silk shirt. I feel so glamorous. Eddie stares at me open-mouthed before letting out a long wolf whistle.

'Err ... wowdotcom. This just got a whole lot more exciting.' He loops his left arm though mine. 'Darling Georgina Hart, let's go and meet our public!' he announces, regally sweeping an arm out wide as if to clear a path for us.

9

We make it on to the shop floor that is lit up like a film set. There are four enormous light bulbs positioned either side of my counter, next to two white paper screens on metal poles, and it feels as though there are people everywhere. Some are obviously from the production company, KCTV; they're wearing funky outfits and flitting around clutching clipboards and various gadgets. The others must be the actors – men, women, a few children; but they all have coats, hats and scarfs on, and a few are even holding Carrington's Christmas carrier bags.

Mrs Grace is hovering by the DKNY display and her beehive has grown a good inch or two higher since I last saw her. And I'm sure her lipstick is more luminescent. Annie comes over to meet me.

'Blimey, you look stunning babe.' She takes my hands in hers and holds them out wide to get a proper look at me.

'And so do you,' I say, smiling at her black fitted maxi dress with Audrey Hepburn style hairdo – the high bun is perfect and the expertly applied smoky eyes with flicky eyeliner make her look stunning.

'God, I'm so excited. But that Zara said we're getting a complaint. You know I hate dealing with complaints,' she whispers, leaning into me.

'Don't worry. We'll just do what we always do. I'll deal with it. If they come to you, then call me over as you normally would. I think it's important that we keep this as real as possible, even if we are dressed up like movie stars.' I smile and give her hands a quick squeeze for reassurance.

'Is it a real complaint then, do you think?' She raises her eyebrows.

'I have no idea, but let's treat it as such. That way we can't go wrong and get portrayed as inefficient like we were in the pilot show.'

'Good thinking,' Annie grins, before being shepherded away by a production assistant.

I take up my position by the counter, wishing I could wear sunglasses as the lights are so bright. I can already feel a trickle of sweat snaking a path down my back, it's that hot in here. I'm contemplating plumping up a few bags as I normally would before we open up, when Hannah appears in front of my counter, bouncing around like an overexcited puppy.

'OK Georgie, as we said on Friday at the rehearsal ...' I try not to smile. 'Rehearsal' is stretching it a bit, more like five minutes in the staff canteen in between bites of her tuna melt panini; she said to 'keep it real' and to 'go with the flow', whatever that means. I nod instead.

'If you screw up then just carry on, we can always edit out any gaffs. You'll be fab, but most of all – be yourself! Like I said before, you're a natural and the viewers are going to *lurrrrrve* you. We've already had enquiries about your status,' she adds enthusiastically, and the bouncing intensifies.

'Status? What do you mean?'

'Single. Married. That kind of thing. You never know, we might be able to get you filmed out on a few dates. Viewers love all that. And we'd foot the bill, of course.' She elbows me affectionately as if we're best friends chatting over coffee and cake.

'But I'm not single.' I bite my lip.

'Oh!' She frowns. 'Are you sure?' She stops bouncing, tilts her head to one side and wrinkles her nose instead. 'I thought you were. I'm sure Kelly mentioned it.'

'Well ... not exactly. Maybe. Sort of ... err, well it's complicated,' I mutter before glancing away, feeling like an absolute idiot.

'Oh don't worry, I'll chat to Kelly and see what she has in mind,' she says, lifting her eyebrows suggestively.

'But I thought the show was abou—' She dashes off, so I end up mumbling 'helping Carrington's to up its game' to myself. My heart sinks. I feel duped all over again. I only agreed to be in the show because I thought it was about Carrington's. Not my love life. Maybe I should have kept out of the spotlight and gone downstairs to sell washing machines instead. I suck in a big gulp of air.

Well, they can't make me be filmed on dates – I know there definitely wasn't a clause about that in my employment contract. Hannah stops and dashes back to me.

'And, ooh, I nearly forgot, what's your writing like?' she puffs.

'My writing?' I ask, momentarily stunned by the randomness of her question.

'Not that it really matters, we can write it for you. A celebrity gossip mag, I forget which one, wants you to do a guest column, write about accessory tips, that kind of thing, tell their readers which bag goes with which outfit. You up for it?'

'Err, yes please! Thank you.' *Wow, my own column.* My mood instantly lifts as I try to take in this exciting new development. Maybe I was a bit hasty in dismissing my involvement in the show after all. This is a once-in-a-lifetime opportunity. 'I'd love to.' I grin.

'Good. They'll pay of course. Won't be much, two grand-ish if you agree to a photoshoot too.'

Whaaaat? £2,000. Oh my God. Amazing.

I'm mulling it all over and feeling really chuffed when a pumped-up version of Wham's 'Last Christmas' bellows through the speakers and the people in coats jump into action – chatting and wandering around the store, looking at and touching the festive merch, creating an authentic busy Saturday afternoon feel. For a moment I'm transfixed at the show unfolding in front of me; it's like being in an actual film or a modern-day episode of

Mr Selfridge – the atmosphere is buzzy and electric, and very, very exciting. My pulse quickens. I think I'm going to love doing this, after all.

The music reaches the '*gave you my heart*' bit, when a woman appears by the Marc Jacobs display. She seems just like a real customer and not how I imagine an actress to look like at all. She's wearing a black mohair coat and even has droplets of rain on her red patent handbag. I can't decide whether to approach her or not. Annie catches my eye and I can tell that she's thinking the same thing. In my peripheral vision I see a camera gliding up behind the woman, who's looking directly at me now, so I decide to go for it.

'Good morning, were you looking for a particular bag?' I give her a smile, and she responds with a poker face. I plough on. 'Just give me a shout if you see anything you like,' I add, retreating back to my counter, knowing that customers like this are best left alone until they're ready to engage. Only she isn't a real customer, and I have no idea what her agenda is. I busy myself with labelling up a new delivery of chunky cocktail rings to go in the display board on the counter. They arrived on Friday but we didn't have time to unpack them then, so I might as well make use of being here on a Sunday. Besides, it will make the show look more authentic if I'm doing what I normally would at work. I've just placed an exquisite sunshine-yellow daisy design ring into place, when the woman beckons me over.

'At last! I've been standing here for ten minutes. I want that bag,' she says rudely, pointing to a gorgeous chocolate leather tote up on the top shelf.

'Oh good choice,' I say, grabbing the stepladder to retrieve the bag.

'No. Not that one. This one.' She wags her finger along the shelf towards the same bag, but in navy crocodile leather. I move the stepladder along and start climbing up. The camera shifts around until it's positioned at the first rung looking up at me, and a sudden moment of panic sets in. What if they're filming my bottom again? There's no backing out now so I leg it up the ladder, retrieve the bag and make my descent in record time, figuring that if I keep moving then at least there won't be too many static shot opportunities, but my left Loub catches on the carpet as I step down and I end up catapulting myself backwards across the floor. The bag does an Olympic standard high-dive somersault before landing in the real pine Christmas tree next to the Lulu Guinness display. Feeling mortified, I fling myself back into a standing position, quickly straighten my jacket and push my big hair extensions away from my face before retrieving the bag, brushing off the pine cones and handing it to the woman. I swear I can hear someone stifling a snigger in the background. 'No, I don't think so,' the woman says, after inspecting the bag. 'It has a scratch.'

'Oh.' I study the area near her pointed index finger.

'Right there.' She taps the leather a couple of times in quick succession.

'I think that's part of the actual crocodile skin,' I state, diplomatically. I can't see a scratch.

'It isn't.'

'No problem, I can easily get another one from the stock cupboard. In the original packaging,' I offer, not wanting to argue about it, especially on camera.

'But I want this one,' she says, taking the bag back and flinging it over her shoulder.

'Of course.' I smile and she stares at me for a bit.

'How much is it?' she asks, pulling it open to inspect the monogrammed interior. I tell her the price and she nods.

'I'll take it.'

'Are you sure? I'm more than happy to get another one for you, if you prefer.' She shakes her head before glancing at the camera.

'This one.'

'Great. Would you like it gift-wrapped?' I remember to keep smiling, thinking this is a bit bizarre; one minute she's complaining and now ... but I decide to 'go with the flow' as Hannah instructed.

'Yes,' she says, and I head towards the counter. She follows. The camera too. I pull out the dustbag and place the tote inside, before selecting a suitably sized box from under the counter. Just as I place the bag inside the box she slaps her hand down, making me jump. 'I've changed my mind.'

I open my mouth to speak, but she turns and marches away, leaving me gaping after her. The cameraman zooms in for a close up and I realise that my mouth is actually hanging open, but before I can figure out what just happened – somebody shouts, 'Cut', and Kelly appears from behind a camera.

'Bravo!' she says, clapping enthusiastically. 'This is TV gold, just what we like. But you must remember to stand up tall and smile, sweetie. *Smile*. It's all about the tits and teeth! Say it after me. And shake your hair back too,' Kelly commands, so I mutter 'tits and teeth' and flick my hair around like a performing show pony, willing my cheeks to stop burning. 'That's it. Tits and teeth. Hair shake.' She makes the jingle-jangle sound as she dances from one foot to other, grinning like a loon as she thrusts her cleavage up in the air.

'Sure. And sorry about my fall.'

'Don't be daft.' She flaps a hand around for a bit.

'Will it be edited out?' I ask, keeping my fingers crossed behind my back.

'Probably not.' My heart sinks. *Great*. My YouTube hits are going to be stratospheric at this rate. 'But don't worry. The viewers will adore you even more.' Leaning in to me, her faces changes to serious and she whispers, 'You are wonderful. A natural. And if you keep this up you will find your life transformed. I promise you that. I'm going to help you.' She pats my arm discreetly.

'Um, thank you,' I breathe, as another wave of

excitement fizzes through me, even though I'm not entirely sure what she means by 'transformed'; but if it has anything to do with me writing magazine columns, then I'm up for it. She may be bonkers and a bit scary, but I can't help warming to her. Maybe she isn't the enemy after all.

'Right. Positions please,' a guy shouts out. Kelly disappears and the camera is rolling again. The guy who bought the Chloé bag on Tuesday is striding towards me.

'I bought this the other day,' he says, not bothering to even say hello.

'Oh yes, I remember. How are you? How is your wife? And Declan?' I ask, fixing a smile on my face.

'It's broken so I need a refund,' he says, ignoring my questions and dumping the Carrington's carrier bag on the counter.

'OK, I'll take a look,' I say slowly. *So this must be the complaint that Zara mentioned.* He's a very good actor, because he seems genuinely ruffled, a stark contrast to the easy-going, laidback, loving husband and Dad thing he had going on before.

'Right there. See, the zip on the inside pocket is stuck and there's a lipstick stain on the fabric. It's been used,' he states, folding his arms.

'But it can't have been,' I say, feeling confused. There's no way Carrington's would sell a used handbag. Even a return would have been checked over thoroughly before being put back into stock. I look at the camera, unsure of

130

what to do next. I've never encountered a real situation like this before, let alone a pretend one. I scan the crowd, desperately searching for Hannah, but she's not here. I swallow and inhale hard through my nose, figuring it best to treat him just like any other customer.

'I'm really sorry, but the bag wasn't like this when it left the store,' I say, knowing that I can't just give him a full refund. It's an expensive, high-end bag, and it definitely wasn't like this when he bought it. And the tags have been removed.

'Well how did it get in this state then?'

'Err, I'm not sure, perhaps somebody used it,' I suggest, cringing and wishing I was anywhere but here. My brain seems to have gone all foggy, and why does it have to be so blooming hot in here? I run a finger along the inside of my collar, conscious of the camera just mere centimetres from my face.

'Are you saying that I've used it?' he asks, staring straight into my eyes.

'No. No, of course not. Sorry, that wasn't what I meant.' I can feel my cheeks burning again now. This is horrendous; I'm not normally so feeble with customers, but with the cameras and the production people all around me, I'm like a rabbit caught in the headlights, literally. And I'm sure another light bulb just went on. Suddenly a dazzling circuit of white light surrounds me and I feel panicky. My pulse quickens and my head spins. I place a hand on the counter to steady myself and realise that I'm actually holding my breath.

'Good, because that would be ridiculous. I'm not in the habit of using ladies' handbags.' He glares as a camera moves in for a close-up.

'Of course. But didn't you say it was a Christmas gift for your wife? It was gift-wrapped, and now it isn't?' I say, quickly pulling myself together. *Ha! Wriggle out of that one.* Two can play this game, which is exactly what this is, a game; he's not even a real customer. He's an actor. I've a good mind to shout 'CUT' just so we can get this farce over with right away.

'I wanted to check it before I gave it to my wife. And good job too. She would have been devastated if I'd presented her with a special bag in such an appalling state. Maybe it's you that used it. Or what about her?' he says, jabbing a finger at Annie, who drops her jaw in silent protest. A camera immediately glides up close so as not to miss a nanosecond of Annie's indignation. I open my mouth. I close it, willing my cheeks to stop flaming. I take a deep breath. I've had enough of this.

'Zara, more like.' But the minute the words come out of my mouth, I want to run away and hide. She already hates me. Silence follows.

'Cut!' It's Leo Afro who breaks the moment. The guy in front of me starts laughing. His shoulders are actually pumping up and down like a cartoon character. He must think the whole thing is hysterical.

'Nearly had you then,' he says, winking at me as he pulls off his outdoor coat and wings it at a production assistant. 'God, it's boiling in here. I'm Lawrence, by the way.' He places an elbow on the counter and leans into me. 'Fancy a drink sometime?'

'Err. No, not really,' I say, dragging myself up to speed. Talk about surreal. Everyone starts clapping. I force a smile, but can't help feeling that I've been had, and not in a good way. I take off my jacket and grab one of the Santa's grotto promotional leaflets from the counter to fan my face, when Hannah appears.

'Well done. That was amazing. Kelly is thrilled,' she says, lifting my free hand and pumping it up and down.

'*Really?*' I make big eyes.

'Deffo, she just called to say that she's left a little something in the dressing room for you. A thank you for being such a shiny star.'

'OK. And thank you,' I say, feeling surprised. 'But what about the ladder incident and the ... ' Oh where do I start? The whole scene was a complete and utter shambles.

'No probs. Anyway, must dash, need to get over to the pet spa now for the scene with Eddie.'

'Sure. Can I see Kelly before I go?' I ask quickly. With a bit of luck I might manage to persuade her to cut the ladder bit after all.

'Sorry, she's already left.' Hannah shrugs before glancing down at my feet. 'And don't forget to drop the Loubs back to the dressing room. They have to stay, I'm afraid.'

10

Crossing the road into the cul-de-sac, I head towards the retirement complex overlooking Mulberry Common. Two floors of net-curtained, brand-new sheltered housing, where each resident has their own self-contained flat. It's amazing: there's a communal lounge with an enormous flatscreen TV, onsite medical centre, a minibus to take the residents down to the supermarket and back – but best of all, Dad has company; he's not sitting alone in the tired little studio flat on the sink estate where he used to live. The council condemned the block when somebody discovered asbestos, so now he lives here, and he was lucky enough to get a ground-floor flat – so he has a pretty garden and was allowed to bring his black Labrador, Dusty, with him too.

After saying goodbye to Annie and reluctantly returning the Loubs, I collected the present from Kelly, a gorgeous bunch of hand-tied russet and plum-coloured seasonal flowers with a card saying:

I'm going to make you a HUGE star! Love Kelly x

I'm not really sure how I feel about being a star, to be honest. Writing the column is more my thing. And yes, it was pretty exciting walking onto the shop floor and being part of it all, but the thought of seeing how they actually portray me on TV this time is utterly petrifying, especially if the pilot is anything to go by. I'll be a laughing stock all over again, I'm sure of it. Eddie can't wait, of course, and sent me a text suggesting he comes over to my flat on Wednesday evening so we can watch the first episode together.

I hoist the flowers further under my arm. Mum would have loved them, which gives me an idea – maybe Dad and I could put them on her grave, it's still early. I'll suggest going after lunch before it gets dark. I'm sure Dad will want to. I take the card from the cellophane and stow it inside my handbag, there's a newsagent's near the entrance to the cemetery where I can buy another one just for Mum.

Heading up the path, I see Dad coming towards me with Dusty bouncing along beside him, and he looks really well. Sort of sprightly and more energetic than when I last saw him a couple of weeks ago. He's standing taller, not stooping like before, and I'm sure his hair looks darker and less grey – maybe he's been at the Just For Men. Well, good for him, it's nice seeing him garner back some self-respect, and Dusty looks good too, her coat is super-shiny. She wags her tail on recognising me and nuzzles my gloved hand affectionately; I respond by stroking her silky ears.

'Georgie! It's so good to see you love, and you're looking well. Have you changed your hair? It was on your shoulders last time I saw you, it looks much longer now – how can that be in the space of a week or two?' Dad asks, confusion creasing his forehead as he kisses my cheek and slings an arm around my shoulders, drawing me in close, the spicy fresh scent of his woolly scarf comforting and reminiscent of my childhood, before everything changed and he went to prison. I remember visiting him a couple of times, but it wasn't the same. In there he just smelt of boiled cabbage and institution. We carry on walking side by side.

'Hair extensions, Dad,' I explain.

'Well I never.' He shakes his head in disbelief. 'Oh, before I forget, I've got something for you.' He pulls a scrunched-up Asda carrier bag from his pocket.

'Oh Dad, you don't have to buy me gifts,' I say, unravelling the bag after giving him a kiss. There's a used bottle of YSL Opium inside. The glorious, original, warm musky one. Neither of us speaks. My chin trembles momentarily.

'Mum's perfume.' The words catch in my throat as I'm instantly transported back in time – sitting crossed-legged on the edge of the bed as Mum got ready for an evening out; once satisfied that her hair and make-up were perfect, she'd let me spritz the fragrance onto her wrists.

'I found it in an old suitcase when I was unpacking after the move. Thought you might like it,' Dad says, softly.

I manage a nod as I pull off the cap. The perfume is

old and stale, but I can still, just about, inhale Mum's scent. I know she died a long time ago, but with Dad in prison when she went, and then not really back in my life until recently, we've only started talking about her – it's as if part of the grieving process has started all over again, only far nicer this time, now that we can remember her together. Fondly.

'Shame to waste it, the bottle is almost full,' Dad says to lighten the moment, and for some reason it makes me laugh. He gives my arm a squeeze and I bob my head down onto his shoulder as I slip the perfume into my coat pocket. I'm so glad we have each other again.

'So how are you, darling?'

'Oh not bad, Dad, thanks. How are you?'

Our breath puffs out into little clouds against the chilly winter air.

'I'm fine, but come on … tell me what's up.' Dad stops walking and turns to look at me. I pull my coat in tighter.

'Nothing, honestly, I'm OK.' I smile.

'Are you sure? You sound tired. Is that it? Have they been working you too hard down at that shop?' he asks sternly.

'No, no, nothing like that. Let's go inside and I'll tell you all about it,' I say, knowing that he definitely doesn't watch TV programmes like *Kelly Cooper Come Instore*, much preferring wildlife or gardening documentaries, and he doesn't even know about Tom. I had wanted to wait a bit before mentioning him, and if recent events are anything to go by, then it's a good job too! What's the point of introducing a boyfriend to Dad if he's just going to disappear without warning? Dad will only get disappointed; he's always saying that people are meant to be together, in pairs, as nature intended, and that it's time for me to 'let a man come close' ... only a decent one of course. When I told him recently what happened with Brett, he wasn't impressed.

'Good idea, love, it's perishing out here.' Dad rubs my arm briskly as we step inside the communal hallway. After pulling off my gloves and pushing them into my pocket, I head towards his front door.

'This way. I've got a surprise.' Dad smiles and gestures towards another door in the opposite direction, and a little further down the corridor. There's a mat saying HOME SWEET HOME beside a canary-yellow front door and a window box containing plastic pink begonias.

'OK, but what about Dusty?' I ask, and she wriggles her body excitedly.

'Oh she'll be fine, everyone here loves her, and she's like a communal dog really, always in and out of the flats.' He chuckles and rings the bell. Dusty waits patiently at his feet, her tail sweeping from side to side on the carpet.

A few seconds later, the door is opened by a plump, mumsy-looking woman wearing a stripy apron over a floral dress. Her blonde hair is short and wavy and she has a full face of make-up.

'Oooh, perfect timing. I've just pulled the Yorkshire puddings out of the oven. I hope you're both hungry, I've got enough here to feed you each for a week, with second helpings as well!' she says brightly, wiping her hands on the apron. A delicious waft of roast dinner greets us.

'Nancy, I'd like you to meet my wonderful daughter, Georgie.' Dad squeezes my hand, puffs his chest out a little and smiles at the woman.

'Lovely to meet you, dear. I've heard so much about you – it's very nice to finally put a face to the name. And you are very glamorous; I bet the nets were twitching as you arrived. Lunch won't be long,' she says jovially, twiddling the gold chain around her neck with a letter N dangling on the end.

What's going on? I thought Dad was cooking and it was going to be just the two of us, but there's no time to ask, so I quickly push out a hand to shake hers, really wishing I didn't feel like a sulky four year old all of a sudden. The flowers nose-dive from my elbow and end up batting her on the shoulder instead. I open my mouth to apologise, but she beats me to it.

'Oh, you shouldn't have.'

And before I can protest, explain that they're Mum's flowers and not hers, Nancy rescues the bouquet and presses her nose into it. My heart sinks.

'Mmmm, they smell just like a basket of fresh laundry,' she says on surfacing. 'And such a treat. The bingo girls are going to be so jealous. Thank you, my dear.' Nancy leans forward and gives me a big kiss on the cheek. A short silence follows and, as if sensing my disappointment, Dusty gives me a quick lick on the back of my hand. 'Come in, come in. Where are my manners?'

Nancy leads us into her sitting room where there's a real fire crackling in the grate and two big squishy armchairs either side of a silver Christmas tree with twinkling red and blue fairy lights. And it's laden with chocolate snowman decorations wrapped in foil, hanging on gold threads. The room is toasty warm and sparkly pristine, with white lacy doilies everywhere. There's an old-fashioned glass cabinet in the corner crammed full of mementoes – picture postcards, a sprig of lucky heather with its stem wrapped in tin foil and framed photos of people who I guess must be members of her family. On the mantelpiece above the fire is a picture of a pretty girl with long auburn hair next to a black-and-white picture of a young man in a policeman's uniform with a helmet under his arm. 'That's my Bob, God rest his soul – passed two years ago,' Nancy explains on seeing me looking.

'Oh, I'm so sorry,' I say, unbuttoning my coat.

'Don't be, love. He had a good innings, was quite a bit older than me.' She pats her hair and smiles sheepishly at Dad, who for some reason looks away. 'Anyway, make yourselves at home. I'll give you a shout when I've plated up,' she adds cheerfully, before disappearing.

140

I am absolutely stuffed. Having eaten my way through the biggest roast dinner ever, with second helpings of everything, including treacle tart with custard *and* ice cream, I just about manage to roll off my chair and stagger back to the sitting room. Nancy insisted. I offered to clear the table and wash up, but she was having none of it, so now she's in the kitchen loading her slimline dishwasher while Dad and I drink tea from china cups with saucers.

Dad motions towards an armchair for me to sit down. Dusty is stretched out on the rug in front of the fire, basking in the heat.

'So how long have you known Nancy?' I start, glancing up at him, and then quickly stop when he presses a hand onto my shoulder.

'Darling, she's a friend,' he says, and I instantly know that it's his way of saying she'll never replace Mum, but I saw the way he looked at her when she answered the door, and what about the spring in his step, the hair dye – it all makes sense now. And I guess this is the news he wanted to share. I'm pleased for him, really I am, and it's nice that he has a friend, especially as his old friends all disappeared when he went to prison. I want to be supportive, but there's something else too – a weird feeling, making me kind of twitchy and unsure, one I haven't felt before and I can't work it out. I'm staring at the flames when Nancy appears in the doorway with a plate of chocolate Christmas Yule logs in her hand and a tin of Quality Street under her arm, Dad groans before patting his paunch, so I decide to park the feeling for now, and make a mental note to think it all through later on – when I'm alone and can get my head straight. Nancy seems really nice, even if she has taken Mum's flowers.

11

It's Wednesday evening in my flat, and the atmosphere at work this week has been really buzzy, mingled with lots of anticipation. There's a rumour going around the store that Mulberry-On-Sea council want the cast of *Kelly Cooper Come Instore* to switch the Christmas lights on in town. Now that would be epic. Last year, they had the utterly lush country singer and local guy, Dan Kilby, do it. He turned up looking hot in leather jeans and a checked shirt, with his guitar slung over his shoulder, just like Gunnar Scott in *Nashville*.

All week, the regular customers have been instore, dressed up in their best gear hoping to get their faces on camera. Mr and Mrs Peabody even turned up on Sunday, and Kelly let them in to mingle as background shoppers. And a reporter from the *Mulberry Echo* popped instore yesterday hoping to get an exclusive about the TV show, but one of Kelly's minions appeared from behind the Missoni mannequin and shooed her away. Apparently, Kelly doesn't do local rags, much preferring big glossy sleb magazines with three-page photoshoots. Serena, one of the Clarins concession girls, and absolutely stunning, did *GQ* after the pilot and got to keep the Calvin Klein jewellery collection she modelled. I wonder if I'll get to do one – I'm still holding out for a free diet delivery service, especially as my tiny freezer is now jammed with a turkey that serves 10–12 people (I didn't read the label properly) and one hundred and forty-eight cocktail sausages. Tesco had them in the 'buy one box get two free' deal. And my fridge is brimming with buck's fizz for the festive period – it was such a bargain that I'd have been a fool not to, a case of six bottles for only £9 – I got two. So even if I did want to stock up on healthy food to cook from scratch, I've got nowhere to store it.

Eddie and Sam are here, and we've just polished off an enormous pepperoni pizza while waiting for *Kelly Cooper Come Instore* to start. Sam and Eddie are lounging side by side on the sofa, with Mr Cheeks kneading Sam's thigh. I'm snuggled in the beanbag next to the radiator, wearing my fleecy leopard-print onesie and Ugg boots, and I'm still freezing.

'Ooh, it's *soo* exciting,' Eddie says, wiping his fingers on a paper napkin. 'You know, Claire could be watching right now, scanning her flatscreen searching for the next reality TV star to manage – yours truly, natch.' He pulls a compact mirror out of his man-bag and preens for a bit.

'You know, I think Dad knew Claire. She's Peter Andre's manager, right?' Sam says, casually, and I remember Alfie had lots of celebrity friends, so it's highly likely.

'*Whaaaat?* Faints. You mean to tell me that you've

been sitting on this highly prized piece of information and didn't even think to mention it?' Eddie is outraged.

'Sorry, didn't realise it was important.' Sam shrugs.

'*Important!* This revelation could change my whole life. Can you call her?' Eddie asks, leaning forward.

'What now?'

'Yes.'

'No.'

'Why not?'

'Because I don't know her. And I don't have her phone number.' Sam shakes her head and Eddie slings the mirror back in his bag before sidling into her.

'But you could get it for your very best GBF, couldn't you? Have I ever told you that I love you, and how your hair is looking *sooo* luscious these days, darling, and you're going to be such a fabulous yummy mummy,' Eddie purrs, working it to the max as he strokes Sam's arm with a wicked glint in his eyes.

'Stop it, you big schmoozer.' Sam laughs. 'I could ask Dad's old PA, I guess. What's it worth?' She slurps the last of her orange juice through a pink bendy straw.

'Err ... a free stint in your delightful café!' Eddie immediately offers.

'Blimey, you must be keen. Not like you to volunteer for extra work, Ed,' I interject, before swallowing an enormous mouthful of buck's fizz. Thought it best to make a start if I'm to work my way through all of it before New Year's Eve, when I'll need the space for a bottle or two of champagne. I pour a generous measure into Eddie's flute too.

'Ha-ha.' He sticks his tongue out.

'Washing up?' Sam asks hopefully, and Eddie winces. 'I was thinking of something more ... customer facing! Seeing as I'm such a wonderful raconteur, as you know ... ' He pauses for maximum impact. 'So you might as well utilise my key skill, darlings.' He flashes us both a look as we stifle a snigger. 'Front of house, stirring drinks, that kind of thing.' He makes pleading puppy-dog eyes at Sam and speeds up the stroking.

'God, you're incorrigible. I'll see what I can do,' she says, yanking her arm away. Eddie plants a kiss on her cheek and Sam laughs.

'You won't regret it.'

'I think I already am.' Sam rolls her eyes.

'Will you two pack it in, the show is about to start,' I say, taking the TV remote and turning the volume up. I grab a cushion to hide behind – just in case. I've got butterflies in my stomach and I can't stop shivering, but I'm not so sure it's the winter weather now as it's actually roasting in here. I guess it must be nerves. Eddie throws himself upright so he's perched on the edge of the sofa.

A funky version of Dolly Parton's 'Working Nine To Five' starts playing and, as he whoops, Eddie practically leaps across the room, he's that excited.

'Oh my God. I just knew this was going to be

sensational. Kelly said as much when we were filming in the spa. She even gave me a speaking part,' Eddie gushes.

'What do you mean a "speaking part" – aren't you all talking while you're being filmed then?' Sam asks, stating the obvious.

'Well, yes, I suppose so, but given my natural flair for the limelight – Kelly's actual words ... ' He pauses to strike a pose in front of the balcony patio doors, and I try not to laugh. 'Yes, Kelly upgraded me to "staged spontaneity".' He makes quote signs with his fingers. 'So, I got to act out a completely fabricated scenario. The whole crew were very impressed with my ability to ... ad lib,' he finishes with a flourish. Sam and I stare at him for a few seconds before clapping enthusiastically and then turning back to the TV.

Sam reaches her hand out to grip mine, and there on the screen is Kelly, standing on the pavement in front of the main entrance to Carrington's, with her arms folded, talking about olde worlde charm and how it has no place in the modern retail world, and if Carrington's wants to thrive and be part of the future then we really must up our game. And she's the woman to show us how. I knew it! There'll be glass lifts replacing the wooden escalators before we know it, and the cherry-wood panelling will be ripped out to make way for tiles and chrome. She's going to sterilise Carrington's. Oh God. Maybe us being on *Kelly Cooper Come Instore* isn't such a good idea after all, and I so wish Tom was here so I could make him see sense before it's too late.

I grab my phone, and without hesitation I press to call his number, one last time. I PM'd him on Facebook days ago which he's ignored, I even tried Skypeing him but that request was ignored too. I'm going to try again, if not for our fledgling romance, then for Carrington's, before it's too late. The number rings out. Sam and Eddie stare at me. Eddie swipes the remote from the coffee table, pauses the programme and frantically mouths.

'What the hell are you doing? We're going to miss the start.'

I'm just about to hang up when the international ringing tone stops. Tom's voicemail doesn't kick in this time. I hold my breath. Silence follows.

'Hello, Tom?' I eventually manage. Sam is shaking her head.

'Hang up,' she whispers quickly, and tries to take the phone from me. It ends up being suspended midway between the two of us when a voice talks out into the open air of my lounge.

'He is busy.' It's a woman's voice. With a French accent. Sultry and breathy-sounding. Sam wrenches the phone from my hand and quickly presses the button to end the call.

'What are you doing? You can't chase him,' she says, with a horrified look on her face.

'Calling him, like you told me to,' I say, desperately trying to keep my voice even. I want to yell. *Who is she?* He's only been gone a little while and already another woman is fielding his calls. Answering his mobile – doesn't get more intimate than that. Unless they're actually having sex. The thought makes my vision filmy and my chest tighten.

'But that was then, hun,' Sam says, gently.

'And now is now – which explains why he's ignoring you,' Eddie butts in, wagging a pointed finger in the air.

'*Eddie!*' Sam snaps.

'Sorry, was just saying ... ' He shrugs his shoulders.

'Well don't.' She glares at him.

'Oh, I'm only joking. Georgie knows I adore her and, well, if I'm totes honest, then I'm cross – how dare Tom do this to her and then swan off?' Eddie grabs my hand and gives it a squeeze. 'Push it out of your mind, babycakes. You know how easily you jump to conclusions – she's probably a production assistant and ugly as hell, with a Cyclops eye and a snaggle tooth. Maybe Tom was on the loo or something.' He grimaces. 'Tell you what, let's watch the show and then you can see for yourself. They might show him scouring the Champs-Elysées looking for gorgeous handbags for you to sell. That would be nice, wouldn't it?' Eddie pats the back of my hand as if he's placating a toddler.

'Yes, maybe,' I manage, calming down a bit. He's right, the sexy-sounding woman could be anyone, and I mustn't judge all men by my ex's, Brett's, standards. I take my phone back from Sam and surreptitiously swipe through to the world clock app. It's ten p.m. here, which means it's eleven p.m. in Paris – surely Tom wouldn't be filming this late in the evening? The thought lingers as Eddie presses play on the remote control, and Kelly comes back onto the screen.

The first half of the show is mainly Kelly talking about her years of experience serving customers in the fashion and retail business, with clips of old film footage from the Sixties of her strolling down Carnaby Street in London, dressed in a mini dress and long white vinyl boots on her way to work in a trendy boutique with freaky-looking mannequins in the bay window. And now she's talking about Carrington's staff, introducing each of us as if we're celebrities.

'Remember to look out for the gorgeous Georgie Hart who runs Women's Accessories; she'll also be sharing her fashion and beauty tips next week in *Closer* magazine.' Wow, how nice of her, and I find myself smiling, despite still feeling disgruntled over the French woman answering Tom's mobile, and the very real possibility that Kelly may change Carrington's beyond recognition – and not necessarily in a good way. Eddie and Sam give me a round of applause. 'And Eddie, the boss's BA. What can I say? He's a natural star. Born for this.' Eddie glows as he beams at Sam and me.

'See! I told you she adores me,' Eddie says. 'You too Georgie.' And maybe he has a point. I glance at the bulging goody bag nestling under my little silver Christmas tree (I couldn't wait to put it up) which arrived from a PR company. It's crammed full of lotions and potions for me to try out and talk about in the column. Hannah said not to worry if I can't be bothered to actually test the products and then write about them, as she'll get one of KCTV's people to do it for me. But I *can not* wait to dive in. I've already had a peep and saw a Jo Malone candle in a new gingerbread Christmassy scent, a beautifully fragrant Soap & Glory strawberry body scrub, there's even a full-size pot of that new CC cream that everyone is raving about   it costs a fortune and they gave it to me for free! I really could get used to this celebrity lifestyle, especially as ASOS are couriering a selection of accessories for me to try out and write about too.

Next up on screen is Zara, donning her floppy hat, which is pretty pointless, given that all of the Carrington's staff know who she is now. She does a spiel about having identified several areas of Carrington's customer service that 'need work' – flaming cheek. And now I'm on the screen, with the poker-face woman going on about the scratch on the crocodile skin bag, and I don't believe it. The voiceover guy is wittering on about me just not getting it. *Not getting what?* Sam tuts. Eddie is up and pacing around now, and I've got my face half hidden behind the cushion. I don't look too bad, my hair and make-up is fab, and the DVF suit nicely accentuates my curves. That old adage of the camera adding on ten pounds doesn't seem true, as I still look fairly slim – not as slim as Annie, of course, she's tiny, but not too bad, even if I do say so myself.

Zara is back now and is saying that I should have offered the woman a substantial discount to compensate for the scratch, and that's why I lost the sale! Unbelievable. If she was half the retail expert that she thinks she is, then she would have familiarised herself with Carrington's pricing policy – if there's any kind of hesitation over the quality of the bag, then we always offer another unopened one from the stockroom, which I did. Every decent sales assistant knows that knocking money off the high-end bags just depreciates their value and perceived specialness. It's a basic. I take a big gulp of buck's fizz. At least they cut the ladder incident – something to be grateful for, I suppose.

After the ad break, they show me dealing with the complaint, but have cut out the bit where the actor accuses Annie of having used the bag, and also my 'Zara' comment. And now Kelly is talking about the new pet spa, and how it's already boosting revenue for Carrington's. Eddie is silent, he's actually got his palms pressed together in a kind of meditative state as we watch him appear on the screen, and he looks fantastic. Really suave, and sort of ... illuminated. He's got a ton of make-up on and has the 'tits and teeth' thing going on too, with his shoulders back and an enormous gleaming white smile fixed into place, and the camera really loves him. It's amazing. It's as if he was born to it. He's parading around the spa now, pretending to be looking for a mate for Pussy – introducing all the dogs by name and telling the viewers about each one's personality. Trixie the poodle loves cuddles. Albert the puppy mutt likes lots of exercise. And oh my God – Eddie is looking directly into the camera now, adopting Kelly's pointy finger pose and asking the viewers to go online after the show to vote for their favourite friend for Pussy. He's just like a pro.

'Genius, Eddie. Well done,' I cheer, feeling relieved that my bit is over. I'm made up for him. 'Are you OK?' He has actual tears in his eyes and I've never seen Eddie cry before. Never.

'Oh it's nothing. Stupid queen,' he says, quickly brushing the tears away with the back of his hand before topping up his glass with more buck's fizz.

'Wow. Think I'd better call Claire, first thing tomorrow.' Sam smiles. 'A star is born! Don't forget us two when you're lounging by an infinity pool somewhere exotic with your pool boy bringing you piña colada spritzers.' She gives him a nudge with her foot.

'*Oooh yes*, now wouldn't that be fabulous? Eddie says, perking up. 'Say it again,' he insists, pulling his mirror out to preen some more, and we all laugh.

Turning back to the TV, my smile instantly freezes. Tom is on the screen. He's wearing the midnight blue Mr Carrington tuxedo, which frames a crisp white shirt, the collar of which is undone to reveal a teaser of his black-curly-haired and very firm tanned chest that has just the right hint of sheen. His dark curly hair is gelled back and he has a shadow of stubble on his chin. His cheeky smile is in place and his eyes are twinkling. My stomach flips and my pulse quickens; he looks utterly gorgeous, as always, and all my doubts about him melt in an instance. It's as if everything that's happened between us is irrelevant, silly and inconsequential. I just want to touch him and feel his arms around me, talk to him, share a joke, inhale his delicious chocolatey scent and let him tickle me all over. Oh God, I miss him so much. And I don't think I realised just how much, until now. Silence follows.

'Cor! He scrubs up well.' It's Eddie who breaks the moment. Sam squeezes my hand tighter as we watch Tom's scene unfold. He's being shown around the actual House of Dior! Oh my God. I'm riveted to the screen. I'd love to go there. The bags are divine, and now he's being shown the exquisite Granville in cruise blue, named after the fashion designer's home town. I wonder if this means we'll be stocking Dior bags – my pulse races at the prospect.

The camera follows Tom into a waiting car and we see him being shown the sights of Paris: iconic Métro signs, the Eiffel Tower, of course, the Moulin Rouge with its famous red windmill on the roof. The opulent Pont Alexandre III bridge with gold statues over a tree-lined River Seine, with bobbing houseboats at the water's edge. Past cobbled narrow alleyways opening out into squares full of chic cafés with striped awnings and seats outside, mingled in with buckets of glorious

154

multicoloured blooms from the many flower shops. Oh, I so wish I was there with him to share a croissant and drink espresso. It looks glorious and really romantic.

Tom arrives at a studio where he's about to meet a jewellery designer, when the ad break starts.

'Top-up,' I say to Eddie, hoping neither of them notices my trembling hands. It's incredible the effect Tom has on me. And then a thought pops into my head – I wonder if he misses me, I wonder if he's watching the show. I know it probably isn't broadcast in Paris, but he could be watching online. I hope he is, then he'll have seen me looking my best – with the big hair and lovely outfit, and not the ladder bit, thankfully. And I'm not bothered about Zara saying I should have given the woman a discount, Tom knows that isn't Carrington's policy, and he's the boss, not Zara, despite what she may think.

We've all been to the bathroom and topped up our drinks when the show comes back on. And I freeze. With the glass halfway to my mouth, which is hanging open, a horrible hot sensation trickles right through me. I place the glass down and hold my breath. There, on the TV screen in my shoebox lounge, is Tom, laughing and looking utterly beautiful in a white shirt and brown leather riding boots over tight white jodhpurs. He's on a moonlit sandy beach under a starry night sky, riding bareback on a fiery steed, just like a hero in that Bonnie Tyler song ... which incidentally is bellowing out in the background. And if that wasn't enough, there's an exquisite, olive-skinned, barefoot woman in a flimsy flowing gypsy dress that's ridden up to show off her toned thighs – her arms are wrapped around his back and her long luscious dark hair is splaying all around them. *But he's supposed to be in Paris? Last I heard, they didn't have beaches in Paris.*

As if reading my mind, the voiceover guy explains, 'Mr Carrington is enjoying a rare moment of R&R on the stunning shoreline along the French island of Corsica.' He then introduces the goddess as Valentina Fernandes – even her name is romantic and exotic sounding. She's a jewellery designer. I swallow hard and blink a few times on realising that I'm actually staring at the screen. Transfixed.

'Isn't she the one who designed the jewellery collection that you palmed off on that dodgy Russian customer? You know, the one who wanted you to launder his dirty money by sending merch he'd purchased to Moscow? He had a limp and a penchant for high-end handbags,' Eddie says, flaring his nostrils.

'Don't remind me,' I say, shuddering at the memory. 'And yes. Her costume jewellery is hideous. So garish that Mrs Godfrey from the WI complained of a headache when she caught a glimpse of it under the spotlights.' But what's she doing in Corsica? And with Tom! I can't help wondering if this is the reason he was so quick to suggest we call it a day. Maybe he had already set his sights on her, knew they'd be meeting up as part of the

156

show and wanted to be single so he could get it on with her. The thought lingers.

'Oh Georgie, please don't get upset,' Sam says. 'We don't know who she is, I'm sure there's a simple explanation.' And I know she's just trying to soften the blow. The man of my dreams, or so I thought, is cavorting with probably the most beautiful woman in the world. If it was Nathan up there on the screen with Valentina, then I guarantee Sam would devastated too.

'That's right. Anyway, we don't even know that he's sleeping with this bird who makes trashy jewellery for nobody to buy.' Sam nudges Eddie hard and flashes a 'shut up' look. 'This footage of them together could just be scripted reality.' Eddie sniffs and crosses his arms, as if he knows all about it. Since when did he become an expert?

'What do you mean?'

'A showmance!' Eddie says, and my forehead creases. 'Set up purely to entertain the viewers. KCTV could have staged the scenes to imply something else entirely, just like they did with you and your Beyoncé moment in the pilot.' I give him a blank face. 'The bottom wriggle, the Anya bag?' he says, as a reminder. 'All fabricated, wasn't it?'

'Yes. I do remember – I just had been trying to block it out of my mind. So you think that's what's going on?'

'It's entirely possible,' Sam joins in, 'and I really didn't think Tom was like that. He didn't strike me as a player at all. Nathan has always said that he's a true gentleman. Admittedly, he doesn't know him that well – only from the squash club, but still … '

'Then why hasn't he bothered to take any of my calls? And who was that woman who answered? I bet it was her, the one on the horse.'

'You don't know that. Try not to jump to conclusions,' she says.

'I'm trying. I'm trying really hard here, but it doesn't look very good, does it?' My heart sinks all over again.

'Well I guess not,' Eddie says. 'But don't be down. Look at your options. What about James? He's here and you know he still holds a candle for you. I'm sure of it, I've seen the way he looks at you,' he adds.

'Don't be daft. James is a good friend, nothing more. Besides, I can't just flit from one man to the next,' I snap angrily, quickly followed by, 'Look, I'm sorry. This has really got to me, I didn't mean to—'

'We know, honey.' Sam rubs my arm and gives Eddie a look. 'But seriously, maybe Eddie has a point. Why shouldn't you date someone else? If Tom is off gallivanting with the jewellery designer, then that means you're a free agent too, surely. If it's good enough for him … ' Her voice trails off, and I ponder on what she's saying. Maybe she has a point, why should I moon over him when he's clearly having such a fabulous time without me?

'Why don't we press on and watch the ending? Only

five minutes left,' Eddie says to change the subject. 'No need for hasty decisions.'

I finish the last of my buck's fizz and wiggle further down into the beanbag. My head feels as though it might explode with all these developments. I try to focus on the TV screen. The voiceover guy is talking again now. The three of us watch in silence as snippets of what's coming up in next week's show appear. And, oh God, I thought it was too good to be true – there's a clip of me hurling the crocodile skin bag into the Christmas tree next to the Lulu Guinness display. And they've done something to the film – speeded it up, and now keep showing the bag spinning into the tree, over and over, with comic-book-style bubbles flashing onto the screen with words like 'pow' and 'thwack' inside. And I knew I wasn't mistaken – you can actually hear someone sniggering loudly in the background. Great.

Now they're showing a clip of Tom in the boardroom at Hermès, where the table is swathed in a selection of exquisite silk scarfs. The voiceover guy is talking again. 'Will Mr Carrington find love on the sensual sandy shores of Corsica?' Cue another clip of him and Valentina on the horse. My stomach tightens again. 'Or will Tom rekindle his romance with an old flame? Don't miss next week's episode to find out … '

Whaaaat?

Old flame …

It's Zara! I knew it. And she's snuggled up in a

chocolate-brown fur coat looking stunning in a horse-drawn carriage in a twinkling, snowy Central Park. New York. Guess that's Tom's next stop then; unless he's there already. Eddie did say they were filming all his scenes upfront. And then it's confirmed. My heart sinks. Tom is back on the screen, with his boyish smile in place. He looks relaxed and laidback, just like he did on our last date, and I so wish he was here, tickling and teasing me. Messing around together just like we used to. He shares a joke with a couple of fit-looking American guys who look as if they've just stepped out of an episode of *Revenge*. They're watching a giant Norwegian spruce Christmas tree being hoisted up into position at the Rockefeller Center. The film cuts to another scene, where the tree is decorated now, and it's breathtaking. With a beautiful sparkly Swarovski star at the top and row upon row of gorgeous rainbow lights glittering in the dark evening sky, it's magical. The Americans sure know how to celebrate the holidays. And I've always wanted to go to New York.

Sam grabs the remote control and quickly presses a button to make the screen go black, before she's off the sofa and giving me a hug.

'I think we've seen enough,' she says, squeezing me tight.

'Well, that settles it then. If *Mr Carrington* can go on dream dates and hook up with exes, then why shouldn't you?' Eddie huffs indignantly, before putting his arms around me as well to make a group hug. He pulls back to look me in the eye and Sam does too. 'Let him see you whooping it up for a change.'

Sam nods in agreement.

'What do you mean?'

'I mean, find yourself another man and flaunt him honey. F-L-A-U-N-T! It's the only way.' Eddie states.

'Like I said before Eddie, that's not my style – I'm not just going to flit between Tom and James. Besides, James is seeing someone.'

'No he isn't, that's old news – Vicky is back with her ex. Flashing an engagement ring around too, she was, in the staff canteen just the other day.'

'That's nice,' I murmur, feeling like a sad old sack all of a sudden. Vicky is years younger than I am. And Sam's married, Eddie is settled down, and now even Dad seems to have found himself someone new. What's wrong with me that I can't even find a decent steady boyfriend and keep hold of him?

'Anyway, it doesn't have to be James if you don't want to go there again. It can be anyone. Think of the end-of-show wrap party – you really don't want to turn up all on your Bridget Jones, not when Tom might have the Brazilian goddess in tow, or worse still, that man stealer, Zara!' Eddie purses his lips. 'I knew she was up to no good.'

I down the last of my drink and press my fingernails into the palm of my hand to stem the tears that are threatening, knowing that Zara isn't really a 'man–stealer' as Eddie says. Tom has a mind of his own; he must have at least wanted to be 'stolen,' to be with someone else, I can't imagine she forced him to be with her against his will. So, it really looks like we're over, then. Properly over. I don't believe it. I had been holding out for it to be just a horrible misunderstanding, heat of the moment brought about circumstance, and giving him the benefit of the doubt when he didn't take my calls – telling myself he was just busy working and travelling. No time to himself. But I guess, deep down, I knew it was a fabrication. He wanted to call it a day, and now he's moved on – or, more accurately, backwards ... to his childhood sweetheart, with a beautiful Brazilian goddess on the side.

12

It's Thursday and Annie is at the laser clinic, so I'm here behind the counter on my own and I can't stop thinking about last night's show. After Sam and Eddie left, I watched it again. And again. And again. I'm obsessed! I searched for clues to the seriousness of their relationship scanning Tom's face; I even freeze-framed a couple of shots of them on the horse just to see the look in Tom's eyes – but I really can't be sure if he's into her or not. It's driving me insane. And if he is, then why is Zara in New York? Tom must have invited her, or at least know she's there; he could have put a stop to it, but he hasn't, so he's obviously fine with it. Happy about it, most likely. They could have been planning it for weeks – no wonder she was offish with me in his office ... She already had her sights on him and didn't want me hanging around, getting in her way. And then it dawns on me! I can't believe I didn't see it – of course, it all makes sense now, that's why he was so quick to call it a day, to make way for Zara! I just made it easier for him by being so cross about my embarrassing debut on TV. I take a deep breath in a desperate attempt to stop my mind from spinning out of control with all the horrible possibilities.

And I feel like I'm in a goldfish bowl, with everyone watching me. There was a group of girls huddled by the staff entrance this morning when I arrived at work, one of them asked for my autograph and wanted to know a) where my new boots were from. She didn't look impressed when I said River Island, and that they were a bargain in last winter's sale, and b) is it true that Eddie is my GBF? And if so, then I'm the luckiest girl alive, apparently, and can I tell him that she's set up a fan page for him on Facebook, and it already has four hundred and ninety-three 'Likes'.

When I eventually made it to the staff room and changed the fleece-lined boots for my usual New Look heels, I overheard someone behind the lockers giggling about the bookmaker's over the road from Carrington's. Apparently, they're taking bets on who Mr Carrington, aka Tom, will turn up with at the end-of-show wrap party – Valentina or Zara. No mention of me! Of course, they stopped talking when they realised I was there. I feel like such a fool, with people whispering and skulking around me.

I'm rearranging the Michael Kors display when Eddie appears; poking his head through the back of the open shelf unit, in between an oversized clutch and a signature monogrammed tote.

'Cheer up, dollface. I have news,' he says, quickly

repositioning the bags back into place before darting around to stand opposite me.

'What do you mean?'

'You're going on a date! It's all organised.' Eddie looks charged.

'Don't be ridiculous.' I head back to my counter and start shoving cocktail rings into their rightful slots in the tray – '*I wish the customers wouldn't mess around with them,*' I mutter angrily to myself, then suddenly feel paranoid that KCTV might have a lip reader watching me. You never know. I remember the row of little TV monitors in Tom's office. It's like being in a giant bubble, or a series of *Big Brother* without the audition or psychiatric evaluation first.

'Oh don't be like that, there's nothing wrong with diving straight back into the dating pool to get you over a messy split.'

'Do you have to sound like a trashy tabloid? Besides, I might not want to get "over a messy split", as you so dramatically put it.' I stop sorting the rings to look him in the eye.

'Why on earth not?'

'Because ... well, just because,' I say, feeling confused and unsure. I don't really know what to think any more. I've got so many things whizzing around inside my head. 'Anyway, I can't talk now, customers to serve.' I nod towards a loved-up couple, holding hands and sharing a joke, as they browse through the purses. A dart of longing shoots through me; they look so cosy and happy in love, and looking forward to a romantic Christmas together. And I still can't believe that that was me, too, not so very long ago.

'OK. But you must come and see me later. It's vital.' Eddie gives me a quick kiss on the cheek and heads towards the staff lift.

'Maybe,' I call out, as I walk towards the couple.

Later, on my lunch break, I push open the door to the anteroom outside Tom's office. Eddie isn't at his desk, but he can't be far away, as Pussy is lying on her bed under the desk, dressed up in a Little Bo-Peep outfit. I decide to wait. She stretches majestically and then nuzzles my leg before spinning in a circle on seeing me. I scoop her up and snuggle in, grateful for a cuddle.

I'm hovering by the Christmas tree when I hear voices in Tom's office. The door is ajar. I sidle closer and peep through the gap. Kelly is sitting at Tom's desk, as if she owns the place – she even has her jingle-jangly feet up next to a laptop in front of her. I think she must be on a Skype call as there's a female voice coming from the laptop, saying something about a hotel with underground parking. I wonder if Kelly is lining up her next series. Perhaps when she's done with Carrington's, she plans on filming in a hotel. But just as I lean in closer, the door slams shut. I instinctively clutch Pussy to me and jump back before ducking behind the tree out of sight, wishing my cheeks would stop burning. How embarrassing if Kelly actually caught me snooping. I wonder if she would insist on me being sacked, just like those people from the cruise ship in her last series.

'Oh there you are.' Eddie comes into the anteroom, bottom first, pushing the door open, and carrying a plate with two enormous cream horns on. 'Hope you're hungry. I've been all over looking for you. That girl from Lingerie, the one who's covering your section, said you were in Sam's café, but then Sam said she hadn't even seen you today,' he puffs excessively, as if he's just run a half-marathon. 'Here, pull up a chair and tuck in, this will cheer you up. Everyone loves a horn.' He sniggers and gestures to the cakes. After placing Pussy back in her bed, I take one of the cakes and lick the gooey cream before sitting down opposite his desk.

'Mmm, thanks,' I say, biting off the bottom of the cake, savouring the sweet sensation on my tongue. 'Sooo, why do you want to see me? And before you start, I'm not going on a blind date.'

'But you must, it's all arranged, and besides, it won't be a "blind date" as such.' He scoops some cream onto his fingertip for Pussy, who laps it up and then works off the sugar rush by hurtling around his office, the hem of her Little Bo-Peep dress flapping wildly.

'What do you mean?'

'Weell.' His eyes dart from side to side. 'It will be with me!' he says triumphantly.

'Don't be silly.' I crease my forehead.

'That's right. And ... ' He looks shifty now.

'Who?' I give him a nudge with my foot.

'An actor.'

'Nooo!' I cross my legs and lean back in the chair. I know where this is leading – straight to YouTube.

'But it's all part of the show. Hannah was chatting about it and, well, Kelly is insistent. And we don't want to upset her now, do we? She's going to make us stars, plus you'd be doing me a massive favour.'

'How come?'

'I'm going to propose to Ciaran ... on camera!'

'Wow! *Really?* How romantic. But will Ciaran like that?' I ask, knowing how he hates the limelight, in complete contrast to Eddie.

'Absolutely. And he's definitely going to say yes,' Eddie states, swinging one leg over the other and looking very pleased with himself.

'He is? But how do you know?' I frown.

'We've talked it all through – planned it out, if you like,' he says, nonchalantly.

'Doesn't sound as romantic now.' I polish off the last of my cream horn. 'And isn't Ciaran already married?' I ask, remembering his disastrous wedding day to Tina. She used to work here in the cash office, and was after Ciaran's money. He married her because he wanted to 'fit in' and, well, it's a long story, but anyway, he's come out now and is definitely gay and definitely committed to Eddie, even if the majority of his devout Irish Roman Catholic family refuse to talk to him any more.

'Oh, but it totally is. We've been thinking about it ever since Ciaran's annulment came through, and I guess when you meet your one, you just know ... ' I glance away and fiddle with my big hair. 'Oops, so sorry, lover. Didn't mean to rub salt in the wound.' Eddie darts out from behind his desk to give me a hug.

'Don't be, I'm made up for you, really.' I manage a wry smile.

'Fabulous. And the most amazing bit of all – KCTV are going to film the wedding and pay for it all, natch. They're talking Vegas *babeeee*. I can just imagine it all now, the Bellagio Hotel fountain and fireworks as a backdrop with a rodeo of topless cowboys, ooh ... it's going to be such a treat; maybe Liza Minnelli will swing by and belt out a show tune for us.' He claps his hands together. 'You'll be my best girl, won't you darling?'

'Err, yes. Guess so,' I say, quickly followed by, 'Sorry, I'd be honoured to.' I don't want to spoil his moment. It's not his fault I'm a dating disaster.

'So why the long face then?'

'Ed, are you sure about this?' I ask, wondering what KCTV will want in return, and what if they fiddle with the filming? Who knows what they might do?

'Of course, why wouldn't I be?'

'Well, it just doesn't seem ... very special. It's almost as if you're only doing it for the show. You know, to be on telly. It won't be private, and think of all the viewers watching.' I'd much rather have a romantic, intimate ceremony with just close friends and Dad there to give me away. But then I guess everyone's different. I allow myself a moment to fantasise before snapping back to reality, because with my relationship track record, I'm far more likely to end up a wizened old woman, all on my own.

'Exactly! Such a fabulous opportunity. And Ciaran agrees – why have boring old Mulberry-On-Sea register office when we can have *OK!* magazine?' He makes big eyes. 'Kelly reckons we'll easily get a six-page spread, and they'll pay us thousands for exclusivity.' He laughs, and I can't resist smiling at how he has it all worked out. 'Now, let me tell you about this actor. In fact, I think you've already met him—'

'*Nooo* way,' I cut in. 'If it's the Chloé bag guy, then definitely not.'

'OK, OK, don't shoot the messenger. Hannah did mention another guy – the sound bloke, big hair with big matching microphone apparently. *Oo-err*, wonder if that's some kind of euphemism.' Eddie smoothes an eyebrow and does kissy lips in my direction.

'*Leo?*'

'Yep, that's him.' I shake my head emphatically and Eddie's shoulders droop, his bottom lip too. 'Georgie, flower, why not? It's not like Tom's here to mind.' I give him a look. 'Sorry, only joking kiddo. Oh *purlease* do it.

All you have to do is walk into a bar with him, to make the scene look more authentic. Kelly said it would be dull for the viewer if I'm just sitting there with Ciaran, when he's not even part of the show. And this is my chance to be really famous – get a free, fabulous wedding to the love of my life. Kelly might not go for it otherwise, you know how she rates you as the real star of the show. And you never know, it could spark something off. Maybe Leo's your one ... ' I flash him another look. 'Your *other* one!' he quickly adds, before nodding and smiling enthusiastically, almost maniacally.

'It won't spark something off, as you say. Anyway, Leo's not my type.' I wonder if I would have been better off flogging washing machines down in the basement after all. I make a mental note to check with Amy. On second thoughts, I don't want to annoy Kelly and end up getting sacked or something, like those sailors did. Probably best to suck it up. I'll just make sure I steer clear of ladders from now on and do everything I can to not look like an idiot during filming. Plus, I'm really looking forward to doing the magazine column. I went through the goody bag and there must have been over thirty items inside. And Hannah cornered me in the staff canteen earlier to say that one of Kelly's VIP friends has invited me to a red carpet event in London – the opening of a new cocktail bar. I just have to turn up and make sure the paparazzi snap me. Then share a few cocktails with the owners inside and give a short glowing review to a journalist. I'll be paid four thousand pounds – I nearly passed out by the help-yourself salad bar when she told me that. Anyway, it's all very exciting – but if I don't do what Kelly wants, then that would all disappear in an instance.

'Might make Tom wake up ... ' Eddie adds slowly, in a perky, persuasive voice, and changing tack now. 'Nothing like another man on the scene to make you want someone and, trust me, honey, I should know.' Eddie folds his arms and tilts his head to one side.

'Hmm, let me ponder,' I say, taking it all in. I think of the betting shop over the road. Valentina or Zara! And with only six weeks until the wrap party on Christmas Eve, I need to find a date – if only to save face. I couldn't bear it if Tom walked in with Zara all over him, or Valentina or, worst still, both. Or all three of them crammed onto a horse with Bonnie belting out a power ballad in the background. And nothing would surprise me any more in this crazy, real-but-made-up world, I've found myself living in.

13

Six shopping weeks until Christmas

'OK everyone, listen up. Change of plan. For today's filming, we've got some real customers spending their own money, hopefully – Kelly's friends down from London, special VIP guests mingled in with the actors – to liven things up a bit. Viewers love a bit of glitz. So be nice, and remember ... keep it real.'

We're in the staff canteen waiting to start filming, and one of the production assistants is shouting out instructions from over by the soup urn. Everyone is here. Mrs Grace is sitting next to me, wearing a Wedgewood-blue trouser suit with a jaunty chiffon scarf knotted at the side of her neck. Millie has made her up with flattering, youthful pastels and her beehive has been replaced with a feathered crop. She looks just like Julie Andrews.

Someone shouts out 'tits and teeth' and we all laugh, even me – I've decided to make the most of this once-in-a-lifetime opportunity of goody bags, red-carpet events and magazine columns, and nobody likes a misery. And I might meet someone else; I don't want to be like I was after the split from Brett, single for nearly two years, not when everyone else is settling down. And I certainly don't want to end up an old spinster – alone, with a feline family and a motorised scooter to look forward to. Plus Eddie and Sam have a point: what will Tom think if he sees me with another man? He's not the only one in demand now – I've had seven Facebook PMs from guys wanting to date me after seeing the show. Besides, I've got nothing to lose, especially as I haven't had a reply to the text message I sent him after watching last week's show for the trillionth time. It was late, I was home alone and I'd been at the buck's fizz. I caved in and sent a message saying:

I miss you so so so sooo soooooooooooooo much, but see that you've moved on. I hope you're very happy Dirty Harry ☹☹☹ ps – Mr Cheeks really misses you too!!!!

I shrivel every time I look at it. What was I thinking? It sounds desperate, and sarcastic and ridiculous, and why-oh-why did I have to mention his great grandfather, Dirty Harry? Everyone in Mulberry-On-Sea knows what a philanderer he was, I may as well have just come out with it and called Tom a two-timing snake, even though I don't have concrete proof as such, like an actual televised snog or whatever. And it's hardly the way to win back his heart, by insulting him and stalking him like an infatuated schoolgirl. I sent the message seven times. Epic cringe!

'Don't worry lovey, everything will be all right,' Mrs Grace whispers, as if reading my thoughts. 'You'll see. Push him out of your head and enjoy the moment. Adventures like this are a rare treat. I've been asked to go on *Alan Titchmarsh* – fancy that. At my age.' She chuckles and pulls a powder compact from her granny bag before checking her hair in the little mirror. 'And my Stan says it's just like having a new dolly bird on his arm.'

I'm in the usual place at my counter, wrapping a length of silver tinsel around the ring display, when 'Deck the Halls' starts playing and the actors move around, suddenly animated and enthralled in the merch. The spotlights are shining bright as before, making the spiced cinnamon scent from the pump under the Christmas tree even more intoxicating. I'm wearing an exquisitely cut black Donna Karan dress, with matching faux fur collared jacket, new instore this week. The girls in Womenswear were thrilled when the stock trolley turned up. Libby, the supervisor, said the suit comes in mink and aubergine too, and Kelly's new rule about staff wearing Carrington's clothes is an absolute must for them, which they're all delighted by.

We've reached the '*fa la la la laaa*' line when a very attractive, petite woman, dressed in a navy abaya with Swarovski trim at the wrists, approaches my counter flanked by two men in dark suits carrying briefcases.

The woman has a headscarf on with a discreet Gucci logo, and a puff of ultra-expensive Oud perfume floats around her. I immediately sense that it's the high-end bags they'll be interested in. They could be from the marina. Taking a break from their super-yacht, perhaps. Excitement rushes through me.

'I come to buy gifts please,' the woman says politely with a Middle Eastern accent. She fixes her heavily kohl-lined brown eyes on me. I do a quick scan of the floor, but the production team aren't here, so I instantly assume she must be one of Kelly's friends. Last week the actors made absolutely certain a camera was on them before they started performing.

'Of course, I'd be happy to help you. Do you have anything in mind?' I ask, relaxing into it. I'm in my comfort zone serving proper customers.

'Bags. Louis Vuitton. The newest collection please.'

'Certainly, if you'd like to come this way, please.' I gesture to a cabinet housing six exquisite top handle bags in a variety of colours, nestling amongst a selection of Louis monogrammed scarfs and purses.

'Would you like to look at one?' I ask, reaching for the key to unlock the cabinet.

'OK.' The men move in closer as the woman reaches into her Chanel clutch to retrieve a diamond-encrusted iPhone. I place a signature biscuit-brown bag on the counter.

'I buy it,' she says, barely glancing at the bag. She takes a quick photo of it with her phone.

'Thank you, would you like it gift-wrapped?' I ask, wishing all of our customers were this decisive.

'No no! I want *aalll* of them.'

'All of them?' I ask, wondering if I've heard her right. Perhaps she doesn't understand about the gift-wrapping service.

'Yes, this one and this one and this one and ... ' she says, pointing a perfectly buffed fingernail to each of the handbags in turn.

'Six bags?' I say, keeping my voice steady. Annie saunters over, her interest obviously piqued.

'No no! *Aalll* of them,' she says, sweeping a heavily jewelled hand in the air. A rock the size of a sugar lump clings to her wedding finger. 'Every colour. Every style,' she says, casting an eye over the adjacent counter housing the Louis luggage. 'And scarves, purses and keyrings too. The whole collection.'

'Um.' I'm momentarily stunned. 'Certainly,' I quickly add, beaming from ear to ear. I discreetly flap a hand in Annie's direction. She immediately dives into the little stock cupboard behind the counter to retrieve a pile of dust bags as I start unlocking the security ropes and emptying the Louis handbags from the cabinet. We both wrap. Fast!

Adrenalin is pumping – I've never had a proper VIP customer like this before. I imagine this is how the sales assistants up in the big London stores feel all the time. I've heard about Saudi customers coming to England in the summer to escape the heat at home, but never at Christmas and certainly not to Carrington's, in the quant, seaside town of Mulberry-On-Sea. Things are really looking up – maybe Kelly's plan to rejuvenate the store might work after all. I hope so. It's exciting, even if I am to be single again. I'll just have to live vicariously through my new glamorous and seriously wealthy customers while trying to avoid Tom. He's bound to return at some stage, and it'll be hard seeing him every day if we're not going to be together any more, but I guess I'll just have to deal with it. I just seriously hope Zara or Valentina or, worse still, both, don't rock up here and start hanging around instore. I'm not sure I could bear that.

We've finished gift-wrapping; Annie had to get a stock trolley to house all the Louis merch. The woman has bought the whole lot, including the monogrammed luggage collection, plus every Louis item from the big secure stockroom downstairs. Annie had to leg it over to Mrs Grace to collect the key before racing downstairs (taking the customer lift for extra quickness) so we didn't risk losing the woman's interest by making her wait a moment longer than necessary.

The woman beckons to the men with the briefcases, who are hovering by the trolley.

'Err, do you have ID available please?' I ask, praying that she has, but knowing the total is way over the floor limit for one customer transaction. The woman produces her passport and I give it a polite cursory glance, not wanting to inconvenience her for a moment longer. The men flip open the briefcases and start unloading wads of cash. Annie does a little gasp before swiftly turning and burying her head in the cupboard behind us to conceal her flushed cheeks. I do a quick scan of the floor, wondering where the security guys are – I can't have this much cash stashed in my till. Besides, from a purely practical perspective, it just won't fit! I wonder how Harrods copes with all its big sales. Maybe it has extra large tills with safes underneath or something. Well, whatever they have, Carrington's will need to find out and upgrade, ASAP, as our tiny old-fashioned tills just won't do at all. Oh no! Not if we're going to be servicing the shopping requirements of über-wealthy customers from now on.

And I don't believe it. I blink again to be sure. Yep. It's Melissa. The sturdy plain-clothes store detective who used to work here. But how come she's back? She left to work at the prison. Melissa catches my eye and surreptitiously wanders over.

'You OK, G?' she mouths discreetly, from behind the Juicy Couture stand. I flick my eyes to the enormous pile of notes in front of me and she pulls out a mobile, presumably to call security.

A few seconds later, Kelly appears; she's crawling on all fours as fast as she can towards the Christmas tree for cover. I make big eyes and pray that my customer doesn't spot her. I bet they don't have Ronald McDonald lookalikes crawling commando-style on the shop floor at Harrods. But then perhaps Kelly's behaviour is perfectly normal in the real-but-made-up world. I bite my bottom lip and try to concentrate on counting the cash instead. It's two hundred pounds over, which I hand back to the woman.

'For you,' she says, placing her hand over mine and gently pushing the wad towards me.

'Oh no, but I can't,' I reply instinctively, holding up my palms.

'I insist.' The woman smiles. In my peripheral vision I can see Kelly flapping a hand wildly, gesturing for me to take the cash. So I do. I nudge it towards the till, unsure of what to do next. The woman says something in Arabic to the men, who fling the empty briefcases onto the stock trolley and start pushing it across the shop floor. Mick, the security guard, appears and offers to give them a hand, and they head towards the side door, which leads straight out to the directors' car park. I make a mental note to see about us getting a proper Carrington's concierge service. This calibre of customer will expect it. We could have a dedicated suite especially for VIP shoppers, park their limos, escort them around the store, load their merch, or we could even deliver to their super-yachts. Fabulous. I'm going to mention it to Kelly.

Annie is practically bursting with delight, and I'm bent over with both hands flat on the counter, taking a deep breath, when the woman returns. I quickly stand up straight and smooth down my jacket. Annie ducks back into the cupboard.

'One for you, and one for your assistant,' she says, handing me a small Carrington's carrier bag.

'Oh,' I start, but on catching Kelly doing the flapping thing again, I immediately take the bag and thank the woman profusely.

'Take me to the cosmetics hall please.' She pulls a magazine cutting from her clutch. 'I want to look like this,' she adds, tapping the piece of paper. It's Taylor Swift!

'Of course.' My mind boggles – never in a million years is this woman going to look like Taylor; she's a totally different ethnic group for starters. 'My colleague will escort you,' I say, hoiking Annie from the cupboard. I figure it best to stay on my section – don't want the voiceover guy saying I shouldn't have abandoned the shop floor, with me being the supervisor and all. Annie starts bobbing from one foot to the other with glee, before quickly calming herself down and gesturing demurely as if the woman is royalty.

'CUT!'

Kelly is up on her feet now, clapping and rushing towards me with her Ronald McDonald hair whipping around like candyfloss in a wind tunnel.

'Bravo. Bravo! Perfect. How do you do it?' she gushes, grabbing my hand and pumping it furiously.

'Do what? I ask, feeling panicky and euphoric all at the same time.

'Exude the perfect blend of exemplary service with such provincially naive wonderment.' She wafts a hand in the air.

'Um.' *What's she going on about?* 'Is that good?' I raise a tentative eyebrow.

'Oh, you are so divine. Of course it is.' She squeezes me tight, almost winding me in the process.

'But I just thought she was an ordinary customer – well, not ordinary for Mulberry-On-Sea, but, well ... ' I say, managing to break free, hoping she wasn't an actor after all. That would be really disappointing.

'And she is. Or will be. I certainly hope she'll become an "ordinary" customer. Carrington's can't be sustained with just the likes of that rain-bonnet woman, whatever her name is, spending a tenner once a year.'

'Mrs Godfrey,' I prompt.

'Yes, whatever.' Kelly flaps a hand. 'Anyway, Princess Ameerah was insistent on not having a camera stuck in her face, hence my covert manoeuvring and the long-lens activity from the filming guys. It was the only way to get her to agree to come here,' she says, and I'm suddenly conscious of being surrounded by the whole crew. They're all laughing and stepping forward to shake my hand or kiss my cheek, and my heart lifts. It feels good to have got it right for a change – perhaps this will earn me a reprieve from the YouTube hall of shame this week.

'Right. On to the next scene,' Kelly commands, and clicks her fingers towards a wardrobe assistant, who immediately steps forward with a sumptuously soft grey cashmere wrap. 'Put this on and follow me.' Feeling like a proper celebrity, I swathe myself in the ultra-chic and super-luxurious wrap.

'What about the money?' I ask as we head off. It's still stacked up on the counter.

'Security can deal with it,' she replies, as if it's mere detail. 'The extra is yours, the contents of the bag too. You must *always* accept Princess Ameerah's gifts with grace and gratitude. *Always*.'

'But that's not Carrington's usual policy,' I say, despite the fizz of excitement bubbling inside me. I wonder what's inside the bag and I'll share the £200 with Annie, of course. She'll be delighted too.

'Well it is now. It's etiquette when serving this calibre of customer. Harrods staff have been doing it for years.' Kelly nods at Melissa as she steps out from her hiding place. 'You can look after it all until Georgie returns.'

'You're the boss,' Melissa says with a hint of sarcasm, and does an exaggerated salute before clicking her heels together and marching over to my counter. I quickly stifle a giggle, hoping Kelly didn't notice, and make a mental note to catch up with Mel later.

'Where are we going?' I ask, having to do a gentle jog to keep up with Kelly, which is no mean feat in six-inch-high Giuseppe Zanotti suede ankle boots.

'You'll see. Don't want to give too much away, will ruin the spontaneity. But trust me, you will *lurrrrrve* it.'

She shakes her hands up in the air. I smile hesitantly. 'And I want you to talk about the council's plans for the Christmas ice rink.' Her face changes to serious.

'Err, OK. But what should I say?' I ask, momentarily thrown by her random flip from wacky Ronald McDonald to serious businesswoman.

'Anything. Just mention it – sure you'll think of something, you're a bright girl. And do it before Eddie proposes, I don't want it getting overshadowed by wedding talk.' Kelly grabs a bottle of mineral water from a passing catering guy, takes a massive slurp and hands it back. 'Chop chop. Time is money in this game,' she says, pumping her elbows up even higher to gather more speed.

Ten minutes later we're in Sam's café, which has been festooned with paper lanterns and flickering tea lights to create a cosy, fairytale atmosphere. Sam is in place behind the counter wearing a new white T-shirt with Cupcakes At Carrington's emblazoned in glittery gold lettering across the front, and a massive smile on her face. Her eyes swivel to the left, practically bulging with excitement, as if she's telepathically saying, 'Look who it is. Right here. In my café! *Faints.*' There's an elegant woman standing next to Sam, with her head down. She looks up. And *oh my God*.

It's Mary Berry. Baking queen. The actual, proper ledge herself, Mary Berry. I *love* Mary Berry. She's brilliant on

TV and now here she is right in front of us. Incredible. I do a speedy silent scream at Sam, when Mary isn't looking. Sam reciprocates.

Mary holds up a cake stand bulging with red velvet cupcakes smothered in butter cream icing with miniature snowflakes scattered on top. Striped candy canes are hooked around the edges of the cake stand and Mariah Carey is singing 'All I Want For Christmas Is You' in the background. This is amazing. I just about manage to resist the overwhelming urge to blurt out, 'Hey, look everyone, it's Mary Berry.' Now, that would be so uncool. And it's true then, Kelly really does know all the famous people. Wow!

I flash Sam a 'what's going on' look? But there's no time. A camera moves in as a guy counts down – three two one with his fingers – before Millie appears, sweeping an enormous blusher brush over my cheeks, flicking a lock of hair away from my face and straightening the wrap. She gives me a quick wink and mouths, 'Break a leg.' Eddie and Ciaran are sitting in a booth, laughing and chatting as if it's just any other day in the café, seemingly oblivious to the cameras, Mary the Ledge, and the crowd all around us. And I feel so excited.

Eddie catches my eye and smooths his already immaculate hair. Now he's fiddling with his cuff links as if he's nervous, which is extremely unusual for him. I know he's about to propose, but I thought he couldn't wait … he's that keen to get to Vegas and have his moment in the spotlight.

In the space behind my head, I sense Kelly clicking her fingers.

'Her date! Her date! Where is he?' she whispers furiously. A girl with a clipboard and a blank face appears. 'Oh never mind. If you want something doing ... ' Kelly puffs, before shooing the girl away. 'Get ready to grab his hand and walk towards the gays,' she hisses in my ear. 'And look happy.' She disappears.

My heart sinks. I don't really want to grab Leo's hand and look happy with him, but I guess it's only show business, and if it's OK for Tom ... I inhale sharply through my nose.

'Go. Go. Go.' Kelly is back. I spin around, but I can't see Leo. An arm reaches out through the crowd. Kelly pushes the crew guys out of the way. And then I see him. My fake date.

Oh my God.

Oh my actual God. It's not the actor. It's not Leo.

It's Dan Kilby.

Singing star. Sexy and soulful. *Proper famous*. But there's no time to react. He takes my hand. His fingers feel warm against mine as he leads me over to join the others. My pulse quickens, not because of Dan (I don't think so, well, maybe a bit – he is utterly gorge with his messy brown hair and soft grey eyes) but because all can I fathom is: what will Tom think when he sees this?

186

14

'Why didn't you say something?' I'm on the bus and Dad's on the phone. He sounds delighted. Nancy has just started on the silver surfers' course and was messing around on her new iPad mini when she spotted a picture of me plastered across the front page of an online gossip magazine above a caption saying:

Recently heartbroken Georgie Girl, star of new reality show, Kelly Cooper Come Instore, *finds love with sexy singer ...*

I want the ground to open up and drag me in. It's not true – I haven't found new love. It's surreal having my private life dissected in the media. I'm mortified. And where did they get the picture? Dad says it's of me standing outside Carrington's chatting on my phone, so I can only assume I was on a tea break and that I'm being stalked by paparazzi. Oh God. And they don't hang around, these sleb hunters – the scene with Dan Kilby was only this morning, which just goes to show how quickly they pounce. I'm not sure I can keep up with it all. Not so long ago I was ordinary Georgie Hart from Mulberry-On-Sea, looking forward to spending Christmas with my new boyfriend, and now ... well, it seems I'm a reality TV star linked to one of the most famous singers in the country.

'Dad, you know how the media make things up, embellish the facts,' I say quietly, turning towards the window, conscious of the other passengers all whispering and nudging each other before glancing in my direction. Dad should know more than anyone what it feels like to be suddenly thrust into the limelight. From the moment he was arrested back then, the newspapers wouldn't leave him alone. Mum used to get so upset on reading lies about him having had secret women on the side, or how he'd 'been fiddling the books' at the bank where he worked for years – I guess that bit is sort of true, but not the rest, I'm sure of it. Even after Dad went to prison, he still sent Mum cards saying how much he loved her. And Mum still loved him – right up to the day she died. She told me so at the end.

'Yes, of course,' Dad says. 'But this is different, darling. If you're on the telly, then you're a celebrity, famous, and we all love celebrities. Everyone here is so chuffed. The curtain-twitchers are all saying they could tell right away, just from your movie-star hair and stylish clothes. We all knew there was something going on in town, but nobody guessed it would involve Carrington's department store. You know, Georgie, one of the old dears even wants me to get your autograph for her niece.'

'Oh stop it, Dad,' I chide, and then smile at how he always refers to people his own age as 'old', as if he's a mere boy.

'Enjoy it, Georgie. A bit of the high life doesn't come around very often,' he replies, echoing Mrs Grace's words. 'And who is this "sexy singer"?'

'Um, he's called Dan. I'll tell you about it later. But it was all set up for the cameras, Dad.'

'Phew. I was worried it might be that no-good what's-his-name, Brett. He liked singing; didn't you meet him in one of those karaoke bars?' Dad sighs.

'Yes. But don't worry, he's definitely history.' I pause. 'Dad, sorry, I'll have to call you back.' I quickly shove the phone in my pocket as a group of teenage girls run down the bus and occupy all the seats around me.

'Are you Georgie from Carrington's?' A girl with a pierced eyebrow and a red Santa hat over dodgy hair extensions asks me.

'Why do you want to know?' I reply cautiously, just in case she's some kind of *crazeee* looper about to happy-slap me in front of her crew.

'Don't be anxious babe, it's me, Madison.' She grins as if we're BFFs and grabs my arm, making my heart speed up. 'Me and the girls saw you on the telly. Can Leanne take a picture of us?'

'Err, sure ... who's Leanne?' Madison points to a pretty

girl with a seriously extreme Ronseal tan wearing a neon pink Juicy tracksuit under a faux fur gilet. She legs it down the bus clutching her smartphone and, before I can say 'cheese', Madison has flung her arm around my shoulders, pulled me in tight, and several pictures have been taken.

'Thanks babe.' Madison jumps up. 'Nice to see you keeping it real.' I raise one eyebrow and smile vaguely, wondering what she means.

'The bus!' She points a long acrylic fingernail around the top deck. 'Thought you'd have a driver, now you're a sleb.'

'Oh no, nothing like that,' I grin. Talk about surreal – a few weeks ago, celebrities were just people I read about in magazines, and now I'm one of them.

The bus stops and the girls leave, so I call Dad back and he tactfully chats about the weather and his neighbours, before asking if there's anything special he can get me for Christmas. *Yes, Tom! Preferably naked, lying on a sheepskin rug in that log cabin we mused about before he went weird and dumped me* ... Hmmm, I suggest a woolly hat and scarf gift set instead, and Dad seems happy with that.

'So when will we see you again?' The twitchy, uneasy feeling from that day in Nancy's flat returns. I'm not used to Dad saying 'we'. I feel as if I'm betraying Mum somehow. Even though she's not here any more. 'Nancy is going to cook her outstandingly delicious beef stew and dumplings,' he adds. 'So make sure you come hungry. I'm still full after last Sunday's feast,' he chuckles.

'Can I let you know Dad? I haven't got my diary to hand,' I say, quickly rummaging in my bag to check.

'Of course, darling. Oh hang on. Nancy's saying something.' There's a muffled, scratchy pause, as if Dad has the phone pressed into his jumper. I stop rummaging. I can just about hear Nancy's voice in the background – she's saying something about 'understanding' and 'best do it now'.

Do what now?

But before I can work it out, Dad is back on the line. 'Just let me know when suits you, sweetheart. I know how busy you are.'

'Dad?' I ask, and then hesitate.

'What is it, Georgie?'

'Err, it's ... oh no, don't worry, it's nothing.' I bite my lip.

'OK. But you know you can talk to me. I'm always here for you.'

'I know Dad.' My voice softens. It's lovely having him back in my life. 'Well, there was something – I was just wondering if we could visit Mum's grave some time.'

'Of course, sweetheart. That would be wonderful. We can make a day of it. Go for lunch or a stroll along the promenade, if the weather isn't too chilly, that is, just like we used to when you were a little girl. Do you remember? Mum used to make banana sandwiches and we'd eat them on the benches next to the pier, and drink cans of ginger beer before devouring those massive Mr Whippy ice creams with chocolate flakes on from the van. And you never see those ice-cream vans any more.'

'Yes. I remember. Mum used to say that when the music was playing it meant the man had run out of lollies, and then spoil it all by laughing, so I always knew she was joking.'

'But you still fell for it every time, if only for a couple of seconds,' he says, sounding animated and light. And for some reason, tears sting in my eyes. I wonder what Mum would have thought of me being on the telly. Proud, I reckon, and it's such a shame she's missing out. Mum was always a little in awe of anyone out of the ordinary. It was my thirteenth birthday not long before she died, and the nurses in the hospital organised a little party; they even invited someone from the local football team to turn up and give me a teddy bear – Mum went all fan-girl. I chew the inside of my cheek as a horrible, immature thought pops into my head. I hope Dad doesn't invite Nancy along on our day out. I quickly shove the thought away – I like Nancy and it's nice that Dad has met her.

We say our goodbyes and the bus reaches my stop.

After closing the door to my flat, I unzip the boots (the wardrobe woman said I could keep them, which I'm thrilled about) and stow them carefully on my shoe rack. They're beautiful, extra-soft purple suede with little tassels down the side, and most likely cost a fortune. I place the Carrington's bag from Princess Ameerah on the hall table; inside is a divine Louis wallet in a beautiful seasonal berry colour with cream detailing. I thought I might give it to Sam as a Christmas present. I could get her initials put onto it. I'm just hanging my coat up, when my mobile rings again. This time it's Sam.

'Georgie! I'm sorry,' she says, sounding worried.

'What for?' I ask, making my way into the kitchen. I'm starving.

'For not saying I'd be there this morning, or warn you that Dan Kilby had been roped in. I only found out very late last night – Kelly called me herself and made me promise to keep it a secret; she wanted you to be surprised. Something about it being more authentic, you know, when they filmed your face on seeing that Dan was your surprise date.'

'Oh don't worry about it. It was pretty exciting and a fantastic distraction from thinking about *you know who*,' I laugh.

'And what about Mary Berry?' Sam is practically hyperventilating, she's that excited. 'She's like my idol. In fact, scrap that, I actually want to be her – she's that amazing. Kelly arranged for her to come and film a Christmas cupcake masterclass in the café, I think they're showing it in the next episode. She was just so lovely and shared some baking secrets with me – we even had a chuckle about the best ways to avoid the dreaded 'soggy bottom' when baking pastry. And there's even talk of me being involved in a special celebrity series of the *Great British Bake Off*.'

'Wow! As a judge?'

'I don't know. Or maybe a contestant – nothing has been agreed ... '

'That's incredible. I'm so happy for you,' I say, knowing one of Sam's dreams just came true. Right there.

'Thanks, hun. Anyway, I tried calling as soon as Kelly hung up last night, there was no way I was keeping it from you.' She pauses for breath. 'I left a voicemail, but could tell from your face you hadn't got it when you turned up at the café.'

'Oh, you know what the signal is like in my flat. It'll probably arrive next week or something,' I say, feeling relieved. I had thought it a bit odd that Sam hadn't said she'd be there, let alone keep Mary Berry and Dan Kilby a secret, but it's not the end of the world. Besides, I'm hardly in a position to take offence: we usually tell each other everything, but that didn't stop me from keeping my passionate night with Tom a secret. A sudden rush of longing engulfs me. After balancing the phone in the crook of my neck, I pull open a Terry's chocolate orange (buy one get two free – I have fifteen) and stuff two segments into my mouth.

'As long as you're OK. Where did you rush off to after?' Sam asks.

'Oooh, hang on a sec,' I reply, in between chewing and swallowing. 'Sorry about that.' I lick melted chocolate off my fingers. 'Kelly rushed me back to the shop floor to do a couple of publicity shots behind my counter – to send out to all the magazines and newspapers. Apparently, she's had enquiries from tabloids wanting to interview me and *FHM* have even asked about a bikini photoshoot.'

'Wow, how exciting. Are you going to do it?'

'I'm not sure.'

'Why the hesitation?'

'Everything's changing so quickly. I'm already in some online magazine linked with Dan. What if they airbrush my clothes off and flog naked pictures of me to a dodgy men's mag, for the curvy girls' page,' I snill, letting my inner drama queen run riot with my imagination. I've read about stuff that happens to celebrities – leaked sex tapes, kiss-and-tell stories. Even fake pictures. And it's not just celebrities: Kate and Will can't even sunbathe in private!

'I bet you'd look glorious,' she immediately replies, not missing a beat.

'Aw, thanks for the cheerleading, but I'd rather not appear naked in a magazine with a Carrington's carrier bag or whatever covering my Aunty Mary.' I shudder at the thought, and Sam giggles.

'Totes agree,' she says, before pausing and then adding, 'They wouldn't really do that, would they?'

'No, probably not – just my feeble attempt at a joke. Besides, I definitely didn't see a clause about getting naked in my employment contract, but hey ... you never know; anything seems to go these days.'

'Sounds to me like you might need a manager, someone to look after that side of things.'

'Really?'

'Absolutely. I know Kelly seems to be passing some amazing opportunities your way, but she also has her own interests to look after.'

'I guess so, don't suppose you managed to get a number for Claire?' I laugh. Talk about mad – I can't believe I'm even having this conversation with my best friend. It's as if I've stepped onto a massive rollercoaster and now can't decide if I want to ride on it or not. I love the goody bags, the freebies (shoes, clothes, makeovers, etc.), the magazine column, which I've written and emailed to Hannah (after sampling every single item in the goody bag, all of which were divine, the ASOS stash too). But the online article that Dad saw before I had a chance to, has really unnerved me. Makes me feel vulnerable and exposed. And maybe I shouldn't travel by bus on my own. Madison and her friends were lovely, but what if the next group of girls aren't? Perhaps I do need someone to guide me.

'No, I tried Dad's old PA, but she couldn't find any details for her. Don't tell Eddie, though, he'll be devastated. Why don't you ask Kelly? I'm sure she could put you in touch with someone.'

'Sure, maybe I will. Thanks for the advice. Anyway,

how are you? How's Nathan?' I say, to change the subject, making a mental note to invest in a new coat with a large hood, or a snood, or, better still, a balaclava, to shield my face whenever I'm outside my flat or Carrington's from now on. I don't want any more random pictures of me turning up online.

'All good here. I haven't had the dreaded morning sickness for days now. And Nathan is such a sweetheart, you know he's getting very good at foot massage.'

'Aw, that's lovely. Are your feet getting very swollen?'

'Oh no, it's way too early for all that, but he likes to feel involved. And he was thrilled to bits when the first scan appointment arrived.'

'Oooh, how exciting – when is it?'

'Monday ... in a couple of weeks' time. I can't wait. It's in the morning at the hospital and then we're going for lunch afterwards, followed by a pay-per-view session at the private clinic. Jenny went a few days ago and said it's fantastic. They even let her set up a Skype call from her laptop so that Tony could see the baby on the plasma screen, all the way from Helmand.'

'Wow. It's incredible what they can do these days,' I say, feeling really happy for Sam, and sad for Jenny that she doesn't have Tony here with her at such a special time.

'And I'm sure I felt the baby moving around. Maybe I'm more pregnant than I originally thought. It said in the baby book that it's around sixteen weeks for the first kick, if I'm lucky, but sometimes later for a first timer like me.'

'Oh my God, that's amazing,' I say, thrilled for her. 'What did it feel like?'

'Tickly. Like popcorn popping in a microwave,' she says, her voice sounding soft and bubbly.

'Well, that makes sense. She is baking inside your tummy, I guess.' We both laugh.

'True. And I like that analogy. Aw, my little cupcake,' Sam says, and there's a short silence while I imagine her rubbing her stomach lovingly. 'Going back to KCTV – you'll never guess what Kelly also asked me last night?' She pauses. 'Only how I felt about being filmed in labour!'

'*Whaaaat?* Nooo!'

'Exactly. I said no way. End of. Not even discussing it – that was after I asked how she even knew I was pregnant, of course.'

'I didn't breathe a word, I swear,' I quickly tell her.

'Oh, I know hun. Kelly told me she just knew, has a knack for guessing these things, apparently. Reckons she has psychic powers inherited from her great aunt or something. More like she heard on the Carrington's grapevine that I'd been puking in the staff loo.'

'Well, she does seem to know everything that's going on; it's probably all there on those little TV monitors she loves so much.'

'Talking of Aunty Mary's – I'm not having mine broadcast to a film crew. Ew. Hideous. I mean, I love watching *One Born Every Minute*, but it doesn't mean I want a starring role in it.'

'They could always put one of those blurry things over your bits,' I suggest, and we both crack up.

'Oh stop it, or you'll make me need the loo again. I can't stop going at the moment,' Sam manages in between wheezes.

'Oh dear. Anyway, the baby isn't even due before *Kelly Cooper Come Instore* ends,' I laugh, relishing in the banter that makes me feel just like I did before everything changed, and it's nice. Normal. There's a lot to be said for anonymity. If I go down the *FHM* route, I'll never be anonymous again.'

'She said it could be part of her next show!'

'The one in the hotel?' I ask, wondering how that will work.

'What do you mean?'

'Oh, I overheard Kelly talking to someone about a hotel with underground parking – presumed it was for her next show,' I say, wondering if Eddie knows.

'Sounds intriguing, but no, she didn't mention any of that. And Nathan was outraged when I told him. Said Kelly is a sensationalist and will stop at nothing to garner publicity and notoriety with her reality TV shows.'

'Well, he has got a very good point – her setting me up with Dan like that, and without any warning.'

'Talking of which, how was it, being with him? Stir up any lustful feelings?' Sam says, adopting a sultry voice now.

'It was OK,' I say evasively.

'Bet it was better than just OK. He's hot. And he plays guitar – that's just sexy as ... ' she teases.

'*Weell*, I'd be lying if I said my heart hadn't skipped a bit. Just a teeny-tiny bit.'

'I knew it!' she screams. 'Go on ... '

'All right, but on one condition.'

'OK.'

'You understand that just because I want Tom back, doesn't mean I'm immune to other men, does it?'

'Of course not, you're a typical twenty-something woman, not a nun! Stop worrying. I'm not going to think any less of you for fancying Dan, or even going on a date with him, not after Tom's "knight in white jodhpurs" performance on the TV screen the other night.' She huffs. 'I'm not being funny, Georgie, but he must have known you would watch the show. To be honest, it doesn't look very good, does it?'

'No, I suppose not.'

'Good, because I'm still sure you'll sort everything out when he comes back, but in the meantime, why shouldn't you have a bit of fun? He obviously is.'

'Well, there was a moment.'

'Oooh, what kind of moment?'

'The kind where, after the photos were done, Dan was waiting for me and asked if I fancied getting together some time; that he'd heard about me breaking up with Tom, from Kelly I reckon ... '

'See, she really does know everything,' Sam sniffs.

'True. And I know she's a bit bonkers, but I can't help liking her. She has a serious side, too, and seems to want the best for me.'

'Good. So tell me more about Dan.'

'Well, we chatted a bit and he seems like a really nice guy. Not flashy or full of himself, given how famous he is. He was really down-to-earth.'

'Aw, that's nice. When are you going out with him then?'

'Steady on, I still want Tom. And if I'm honest, seeing him with Valentina just made me want him even more. I was a stubborn idiot that day in his office, and I think he was too.'

'Fair enough. For what it's worth, I think you have a point, but you don't want to miss out on a date with Dan Kilby. Tom will keep, especially if you two are meant to be together. Remember that old adage ... if you love someone, let them go, they'll come back, and all that. Plus, it will do him good to have a bit of competition.'

'Maybe. Anyway, I told Dan I'd think about it.'

'*Whaat?*' Sam is outraged. 'Georgie, please tell me you're joking and that you didn't really tell *Dan Kilby* – the man of many girls' dreams, that you would think about going on a date with him.'

'Well, I didn't want too look keen. Besides, I'm in demand now ... didn't you know?' I laugh.

'True, but just don't think for too long. There's the wrap party, remember, and a trillion women that wouldn't mind going with Dan on their arm. Have you seen the number of "Likes" on his Facebook fan page?'

'We'll see,' I say, wondering if I am actually ready to go on a proper date with another man. I'm not sure. I just hate the way things were left with Tom. If only I could talk to him for a few minutes to find out if it really is over – I need closure, if nothing else.

'OK. Hun, I'm going to have to love you and leave you as Nathan's just walked in.'

'OK, chat tomorrow. Oh, really quickly, before you go. Did you know Melissa was back working at Carrington's?' Sam always hears what's going on, from the café.

'Yes, apparently she didn't like it at the prison – too many psychopaths for her liking, said she found it very hard not to want to fight them. You know how she's into all that ninja warrior stuff ... ' We both laugh. Typical Mel.

We end the call and I make my way into the bathroom, smiling to myself at Sam's comments. She's such a queen of hearts, always trying to pair me up, ever the romantic. I turn on the bath taps and plop in my favourite vanilla-scented Lush bath bomb and take off my clothes, carefully hanging the dress and jacket on the back of the door, which I've left ajar, so the steam doesn't ruin them.

I've submerged my body into the blissfully warm water and relaxed for a few minutes, when my mobile vibrates across the vanity unit next to the bath. After drying a hand on a towel, I reach for the phone and turn it over to see the screen.

And I don't believe it.

It's a text message.

From Tom! Just like that.

Seems Sam was right – let him go and he'll come back ...

I hurl myself up into a sitting position. Water splashes everywhere. My heart soars as I press to see the message. At last! Maybe he has been missing me. Maybe Eddie was right and KCTV engineered the horse-riding scene. Tom isn't interested in Valentina at all. It was just for show. Of course it was. And he's not interested in Zara, why would he be when he has me? I've been an absolute fool. Maybe he genuinely thought I'd love doing the show, a nice surprise, and to be honest ... I'm not exactly hating it. I should never have doubted him. Or what we have together. He just needed a bit of time to get his head straight and now he wants to sort things out. All that rubbish about calling it a day – it was said in the heat of the argument, nothing more.

I'm so excited. Everything's going to be wonderful after all. We'll spend Christmas together and it's going to be amazing. It will be all of the gorgeous romantic things we talked about. Hot chocolate. Tartan rugs by the fire. Bing singing in the background. There's still time to find a log cabin. I could get on Lastminute.com. *I can not wait*. I read the message.

Yes I have moved on! I'm with somebody else now so stop stalking me, or you'll lose your job too.

Stunned! I sit motionless in the water staring at the screen. Saliva drains from my mouth. Silent tears trickle down my cheeks. Is that what he thinks of me? A stalker! Oh God. How hideous. I feel like utter rubbish – humiliated too. Nauseous even. I've never been called a stalker before. And I've never seen this side of him. It's horrible. I don't believe it. And I don't know what to do. And he has somebody else. A sob catches in my throat. *Who is she?* Valentina or Zara? And how can he be so callous? He knows how much my job at Carrington's means to me. I stare again at the message. I type out a reply. I delete it. I type another reply. I delete it. And I type another. I delete it too. A hideous cold trickle of realisation seeps through me. This is it! Over. Really over. So he meant it after all. I can't contact him again. Not now. Not ever. Because if I do, then his words will be true – a stalker! A bunny boiler. Whatever spin you want to put on it. And nobody wants to be likened to a looper who shoves a rabbit in a saucepan and freaks everyone out.

After what feels like an eternity, I place the phone back on the vanity unit and pull my knees up under my chin, wrapping my arms around my legs, I hug them into me. I'm shaking all over. I guess I really did get him completely wrong. I feel like such a fool. And then it occurs to me – this is like Brett all over again. I've been dumped for another woman. For all I know, Tom could have already had his sights on Valentina – he did say he had a Skype meeting with a foreign supplier the morning after our hat trick; maybe it was with her. My mind races, mentally scouring our time together, searching for clues of his infidelity. Cold, miserable tears trickle down my face, slowly at first, but fast now, and they won't stop. My chest heaves, in and out, until I'm sobbing uncontrollably.

Eventually, I manage to calm down. The water is cold, I feel trembly and weak with emotional exhaustion – euphoric elation, quickly followed by crashing devastation, does that, I guess. I manage to haul myself out of the bath and scrub myself dry before pulling on my oldest pair of Disney-themed fleecy pyjamas. They're practically threadbare, with a hole at the knee and a button missing – *but what does it matter, it's not like I have an actual boyfriend to impress any more ...* just a fake date, and a list of Facebook strangers who are probably only interested because I'm on the telly.

Feeling numb now, and very sorry for myself, I grab my phone and quickly delete Tom's message. I can't bear to read it ever again. Then I delete every single one of his other messages – even the ones from the start, where we joked together, where he flirted, where he asked if I fancied having lunch with him, where he thanked me for a lovely evening, right through to his actual numbers – home and mobile. Until it's as if he never existed in my phone, or my life at all. And then the penny drops – no wonder he wanted me to have Mr Cheeks, he bloody knew he was going away, he must have been talking and planning with KCTV for months. Well, I get the message, Tom! I hear you. Loud and clear.

I head into my bedroom and slump down on the bed, wondering what to do next. I try to think straight. The shock is subsiding into anger now. If I look at this rationally, then I haven't done anything wrong, not really. All I did was ask him why he didn't tell me about the filming. And he can't blame me for retaliating when he said he wanted to call it a day. OK, I've tried to contact him a few times since, and yes, I did send a drunken text – well, seven times, to be precise! But then who hasn't done that when they've had a few too many buck's fizzes while trying to heal a broken heart? It's not a crime. It's not illegal. Because if it was, then the prisons would all be high-rise tower blocks, or makeshift cells would have to be set up all over the place, in sports halls, aircraft hangers and suchlike. They'd have to utilise those empty retail units down in the pedestrianised part of town, stack bunk beds in and install communal showers. And that would be totally ridiculous.

I turn my phone over and over in my hands, until I come to the realisation that I'm stronger now than I was after the split with Brett. I'm not going to sit around moping and worrying about what might have been with

Tom. And I'm sure as hell not going to the wrap party on my own like some saddo, not while Tom's there whooping it up with his new 'somebody'. Eddie was right, I need to dive straight back into the dating pool. And that's exactly what I'm going to do.

I take a deep breath before letting out a big long puff, and scroll through my contacts list until I find the number. It rings twice before he answers.

'Georgie. Hi, how are you?'

'Not bad thanks. How are you?' I say, doing my best to sound assured and breezy, even though I still feel wobbly inside.

'Good, much better for hearing from you.'

I brush away the last of the tears and swallow hard, remembering Sam's words from our conversation earlier, which seems like an eternity ago now.

'I was wondering about us getting together. And if the offer still stands, then I'd love to, Dan.'

15

It turns out that the council have had to scrap their plans for an ice rink in the centre of town. Sam found out from Mandy, who works in the town hall. She came in for her weekly chocolate orange cupcake with banoffee coffee and told Sam all about it – not enough funds left after their budget was slashed, apparently. But Mandy also said that KCTV had stepped in and offered to stump up the money instead, on one condition, that it's built on the roof of Carrington's, and that customers access it via the store after buying a ticket for a fiver, or merch costing at least the equivalent amount. So that's why Kelly insisted I mention it on camera; she wanted to make sure Carrington's and KCTV garnered as much kudos as possible. She's certainly shrewd when it comes to business and publicity. And someone from Footwear said they heard her plugging it on the local radio station too, so now the whole of Mulberry-On-Sea is delighted with Kelly and KCTV, especially as she has agreed to let the first fifty shoppers have a twirl on the ice for free.

So, due to health and safety regulations, the store is closed this afternoon, with Friday being our quietest time. KCTV are covering the estimated loss of takings. It was the only way the board would agree to Kelly's plan to have scaffolding erected up the back of the store, so the builders don't have to come inside to reach the roof.

Sam and I have decided to make the most of the bonus time off, and are heading into town for a late lunch followed by a pamper session in the Mulberry Grand Hotel spa. Sam's booked herself in for the special Mum To Be package, and I'm having the Ultimate Night Out package, ahead of flicking the switch with the rest of the Carrington's staff, for the Mulberry Christmas lights on Saturday. The rumour was true and I'm so excited. Dad said he might come down to watch – if it's not too cold.

'What do you reckon on these?' We're in the changing room of a little boutique called Bumpalicious, just off the market square in the centre of town, and Sam is trying on a pair of maternity jeans. 'Plenty of room for Cupcake to grow into them,' she adds, holding out the enormous elasticated waistband like a super slimmer in one of those 'post-weight-loss' pictures.

'They look nice on the legs, are they comfortable?' I say, diplomatically.

'I suppose so, but I'm not sure they're me. I don't really do "nice".' Sam wrinkles her nose and I giggle.

'*Weell*, I was wondering why you were buying jeans when you never wear denim.' I smile.

'I know. But I really want some maternity wear. You

know, to feel properly pregnant,' she says, stepping out of the jeans.

'How are you getting on?' It's the sales assistant, calling out from behind the curtain.

'Have you got anything else, please? Something with a bit of a sparkle would be good,' Sam says, grinning as she pops her head around the curtain. 'Jeans aren't really my thing.'

A few minutes later the assistant returns with a beautiful bright red maxi dress, a black shift dress with sequin trim, a purple silk blouse and a grey woollen poncho with silver flecks in – Sam buys the lot.

We're just leaving when the shop's owner stops us.

'Oooh, I've just realised. I thought I'd seen your faces before. Aren't you the two from that programme? Ohmigod! How exciting. Slebs inside my shop,' she gushes. 'And you are *sooo* funny, but I don't know how you put up with those customers, and I think I would have thrown that sleazy guy out – it was totes obvious that Chloé bag had been used,' she says, glancing at me sympathetically. 'I have those types in here all the time; use the merch and then bring it back looking for a refund. Must think we're daft – I even saw one customer on Facebook wearing the top I sold her just the day before she brought it back in, saying it didn't fit. Good for you, standing your ground.' She shakes her head and I don't have the heart to tell her he's an actor, plus I can't remember if we're allowed to say or not. Before we started filming, KCTV handed out contracts to everyone taking part, with a big list of confidentiality clauses. I'm sure I saw something about not 'spoiling the magic' for the viewers. 'Can I take a photo?'

I hesitate.

'Sure,' beams Sam, before I have a chance to answer. 'Come on Georgie.' She loops her arm through mine and stands next to me. I smile politely.

'Can you sign something? What about this?' She hands us a magazine, and we both oblige before saying goodbye.

'What was that all about?' Sam whispers as we head out onto the pavement.

'I don't know, I just feel like a bit of a fraud, I suppose. We're not really proper famous people. We haven't actually done anything as such ... you know, like talented actresses or Olympic athletes.' I pull up my hood, and grip my oversized tote in closer before taking Sam's carrier bags – she's laden down. In addition to the clothes, she bought a really cute cot set with matching mobile, various other bits of baby paraphernalia and an enormous pile of zebra-print washable nappies The assistant said they were the latest baby must-have, and that all the eco-mummies are stocking up on them and signing up to a scheme, where they collect the used ones and bring them back freshly laundered. Sam was keen to be a part of it.

'Are you sure that's all it is?' Sam gives me a concerned look.

'Um, well, I still feel a bit down after Tom's text, but

I don't want to talk about it and spoil our afternoon together. Especially as you look so happy, glowy and radiant, and just like a pregnant woman should be.' I grin. 'This is what you've always wanted and I'm not spoiling it for a single second by moping over a man.'

'Aw. Well, I still can't believe Tom was so heartless. It just goes to show, and I feel partly to blame.'

'Oh please don't. It's not your fault. Let's change the subject.' I smile.

'Well, if I'd have known what he was really like, then there's no way I would have invited him out to the wedding to surprise you. I just wouldn't have encouraged you to get together with him at all,' she says, ignoring my plea.

'I know.' I touch her arm and smile. 'You're a wonderful friend.'

'Thanks, hun, and so are you. And it sounds to me as if you've had a lucky escape, if he can be that mean. I can't believe he was so harsh in the text message – talk about using a hammer to crack a nut. But look on the bright side – you have a date with Dan Kilby. There are women all over the country that fantasise about sleeping with him.' She gives me a cheeky wink and I smile, but know inside that won't happen. Not so soon after Tom. 'Come on, let's go to that new restaurant in the marina for lunch. We could ask the maître d' to seat us somewhere quiet, away from the crowds, *daaahling* – seeing as we're slebs now!' Sam laughs to lighten the mood and change the subject. She pulls out her Gucci shades and puts them on before shaking her curls back to complete a proper celebrity look, even though it's a cold, dark wintery day. And I laugh too, which is something I haven't felt like doing for far too long now.

'That's better. Georgie, I really hate seeing you down, especially in the run-up to Christmas. Talking of which, I'd love you to come to mine for lunch on Christmas Day. Gloria is coming, Nathan's dad too. We were planning on going to Italy, but Gloria was having none of it. "What if you go into labour on the aeroplane?" she said. Nathan told her it's highly unlikely at this early stage ... but anything for a quiet life.'

We join the queue for a taxi, and the atmosphere is really friendly and Christmassy, with the Salvation Army choir singing carols beside a twinkling tree. A guy is roasting chestnuts on an outdoor barbecue and shoppers are milling around, all smiley and happy with their festive goodies, giant rolls of snowman-print wrapping paper tucked under their arms alongside Argos bags crammed full of boxes. One man even has an oversized felt reindeer hat with flashing antlers on, entwined in tinsel. Sam huddles in closer to me. It's freezing and the sky is swirly white – maybe it will snow for Christmas, after all. I place the bags on the pavement and put my arm around her shoulders to keep her warm.

'Thanks for the invite, but I was hoping to spend it with Dad – with it being our first one together in years,'

I say, through chattering teeth, then immediately feel like kicking myself on forgetting that Alfie won't be with us this year. And it feels so sad. He was the ultimate life and soul of the party, always turning up laden with gifts for everyone, and he was the perfect host, the perfect dad, making sure our glasses were full and that we all felt happy and carefree, laughing as we listened to tales of his international travels. And he had a knack of making every female he met feel like the only woman in the world. 'I'm so sorry, I didn't think ... ' I quickly add.

'It's fine, honestly. You must spend it with your dad.' Sam blows on her hands, attempting to warm them up. 'It's important,' she says, wistfully.

'You really don't mind? I'm sure Dad would under-stand ... '

'Of course not. Don't be silly.'

Our taxi swerves up to the kerb and we bundle into the back seat, wedged either side of all the shopping bags. Sam turns to face me.

'I know ... ' she starts, her eyes all sparkly. 'Why don't you bring him with you? I'd love to see him, and he kind of reminds me a bit of Dad. With him giving me away at the wedding and all.'

'Aw, that's really nice. He'll be thrilled, I'm sure. Although, I think he has a girlfriend,' I say, slowly. It feels weird saying it out loud.

'Wow! Good for him, sly old fox.' Sam claps her hands together, seemingly thrilled to hear of another

214

new romance, quickly followed by, 'What's up? Don't you like her?'

'No, no, it's not that, Nancy's really nice, lovely and warm, and I want to be supportive, but it's ... well, I don't know. He's my dad, I suppose.' I shrug.

'And he'll always be your dad,' Sam says, softly. 'But he's a man too. You want him to be happy, don't you?'

'Yes,' I nod. 'But what about Mum?'

'Georgie, she died a very long time ago. And it doesn't mean he loved her any less. He's still here and very much alive, and you being happy for him doesn't diminish your mum's memory.'

'But sometimes it seems like only yesterday to me,' I say, immediately feeling feeble. Sam's dad died less than a year ago and she seems to be coping far better than I ever did.

'And you were a child, you cared for her before she went, then you had to live with strangers who didn't know her or miss her like you did. No wonder it's still so raw, your whole world shattered and you had to deal with that pretty much on your own ...,' Sam says, as if reading my mind.

'Some days I just miss her so very much.'

'Of course you do, and I bet your dad does too. Nancy won't ever replace your mum – and I bet she's worried you might be thinking like this. Why don't you talk to her?'

'Oh no, I've only met her once, I couldn't.' I shake my head.

'Well, talk to your dad then. I bet he'll put your mind at rest.'

'But what do you think I should say? I can't just blurt out, "What about Mum?" I'll sound like a silly little girl. I'm a grown woman – surely I shouldn't feel this way, and it's not just Nancy. It's almost like I'm jealous that he has someone else in his life. After so many years apart, I want to be the important one. I want all his attention for myself. Do I sound ridiculously immature?' I bite my bottom lip.

'Don't be silly. I was just the same. I always felt put out for a bit whenever Dad had a new girlfriend, but he was a ladies' man; women flocked to him like moths to a lamp. I got used to it as I got older; in fact, I got quite close to a few of them, as you know.'

'Yes, Ava. I remember her. Wasn't she at your wedding?'

'That's right. And I truly believe she loved Dad. She adored him, made him happy and that made me feel happy.' Silence follows. 'Georgie, talk to him. It'll make all the difference. I bet he'd be upset if he knew you felt this way.'

'You're right,' I say, feeling a bit brighter about it.

'Tell you what – next time you see him, ask if he wants to bring Nancy along too, for Christmas lunch. That can be your lead-in … '

We've just polished off a delicious crispy duck stir-fry followed by *crème brûlée*, and I'm enjoying a large glass of mulled wine, when Sam reaches across the table to clutch my hand.

'Don't look now. But guess who I've just spotted at a window table in the far corner?'

'Who?' I ask, immediately desperate to know.

'Only Zara!' she makes big eyes.

'But that's impossible. She's in New York. With Tom,' I add, not wanting to be reminded of the fact.

'Well, I'm telling you, it's definitely her. She's sitting with a group of Arabic-looking men, and that woman from the last episode, Princess something or another.'

'Ameerah.'

'That's the one! Oooh, it looks very formal, they're going through a pile of paperwork.'

'Really?' My mind is racing. What's going on? My heart starts pounding, what if Tom is here too?

'No idea, and now she's pointing to something.'

'Who is?'

'The princess. Hang on.'

'What are you doing?' I say, keeping my voice low as Sam pushes her chair back and flings her napkin on the table.

'Finding out what they're up to, of course.'

'*Nooo*, you can't. What if they see you, they'll think we're spying,' I whisper quickly, but it's too late. Sam is off.

I sit for a few seconds, trying to take it in, before I risk swivelling round in my seat, to see what's going on. And Sam was right – it's definitely Zara! Right here. In

Mulberry-On-Sea, and sitting mere metres away from me. My mind races, what's going on? Why is she here? And what does this mean for me? And Tom? Sam is loitering by their table now, with her back to Zara. She ducks behind a giant shoji screen, presumably within listening distance – it's right behind Princess Ameerah's chair. I circle the bottom of my wine glass with an index finger; silently praying that Sam doesn't get caught. What if Zara spots her and tells Kelly? She might sack her – well, not sack her as such, but she could make the board give Sam notice on the lease of the café or something, I suppose. And I wouldn't put it past Sam to have a word with Zara, ask her what she's playing at with Tom. She's always been a loyal friend.

A few minutes later, and Sam is back. She has her shades on and her hair pulled around the sides of her face, attempting to look inconspicuous. She hunches down in her chair before leaning into me.

'Sooo?' I breathe, as she draws out the moment of revelation. She peers at me over the top of her shades, swivelling her eyes around like an undercover secret agent.

'I don't believe it!' Sam pants, eventually.

'Tell me. What's going on?' I ask, absolutely desperate to know.

'The papers are floor plans for a hotel. They were talking about bedroom numbers, concierge services … stuff like that.' Sam flaps her hand dismissively.

'Ahh, that makes sense. They're lining up the next show. Probably going to call it *Kelly Cooper Room Service*. I told you, didn't I, that I overheard her talking about a hotel with underground parking?'

'Yes, I remember. But that's not all.' And Sam's face suddenly pales.

'Are you OK?'

'Yes, I'm fine. But Eddie was right – Zara is up to something.'

'What do you mean?'

'Georgie. I'm so sorry.' Sam takes a gulp of air and glances downward to avoid eye contact.

'What is it?' I ask, the look on her face making me nervous now, scared even.

'Are you sure you want to know?' Her forehead creases with concern.

'Yes. Please, what is it?' I inhale sharply through my nostrils, desperate to quell the creeping sense of unease.

'I need some of your wine first?' she says, her voice tinged with panic.

'Now you're really scaring me,' I say, placing my hand over the top of the glass.

'One sip won't hurt the baby, give it to me,' she says, pushing my hand away and taking the glass. She takes a mouthful before wiping her lips on the napkin. 'OK. It's not good, hun. But better you hear it from me, right?' She grabs my hand and squeezes it tight. I nod, and hold my breath.

Sam closes her eyes and tells me really quickly without even pausing for air.

'Zarawastalkingaboutheirengagement.' She gasps. 'To Tom!'

Sam flings her eyes open and rubs the back of my hand.

'It's going to be fine, Georgie. You're going to be fine. I promise you. Who needs Tom? Let him get engaged to Zara. It's his loss, he's just … ' But I can't hear her voice any more, only a buzzing sensation all around me.

Tears sting in my eyes. I gasp and then swallow hard. It's as if time has stood still. My instinct is to run away as fast as I can. But instead, it's as if somebody has flicked on an autopilot switch. Slow motion. I down the rest of the wine in one huge gulp. I pull out my purse, place some notes on the table, push my chair back and apologise to Sam. She grabs her bags and follows me out of the restaurant.

16

Five shopping weeks until Christmas

I'm standing on the balcony of the town hall overlooking the market square, with a gloved hand poised over the big red plastic button, and a massive smile stuck firmly in place. I feel far from happy inside, but this is proper celebrity stuff. It's meant to be exciting. Fun. Plus, it helps take my mind off wondering how Tom managed to move on so quickly. It still hasn't sunk in. I have to deliberately force myself to stop analysing – in fact, I've given myself a rule: I can have five minutes per hour *max*, to work out when and how he could have got engaged so soon after we split up. It's the only way. I'm in danger of driving myself crazy otherwise. But it explains why he wouldn't take my calls, or reply to my Facebook messages.

Everyone's here from Carrington's including Annie, Mrs Grace, Doris, Suzanne, Lauren and Melissa. Kelly is telling Eddie how wonderful he is, just inside the door behind me. Three KCTV cameras are positioned, ready to capture it all for *Kelly Cooper Come Instore*, and the mayor of Mulberry-On-Sea is making her way towards the front of the balcony. As the mayor starts the countdown, I scan the crowd below – groups of teenagers, families with young children, pensioners, Carrington's customers, Mr and Mrs Peabody, I give them a quick wave and they both wave back enthusiastically. Everyone's happy and smiley and getting in the mood for Christmas; even Mrs Godfrey from the WI is here, wearing her rain bonnet.

Around the square are several Christmas trees covered in sparkly baubles. On my right is a Santa's grotto, with real reindeers in a straw-lined pen next to a sleigh swathed in tartan blankets and crimson sacks stuffed full of presents. Students from the local college are dressed up as elves, helping to supervise the lengthy queue of children, handing out balloons and offering photo opportunities. An assortment of delicious aromas waft up from the many wooden food cabins dotted around – selling roasted chestnuts, hot chocolate with swirly peaks of whipped cream, roast turkey and cranberry rolls and mulled wine. It's all here. I spot Sam's cabin decked out in garlands of twinkling fairy lights with boxed panettone and slabs of Christmas cake piled up high on the counter. The whole place is like a picture-perfect Christmas card, or a scene from a Hollywood movie. The music stops. The crowd cheers before counting down the numbers being displayed on a massive electronic billboard.

'Five. Four. Three. Two. One … '

The mayor starts clapping and I press the button. And, as if by magic, Mulberry-On-Sea is illuminated from one side of the town to the other in a rainbow of colour linking each streetlight to the next. It's incredible. It's amazing. And it literally takes my breath away. The crowd goes wild – whooping, cheering and clapping. Kelly is standing next to me now. She swings my left hand up in the air before grabbing the microphone and bellowing out to the crowd.

'Happy Christmas everyone, from *Carriiiiiingtons*.' Kelly leans in to me, and whispers, 'Tits and teeth, darling. Tits and teeth. Hair shake. Look at them all down there while you're up here. They adore you. Told you I'd make you a star. You too,' she says through a fixed smile, all the while posing for the crowd as she turns to face Eddie, who's standing the other side of her now. 'Didn't I tell you? Stars. Huge. The pair of you. Wonderful!' We all clap some more and blow kisses as the opening notes of Slade's 'Merry Xmas Everybody' starts belting out from four giant speakers erected on scaffolding.

'Right. That's their lot. Come on inside. The media pack are waiting for you.' Kelly ushers me, Eddie and Mrs Grace away from the balcony and into a lounge area, closing the doors behind us. We take off our hats and coats, and Hannah piles them up into a mountain on a couple of wing chairs. I scan the room. It's crammed with press people wearing plastic ID badges on chains around their necks. Some are holding pads and pens, others have Dictaphones primed to record.

'Ooooh, this is the best night of my life.' Mrs Grace

helps herself to a flute of champagne. 'Did you see the Peabodys? Turn up to an envelope opening, those two. And that snooty one from the WI? She won't be looking down her nose at me again,' she sniffs, before pushing her granny handbag into the crook of her elbow and turning towards a waiting journalist. 'Yes dear, that's G-R-A-C-E.' I smile as Mrs Grace peers over the journalist's shoulder, making sure she gets all the details correct. 'Did they tell you that I'm "in talks" ... ?' she pauses to do quote signs with the fingers of her free hand and the journalist smiles patiently. 'That's right, with *Good Housekeeping* magazine regarding a regular column, which is a huge honour as it's a marvellous publication and everyone holds it in such high regard. You know, I heard the queen reads it and there's no higher endorsement than that!' Mrs Grace purses her lips and makes big eyes. 'And I served her once. Such a charming girl she was.'

'Did you? When was that?' the journalist asks, looking interested now.

'Oh, this was back in the Sixties when she was here on official business – a "meet and greet", I think they call it, dear.' She pauses so the journalist can catch up in writing it all down. 'Anyway, Her Majesty came to Mulberry-On-Sea and ... '

Kelly loops her arm through mine.

'Come with me.' She steers me over to the other side of the room. 'Oh, hang on a sec.' Her mobile rings. 'Yes. What is it now?' she says on answering. A short silence

follows. 'Zara, you can be so obnoxious sometimes ... '
Another pause. *Hmmm, ain't that the truth?* 'Fine. I will tell
François that the seven thousand pound Birkin bag that he
gifted to you is the wrong shade of pewter.' She snaps the
phone shut and lets out a huge sigh before turning back
to me. 'Now, the next person I'm going to introduce you
to is very important, a handbag designer, and if you play
your cards right, then you may get to help design some
bags.' Oh my God. Thoughts of Zara instantly vanish from
my head and my heart actually misses a beat. Designing
handbags, I'd love to do that. Instinctively, I smooth down
my top and check my hair before swigging a mouthful of
champagne. 'Here she is. Now, five minutes only darling.
Georgie's in demand,' Kelly says to an attractive blonde
woman, who looks vaguely familiar. I'm sure I've seen her
in magazines. And then I realise ... it's Anya Hindmarch,
designer and manufacturer of exquisite handbags and
purses. I've read her Wiki page. Oh my God. I *love* her
bags. Annie and I always squeal with delight when a new
range arrives for us to sell.

I resist the urge to do a little courtesy in reverence,
and shake Anya's hand instead. We chat about bags
for the allocated timeslot and she gives me her business card before Kelly ushers me away. I'm introduced
to journalists, brand managers and magazine editors.
Someone from *Closer* magazine thanks me for my
column, congratulating me on the in-depth detail and
star rating I gave to each product, and promises to send

me more goody bags, if I'm interested in doing a few more features – she suggests a special celebrity 'what's in your handbag' piece, where I get to scrutinise the contents of A-list women's handbags? *Err, what do you think?* Who wouldn't want to get a glimpse inside someone like Victoria Beckham's handbag? I bet it's crammed full of luxury items and that special tea she likes.

I'm having such an amazing time that when I glance at the crystal clock on the wall at the far end of the room, I'm surprised to see that it's almost ten p.m. – I haven't thought about Tom for at least four hours. But then, as if reading my mind, my mobile vibrates in my clutch. I pull it out. Unknown number. I hesitate. What if it's Tom calling to explain? I'm not sure if I even want to speak to him now. I swallow hard and decide to go for it. I can always hang up if he starts on about having always loved Zara and how he wanted me to hear about the engagement from him first, bla bla bla ...

'Hello?' I say, finding a quietish corner of the room.

'Is that Georgie Hart?' It's a woman's voice, but I can barely hear her. I put a finger in my free ear and duck behind a heavy velvet curtain.

'Yes it is.'

'Great. Georgie, I'm calling from CAN Associates. Claire would very much like to meet with you.' *Oh my actual God.* It's Claire. Peter Andre's manager. My jaw drops. I fling the curtain back. Eddie waves over. He is going to S-C-R-E-A-M when he hears about this.

17

Four shopping weeks until Christmas

There's an actual courtesy car waiting for me! KCTV have sent a limousine to take me all the way to London, and it's just arrived outside my flat. I'm off to the red-carpet opening of the cocktail bar in Soho, and Dan Kilby is meeting me there. Kelly suggested I invite him, and when the wealthy Chinese owners of the cocktail bar heard about my properly famous plus one, they trebled the fee, just like that. I check my hair in the hall mirror one last time. Perfect. KCTV also arranged for me to be styled – super big hair, tan, nails, make-up, lashes, and even arranged for me to borrow this exquisite crimson playsuit by Alexander McQueen. It clings in all the right places. A generous spray of the new Dior perfume (there was a 100 ml bottle in the latest goody bag) and I'm ready to go.

We're in the cocktail bar, which isn't like any cocktail bar I've ever been in before, it's more how I imagine a gentlemen's club to be. There is a selection of podiums dotted around, with women in bikinis gyrating around poles. Black flock paper hangs on the walls, with strategically placed mirrors ensuring the audience gets to view everything on offer. And there must be at least four fountains pumping a creamy piña colada concoction up in the air that slides down into goldfish-bowl-sized glasses for people to help themselves to, before popping in straws to sample. At one end of the club is a stage set up on a flight of stairs, each with twinkling blue sparkly speck lights pulsing away in a light show extravaganza. Chinese businessmen in suits are milling around, and everyone else is trying not to stare at Dan, who is leaning casually against the bar next to me with two of his security people hovering nearby.

'Have you tried one of these?' he says, pointing to a caramel-coloured mixture in a tall frosted glass.

'I don't think so. Is it good?'

'Sure is. It's a Baileys Biscotti milkshake. It's their signature cocktail especially for Christmas,' Dan explains, over the loud music. He offers me the straw and it tastes divine. Mm-mmm. 'Shall I get you one?'

'Sure,' I say, nodding and smiling.

'Or we could get out of here?' he grins, glancing around the club and surreptitiously pulling a face. 'Not really my thing ... '

'Or mine.' I grin too. 'But aren't we supposed to have pictures taken with the owners and talk to the press?' I say, remembering the enormous fee I'm being paid. I can't really just leave.

'Probably. But I reckon they have enough publicity shots, don't you? That guy over there hasn't stopped taking pictures of us.' Dan indicates over my right shoulder. I turn around to see a man in jeans and a T-shirt with a zoom camera pointing directly at us.

'Is he allowed to do that?'

'The owners are most likely paying him; we've been directed to the perfect spot for him to capture us underneath the bar's logo on the wall behind us,' Dan explains. 'Come on. Let's go. I know the perfect place and I'll get my manager to square it with the owners, give them a glowing review from us both. This cocktail is awesome, so we'll make sure we mention that.' He laughs and takes my hand, nodding at his security men as we leave.

We're sitting on a squishy double seat in the back row of an old-fashioned cinema, sharing a box of Maltesers. Organ music is playing as we wait for the film to start. *It's a Wonderful Life*. A special late-night showing and part of the cinema's Christmas-themed programme running right up until 24 December. And we're the only people in here, apart from Dan's security guys down in the front row, which isn't surprising as this cinema is tiny and old-fashioned compared to the multiscreen complex over on the industrial estate. In one corner of the stage is a glorious 1950s drinks cabinet complete with chrome cocktail shakers behind sliding glass doors; in the other corner is an old Chesterfield sofa, and the screen is swathed in shimmery gold satin curtains. There's a lovely, halcyon atmosphere of days gone by. I can just imagine the men in Trilby hats and pinstripe suits with sweethearts in floaty tea dresses, hair set in starlet curls framing rouged cheeks and crimson rosebud lips. The nostalgic images make me feel calm and relaxed.

'So, what do you think?' Dan says, turning his head sideways to face me. 'Better than a sleazy cocktail bar, isn't it?'

'It sure is. I love it, and I can't believe I haven't been here before,' I say, taking in his physique – tall and slender. A total contrast to Tom's muscular athletic build. Stop it! I shove the comparison out of my head. There's no point. Tom has made his choice, and I just have to accept it. Move on. And Dan is lovely. He chatted all the way back here to Mulberry-On-Sea – about how it's still his home; he has a beach house in the private development. And how living here keeps him sane. He's tried the whole fame game, even moving to LA for a bit, but he said that he just felt shallow and miserable most of the time.

The lights dim and the curtains swish back to reveal the screen. I sink into the seat, grateful for the opportunity to switch off and relax for a while, and quieten the analytical voice from going over and over everything inside my head. Dan puts his arm around my shoulders and I lean into him. A feeling of bittersweet happiness trickles through me. And, for just a glimmer of a second, I can't help wishing it was Tom sitting here beside me. I instantly feel ashamed. I force myself to get a grip.

Dan's a sweet man, and bringing me here is kind and thoughtful. Romantic.

As the credits roll, we smile at each other and stand up. The film was so uplifting. Just what I needed. And it made me think about what's really important. I do have a wonderful life. I have Dad back and I know he loves me, he thinks the world of me. I have amazing friends. A job I love. And I'm getting to do once-in-a-lifetime things that not so long ago I could only dream of. Like going on dates with famous singers ...

Stumbling and bumping into each other, we make our way down the dimly lit stairs and out into the cinema's tiny foyer. Dan crunches up the Malteser box and drops it in a bin before pulling his hat low down on his forehead and pulling his scarf up around his chin.

'Disguise,' he says, smiling. 'Means I can usually walk from here to the seafront without being recognised.' He takes my hand.

'What did you think of the film?' he asks, smiling and pushing his hair out of his eyes.

'Dan, it was perfect. Thanks for bringing me here.'

'My pleasure. You seemed a bit down earlier on. Is everything OK?' We leave the cinema and start walking towards the seafront. 'Is what happened with the other guy on your mind?' His eyes search mine and I look away.

'Err, yes, a bit, I guess so. Sorry,' I say, wondering how much he knows.

'Ahh, don't be. When KCTV got in touch about me making an appearance on the show, they said you had just split up with your boyfriend.

'Oh, I see … ' I start.

'No need to explain. It's none of my business, unless you want to talk about it.' He glances sideways at me and I shake my head. 'It's really hard when something you thought you had turns out to be nothing very much at all.'

'Sounds as if you've had a hard time too,' I say, as we cross the road and walk along the promenade.

'Yes. I split up with my ex in the summer.'

'Oh, I'm sorry.' There's a short silence.

'So, how do you feel about being on a reality show?' Dan says, pulling my hand inside his coat pocket to keep warm. I snuggle into his arm, drawing in his citrusy scent, and make a conscious effort to focus on enjoying the moment, instead of worrying about what might have been with Tom.

'Well, it was a shock at first, seeing myself on TV without warning,' I say, looking at the pavement. 'And then I felt let down by … ' My voice trails off.

'But you're having fun now? It's changed your life,' he says.

'Yes. It has.'

'Will you pursue a career in the spotlight, once the reality show is over?'

'I'm not sure. I like some things about it, others not so—'

'Ah, let me guess ... YouTube. I was shown a clip of you.'

'Oh no.' I cringe.

'You made me laugh, which is why I agreed to be your surprise date, and I'm glad that I did. We're having a good time, aren't we?'

'Yes. But it is a bit surreal, though, if I'm honest.'

'Really? Why?'

'Well, you know ... you're famous.'

'So are you.' He nudges me and I smile.

'So why did you agree to be on the show?' I ask.

'Guess I just wanted to reach a wider audience.' He shrugs his shoulders and laughs at his own joke. 'Besides, it's fun, especially if I get to hang out with you. You're normal. It's refreshing, and makes a change from the people I usually meet.' He swings my arm playfully and it makes me laugh.

'Ahh, thank you.'

'My pleasure. Seems to me we're in similar places right now, relationship-wise, so we might as well keep each other company.' Dan stops walking and we turn to face each other. He takes my other hand in his. 'If that's OK with you?' He grins, and I grin back. I'm having a really nice time with him, and it sure beats sitting at home alone on a Saturday evening with my phone at the bottom of the laundry basket, just so I'm not tempted to send Tom another trivial text message to like *congratulate him on his engagement*', or ask if I can have my Adele CD back – that was a particularly low moment when I just wanted a response from him. A reaction, anything, even a short, sharp 'NO' in reply would have been a comfort. It's so rubbish that I haven't even had a chance to ask him why we ended up the way we did. But it's done with; I'm drawing a line under it. I take a deep breath and puff a big cloud out into the frosty night air, as if to mark my decision.

'I'd like that, Dan.'

'Good. Me too,' he says, and we carry on walking.

We reach the bandstand on the promenade, which is illuminated by a trillion tiny golden lights set in snow-flake shapes against the inky night sky. The rhythmic swirl of the sea laps the shore. The icy air makes my cheeks numb. I press my free hand up to my face in an attempt to keep warm, when Dan swings me around to look me straight in the eye.

'Georgie, can I kiss you?' He pulls me in close.

'Um, yes. OK,' I say, instantly wishing I'd thought of something slightly more inviting to say, but before I can utter another word, his lips are on mine. Soft and warm. It feels nice. Not electric. Just nice and comfortable. Instinctively, I close my eyes and melt into the moment. My pulse quickens. We finish kissing and pull apart. A spark of light catches my eye. Dan sees it too and, as we turn together, there's another spark. A camera. He grins at me. I grin back.

'Are you thinking what I'm thinking?' he says, raising

an eyebrow and lifting a lock of hair away from my face. I nod. 'After three,' Dan whispers in my ear, and a few seconds later he moves one hand up between my shoulder blades and circles my waist with the other. 'Let's give them something to talk about.'

And in one swift movement, he leans forward, dips me back, and plants a massive kiss on my lips, holding it for several seconds in true, sweepingly romantic Hollywood movie-style, almost taking my breath away. As my hair swings back in the breeze, my right leg pops up against the side of his thigh, and I cherish the feeling. It's exhilarating. Glamorous. Fun. A wonderful life ... or so it seems.

18

Three shopping weeks until Christmas

It's Monday, my day off, so I've decided to surprise Dad with an impromptu visit, I've brought banana sandwiches and ginger beer just in case he's free and we can take a trip to Mum's grave, followed by a stroll along the promenade. Just the two of us. It will give us a chance to talk, for me to let him know I'm pleased he's met Nancy, and see if he wants to invite her to Sam's house for Christmas lunch.

I press the intercom and wait for him to answer. There's no reply. I press again; perhaps he's in the bathroom. But still no answer. I rummage in my bag to find my mobile. His number rings before going straight to the answer service. My heart drops with disappointment. I'm just about to leave when an old woman wearing a festive red Santa hat decorated with tinsel, and dragging a tartan wheelie shopper, comes to the door. She presses the security pad.

'Ooh duck, you'd better come on in – can't have you standing out in the cold. Not when you're, well, you know ... ' she says, standing aside as the automatic door buzzes open.

'Thank you. Err,' I mutter, wondering what she's going on about, but before I have a chance to ask, she's off up the path, bellowing out to the minibus driver to make sure he waits for her. I'm hovering in the hallway when my mobile rings. It's Dad.

'Georgie, I'm so sorry, I missed your calls. Are you OK?' he says, sounding different – panicky, edgy perhaps.

'Yes, I'm fine thanks, are you?' I brace myself, desperately hoping he hasn't slipped back into his old ways and got in trouble again – gambling is an addiction, after all. And I know he's never missed a meeting since he left prison all those years ago, but it's still there, secreted in the back of my head as a possibility, I don't think that will ever go away. And I couldn't bear it, for his sake too, if he succumbed again. I know he'd be devastated. And what would Nancy think? Dad could lose everything he's worked so hard to rebuild.

'Oh, don't worry about me,' he quickly replies.

'Dad, I'm actually outside your flat, but you're obviously not here. I'll come back another time.'

'No no, don't be silly darling, knock on Nancy's door, I'm in with her.' I press to end the call, and for some ridiculous reason, tears sting and a lump forms in my throat. There's no way I can go to Mum's grave and talk to Dad on my own now. The disappointment is crushing. I quickly find a squashed tissue in my bag and dab at my eyes; it'll have to do. I don't want Dad seeing me upset. He'll only worry and, besides, I'm a grown, confident woman, I need to get a grip. I'm not normally this emotional. It must be everything that's happened recently. I'm exhausted by it all. And with the filming, and being in the public eye – well, it makes me feel exposed. Vulnerable.

'There you are.' Dad is coming along the hallway, with Dusty right behind him. 'Come in. Nancy would love to see you. What a nice surprise.' Shoving the tissue inside my pocket, I put a smile on my smile and follow him back to Nancy's cosy flat. She's waiting by the front door and Frank Sinatra is singing 'Strangers in the Night' from the bedroom. After giving me a kiss on the cheek and taking my coat, Nancy dashes in and turns the music off. Dusty nuzzles my hand to greet me, and I give her silky ears a stroke.

'We were just, um ... dancing,' Nancy puffs, patting her hair nervously when she reappears. There's an awkward silence.

'Oh, don't turn it off on my account. I love the old songs. Dad used to play them all the time before ... ' My voice trails off as I wonder if she knows. He may not have told her about his time in prison for fraud. Yes, it was a long time ago now, but still, it's his personal business, not mine to tell. It makes me feel strange – I'm worried she'll judge him. I don't want him getting hurt, rejected, like I have been. For all his faults in the past, he's my dad and I love him.

'Come and sit down, dear. Put your feet up,' Nancy says, giving me an odd look. I do as I'm told and follow her into the sitting room. Dad follows behind and sits in the armchair opposite. 'I'll give you two some privacy.' Nancy disappears and I crease my forehead, wondering why she's acting so strangely. First the old woman at the door. Now Nancy. And Dad too, if the look on his face is anything to go by.

'Dad, is everything all right?' I ask, rattled.

'Err, yes, yes of course. Why wouldn't it be, sweetheart?' he says, and I know I'm not mistaken, there's definitely something weird going on, and it's more than him having been in Nancy's bedroom and feeling a bit embarrassed about it. I'm not stupid, they could only have been cuddling, or dancing, as Nancy said, but there's no way they were naked – unless they hold the world record for getting dressed in record time. Dad is wearing a shirt, tie, V-neck jumper, trousers and lace-up shoes – he'd have to be a contortionist ninja to have got dressed that quickly. Not that it really bothers me if they were naked – good for them; it's more action than I'm currently getting in the bedroom department. No, there's definitely something strange going on. Oh God, I hope Dad's OK. I decide to probe him.

'I'm not sure Dad – maybe it's my imagination, but you all seem to be acting really uncomfortably around me. If it's because you're worried about how I feel about you and Nancy, then I want you to be happy, Dad. I know

Nancy won't ever replace Mum, you said so and that's good enough for me. I like Nancy and I understand that you can't be expected to be on your own for ever more and, well, if we can still go to Mum's grave sometimes, and the pier, like we said we would, just us and well—'

'Georgie. Stop talking,' Dad interjects, and I close my mouth before opening it again and sucking in a massive gulp of air. I hadn't realised I was babbling without drawing breath. I actually feel dizzy. Silence follows.

'I'm sorry. It's probably not my business,' I mutter, to break the awkward atmosphere.

'Of course it is. And we do need to talk about my relationship with Nancy,' Dad starts. 'But there's something else first. Something far more important.' He cups his chin with his thumb and forefinger, and I know it must be serious; he used to do this when I was a child and had done something I shouldn't have, like the time I poured a tester pot of apple blossom paint into Mum's handbag. But I'm not a child any more, and I haven't done anything wrong, as far as I know.

'Oh, Dad, what is it? Are you OK? You're not ill are you? Oh my God, why didn't you say?' I leap up and dart across the room to crouch down in front of him. I put my hand on his knee. 'Dad, please tell me ... ' A lump forms in my throat. I've just got him back in my life. Tears sting. I couldn't bear it if—

'No, no, it's not me Georgie. I'm fine. Honestly sweetheart, no need to put two and two together ... ' He smiles kindly and shakes his head. 'I remember you doing exactly the same as a little girl, but please don't worry, I'm as strong as an ox, me.' Dad pats my hand reassuringly and relief rushes through me.

'Georgie, you know I love you very much and I'll never judge you – not that it's a big deal these days anyway, but just so you know, I'm always here for you, I'll support you every step of the way.'

'What do you mean?'

'Darling, you don't have to hide it. Dad looks away. I'll support you no matter what.'

'Dad, what are you talking about?'

'Oh sweetheart, shall I make it easy?' Dad says softly. He stands up and walks out of the room.

I'm still trying to work out what's going on when Dad returns with a glossy magazine in his hand. He passes it to me. I glance at the page. And freeze. I can hear my own blood pumping in my ears.

Is new reality star, Georgie Girl, of Kelly Cooper Come Instore *going to be a yummy mummy soon? Here she is outside Bumpalicious laden down with baby goodies!'*

There's a picture of me below the headline. *Alone.* They must have cropped Sam out. And I've got all the maternity shopping bags in my hands and I'm standing right next to the Bumpalicious shop sign. And then, if that wasn't bad enough, a reader has posted a comment underneath.

*I bet she's holding that oversized tote in front of her belly
to hide the bump, oldest trick in the book, all the slebs do
it. PS – I love her coat; does anyone know where it's from?*

'*Dad!* You think I'm pregnant. Oh my God!' I don't believe it. Talk about surreal. No wonder he's being weird. I bet he thinks it's a secret love child or whatever, especially with me not being married. In his day, this would have been a total scandal, and he can be a bit old-fashioned when it comes to stuff like this. Only a few months ago he was telling me how shocking it was that a woman in the post office he goes to is rumoured to be pregnant after a one-night stand – Dad was outraged that 'the scoundrel responsible' hadn't offered to marry her.

'It's OK, darling. Really it is. And thank goodness it's with the singer and not that lad Brett,' Dad puffs, leaning forward and pointing a finger in the air as if he's marshalling a damage-limitation plan. 'Do you think you might marry him?' he quizzes.

'Dad. Please. Will you just stop it? I'm not pregnant. And even if I was, I know how to look after myself. I'd deal with it, decide what's best for me. I'm not a little girl without a mind of my own. I'm a grown woman. And nobody cares if people are married or not these days.'

I'm up on my feet now, my mind racing as I pace around Nancy's sitting room. She appears in the doorway. I knew I should have moved down to the basement to flog washing machines. It might not be as glamorous as selling high-end handbags and being on TV, but I bet it's dull, discreet and just what I could do with right now.

'Is everything OK? Shall I get the cakes?' Nancy gives Dad a furtive glance. 'It's all pasteurised cream,' she quickly adds, giving me a look. I stare at her, goggle-eyed and speechless. I turn to look at Dad. His face gives nothing away – *Oh my actual God*, he's not even sure I'm telling the truth.

This is madness. And then my mind starts racing, back to my night with Tom. He was sensible. We both were. I'm on the pill, for crying out loud – I'm not pregnant! I'm definitely, definitely not pregnant. Sweet Jesus, the real but made-up world has finally gone and addled my brain. I can't even tell what's fact and what's fiction any more. I'm even doubting my own sense of reality. It's official. I need to sit down. I slump back in the armchair, exhausted by it all. And I need a drink – I pull a ginger beer from my bag, open it and guzzle half in one go. The alcohol content is practically negligible, I know, but it's all I have right now, it'll have to do. Maybe the pending sugar rush will help ...

Once the initial shock wore off, I talked Dad through it all. Explained that Sam is the one who's pregnant and how the magazine had cropped her out of the picture. It took him a while to get his head around how that could be and he's vowed to ask his teacher on the silver surfers' course to show him how it's done. And Dad was delighted for Sam and Nathan, naturally. I've told him that it's early days and that she had wanted to wait to share the news with him, but I guess it's too late now. Sam was OK about it. I checked with her first – went into Dad's garden to call her, to quickly explain what had happened as she had just arrived at the hospital for her scan. I told her about the magazine, the misunderstanding, and after she'd stopped screaming with laughter, she said it was fine for Dad to know.

'Oh Georgie, I'm so sorry for jumping to conclusions,' Dad says, holding his head in his hands. 'I've been such an idiot.'

'We both have.' It's Nancy, hovering in the doorway with a mountain of cream cakes piled up on a silver foil platter.

'It's not your fault,' I say, looking first at Dad and then Nancy. 'The paparazzi are very good at distorting the truth.' I shake my head.

'Well, I shan't ever bring up your tendency for putting two and two together again, that's for sure. And now we know where you inherited it from – I'm the one with the drama queen gene. Sweetheart, it's all my fault.' Dad lets out a big puff of air. 'I feel like such an old fool. And you know, I was thinking about asking the council to rehouse me again so I could be nearer to help out with the baby. And Nancy had even dug out her knitting needles, hadn't you love?' We all laugh. I've calmed down a bit now.

'That's right. Oooh, I'd love a grandchild ... ' Nancy stops talking abruptly and there's an awkward silence.

'I'm sorry, I err ... didn't mean, that's not ... ' She places the platter on the coffee table and her cheeks flush rhubarb-red.

'It's OK, Nancy. Really.' I smile and Dad looks up. Nancy fiddles with the gold letter N on the end of her chain.

'Why don't you two get stuck in and I'll put the kettle on.' Nancy nods and makes big eyes at Dad, as if she's telepathically giving him a message. What's going on now? He waits for her to disappear before getting up to close the door.

'We need to talk sweetheart.'

'I know Dad.'

'Please hear me out. Is that OK?' I nod, eager for everything to be out in the open.

'I loved your mother with all my heart. I still do. And that will never change.' I nod and smile. Nancy is very lovely, but she'll only be second best, a companion; she'll never take Mum's place.

'I know Dad. And you were the only man for Mum, she told me so.' Dad smiles wistfully.

'But, I ... I've always loved Nancy too.' His eyes are searching mine now, gauging, waiting for my reaction. What does he mean?

'*Loved?*' I ask, wondering if I heard him correctly.

'And I still do. Very much so.' He's glancing at the carpet now.

'But, I ... I don't understand.'

245

'I think you do, sweetheart,' Dad studies the swirly patterned carpet intently, and the ramifications of what he's just said sink in. He didn't meet Nancy when the council condemned his old flat and relocated him here. He hasn't been on his own since he came out of prison. And no, Frank Sinatra ... they're not *strangers in the night exchanging glances*, at all. Oh no, they're seasoned lovers all day long. He's known her for years!

'How long?' I ask, holding my breath.

'Georgie, it was a difficult time. I was ... the gambling was—'

'How long, Dad?'

'Twenty years, give or take.'

'*Whaat?* But it can't be. That would mean Mum was still alive. I must have been a child when it started. You knew Nancy before you went to prison?' That twitchy, uneasy feeling from the first time I met her returns.

'That's right. And I'm so ashamed.'

'And so you should be,' I snap. 'Poor Mum. She adored you.' I take a deep breath, desperately trying to take it all in. 'Oh please, God, tell me she didn't know ... ' Dad shakes his head and the feeling of relief is overwhelming. She had enough to contend with, with the MS and Dad gambling away everything we had. 'Well, that's some-thing, I suppose. But Dad, how could you? Mum was ill. She needed you. And then you left ... you left us all alone. Do you know what that did to her? To us?' I'm conscious that I'm almost shouting.

'I know, darling. And, like I said, I'm truly ashamed. I'm so sorry. Nancy is too, that's why she urged me to be honest with you. She's hated keeping it from you. Me too. Of course it all stopped when I went to prison, but we, well, after Mum died, we were back in touch.' He looks up and then I remember, there were rumours of other women. So it was true. They weren't lies made up to discredit him and upset Mum. It was even in the newspapers at the time.

'And what about Nancy's husband? Did you even stop to think about Bob, or Mum for that matter?' I say, my voice all shrill and accusatory, but I have to stand up for them, it's not as if they can do it themselves.

'Bob knew,' Dad says, flatly. His shoulders drop.

'*He knew?*' A short silence follows. 'But how? What? Did he *condone* it?' I say, incredulously. Nothing would surprise me. I push a hand through my hair. Talk about the day that keeps on giving, first my faux pregnancy and now this – it's beyond surreal.

'It's why I went to prison.' The room sways. I grip the arm of the chair. 'He found out about the affair and wanted revenge. He launched an investigation into me and my business affairs, unravelled everything, and, well, you know the rest.' Dad's voice is barely audible. And I notice a silent tear slowly trickling down his chin. 'I don't expect you to forgive me, or Nancy. But I had to tell you. I had to. I couldn't keep it from you any more. What if these celebrity hunters had found out before you knew? How would that have made you feel? I wanted you to hear it from me, not from some scurrilous hack looking to make a quick buck without a single thought for who they might hurt in the process.'

I stand up, practically panting for air. Why is the room so hot? I feel as though I'm suffocating. I push my sleeves up. I can't breathe. And my head feels as if it might explode. So Dad went to prison because he was having an affair with a policeman's wife, and my whole life – Mum's too – changed because of it. Abruptly. And horribly.

'Dad, I have to go. I'm sorry. I can't do this. Not right now. I have to go ... ' The rollercoaster of emotions is overwhelming. I pull the sitting room door open, race down the hallway, grab my coat from the peg on the wall and run from Nancy's flat. The crisp fresh air hits me like a shot of adrenalin, and I gasp.

I'm running along the slippery ice-covered pavement when my mobile buzzes inside my pocket. I pull it out. It's Sam. I press to see the text message. I stop running. My hand freezes around the phone. And everything that's happened today, and in the last few weeks, evaporates in an instance. Inconsequential.

No heartbeat

Oh God. Oh no. Oh no no no no ... Tears sting my cheeks, collecting on my chin before snaking down and pooling in the groove above my collarbone. I have to go to her.

248

But I can't move. I'm standing motionless against a brick wall. The phone still clasped in my hands. I send another text.

Ps – I love you xxx

19

Sam is devastated. Nathan too. But he's holding it together, trying to be strong for her. I've taken time off to be with them, Annie is holding the fort at work with Denise from Home Electricals helping out, and we're in the lounge of their villa on the private beach estate just along the coast from Mulberry-On-Sea. Sam blames herself, says she feels like a failure. Or that she's being punished – for working too hard, for tempting fate by getting excited, for buying baby clothes so early on, for letting herself imagine a whole lifetime in a few short weeks. At one point she even convinced herself that the miscarriage was down to the sip of mulled wine she had in the restaurant that day. Of course, both Nathan and I have told her that it definitely, *definitely* wasn't the reason, it absolutely wasn't anything she did, but she can't help going over and over, searching for an explanation. A reason. Something to help her make sense of what happened.

The sonographer started doing the scan before calling the doctor in, who explained that Sam was right – she was more pregnant than she first thought, but the baby had stopped growing at around eleven or twelve weeks. But she'd felt the baby move. She was convinced of it. The doctor said it was most likely wind. Nathan stepped in then and promptly brought her straight home, determined they be allowed to cherish at least some memory of the pregnancy. And Gloria is on her way over from Italy. Sam has stowed the scan picture in a keepsake box, with the tiny clothes she had already bought, to show Gloria; she really wants to do that, she says it means the baby was real, even if she was only here for a short time. And Sam is still convinced that Cupcake was a little girl.

Sam was given the option of going back to the hospital for an operation, but decided she'd rather stay at home and let nature take its course, which it did soon after. We sat up one night and she told me that even though Nathan and I were here with her, she just felt numb and alone, that she needed to talk to someone who knew how she felt. Who understood. Someone who had been through it themselves – so I got on Google and got her the number of a couple of support organisations who've put her in touch with a woman who lives here in Mulberry-On-Sea. Sam called her and said she was very calm and kind, and gave her hope.

At first, Sam was adamant that she wasn't putting herself or Nathan through the heartache again, but in the last few days she's been talking about trying for another baby. She says it's a comfort to know that although this time it wasn't meant to be, next time it very much could be. Sam's always been a positive person, and I'm in awe of the way she's coping, once again, in the face of adversity. Archie would have been so proud of her ...

The doorbell rings. I look over at Sam sitting on the sofa next to Nathan, but they are oblivious. Sam has her head on his shoulder and they both have their eyes closed, their fingers entwined. I leave them to be alone and go to the front door. It's Eddie and Ciaran.

'We won't come in,' Eddie whispers, handing me a massive cellophane-wrapped wicker hamper crammed full of luxury lotions and potions – bubble bath, sugar scrub, exfoliator, scented candles ... 'We just wanted to bring this, for when she feels a bit brighter.'

'Oh Ed, thank you, that's really kind,' I say, stepping outside and pulling the front door to behind me. Ciaran leans across Eddie and gives me a kiss on the cheek.

'And this is for Nathan,' he says, in his lovely Irish accent. He hands me a small package. 'It's a CD, a playlist of songs by artists that I know he likes – I think I've managed to remember most of them from that night in Italy after their wedding, when we all sat around the pool, chatting and laughing about our favourite things.' He smiles wryly.

'In happier times,' Eddie says, giving my arm a squeeze. 'Oh, it's just too sad for words, especially with Christmas so near.' He shakes his head.

'Bad things can happen at Christmas time too,' Ciaran

says softly, before adding, 'but the happy moments will come again. Now just wasn't the right time.'

After saying goodbye, I put the gifts on the hall table and make my way into the kitchen, figuring it best to give Sam and Nathan some time alone. I know they'll get through this, and probably go on to have a trillion babies, but for now it's as if their whole world has shattered beyond repair.

I make a pot of tea and settle on the sofa in the conservatory, which overlooks the beach leading down to the foaming sea – it's high tide, and the waves are furious, rocking and rolling, back and forth over the pebbles. Mr Cheeks nestles in next to me, purring and kneading my thigh with his paws - I brought him with me, rather than leave him in the flat alone, as I wasn't sure how long Sam would want me to stay. I pour the tea and think of everything that's happened recently. Sam and Nathan's heartache has really put things into perspective – at the end of day we all just want to be happy, to have our very own version of 'happy-ever-after'. And that includes Dad. And Tom too, even if it isn't with me. But I just wish Dad hadn't betrayed Mum. I feel so torn. I really like Nancy, she's cosy and warm and, dare I say it, mumsy, and it's true – I've missed having a mother-figure in my life, which just adds to my feelings of guilt over my loyalty to Mum. And knowing Nancy was complicit in deceiving Mum when she was ill and vulnerable just makes this situation so much harder to work out as I try to accept it. And part of me wants to accept it. I love Dad and I don't want there to be any barriers between us; there's been too much of that in the past.

So I spoke to Dad yesterday and, after I'd apologised for running out, not even giving him a chance to explain, he apologised too, and then told me all about it. Seems that all those years ago, Dad was struggling to come to terms with Mum's illness, petrified of losing her, but instead of talking (he didn't want to burden her), he sought solace in his gambling. Nancy had worked in the local bookie's at the time, and she had seen straight away how sad Dad looked, and tried to help him, discouraging him from throwing his money away, chatting instead, which eventually turned into evenings in the pub or a meal in a restaurant when Bob was on night duty. Dad says they talked mostly about Mum and me and Nancy's sorrow over the death of her daughter, Natalie, in a motorbike accident aged only seventeen. The pretty girl with the auburn hair. Dad says it was a distraction from what was happening at home, and the hospital visits, and he swears nothing physical happened until he came out of prison – Mum had died and Nancy was finding it hard going with Bob, seeing as he had assumed back then that she was having a full-blown affair and had promptly launched the revenge campaign against Dad. And of course, the rest is history, as they say.

I take a mouthful of tea and send Dad a text message:

Let's meet up soon. I love you and please say hello to Nancy for me.

I insert a heart icon and some kisses before pressing send. It's the best I can manage at the moment. Mum's gone, I know that, but with everything else that's going on, I can't even contemplate building a brilliant relationship with Nancy right now, not when my head is so crammed full of worry about Sam.

My phone vibrates to signify the arrival of a text.

i love you too very much and thank you it's more than I dared to hope for dad xxx ps i hope sam is bearing up please give her my love too xxx

Smiling, I finish the last of the tea – Dad hasn't mastered punctuation yet, but he can do email now. I was thrilled to get a text message from him last Sunday, even if it was all in shouty capitals. Oh well, I'm just so glad to have him back in my life after all those years apart, and if it means he comes as a package with Nancy, then so be it. At least he's found his happy-ever-after.

Nathan appears, looking tired and drawn. His blue eyes are sore and bloodshot, and his blond hair dishevelled.

'There you are, thought you'd run away. And who could

blame you with so much sadness in the house ... ' His voice trails off as he attempts a weak smile.

'Sorry, I just thought I'd give you a bit of space. Are you OK? How's Sam?' I place the cup on the table and unfold my legs to stand up.

'Please, don't get up on my account.' He waves a hand in my direction. 'We're fine – well, not fine exactly ... but we will be, if you know what I mean.' He sits down next to me.

'Sure I do.' I pat his arm gently. 'No need to explain.'

'Life is crap sometimes. Poor Sam. First Alfie and now this; it's just so unfair,' Nathan says, shaking his head.

'But it will get better. Sam is resilient, she'll get through this. She's already starting to talk about the future, and that's a good thing, yes?' I say with as much conviction as I can muster.

'I really hope so, Georgie. She was so very happy – we both were.'

'And you will be again, I'm convinced of it.' I smile encouragingly.

'A family. It's all she ever wanted.' He stares at the floor.

'And you,' I state.

'What do you mean?' he says, looking back up and turning to face me.

'Nathan, I've known Sam since we were schoolgirls, and she's spent her whole life looking for someone like you. *You* are all she ever wanted too. I know she had a ton of ... ' I pause to quickly rack my brains; I can't remember if Sam ever mentioned her legion of boyfriends before him, so I settle on 'admirers.' He nods proudly, so I reckon I'm on safe ground. 'But at the end of the day, none of them were what she had been dreaming of. You two are perfect together.'

'Thank you. I guess when you put it like that, it does make sense; at least we still have each other.' And he leans across to give me a hug. I give his back a rub and notice how tense he is. They need a holiday – some time away, somewhere hot. Where they can grieve, and just be together in the sunshine, walk on the beach, lie in the sun. Warm weather always makes things seem better. I make a mental note to mention it another time. He sits back, dropping his arms away from me.

'Remember she has you, and that counts for a lot. You make her happy. This is just nature's way, for whatever reason, and one day you'll look back and say, ahh, so that's why it happened at that time. Most likely with several adorable blonde-haired and blue-eyed cherubs driving you bonkers.'

'You truly are an amazing friend, Georgie. Thanks for being such a fantastic support, as always.' Nathan grins.

'Oh don't be daft. It's what we do. Which reminds me, there are some gifts on the hall table for you and Sam … from Eddie and Ciaran.'

20

I'm at home with Mr Cheeks keeping me company, and pondering on whether to torture myself by watching this week's episode of *Kelly Cooper Come Instore* – not sure if I want to see Tom and Zara together, when the intercom on the outside door buzzes. I press to see who it is.

'Only me, sweetcheeks! I come bearing gifts.' It's Eddie, and he's waving a cake box up to the camera outside. I buzz to let him in and head into the kitchen for a bottle of buck's fizz and promptly realise, to my shame, that it's the last one. I guess I have been putting it away recently. I vow to clean up my act and drink more tea instead. And cook proper food too while I'm at it – my fridge and freezer are crammed now with festive food bargains. I even got a whole smoked salmon the other day for a third of what they usually cost. With some blinis, crème fraîche and dill, it will make a lovely starter, and certainly a nice step up from last year's prawn ring. I figured that Sam may not be up to hosting a full-on Christmas lunch this year, so I might as well get prepared to invite them all here instead – Sam, Nathan, Dad, Nancy; it'll be a squeeze, but I'm sure they won't mind.

I've just rinsed two flutes, when Eddie appears, out of breath, with the cake box balanced regally on an upturned palm and Pussy trotting along behind him – she's wearing a festive red knitted polo-neck jumper with a white snowflake pattern on. Mr Cheeks takes one look at her before bolting through the cat flap. Eddie manages to drag himself up onto a stool by the breakfast bar while Pussy charges around my kitchen, sniffing and inspecting everything before settling at my feet.

'What's the matter with you?' I laugh.

'I'm utterly exhausted. Like properly actually knackered.' He yawns dramatically. 'It's the wedding plans. Who knew romance could be *sooo* demanding?'

'What do you mean? I thought KCTV were organising it all.'

'They are, but for some unfathomable reason, I insisted on being consulted on all the minutiae, figuring this way they can't mess it up or make me and Ciaran look ridic.' He huffs. 'So now I've got that totes whiny production girl, Hannah, in my ear all day long, banging on about canapés and suchlike. I said who cares, just feed them already!' he adds, rolling his eyes and sounding like some kind of Hollywood A-list diva.

'And what about the cowboys? And Liza Minnelli?' I say, pouring him a generous measure of buck's fizz, figuring from the state of him that he could sure do with it.

'Oh Kel loves the cowboy idea, has got a troop or

whatever they call them … ' He pauses to ponder while I smile inwardly at how he's quite obviously BFFs with Kelly now, if he's being this familiar. 'A herd, perhaps. Anyway, they're coming in from the Nevada desert – she knows someone who knows someone who knows someone – so they'll be turning up and looking hot. Yee-ha!' He slaps his thigh, Doris Day-style. 'Topless, natch. But between you and me, I've got an inkling that Kel wants to break into the American TV market; hence she's putting on such an extravagant show. She's just like a female Simon Cowell.' And I swear his adulation of her intensifies. His eyes have gone all misty. 'But sadly, Liza can't make it,' he purses his lips. 'Other commitments, apparently.'

'You mean KCTV actually asked her?' I'm flabbergasted. 'I thought you were joking.'

'Oh no darling. Kel knows *eeeeveryone*,' he says, sweeping a palm through the air, but something's not right, I can sense it. On the surface it's as if he's talking about his dream wedding, yet his eyes look sad which is unlike Eddie. It's like he's playing a part. Yes, he can be a bit queeny, but he's not normally this OTT, not when it comes to serious things like weddings and stuff.

'What's up?' I ask, figuring it best to cut to the chase.

'What do you mean?' he says, inspecting his nails.

'Come on Eddie, how long have we been friends? I say, gently.

'Years.'

'*Exactly*. So I can tell when you're putting on a brave face. It's the wedding, isn't it?' I ask, secretly praying that Ciaran isn't having second thoughts.

'*Weell*,' he starts. 'OK. I hold my hands up ... You were right.' He crosses his arms. 'It's all the fluff.'

'Fluff?'

'Yes fluff. I got carried away and now I don't know how to change it. Topless cowboys, who am I kidding? I mean, it's just *sooo* not me.' I manage to stifle a smile.

'I'm sure if you talk to Kelly—'

'I've tried. But it's no use. I'm scared Georgie.'

'Scared of what?' I ask, gently.

'That we'll look like a circus act ... ' he replies, miserably.

'Well then, I'll talk to her. Or, if she won't listen to me, then we'll just contact the cowboys direct to explain,' I say, feeling protective of my friend.

'We can't do that.'

'Yes we can. Don't worry. I'll help you. We'll scale it down somehow and get you the wedding of your dreams. I promise,' I add boldly, inwardly hoping I can pull if off. First chance I get, I'll have a word with Hannah and take it from there. I'm not letting my best friend dread his own wedding. I can't let that happen, so I'm going to make damn sure I do everything I can to sort it out for him.

'Thank you darling, it's such a relief to have you on board.' He gives me a kiss. 'Now, let's grab a muffin and

261

plant ourselves in front of your box. I want to see my performance, if only to take my mind off the wedding,' he says, perking up a bit.

Pondering on how I can best sort out their wedding, I follow Eddie into the lounge and assume my usual seat on the beanbag, gesturing for him to take the sofa as my guest. Eddie flips open the cake box and offers it to me. I gasp. Inside are two massive chocolate muffins slathered in twinkly white peaks of icing with cute miniature reindeers perched on top.

'Well, it is nearly Christmas.' Eddie hands a cake to me. I smile and bite into the delicious creamy mixture that ends up on my cheeks and the tip of my nose. 'Mm-mmm, this is good.'

'They're from Sam's café. I popped in on the off chance of seeing how she was, if she was back at work yet ... ' He stops to dip his finger in the icing and offers it to Pussy, who laps it up before licking her little lips in approval and nuzzling into him.

'Yes, she seemed to be picking up a bit when I talked to her this morning. Was she there in the café when you called in?' I ask, plucking a tissue from a box on the coffee table to wipe my face.

'She sure was, but out back in the kitchen; said she doesn't want to be around the customers yet, especially that pregnant Jenny from Greggs, the one who's about to pop any day now. And who can blame her? I imagine it must feel as if everywhere she looks there are reminders

— pregnant women, babies in prams. You can't walk down the street without seeing children. And Sam is so sweet. Life can be so cruel sometimes.' Eddie sighs and fiddles with Pussy's collar.

'How did she seem when you saw her?' I ask because I've been really worried about her. She's so quiet.

'OK. She was baking – said it helps, that she finds it cathartic. Hence these beauts ... she forced them on me.' He grins before taking a huge bite of his muffin. 'Mmm, exquisite,' he manages, in between chewing. 'What time is it?'

'Nearly ten, why?' I ask.

'The show of course! Flick the TV on, petal.' Eddie flaps a hand in my direction.

'Oh, do we have to?'

'Yes, we do ... why wouldn't we?' He gives me a look.

'You know very well why.' I will my cheeks to stop flaming.

'*Toooom?* Oh babycakes, you need to move on. I know he's probably the hottest man on earth, after my Ciaran, of course, but it's just not good for you hankering after a lost love. Anyway, I thought you had hooked up with that country singer.'

'Well, yes, Dan and I are friends but—'

'With benefits, saucy girl,' Eddie quips, giving me a big wink, and not missing a beat.

'Not exactly.'

'Boring!'

'Stop it. I'm not "hankering", as you say, I err … just don't want to see Zara strutting her stuff,' I mutter into my muffin.

'Good. Then let's get on with the show.' He grabs the remote control and hands it to me. 'Face your demons, darling. You're twice the woman she'll ever be; besides, I don't think she's in this week's episode. Or if she is, then she isn't with Tom in New York.'

'Really. How come?'

'Well, how can she be? Didn't you and Sam spot her in a restaurant, and then she was in my office slagging off her shaman, something about him being out of order after suggesting she try a Tantric massage to ease her stress.'

'A what?' I ask, wondering what she has to be stressed about. She's getting engaged to Tom – hardly stressful; bliss, more like.

'Oh does it really matter? Ignore her. She's nobody. Kelly's the dream-maker,' he sniffs.

'Eddie! You are so fickle … '

'Not at all, darling. It's just business. Show business! Now, finish your cake and settle down.'

Doing as I'm told, I swallow the last of my drink and polish off my muffin as the funky 'Working Nine To Five' theme tune starts. I brace myself, just in case Zara and Tom appear on the screen actually kissing or something. KCTV could have kept back footage from a previous week to air tonight. They don't necessarily show stuff in sequence as it happens. I haven't actually seen them together yet, not properly, and even though I know in my head that he's moved on, I'm not sure my heart truly accepts it.

'Oooh, here we go.' Eddie appears on the screen, he's wearing tight black skating trousers and a sparkly silver top. He's got a microphone in his left hand and he's asking shoppers, aka the actors, if they're having a good time on the Carrington's ice rink. He even does a little twirl before skating over to the other side of the rink to talk to a girl in a swishy red velvet mini Santa dress.

'Wow! Why didn't you say that you'd been elevated to presenter?'

'I wanted to surprise you.' He beams, pushing the muffin aside and pulling Pussy onto his lap.

'But what will Zara think? Isn't that her job?'

'Well not any more,' he says in a singsong voice.

Next up is a shot of the cash office with Lauren, Doris and Suzanne being talked through some new computerised cashing-up process that Kelly wants them to adopt, while the voiceover guy does a spiel about how Carrington's will reap the results once we've embraced the modern technological age. Cue a shot of Mrs Grace in her stockroom showing the viewers a selection of vintage gowns, still hanging in cellophane covers with the old-fashioned swirly 1950s Carrington's logo on. Next on screen is James, escorting a customer through to the Personal Shopping suite, which by the looks of it has had a spectacular makeover – it's now adorned in sumptuous swathes of velvet cascading from an enormous chandelier in the centre of the room. A decadent plum brocade chaise longue has replaced the old white circular sofa and a row of giant mani/pedi chairs have been installed along one wall so customers can be pampered as they peruse our A/W collection. There's even a little elevated runway and a model is strutting up and down in an exquisite Oscar de la Renta embellished tulle dress. Since when did we stock Oscar de la Renta? Wow! But I can't see any of our regular customers forking out over five thousand pounds for a dress, although I guess that's the point – to attract the glamouratti from the marina and send the locals down to the superstore on the industrial estate instead. It makes me feel excited, but a bit sad, as if it's the start of the end of an era. Kelly is certainly upping Carrington's game. Next we'll be selling Prada and being told what shade of lipstick we have to wear to work.

'Quick. Look, did you see that?' Eddie bellows, making Pussy jump. She springs off his lap and dashes over to join me. I scoop her up and stroke her little furry head. She settles down, nuzzling her nose into the inside of my elbow.

'What? I missed it.'

'Zara. Right there, skating around in the background. It was definitely her – hmm, why didn't she let us all know she was around for filming; not like her to be camera shy.' I peer at the screen and there she is, all bouncy big hair and sparkly eyes. She's breathtakingly beautiful. And she's wearing a proper minuscule fuchsia satin skating leotard with white leather skates.

'You're right,' I say, giving my hair extensions a quick bouff. 'And what's she doing?'

'I don't know, but it's freaky whatever it is … it looks like some kind of weird solo dance, a sort of freeform expression thingy. Ew.' Eddie winces. 'And what's with the flailing arms and the dying swan finale?'

'Maybe it's her Boléro impression,' I offer, trying to be charitable. She looks ridiculous.

'*Weell*, I think it's weird that she's even here in Mulberry-On-Sea.' Eddie sniffs.

'How do you mean?'

'Why isn't she with her "fiancé"?' he says, making sarcastic quote signs with his fingers.

'Oh I don't know Ed, and to be honest I'd rather not think about it,' I say, relaxing back into the beanbag.

After the ad break, the voiceover guy is back and he's talking about a reindeer safari and the birthplace of Santa and sourcing authentic Christmas goods for Carrington's to stock next year. Now there's a log cabin on the screen, with twinkly lights at the windows and steam coming from the chimney. It's like something from a fairytale. We're going inside now, and it's enchanting, a real log fire in an enormous inglenook surround beside a sumptuously soft sheepskin rug. It's the perfect setting for a romantic Christmas.

'What's this?' I ask Eddie. He shrugs.

'No idea. Kel hasn't mentioned other locations. Looks divine though, doesn't it?'

'It sure does. All Christmassy and magical,' I say, finishing the last of my buck's fizz.

A giant wooden sleigh comes into focus, and it's being pulled though a snow-laden forest by a pack of huskies with jingle bells on their harnesses. As the sleigh gathers speed, powdery fine snow whisks all around, giving us the illusion of being inside a giant snow globe. As the snow settles, a bubbling hot tub emerges on screen. My heart flutters. My cheeks flush. My thighs tingle. It's Tom. And he's topless, his beautifully honed chest glistening in the golden glow of a trillion flickering paper lanterns swaying in the night air. Steam pumps all around him as he leans back and reaches out a muscular arm to take a pewter jug from the deck. I bite my bottom lip, willing my whole body to stop burning with desire. It's insane. Even though I know we're over, I just can't help myself. I'm consumed with lust. I make a mental note to call Dan first thing tomorrow morning; I can't continue to go on dates with him when I still feel this way about another man. It's just not right.

'Cor! Scrub what I was saying earlier ... he really is the hottest man on earth, and that's the end of it! No wonder Kel had the good sense to get Mr Carrington on screen. Ratings will skyrocket to the moon and beyond after this delicious scene. And takings too! We'll be beating a path into work every day once new customers work out where to find him. I can see it now: hordes of women – men too – bussing in to shop at Carrington's in the hope of catching a glimpse of sexy Mr Carrington. And Security will have to up their game, that's for sure. No more lounging around the delivery bay flirting with the Lingerie girls.' Eddie can't help himself; he's leaning forward and practically salivating.

'OK. I get the message,' I say sulkily, wishing he wouldn't keep on. I get it. I'm doomed! Sentenced to singledom for the rest of my life as, right now, there's no way another man will ever come close to Tom. Eddie is right – Tom is pure perfection. 'Zara is very lucky,' I manage, magnanimously, stuffing the last of the muffin into my mouth.

'I'll say,' Eddie starts, and then quickly stops when we see the rest of the shot. As the camera pans around, Valentina emerges, her perfect long legs sashaying across the deck before lowering her equally perfect body down into the bubbles. He wet hair splays back as she tilts her face up towards the moonlit sky while adjusting the halterneck of her bikini. 'Sweet Jesus, is she getting naked?' Eddie shouts.

'Stop it!' I snap, biting back tears.

'Only joking dollface.'

'Please, Eddie, will you just switch it off?' I say, scanning the coffee table for the remote control. Eddie finds it hidden under a cushion and duly obliges.

'Sorry sweetie. But I thought you were over him, you know, with you seeing the singer and getting involved in all the exciting magazine and PR stuff you're doing now. Lots of distraction.'

'Yes, you're right, I should be over him, but ... '

'Oh, come here.' Eddie jumps off the sofa and flings his arms around my neck, almost squeezing me to death in an enormous bear hug. 'Listen.' He pulls back to look at me.

'What it is?' I say, on seeing the mischievous look in his eye.

'*Weell*, like I said before, something doesn't add up ... Don't you think it's weird that Zara isn't with him?'

'I guess so. But this could have been filmed ages ago. I can't really keep up with it all any more ... I didn't even know Tom was in Lapland. And I thought he was supposed to be visiting all the big fashion houses sourcing new stock for Carrington's to sell, not necking steaming big jugs of hot berry juice or whatever the voiceover guy said it was,' I say in a quiet voice.

'Hmm, well, I suppose Lapland is more Christmassy, and I know KCTV had to cancel Milan at the last minute – Prada got sniffy about opening their doors to TV cameras and there wasn't time to organise anything with the other Italian design houses. But look on the bright side.'

'Bright side?' I ask, failing to see how the scene in front of me could possibly be classed as anything remotely positive as far as my love life is concerned.

'That's right. If you were Zara, would you be happy if your fiancé-to-be was cavorting in a hot tub with a goddess wearing just a grin – for all we know she could have discarded the bikini bottoms and be naked right now under that bubbly water. Maybe Tom's moved on already.'

I let the thought linger for a moment, and in spite of how seriously fed up and jealous I feel right now, I also can't help feeling a teeny bit secretly pleased. Ha! Of course Tom has the right to his happy-ever-after too, just like Dad and Nancy, but if he doesn't want it with me, then I'd sooner he have it with Valentina. At least she's an unknown entity who lives in Brazil – perhaps he'll move there and live happily ever after. Out of sight. Unlike Zara with her horrible attitude and collection of pilfered handbags that she tosses on the floor without a second thought, while dishing out dirty looks in my direction. I imagine she'll be all over Tom, rubbing my nose in it at every opportunity.

21

Two shopping weeks until Christmas

I'm at work, stuffing acid-free tissue paper into a rainbow crystal clutch when Annie sidles up to me with a tentative look on her face.

'Have you heard?'

'Heard what?' I ask, busying myself by placing the clutch in a prominent position near the edge of the display shelf, and right under a spotlight to accentuate the sparkle from the crystals.

'About the engagement?' she swivels her eyes nervously.

'Oh that. Yes, I heard a while ago.' I shake my hair back in what I hope is a nonchalant way.

'Oh good,' she says, before quickly adding, 'sorry, I don't mean good as in *good* good, I mean ... oh God, it's all coming out wrong. I meant, that, well, it's good that you know already. Only Zara has been going on about it to anyone who will listen and I didn't want you to hear via shop-floor gossip. Emma in Stationery got cornered in the lift the other day and said that Zara wouldn't shut up about "her news" and that as soon as she gets the ring she'll let everyone see it. Nobody likes her, you know.' Annie flings a hand on her hip and twiddles her nose stud.

'Really?'

'Yep. And apparently she's been telling people that I'm a "dirty pikey".'

'Oh no, I'm so sorry Annie.'

'Oh don't be, I can handle myself.' She puffs her ample cleavage out. 'But she was also overheard saying that it was a good job Denise in Home Electricals wasn't in the show as she would have scared all the viewers away.'

'Nooo. Poor Denise. I hope it hasn't filtered back to her.'

'Not yet. But what a mean thing to say – Denise can't help having that burn scar down the side of her neck.' Annie looks over her shoulder before leaning in to me with a deadly serious look on her face. 'I could clump her one, if you like. Would wipe that fake smile off her mush.'

'Err, no. That won't be necessary,' I quickly say, dreading to think what Tom would think if it ever came out that I was behind his fiancée getting slapped. I'd be deemed a thug as well as a stalker. I spot a customer trying on a D&G top handle bag and, feeling grateful for the distraction, I apologise to Annie and make my way over.

'Oh good choice, we have it in cherry red too.' I smile at the forty-something woman while admiring her gorgeous swingy poncho as she checks out the bag in the long mirror.

'How much is it please?' she asks, handing me the bag. I check the inside pocket and show her the tag. She ponders for a moment before saying,

'I'll take it.'

'Lovely. Is it a gift?' I ask, impressed with her quick decision-making skills. Customers usually procrastinate for a little longer over bags in the nine-hundred-pound-plus bracket, unless they're Princess Ameerah of course.

'Yes,' she says, fingering the matching purse.

'I'll gift-wrap it for you in that case.'

'Oh no need. It's for me – a Christmas present to myself. And I'll have this to go with it too.' She hands me the purse.

'Great. Are you sure you wouldn't like them gift-wrapped?' I ask, and she hesitates. 'Might as well, there's no extra charge and if you're treating yourself ... ' I say, hoping to persuade her. 'All part of the shopping experience,' I beam.

'Oh go on then. I can put them under my tree and think of my ex-husband as I open them on Christmas Day. After all, he's paying ... even if he doesn't know it.' She flashes me a wry smile.

'I'm sorry,' I say diplomatically.

'Don't be. I caught him with someone. In fact, you might know her, she's something to do with this show your shop is involved in,' she says, in a very breezy voice, while plucking a credit card from her purse.

'*Kelly Cooper Come Instore?*' I confirm, wondering who it could be as I head over to my till.

274

'Yes, that's the one. My husband is an actor and well ... ' She pauses to slap the card on the counter. 'It was only a matter of time. Things have been rocky for a while between us, and Lawrence has always been such an outrageous flirt.' Oh God. She must be Declan's mum, the cute little boy with the Irish guy who bought the Chloé bag that Zara ruined. 'In fact I was thinking of leaving him in any case, but nobody wants to be upstaged by a gorgeous creature less than half their age now, do they?'

'Indeed,' I say, busying myself with the gift-wrapping. I'm used to customers offloading, and have learnt over the years to just listen without voicing an opinion, rather like hairdressers do. I guess it's easier to talk to a stranger sometimes.

'And to think, he seduced her with my son in tow.' Silence follows as I run the transaction through the till. 'He's three years old, for Christ's sake.' I turn the card reader towards her and she punches in the PIN. 'My apologies, I've embarrassed you.' I notice her trembling hands as she stows the credit card back in her purse.

'No, not all. I'm sorry,' I say discreetly, making sure I keep my voice low. I really feel for her, being thrown over for someone else is totally crap. I should know. Maybe it's better to stay single after all; I'm not sure I could bear it if my actual husband was unfaithful. I think of Mum. I'm so glad she never knew about Dad's affair. Although, I have been wondering recently if perhaps she did know, and just chose not to acknowledge it. I've been racking my brains, going over and over things. I distinctly remember sitting on the hall stairs listening to Mum crying on the phone in the lounge to her friend one time. Maeve, in Australia, and Mum was saying something about "she can give him what I can't". I swallow hard, Mum must have assumed they were sleeping together, just like Bob had. How could Dad do it? And in an instance, my feelings about him and Nancy waver. I grab two carrier bags from under the counter and quickly push the thoughts from my head. I focus on tying ribbon around the handles instead. I can't think about it all now.

'Oh don't be. I'm having a fabulous time, next stop the salon upstairs. I'm having the works and then I'm off to Dubai to meet up with an old girlfriend who has some gorgeously eligible bachelor friends lined up for me to meet. I just hope Lawrence's new lover is good with kids as my three darling boys are a handful.'

'Of course. You've just had a baby. Congratulations.' The minute the words come out of my mouth I regret them. She instinctively folds her arms over her perfectly flat stomach.

'I beg your pardon?' she mutters, blinking furiously.

'Err, I'm so sorry. I thought, um … Lawrence mentioned you'd had a new baby, when he came first came into the store. It was a rehearsal scene for the show. He bought a handbag … ' I will my cheeks to stop burning. *Diplomacy. At all times.*

'Oh did he? Well that's nice of him to inform me. No. No babies. Just three adorable but extremely boisterous sons aged ten, seven and three years old. Lawrence is having them on alternate weekends and a whole month in the summer. I'll be making sure of that. Sooo, we'll see how long *Zara* hangs around!' she beams, before taking the gift-wrapped bags and breezing over to the escalator.

Oh my God!

My jaw drops.

I close my mouth and duck into the little cupboard behind my counter to pull out my mobile and quickly tap out a text to Sam.

Are you up for some lunch hun? xxxx

Sam replies straight away.

If you have gossip, then I need to know IMMEDIATELY :) Early Lunch? Like RIGHT NOW??? A girl needs details!!! xxx

I smile, pleased that Sam seems happier. More like her old self. I know she's been quiet, but she has good days too when she says she feels really optimistic, especially after her gynaecologist said that there's no reason why she can't try to conceive again right away, if that's what she wants. She says that's her focus now. Positive action. But then a seemingly random event can set her off. The last time it happened was during a holiday advert about cruises and cherishing memories. She has no idea why it made her cry, other than when she first knew she was pregnant, she had started imagining a whole lifetime, not just for her, but for the baby too, and now it won't happen. Those memories won't be made. I struggle to know what to say to comfort her sometimes, so I figured I should tell her this rather than say the wrong thing. She's my best friend and I want to help her as much as I can. I just wish I could snatch the sorrow away for her. But she said the best thing I can do is not be afraid to ask how she's feeling because she's not going to crumble in front of me. Plus, I should carry on being how I've always been with her, not tiptoe around making her feel fragile. She said the hardest part to deal with is when people avoid her – people who used to stop and chat, but now cross the road or hover in the doorway of the café until someone else is at the counter to serve them. If they only asked how she was, then she could thank them and say that some days are good, some not so, before talking about something else.

I ask Annie to cover while I pop up to the café.

'Sure, no problem. And give Sam my love. Tell her I'll be up later on my tea break and if she wants to chat ... well, it happened to me last year.'

'Oh Annie, I'm sorry. I never knew.' I give her hand a quick squeeze.

'And my cousin the year before and my aunty Sadie has

had three miscarriages. It's more common than we think, only nobody really talks about it. I don't understand why ... maybe we should, and then when it happens we might not feel so alone.'

I give her a hug before pulling back to look her in the eye.

'You're a wise woman, Annie O'Leary.'

22

'So, rewind a bit and start from the beginning.' I'm with Sam, and we're in the best booth, tucked away in the far corner of the café. In the time it took me to get up here, she's made us each a mug of delicious crème brûlée latte, a round of turkey feast sandwiches and sliced up an extra gooey-looking chocolate Yule log. Sam tucks into her second sandwich. I wipe my fingers on a napkin and take another sip of the latte, the swirly caramel and whipped cream topping coating my top lip. 'I need to understand what's going on here,' she says.

'Are you sure? It seems trivial now somehow, after everything that's happened,' I say, worried now that I shouldn't have been so impulsive. 'How are you?'

'Stop it. Please.' She smiles. 'I'm fine. Women have miscarriages every day, I'm not ashamed or delicate. Yes, there'll always be a little part of my heart that's broken, but I'm still me. I'm strong. And I still want to hear all the gossip. Now tell me ... ' She nods for me to continue.

'OK. Well, like I said, Lawrence's wife caught him with *Zara*,' I whisper.

'Nooo ... but caught them doing what exactly?' Sam makes big eyes.

'Well, she didn't go into specific details.'

'Hmm, so it could be nothing at all. A clinch. A hug. Even a friendly kiss on the cheek for all we know. To be honest Georgie, I just don't get it, it doesn't make sense. Not when Zara was so excited about the engagement, I heard her with my own ears, telling Princess Ameerah how much Tom loves her and how he practically begged her to marry him.' I breathe in sharply. 'Sorry hun.'

'I don't think it's nothing at all because Lawrence's wife said she was leaving him and going to Dubai, and she even talked about sharing custody of their children,' I say, my mind working overtime.

'Oh dear, that does sound pretty serious. So what are you going to do?' Sam raises her eyebrows enquiringly and takes another bite of her sandwich.

'What do you mean?'

'I mean, are you going to confront her?' she asks, covering her mouth with her hand as she talks and chews.

'I can't do that. It's not really my business.' I shake my head.

'Of course it is. Ask her!'

'Sam, I can't, really. Besides, it'll just look like sour grapes. And what if Kelly finds out? Zara is her daughter after all. And remember, Kelly and Tom's mother are friends, so it's bound to get back to him. Or, worse still, it turns out to be untrue, or what if it is true and Tom already knows and has forgiven her or something – he could end up hating me for meddling and ruining his "happy-ever-after". Just because Lawrence and his wife are over – I mean, she did say that their relationship had been rocky for a while – it doesn't necessarily mean that Tom and Zara are over,' I say, secretly wishing more than anything that they were. 'And what about Valentina? Where does she fit into all of this?'

'No idea. And you may not want to know what's going on, but I'm sure as hell going to find out. It's the least I can do after playing Cupid and getting you two together in the first place. I can't believe I got him so wrong.' Sam finishes chewing and folds her arms assertively.

'Sooo, what do you have in mind?' I venture, slowly.

'Right. This is the bottom line. Do you still want him?'

'You know I do.' I will my cheeks to stop flushing as, no matter what, it's not my style to go after an attached guy, even if he is my one ... or so I had thought.

'Well, that settles it then. I've had enough of this, and one thing I've learnt recently is that you have to grab every chance of happiness with both hands, no matter how fleetingly it comes your way ... ' She pauses momentarily. 'I can't promise that he'll come back to you, but I'm not sitting back and letting you go through this for a second longer. You deserve a proper explanation. I'll do it at the wrap party.'

'Do what?' I ask nervously, Sam has come up with some truly hare-brained schemes over the years, so I dread to think what she has planned. 'Well, if you don't want to have it out with Zara, then I'll ask Tom!'

'Oh Sam, I'm not sure that's a good idea. He'll think I'm some kind of silly schoolgirl, getting my best friend to confront him. And I'll look like a bunny-boiler for sure.' Panic rises in me.

'No you won't. Besides, that's not all he's been up to.' Sam places her mug down and gives me a serious look.

'Go on,' I say tentatively, thinking of Zara and Valentina and wondering just how many more women there are. Sam turns to look me in the eye. 'What is it? You're scaring me.' I brace myself.

'You'll never guess what Mandy told me.' Sam makes big eyes.

'No?' I bite my bottom lip. I'm absolutely desperate to know. I can hear my own blood pumping in my ears as I rack my brains trying to fathom what it could possibly be.

'Now, this is strictly confidential.' Sam leans in really close to me. 'Mandy could lose her job at the town hall.'

'Yes, yes, of course. I'll take it to the grave,' I say quickly, tilting my head towards her. She covertly lifts my big hair to talk directly into my ear.

'Someone wants to buy the Carrington's building and turn it into a hotel!' she whispers, and the pounding sound is so loud now, my heart feels as though it's going to burst right out of my chest.

Silence follows.

Sam leans back. I gulp. No. This can't be happening. But why? I don't understand. Panic engulfs me. Everything is changing. Everything I thought I had is disappearing, one by one, slipping through my fingers like sand in a timer, and there seems to be nothing I can do about it. And why would Tom do this? Why would he let it happen?

'But why, how?' I eventually manage. My hand is shaking as I place my mug back on the table.

'That's all Mandy knows.' Sam helps herself to a slice of Yule log. 'Apparently a request has been received via a solicitor in London. Something about a mystery person enquiring about a change of use from shop to hotel with underground parking.'

'I knew it!'

'What do you mean?'

'Kelly! I knew it right from the start that she wasn't to be trusted. I heard her, remember? Talking about a hotel with underground parking. I thought she was lining up her next TV series.'

'Yes! I remember,' Sam says.

'But it doesn't make sense. Why would she invest so much money in the store if she plans on closing it down and making it into a hotel?' I ask, my mind racing, desperate for it to be a mistake. For Mandy to have got it horribly wrong.

'Exactly! Now can you see why somebody has to confront Tom? He's the boss, after all. The major share-holder. And this affects all of us.'

'True,' I say, trying to think straight.

'Enough is enough. He can't carry on like this. First

he dumps you, and now he wants to dump Carrington's. And I for one have worked too hard to sit back and lose my lovely café, on top of everything else I've lost.' Her voice falters momentarily. I squeeze her hand.

'But he loves this store. It's his family's business going back generations. The original Mr Carrington was his great grandfather. Why would he even want to sell Carrington's? We have to find out more. Can't you ask Mandy for a name?' I ask, panic rising in my voice.

'I've already tried but she wasn't budging – data protection and all that.' Sam shakes her head.

'Well, there's got to be something we can do. Some way of getting more information before we confront Tom,' I plead.

'But let's look at the facts. A hotel could also benefit from a pet spa; guests could even board their pooches next door and have them walked, too, like a kind of dog hotel. You know there are restaurants and hotels in London that do it – exercise your dog while you dine,' she says, knowingly. 'And why not have an ice rink on the roof?'

'Ahh, but you wouldn't refurbish a whole personal shopping suite just to rip it out again when you turn it into a junior stateroom or whatever. And you know she's even installed a Costa Express machine in there,' I say, still hoping somehow that Mandy really has got it all wrong.

'Well, some hotels have coffee machines too,' Sam sniffs disapprovingly.

I nod, letting it all sink in as I desperately try to push the sickening feeling aside. What if Tom really is selling? He could be. He told me himself he was worried about turning the store around, being able to pull it off. And all those doubters in the business world he had to contend with, watching and whispering about his abilities – maybe he's seen an opportunity, a way out, and decided to sell to Kelly and Zara, and most likely Princess Ameerah is on it too. She's incredibly wealthy; perhaps she's the one putting up the money so Kelly and Zara can film the transition from shop to hotel. And it's not as if doing the show has upped our game that much. Takings are only slightly higher than would be expected anyway for this time of year. I saw the sales chart on the wall of the staff canteen. And not forgetting his horrible text message, is this what he meant about me losing my job too? Because if Carrington's were to become a hotel, then where would that leave me and the rest of the staff – Eddie, Annie, Mrs Grace, Melissa, Lauren, Doris and Suzanne? We all love working here. It doesn't bear thinking about. And in an instance, the wrap party I've been dreading for so long, now suddenly seems so much more appealing – if nothing else, I'll get to see Tom. To talk to him. To confront him, once and for all. To find out exactly what is going on. Sam is right, we can't just sit back and let him sell Carrington's out from under us ... but there's something else I must do first.

23

Five shopping days until Christmas

I'm in the little wine bar tucked down a side street
behind Carrington's. I've decided to meet up with Dan
to explain how I feel. It's only fair. We thought it best to
meet here, discreet, and away from the Mulberry gossips
and the paparazzi. I take a sip of rosé, pacing myself.
It's Monday evening – well, late afternoon really – but I
need something to help me relax. I'm so wound up, even
my shoulders seem to have fused into a spasm. I'm back
on the emotional rollercoaster – one minute I still want
Tom so much it practically takes my breath away, but
then in the next moment I'm consumed with a mixture
of sorrow and anger. Angry with myself for getting it so
wrong yet again. How could I have been so stupid? To
actually think he was into me, that we were really going
to spend Christmas together. It's obvious now, if he is
planning on letting Carrington's become a hotel, that
he never had any real intention of us having a future
together. He can't have done. He knows how much I love
the store, how I grew up with it. It's part of me. And all

those conversations we had, where he confided in me about his plans for Carrington's, schmoozed me with it all – was I just a distraction until someone like Zara came along? Because if that's what it really was, then he really needn't have bothered making so much effort – all those illicit glances across the shop floor, rendezvous in his office, lunch dates, dinner dates, long late-night conversations, even travelling to Italy to surprise me ... I wanted him from the first moment I clapped eyes on him. I wanted to sleep with him. And women can want sex too these days – this isn't the Victorian times or whenever, where they had to pretend they didn't. But it was so much more than that too. I was falling in love with him and you can't just switch that off, no matter how hard you try.

I glance at my watch, and on seeing that I'm fifteen minutes early, I pull out my mobile to try Sam again. I'm getting worried as she hasn't been around. I've not managed to talk to her since that day in the café – whenever I've popped into the café she's not there, and Stacey doesn't know where she is. And when I've called her, there's either no answer or she hasn't returned my messages. It's unlike Sam to go AWOL; we usually talk or see each other every day. I'm just about to hang up when she answers.

'Sam! Are You OK?'

'Oh, yes. I'm fine. Sorry. I've been busy ... just some business stuff. Boring!' She laughs.

'Ah, I see. As long as you're all right. I was getting worried,' I say, feeling relieved. It's most likely something to do with Archie's multimillion-pound estate. As his sole beneficiary, Sam has had loads to sort out since he died earlier this year. Meeting with Archie's lawyers. In addition to his estate agency business, he owned three properties, and that was just in this country. I think she said there were apartments in Hong Kong, Dubai and Sydney too. Archie didn't like hotels, much preferring to stay in one of his own homes when travelling. And then there is the multitude of international business accounts. I remember Sam saying they were a convoluted puzzle that the lawyers were struggling to sort out – Nathan had to call in the help of an international taxation specialist to help unravel everything. 'Anything I can do to help?' I offer, but knowing there probably isn't. 'Paperwork? I could file stuff, or make tea? Or what about phone calls – I could help with those,' I joke, feeling relieved that she's OK.

'Thanks, but not really. Think I've got it under control, just be nice to get everything sorted out by Christmas. Only seven days to go!' She sounds excited, and it makes me feel really happy for her after everything she's been through. 'Are you sure it's still OK to come to yours?' Sam asks.

'Absolutely, you wait till you see the mountain of food I've got in. And Dad is really looking forward to seeing you.'

'Great. I'm looking forward to it too. And the New Year. It's a new start, full of wonderful possibilities ... ' And she sounds brighter than she has in a long time.

Dan arrives, unravelling his scarf and pulling off his gloves as he reaches the table. One of his security people, a tall guy in a duffel coat, scans the room before settling himself on a stool at the bar.

'Not been waiting too long I hope.' Dan leans in to give me a kiss, his cheeks flushed and cold from the icy winter air outside. I smile and shake my head.

'I just arrived. Can I get you a drink?' I offer and go to stand up.

'Oh no, stay put. I'll get them. Same again?' he asks, motioning to my now half-empty wine glass.

'Err.' I hesitate. I really shouldn't, I've got work tomorrow. 'No, thank you. I'm fine,' I say, relaxing a bit.

'Sure. Be back in a sec.'

My mobile rings and on seeing a number I don't recognise, I quickly press to decline the call, and stow the phone back in my bag.

Dan returns with a pint in one hand and a bag of peanuts in the other.

'You don't mind, do you?' He waves the bag in the air. 'It's this winter weather, gives me a ferocious appetite.' He laughs and bites the corner off the packet as he sits opposite me.

'Sure, go ahead.' I finish the last of my wine.

'So how are you?' He offers me the packet and I shake my head.

'Good thanks,' I say, being polite. I don't want to bother him with my stuff. 'And you?'

'Yeah, not bad,' he mutters, before glancing away.

'You sure? You seem a bit preoccupied,' I prompt.

'Well, there is something ... ' He hesitates. 'Err, something I need to talk to you about.' He finishes the peanuts and squashes the bag up into a tiny ball.

'OK. Me too.'

'You first,' he says, keeping his eyes fixed on the table in between us, and suddenly I feel panicky. What am I doing? There are plenty of women who would love to date Dan. He's such a nice guy, and I had a wonderful time on our date. It was romantic. And fun. And I felt happy. OK, not happy in a thrilling way, happy like I was with Tom, but content, and comfortable. Maybe it's enough. Maybe I should forget about Tom, once and for all. If he is planning on getting rid of Carrington's, then maybe it's for the best, to draw a proper line underneath this part of my life and move on.

'It's nothing really. It'll keep ... you go first,' I grin, and he takes a mouthful of his drink.

'If you're sure,' he says, and I nod for him to continue. 'OK.' He inhales before letting out a big breath. He leans towards me. He hesitates as if it's hard for him to say the words. 'My ex-girlfriend is pregnant!' A short silence follows. He downs the rest of his drink in one.

'Great,' I say, unsure of how to react.

'The baby's mine, apparently.' He pushes a hand through his hair.

'Well congratulations, that's brilliant news,' I say hesitantly; he doesn't look overly happy. His shoulders have dropped and his left knee is pumping up and down like a piston.

'Err ... this is a good thing, right? You're going to be a dad,' I say, searching his eyes for confirmation.

'I'm so sorry.'

'Hey, it's fine. Honestly. We had fun, but I totally understand if you want to be with her. This is huge news. Amazing,' I say, feeling a bit relieved, the decision having been made for me. But there's something else too ...

'Do you mind if we go? I need some fresh air.' He stands up.

'Sure. Of course,' I say, grabbing my coat and racing after him as he strides off towards the door.

Outside, and I manage to catch up with Dan near the end of the road. His security man is close behind me. I touch Dan's sleeve and he stops walking.

'Dan, what is it?' I ask, pulling on my woolly gloves. It's dark, but he looks totally crushed in the glow from the streetlight we're standing underneath. The security guy hangs back to give us some privacy.

'Oh Georgie, it's such a mess.'

'Tell me,' I say softly, and he hesitates before clearing his throat.

'Chloe, my ex, got married.'

'OK,' I say, thinking that was quick. I remember him telling me they split up in the summer.

'Last Saturday at the register office,' he adds, as if reading my mind. 'And her new husband is the guy she was seeing behind my back.'

'I'm so sorry.'

'And they felt it only fair to let me know that I'm the father. Even though her husband is going to bring the baby up as his own, Chloe said.' I slip my hand in his and give it a gentle squeeze of solidarity. He stares at the pavement and I wish there was something I could do to help him.

'But what about you? What do you want?'

How could they do this? Cut him out. Surely Dan has a right to be happy too? A baby is a gift, and he should be elated, but instead he looks crushed, as if he has the weight of the world on his shoulders. I feel so sorry for him. Especially at Christmas time – it just makes it a whole lot worse somehow. It's supposed to be a happy time, a joyous time.

'To be a proper dad.'

'Of course you'll be a proper dad. You'll be fantastic.'

'Well, on paper perhaps – that's if she even puts my name on the birth certificate, but then knowing Chloe she probably will, she'll want money from me, which is fine of course, I'll gladly provide for my child … ' His voice trails off. Silence follows. I take a step closer to Dan and he leans forward. We put our arms around each other and hug tightly. Neither of us speaks. I turn my face to his and he looks into my eyes. 'I'm going to need to be on my own ... to get my head around it all and work out what to do,' he says quietly.

'I know.' I put a gloved finger on his lips. 'No need to explain. But just shout if you ever want to talk.'

'Thank you. And you take care. You're amazing. Any guy would be lucky to have you.'

'Hey, everything will be OK. It will, I promise. One day from now, you'll look back and see ... ' I kiss his cheek and close my eyes to shield them from the bright headlights of a taxi as it pulls up close to the pavement opposite. Dan reciprocates with a kiss on my lips before giving me a hug.

We pull apart on hearing voices from a group of men crossing the road towards the wine bar. I glance around Dan's shoulder in their direction and one of the guys looks back. And then I see him. I blink to be sure. And it's definitely him. There's no mistaking the dark curls and gorgeously athletic physique.

Oh my God. I don't believe it.

My stomach flips involuntarily. My pulse races. I feel dizzy.

It's Tom!

I hold my breath for what feels like forever. Stunned. Everything flicks into slow motion. I can't move. He sees me. He stops walking. And for a glimmer of a second our eyes meet. I don't know what to do. Instinctively,

I want to go after him. Talk to him. Be close to him. Touch him. But he just nods to acknowledge me before turning away, pushing his hands inside his coat pockets and following the others into the wine bar.

I drop my arms away from Dan and will myself to get it together. My whole body feels as if it's on fire. My mind is racing. My hands are tingling. Tom is back. He's right here. In Mulberry-On-Sea. Yet it's as if he's even further away from me than ever before.

'Hey, what is it?' Dan leans back and lifts my chin. 'You look as if you've seen a ghost.'

I pull my coat in tighter as the intense surge of adrenalin ebbs away, leaving me feeling drained and panicky. My heart is hammering so fast, it's actually making my chest hurt. I inhale hard and exhale slowly, over and over to calm my breathing, until eventually I'm able to speak.

'Someone I thought I knew,' I manage, still reeling from the intensity of the extremely close encounter.

24

Last shopping day before Christmas

The twenty-fourth of December. It's Christmas Eve and the day of the wrap party has finally arrived. I'm with Sam in Millie's room, 107, in the Mulberry Grand Hotel. The party is in the ballroom downstairs and the dress code is 'glamour'. I've chosen a gorgeous blush pink chiffon skater dress with a crimson faux fur stole teamed with a pair of nude Loubs.

'Ooh, very Christmassy. I love the colour,' says Sam, running a finger over the fur. She's wearing a floor-sweeping gold-beaded goddess dress, and Millie has managed to tease her curls into a sophisticated up-do. She looks absolutely stunning.

'Thank you, hun. And wow, look at you,' I say as she manoeuvres into position on the stool in front of the mirror, taking care not to crush the dress. Millie is doing our make-up, and Sam is going first.

'So, have you decided on an eye shadow?' Millie asks, sweeping a protective plastic cape around Sam's shoulders before selecting two palettes from an enormous three-tiered make-up case.

'Hmm, the shimmery gold I think, what do you reckon Georgie?'

'I reckon you could wear any colour and look incredible, you always do,' I say, keen to boost her mood. She's not been around much all week, and when I spoke to her on the phone yesterday, she seemed really distracted. Vague. As if her mind was elsewhere. I'm worried about her as she's normally so upbeat.

I hand them each a glass of champagne.

'Thanks.' Sam smiles at me in the mirror and I can't help noticing how tired she looks. I make a mental note to chat to Nathan later, to see if there's anything I can do. When I tried talking to Sam in the taxi on the way here, she waved a hand in the air and said everything was fine and that I worry too much. But I'm not convinced. 'And thank you, Millie,' Sam adds, and the three of us chink flutes.

'A pleasure. I love doing make-up; and besides, it means I can avoid the boss for a little longer.' She swallows a mouthful of her drink and rolls her eyes.

'Is she that bad then?' I ask.

'Oh, Kelly is OK really, we've worked together for years now, but Zara – well, she's the obnoxious one.' Millie shakes her head and downs the rest of her champagne. Sam gives me a look. 'What is it?' Millie asks, looking at me first, then Sam.

'Oh it's nothing,' I quickly say.

'It's not nothing. She stole Georgie's boyfriend,' Sam says indignantly.

'She didn't exactly *steal* him,' I jump in. 'He, well, he just got back with her after we split up ... they have history.'

'Hmm. Doesn't surprise me.' Millie purses her lips.

'Why's that then?' Sam asks.

'Well, let's just say that Zara has a lot of "history".' Millie leans forward and drops her voice. 'She has a habit of playing the field.'

'*Really?*' Sam and I say in unison.

'Yes, but I tend not to get involved these days. Kelly knows I don't have time for Zara, not since ... ' Millie's voice trails off and she looks away, busying herself in the giant make-up box.

'Since what?' Sam coaxes.

'It was a long time ago, and she was young and ... ' Millie loads up a plump blusher brush, swirling it furiously, round and round inside a pot of bronzing beads.

'And what? What did she do?' Sam asks, persistently.

'She slept with my boyfriend,' Millie says flatly.

'*Whaaaat?*' I jump in. 'Oh Millie, I'm so sorry.'

'Ah, don't be. Like I said, it was ages ago, and he's happily married now with two children and living in the Cotswolds. Besides, it takes two. I'm sure he was complicit.'

'So Zara's a serial cheater then?' Sam folds her arms. 'Well, she'd better not come near Nathan.'

'I don't think you have anything to worry about on that score, Sam. Nathan adores you.' I glance at her in the mirror and she smiles nonchalantly.

'True.' She takes a sip of champagne. 'And I adore him.'

'But what about Tom? He can't marry Zara and end up heartbroken when she has another affair,' I say, thinking of Mum and how she must have felt that time I overheard her talking to Maeve. And no matter what's happened between Tom and me, I don't want to see him make the biggest mistake of his life, potentially, by actually marrying Zara.

We finish getting ready and make our way downstairs, out through the main hotel exit and over the long windy gravel drive that's covered by a white canopy. A ruby-red carpet winds a path to the main ballroom, illuminated by a trillion flickering tea lights in glass lanterns. The scent of orange and cinnamon fills the air, creating a warm, sensual atmosphere. Sam slips her arm through mine.

'Deep breaths, honey. Deep breaths. You look fabulous. Every man in this place is going to want you ... with whipped cream on,' she giggles naughtily. I flick my big hair back and smile, pleased that she seems brighter and more like her old self.

As we get closer to the ballroom, a lively swing version of Jingle Bells wafts towards us in the night breeze. And wow! Michael Bublé is right in front of me. The actual Michael Bublé himself is singing here in the foyer of the Mulberry Grand Hotel. So it's true, Kelly really is friends with the famous people and, despite my apprehension about the evening ahead, a shiver of excitement radiates though me. Michael winks as we pass by and I can't help gasping like a proper fan-girl. Sam steps forward and gives him a kiss on the cheek, as if they're old friends; for all I know, maybe they are, Sam did go to some very exclusive parties over the years with Alfie, but I'm sure she would have mentioned meeting Michael before now. Cameras swerve into action and I'm immediately reminded that tonight is being filmed live purely to entertain the viewers.

We make it into the ballroom, which is lit up like a theme park, and there's a woman on stage who's a dead ringer for Dolly Parton – she even sounds like her too, maybe it is her. She's singing the funky version of the 'Working Nine To Five' theme tune from *Kelly Cooper Come Instore*. At one end of the room, there's a full-size carousel. Lauren, Doris and Suzanne from the cash office are laughing as they glide round and round and up and down, clinging onto poles in the centre of brightly painted wooden horses. There's also a snow slide – Melissa is sitting in a rubber tyre at the top, looking eager to descend. Next to the slide is a Santa's grotto, inside a gingerbread house that looks as if it's actually made from real gingerbread, apart from the front door that's been created from a trillion striped candy canes.

We're handed flutes of pink champagne as a photographer takes our picture.

'Darlings, there you are.' It's Eddie and he looks as if he's channelling Brad Pitt at a film premiere in a sleek black tuxedo and gold-framed aviator shades, only years younger – and on closer inspection it appears as if he's had more work around his HD eyebrows and gloss-coated lips. Pussy is perched regally in the crook of his elbow wearing a mini crimson taffeta ballgown, complete with sparkly tiara on her fluffy head and a diamanté choker around her neck. I stroke her ear and she preens into the palm of my hand.

'Is this nail varnish?' I ask, touching one of Pussy's paws. Her claws are painted a glittery silver colour.

'Of course. Pussy wanted to look her very best; this is one of her Christmas outfits.'

'*One?*' I ask, bemused and grateful for the distraction – anything to put off the moment I have to see Tom. I was barely able to keep it together when I spotted him in the street that night, so what's it going to be like watching him with Zara, his fiancée?

'That's right. She can't be expected to make it through the whole festive season with just one measly gown. No, a girl needs a selection sweetie. A *se-lection!*' Eddie's waves his free hand in the air flamboyantly, elevating his diva status a notch further. He kisses the air either side of my head before stepping back to get a better look. He lets out a long whistle. 'Sensational. Truly sensational. And you must come and meet Will.' He gestures towards a giant snowman-shaped ice luge to the left of one of the three cocktail bars. Will.I.Am is actually here, chatting to Kelly, and he looks hot in a long trench coat and woolly hat over silver T and black combat trousers. Annie is hovering near him and, on spotting me, she does a silent scream and points to Will's back before placing a hand over her heart and making kissy lips.

'Is it really him?' I ask, in a ridiculously breathy voice.

'Of course it is,' Eddie replies casually, as if it's an everyday occurrence to be mingling with world-famous superstars. 'But honeypie, you might want to reunite your jaw with the rest of your face and tone down that whole fan-girl thing you have going on.' He flashes me a look before whizzing an index finger in a Z-shape around me.

'Oh I'm *sooo* sorry, Ed, I wouldn't want to cramp your style now,' I laugh and nudge Sam. She gives Eddie's cheeks a quick tweak.

'Stop it! Must you be quite so gauche?' he says, batting her hands away. He quickly adjusts his bow tie and grabs a flute of champagne from a passing waiter. 'Honestly, I don't know why I bother. I'll come back for you two when you've calmed down. *Considerably*.'

I down my drink and cast a furtive glance through the crowd, wondering if Tom is actually here yet.

'Relax, will you?' Sam mouths, giving me a nudge.

'I can't help it,' I say, nerves making my voice sound trembly.

'Well try. You want to look poised and breezy, not anxious and scorned.'

We finish our drinks and hand the empty glasses to a waiter. 'Now follow me,' Sam commands, taking my hand and delving into the crowd.

We emerge at the other end of the room near a crimson velvet-covered stage and next to an enormous real pine Christmas tree, swathed in silver tinsel and pink diamanté-encrusted baubles.

'Let's duck in here and take a breather before we hunt Tom down,' Sam says, but before I can protest that I don't actually want to 'hunt Tom down' – I was hoping we might just casually bump into him, preferably without Zara in tow, and then I can confront him over letting my lovely Carrington's go – she pushes open a door and drags me in behind her. And I gasp. It takes me a few seconds to acclimatise. The whole room is dazzling. Brilliant white. Fake snow is swirling all around us; even the floor is covered so we're knee deep in soft, twinkly flakes.

'Oh wow,' Sam breathes, 'a proper snow room! Come on, let's get involved.' She runs into the middle of the room making the snow flurry and flutter, whipping around the room. It's like being inside a giant snow globe. Flakes flick into my eyes, my mouth, my hair – I can even see them on the ends of my eyelashes. It's incredible. I follow Sam, pleased to see her happy, and she grabs my hands and twirls me around, faster and faster, until neither of us can sustain it any longer and we collapse on the floor laughing. Sam is the first to recover and manages to scrabble herself into a standing position, just about; she's slipping and sliding as she struggles on her heels while trying not to trip on her dress. She reaches out a hand and I manage to haul myself up onto my feet. But at the last minute, I lose balance, and my left Loub skates away from me and I end up doing a Bambi impression before landing back on the floor in a sideways splits position with Sam toppled over on top of me.

'Jesus Christ, I've think I've ripped myself in two,' I bellow as a searing pain cuts right though me. Sam is cracking up as she rolls over to the other side of the room, where she lies on her back, hoists her dress up and starts doing snow angels. I'm on all fours now and wading over to her. Snowflakes are making it near on impossible to see – they collect in my mouth, I spit them out and keep wading, tossing my big hair back over my shoulder as I go. I've just made it over to Sam when a sudden gust of ice-cold air blasts down on us, making me gasp; the sheer force of the wind knocks me sideways and I end up in a heap next to Sam who stops moving and curls herself into a ball beside me. A deafening noise makes it near on impossible to communicate. We cling to each other, the wind whipping around us, with me desperately trying to keep my flimsy skater dress about my body, when Sam manages to gesture upwards.

I follow her line of vision and *oh my actual God*. Black night sky is above us. Stars. The moon. The ceiling has disappeared. Walls too. A helicopter is hovering above us, and two giant television screens are broadcasting Sam and me, writhing around on the ground like a pair of crazy loopers with fake snow rotating all around us, tornado-style. LIVE. To the whole world ... if you count all those ex-pat satellite viewers in places like the Costa del Sol, and hotels and laptops. And I just know this is going to end up on YouTube. Global. My hits will be stratospheric. *I officially want to die*, right now, spooning my best friend in a perishing cold field while my new Father Christmas-themed knickers, which have the phrase '*ho-ho-ho*' emblazoned all over them, are projected up onto the big screen.

Fifteen minutes later, and Sam and I are huddled together in tartan blankets with Millie in 107. And I'm still cringing all over. It turns out that it wasn't a snow room at all. Oh no! No no no no no! It was a flaming helipad behind the ballroom that KCTV had put a marquee over and filled with snow to be whipped away by a giant pulley, creating a dramatic James Bond-esque arrival scene for Mr Carrington, aka Tom. It was him in the helicopter. So when Tom actually landed, the first glimpse he got was of me curled up on the helipad with my dress whipping at my midriff and my big hair puffing around my head like I'm some kind of freak with her finger stuck in a plug socket for laughs. He didn't actually speak to me, or anything; no, it was just a horrified glance as he strode past with the film crew.

There's a knock on the door. It's Eddie.

'O-M-A-G.' He plonks Pussy on the bed, puts his arms around us both to draw us into a big group hug. 'You sure know how to make a dramatic entrance. Everyone is talking about it. Even Will said you two were "dope".' He breaks away to do quote signs with his fingers. 'Kel is practically hyperventilating, she's so thrilled. Apparently, the whole scene went viral in under ten minutes. You're international, sweet pea.'

'Oh stop it, please,' I say, dying a little more inside.

'So you're not outraged by our behaviour then, Eddie?' Sam says, shaking her blanket off and brushing down her dress. She sits down and Millie touches up her make-up.

'*Au contraire*. You give exceedingly good visual,' he sniffs, like he's been in the television industry his whole life, and not a mere few weeks.

'Right. That's you restored. Now it's Georgie's turn.' Millie gives me a despairing up-and-down glance, as if she's wondering where to start first. I have mud on my bare legs and my make-up has melted into a ghoulish mask. 'Hmm, I may have to give you an up-do,' she says, with a fleeting look of panic in her eyes as she inspects my hair, which resembles a matted nest. I've even lost a whole chunk of hair extensions, so I now have a weird, conical-shaped head.

I'm back at the entrance to the ballroom with a glass of champagne in one hand and a canapé in the other. I take a bite and wish I hadn't, before surreptitiously depositing it in a pot containing a miniature Christmas tree with silver frosting. Zara is standing beside the luge looking stunning in a sheer Stella McCartney dress that clings to her perfect siren figure. She shakes her glossy mane around for a bit while I scan the room and tentatively pat my high bun, wondering where Tom is; expecting him to be beside her, but I can't see him.

'He's over there,' Sam whispers in my ear and points discreetly in the other direction. And then I spot him. He's wearing a midnight blue tuxedo, the crisp white shirt complementing a perfect, caramel-coloured tan. His curly black hair is a little longer than before, gelled back, making him look just like a gorgeous Hollywood star; after everything that's happened, my heart still flutters and my pulse quickens. He looks so charismatic and charming – the perfect, quintessential, tall dark handsome man. A group of girls are hovering around him, laughing and flicking their hair. 'Weird, isn't it?' Sam says.

'What do you mean?'

'Well, Zara on one side of the room and Tom on the other, and I'm not sure I'd like it if Nathan was surrounded by a group of flirty girls.' I ponder on what Sam has said, and I suppose it is a bit strange, but before I can analyse further, the music stops and Kelly is up on the stage with a spotlight on her, and oh my God, she's calling out my name. My cheeks burn and my heart pumps into overdrive. I quickly finish my drink and turn to leave but a camera is blocking my exit.

'Georgie. Where are you?' Kelly booms into a microphone, and suddenly there's a spotlight beaming down on me and the music peters out. 'Come on now, no need to be camera shy, not after your earlier performance ... which was spectacular, by the way.' A round of applause circuits the room. 'Bring your friend, then we can thank you both properly,' she finishes, before grabbing two giant bouquets from a production assistant who's standing just offstage.

Everyone, except Zara, is clapping as we reluctantly make our way towards the stage. I'm willing my cheeks to stop flaming. I catch Tom's eye in my peripheral vision and I swear a fleeting look of amusement hovers on his face before he turns back to charm the groupies. *Grrreat!* So now he thinks I'm a ridiculous novelty act as well as a stalker.

'I'm right behind you,' Sam says, grabbing my hand. We make it to the stage and are shooed up the steps by Hannah, clutching a clipboard and doing her manic smile.

'Stand on the cross,' she hisses after me, and as if on autopilot I do as I'm told. Sam is next to me.

'*Ho ho ho ...* ' Kelly nudges me and winks, laughing as if it's the most hilarious joke she's ever told in her entire life. 'Ladies and gentlemen, I give you the star of *Kelly Cooper Come Instore*.' She grabs my hand and flings it up in the air. A camera zooms in. 'And her friend, err ... '

'Sam,' I quickly prompt, leaning into Kelly's microphone. I can't believe she forgot Sam's name, especially after the whole *One Born Every Minute* request, but Sam smiles graciously and does a little curtsy to the Carrington's crowd before flinging her arms around my neck and giving me a squeeze.

'Just smile,' she whispers reassuringly in my ear before we break apart. Leo darts across the stage to swiftly pin miniature microphones onto our dresses.

'Speech. Speech,' Kelly says, clapping again, and the crowd starts chanting my name. Saliva drains from my mouth as I look around – Mrs Grace is standing in front of the stage wearing a sparkly fascinator and clapping her bony hands high above her head. Annie is next to her looking gorgeous in an emerald green playsuit. She looks really happy as she leans back against the chest of an incredibly fit-looking, muscly guy. He has a curly wire hanging from his ear and Will is standing behind him – Security! Must be.

I swallow hard and try to think of something sensible to say.

'Thank you,' I mutter, dropping my chin to talk directly into the microphone. 'And, err ... Happy Christmas everyone,' I add, breathing a sigh of relief, and then promptly ruin it by doing a ridiculously feeble little wave. I look back up and see Zara in my peripheral vision. She's staring me out. I shudder. *What is her problem?*

'Bravo. Simple and understated,' Kelly says, kissing my

cheek. 'And how about a word from our other star, Mr Carrington himself.' She scans the crowd. 'Ahh, there you are.' She points at Tom. 'Ladies and gentlemen, I give you *Toooom* Carrington. Whoop whoop!' With both hands, Kelly pummels an imaginary punchbag high above her head.

What's she doing? Oh my actual God. Tom is coming towards the stage. He's mounting the steps. He's within touching distance. He's got the irresistible smile in place. His arm brushes against my back as he walks past, making my stomach flip and my cheeks flame. I dart a look at Zara and her eyes narrow.

'A few words, if you don't mind, Tom. Tell our audience at home a little more about your adventures in Paris, New York and the Christmas capital of the world, Lapland,' Kelly swoons, nuzzling into him. Tom coughs discreetly and waits for Leo to fit a microphone onto his lapel. Sam edges closer to me and I just know she's thinking the same – *yes, why don't you tell us aaaalll about it, Tom? NOT!*

He takes a step forward. Oh God. This is hideous. I'm going to have to stand here in front of all the Carrington's staff, and the viewers at home, and listen to the man I thought was my perfect one go on about the fabulous time he had with other women. And what if he starts on about Zara – talks about their wedding plans, and all that?

'Firstly, I'd like everyone to raise their glasses and join

me in congratulating Kelly on producing such a fantastic programme.' He pauses to allow a resounding, 'hear hear!' from everyone. Mrs Grace is even high-fiving the air and whooping, she's that thrilled. 'But most of all, I'd like to thank all of you. The wonderful Carrington's team that make our department store such a fantastic place to shop. And with the new pet spa, the ice rink and the refurbished personal shopping suite, not to mention all of the other changes that Kelly and her team have introduced – well, I'm thrilled to say that our latest figures are looking extremely healthy indeed. I think we may have managed to turn things around—'

'Hmm, so why are you selling then?' I mutter under my breath, and the second the words come out of my mouth I shrivel inside. The mini microphone amplifies my voice around the ballroom. It ricochets off the walls. I can see myself, practically poster size, on the two giant screens. Now the floor feels as if it's fallen away. My head is pounding. I want to run away and hide. Tom stops talking and glances at me with his forehead creased. There's a collective gasp followed by an eerie silence. The whole crowd stands motionless, staring at me.

'Cut! Cuut! *Cuuut! Cuuuuut!*' Hannah shrieks, each time louder and more frenzied than the last. She looks as if she's having an actual proper meltdown as she flaps the clipboard furiously, and gurns at Leo. Kelly practically dive-bombs in front of me, grips my elbow, turns me around and marches me down the stairs and

311

through a side door into an anteroom that's crammed full of KCTV production people who are staring at a long line of little TV monitors.

'Out. Out. GET OUT,' she hollers, flapping her hands at them as they throw off their headphones, grab their drinks and scurry towards the door. 'Not you.' She hoiks a cameraman back into the room. 'Flick that back on and make sure you get the lot. This is TV gold,' she hisses to him, her eyes glittering with the thrill of ending her *live* show with such an explosive bang.

Kelly strides into the middle of the room, closely followed by Tom, who slams the door behind him. It bounces on the frame before flinging back open. Sam appears and quickly runs towards me. 'What do you want?' Kelly shouts at her.

'To even things up. Two versus one – not very fair, is it?' Sam replies quickly, before flashing a panicky look at me, then back to Tom and Kelly.

'Fair enough. Stand over there and be quiet,' Kelly commands, pointing to a spot beside a wooden cabinet. Sam grabs my flowers, plonks them alongside hers on the cabinet, before standing in the designated spot and glaring at Kelly.

'So, what the hell are you playing at?' Kelly barks at me.

'Well, I ... erm, I'm sorry.' I will my cheeks to stop burning as I bob from one foot to the other and try to avoid the camera that's practically touching my face.

'Sorry! Is that all you can say?' Her eyes look as if

they're going to pop right out of her head. 'I spend months preparing, researching and then filming to save Carrington's for my dear friend, Isabella's son ... ' Kelly pauses to glance at the camera, and then Tom, before flapping a hand around crazily and grabbing a chunk of her wild orange Ronald McDonald hair. 'You destroy it all in a second and then say *sorry*.' She flings both hands on her hips and leans forward to stare at me, goggle-eyed and speechless. And I can't be sure if this is for real. Or is she acting up for the viewers at home?

'Sorry,' I mutter, feeling pathetic and wimpish. The door fly opens and Zara appears; she sashays in and stands proprietorially next to Tom. The camera guy swivels to get a close-up of her face before retreating to the corner. Hannah's back, and flapping for us to stand closer to each other, presumably so they can get us all in shot.

'Stop saying sorry, and stop that incessant bobbing – it's getting on my nerves,' Kelly snaps. I stop moving and fold my arms thinking, *Bloody cheek*. She's the one ruining everything by buying the store so she can close us down and turn us into a hotel. 'I want an explanation. A reason for your sudden ludicrous outburst – I mean, I guessed right from the start that you weren't the full picnic, what with that stupid Beyoncé stunt you pulled.' She lets out a dramatic puff of air.

'*Excuse me?*' I say indignantly, thinking, *This is a turn-around*. Not so long ago she wanted to make me a star. 'You filmed me without even asking and then plastered

313

it all over the telly, *and* the World Wide Web. Hardly a "stunt", I say, trying to keep my voice even, but I've had enough of her parading me like some kind of show pony.

'Oh stop bleating ... honestly, you sound like a—'

'OK. That's enough.' Tom jumps in, darting a look at Kelly before settling on me. 'Let's stick to the point here. What did you mean about "selling" the store?'

'You tell me,' I reply, not missing a beat, my stomach flipping as he stares me straight in the eye. God, he's so gorgeous; even after everything I can't stop fancying him. His chocolate brown eyes, nestling in those sumptuous eyelashes, his broad shoulders, the charisma, just his presence, being here in the same room with him, it's madness ... I wish so much that I could turn back time and start all over again. I bite my lip instead, and spot Nathan hovering in the doorway with a concerned look on his face. And he looks totally out of place in track bottoms and a washed out T-shirt. Sam beckons him in. *What's he doing here?* But before I can figure it out, Tom is standing in front of me.

'But I'm asking you,' he replies, pushing a hand through his nicely dishevelled hair.

'Well, you're the one doing it. Ruining everything.' I flash him a look and dig my nails into the palm of my hand to steady my nerves. 'How *could* you?' And to give him his due, he does look a bit baffled – probably all part of their cover-up. He just doesn't want us all knowing that he's no longer Mr Carrington. Oh no. Mr

Sellout, more like. Well, they're not getting one over me. I steel myself, figuring this wasn't exactly what I had in mind by way of confronting him, but I might as well get on with it, now that it's out in the open. LIVE to the whole country. Eeek!

'Do what?' he asks.

'Oh, don't pretend you know nothing about it. You're in on it. Kelly too,' I pause to point in her direction, 'and Zara.' I can barely manage to look at her. I drop my head and study the swirly pattern on the carpet instead.

'*Zara?*' Tom says, and she steps a little closer to him.

'That's right. Sam even saw her going through the plans with Princess Ameerah. Is she the buyer?' I accuse.

'Princess Ameerah?' Tom repeats vaguely, like he has no idea what I'm talking about. But he's not fooling me. Not again. Oh no.

'I told you to leave it alone.' Kelly steps in hastily, glaring at Zara. 'I can't believe you went behind my back. I said it wasn't happening. I'd never do that to my friends.'

'Don't pretend. I overheard you talking about it, turning us into a hotel with underground parking,' I say, studying Kelly's face for clues. She blinks a few times before letting out a long measured breath and glancing directly into the camera.

'Well, whatever you heard, you were mistaken.' I shake my head in disbelief, barely able to comprehend her audacity. I know what I heard.

'Look, will someone tell me what's going on?' Tom

says. 'Georgie, why would you say something like that? Why didn't you just call me if something was bothering you?' I lift my head to look him in the eye.

'Are you for real?' I murmur, desperately trying to keep up. I feel as if I'm in some kind of crazeee pantomime where everyone knows the lines except me.

'Err, yes. I think so ... ' *Unbelievable. Talk about flippant.* I can't believe I never even got a glimpse of this side to him. He obviously couldn't care less about me, or Carrington's for that matter.

'I tried contacting you but you ignored my calls, messages and Facebook PMs. And then I get a horrible text.' I cringe at the hideous shrillness in my voice.

'A horrible text? What do you mean?' He pulls his mobile from his pocket as if to prove me wrong, but I'm not stupid, he could have just deleted it. I flip open my clutch to retrieve my phone and then I remember – I am the stupid one, I deleted the hideous message, along with everything else that reminded me of him.

'I mean the one where you told me to leave you alone. The one where you said you'd met someone else? The one where you called me a stalker,' I state, practically shouting and desperately wishing that I didn't sound so hysterical. They're all staring at me. I glance at Zara and she looks edgy, pumped – relishing the showdown, no doubt.

'I would never send you a text saying stuff like that, and what do you mean calls and messages? Yes, I ignored

316

one call from you – I was boarding an aeroplane with a steward glaring at me to switch the phone off. And I didn't bother with Facebook while I was away – the Wi-Fi was practically unusable it was that slow on my iPad, and I was on and off flights, in different countries from one day to the next. And given the way things were left between us ... ' he adds, his Downton accent getting a little more pronounced.

'Well if you didn't send it, then who did?' Maybe I'm going mad. I've finally lost the plot and, for some bizarre reason, an image of Dad pops up inside my head. He's wringing his hands as four men in long white coats strap me to a gurney and whisk me off to a clinic.

'I did!'

Whaaaat?

It's Zara!

I turn to face her.

'Don't look at me like that. I was doing you a favour.' Zara looks directly at Tom. 'She was stalking you. Come on, seven messages in one evening with all those stupid little sad face emoticons! Who even does that?' She laughs nastily. 'And then trying to trap you by getting herself pregnant. Talk about desperate ... ' My cheeks burn. I fling my hands to my face and see that they're trembling.

'*Pregnant?*' Tom says softly, his forehead creasing as he fixes his eyes on mine. And momentarily, it's as if we're the only ones in the room – apart from the camera that's practically touching the side of my head, it's that close up. I shake my head and mouth 'no', and I'm sure I spot a dart of disappointment flicker across his face. Tom clears his throat, keeping his eyes on Zara. 'I thought we were friends?' he says to her quietly, before addressing the room. 'It was all very last-minute, the flight to Paris, and it wasn't until I arrived that I realised I'd forgotten my phone. Zara kept it safe and brought it with her to … ' His voice trails off when he realises that not only did she keep his phone safe, but she also used it to field my calls and send a choice message of her own, thereby ensuring I never contacted him again for fear of being deemed a stalker. And I bet it was her who said he was busy, putting on a French accent. I open my mouth but the words won't come out. I swallow and bite down hard on my bottom lip. So hard, I taste blood, metallic in my mouth.

'*Friends?*' It's Sam. She moves close to me, and she's fuming. Her eyes are flashing and her tiny frame is braced in a forward-attack position. 'Oh purlease. Don't be coy. And the rest,' she huffs. 'Engaged to be married more like … until the next fool comes along. Like Lawrence! Married with three children he is, that's right.' Sam points a finger in Zara's direction and she scowls back. 'She's been having an affair behind your back with a married man. And to think I played Cupid for you with my best friend. Honestly Tom, I thought you were a far better judge of character. Anyway, it's your loss. Georgie is

318

worth a million of this spoilt, overindulged tramp.' Sam crosses her arms and stares at Zara, who whips up her hand, but Sam is too quick for her and manages to bat it away before Zara strikes her face. Zara grabs hold of Sam's dress and yanks her up close. Instinctively, I reach out a hand to pull Sam back, but I'm too late.

'Oh bore off. You hideous little troll,' Zara hisses into Sam's face. 'No wonder your baby died, probably couldn't stand being inside you.' There's a collective gasp. Nathan and I immediately step towards Zara. My hand actually comes up to slap her – how dare she hurt my best friend like this? – but it's Kelly who grabs Zara from behind and drags her away.

'That's enough! It shames me to say this, but you've always been an obnoxious madam. And now you really have crossed the line. You need to apologise.' Kelly tightens her grip on Zara's shoulders.

'She started it,' Zara retorts like a sulky teenager, shrugging herself free.

'Apologise godammit!' A loaded silence hangs in the air. '*Just bloody do it,*' Kelly screams, her face turning a violent rhubarb-red.

'Jeez, can't anyone take a joke around here? I'm sorry. OK?' Zara says reluctantly, rolling her eyes and flicking her hair.

'Look, please. Can we all just calm down?' Tom looks around the room. 'Sam, I'm so sorry. Are you OK?' he asks quietly and politely. Sam waves a dismissive hand in his direction before leaning into Nathan. I touch her arm and she mouths 'thank you' at me. I nod my head in solidarity.

'I have no idea what is going on here, but can someone please tell me?' Tom looks around the room, waiting for one of us to speak. Zara's bee-sting lips are pursed tight.

'Oh for goodness' sakes. I hold my hands up – shoot me why don't you? It's only a tacky little shop, for crying out loud. Ameerah and I go way back. Boarding school. Anyway, she's been on the lookout for a project, so I gave her the nod on Carrington's. Perfect location, not far from the marina – only bit of glamour in this twee town, I might add. So why not rip it out and turn it into a hotel? Simple. And Mummy wasn't interested in coming in on the deal, so you can leave her out of it. Serves you right, Tom.' There's a stunned silence. We all stare at Zara. What's she going on about? Hardly the actions of a loving fiancée ...

'But why would you do that?' Tom asks, his jaw tightening.

'Why not?' Her eyes flash around the room before landing on me. 'But it doesn't matter now, Ameerah didn't win the auction,' she shrugs nonchalantly, and I really have to resist the urge to punch her now ugly-looking pinched face.

'And what about my phone? Why would you deliberately hurt Georgie?'

'Well, I wasn't going to just stand by and let you ruin

your life by settling for ... *her!*' she screeches in my direction, 'a ridiculous *shop girl!*' She jabs a heavily jewelled finger in my direction. 'Not when you can do so much better.' She tosses her hair around for a bit, daring any of us to disagree that she is, in fact, the 'better' option. I hold my breath.

'Yes.' Tom steps forward. My heart misses a beat. My palms are drenched in sweat. I discreetly wipe them across the back of my clutch. The room sways. It's as if time has stood still. Suspended. 'You're absolutely right, Zara. I can do better ... than you!' I gasp. 'I told you in New York that I wasn't interested; I suppose this is your way of paying me back – by trying to destroy everything that's important to me. And why would they think you're my fiancée?' He gestures towards Sam and me.

'Yes *Zara?*' Sam says pointedly, as Hannah steers the cameraman into place.

'Fine. You're obviously more stupid than you look. I saw you sneaking around behind that shoji screen in the restaurant, so, well ... I thought I'd toss you a scrap to gnaw on with your pathetic little friend.' She gives me an up-and-down look. I don't believe it. So Tom isn't engaged at all. Zara made it up!

Tom is right next to me now. He touches my arm, sending a surge of electricity to circuit my body.

'I think we need to talk,' he says, his eyes still flashing as Zara storms from the room.

'So you haven't sold Carrington's?' is all I manage to say,

but I have to be sure. He shakes his head and his eyes soften.

'No. It's not mine to sell. Carrington's leases the building. My great grandfather, Mr Carrington, aka Dirty Harry,' he lifts his eyebrows, 'sold the freehold years ago after he got into bother financially – frittered the profits on showgirls, apparently. He had no choice and had to raise funds to save the store. I know the freehold changed hands recently, though, because I was notified of the pending auction and put in a sealed bid right away, naturally, but without success. The board were told of the new freeholder's details, care of their lawyer in London, but that's all we know. I'm sure there's no cause for alarm,' he says casually. But I can't believe he's being so blasé about it all.

'No cause for alarm?' I repeat. They could pull the rug from under us at any time. Give notice and take back the building. What if the new freeholder has the same idea as Princess Ameerah and turns us into a hotel with underground parking? 'Well it bothers me,' I tell him firmly. 'If Princess Ameerah didn't buy it, then who did? We need to find out!'

Another silence follows.

'I did.'

Whaaaat?

Oh my God. My pulse quickens. I can feel my legs wobbling as I attempt to try and cope with this roller-coaster of revelations. My mouth falls open. I quickly close it. What is she talking about? *Oh my actual God.*

Sam steps forward, wiping tears away with the back of her hand.

'Yep. That's right.' She pauses and our eyes meet. 'Sorry I didn't say,' she mouths in my direction, and gives me a watery smile. Tom's jaw actually drops.

'But how? *When?*' I ask, in a daze.

Kelly whips open the door so the cameraman can capture the deafening applause that's coming from the ballroom. The whole of Carrington's is watching us on the big screens. They must have continued filming in there too – I can see Mrs Grace on the row of monitors, with her hand over her face. She's clearly in shock. Melissa is on screen now, chest-bumping Mick, the security guard and shouting, 'Yo, go Sam.'

Annie is up on some guy's shoulders bellowing, 'Sam, I love you babe,' and sloshing a cocktail in the air.

'So you were the mystery bidder who came in at the last hour,' Tom interjects, shaking his head with an incredulous look on his face.

'That's right. And I'm sorry, Tom, we didn't know you were the other bidder.' Sam looks apologetically at Tom. 'As you know, Alfie Palmer, owner of Palmer Estate Agents and, more importantly, my wonderful Dad, passed away at the start of the year and left his fortune and his business to me. So, after overhearing Zara talking about a hotel on the Carrington's site, I asked the managing director of Palmers to find out what was going on. Then, when Mandy from the town hall told me about the enquiry, and after a bit of delving with the help and expertise of my brilliantly clever legal advisor, aka my husband, Nathan,' Sam pauses, 'we came up with a way to save Carrington's.'

'That's right.' Nathan steps forward. 'My wife liked it so much, she bought the store.' He laughs and shrugs.

'Err, not the actual store … just the freehold for the building. The store still belongs to the Carrington family and I have no intention of giving notice on the lease. Absolutely not. Ever! Freeholds don't come cheap, I'm relying on your rent to pay me back,' she grins, and offers her hand to Tom, who shakes it enthusiastically.

'Sorry Georgie.' Sam moves close to me.

'Um, what for?' I just about manage.

'For going AWOL on you recently.'

'Hey, no need to apologise,' I say, in a soft voice, thinking how magnificent she is. Her whole world fell apart when Archie died, and then the miscarriage – I can't imagine the feelings of loss will ever disappear; yet she's keeping on. Strong and strident. Buying up freeholds in her spare time. No wonder she wasn't around or answering her phone – she was blooming busy!

'I had to move fast. I was up in London trying to sort everything out quickly, and I really wanted it to be a surprise, for, well … for Christmas,' Sam says, taking my hands in hers. 'For the both of us. For you, and for your mum,' she drops her voice and my eyes fill with tears. Happy tears. 'I know how much you love Carrington's.

Me too. And, like I said, I wasn't going to stand by and lose my café, the same café that Dad helped me set up, not on top of everything else I've lost ... ' Her voice wobbles. I throw my arms around her and squeeze tight.

'Oh Sam, you're incredible. This is the best Christmas present ever,' I breathe, pulling back to kiss her cheek. 'But tell me something.'

'Sure.' She raises one eyebrow.

'How on earth did you manage to keep it a secret? I thought we told each other everything,' I pretend to chide.

'With a lot of difficulty, I can tell you.' She laughs and rolls her eyes. 'But I just couldn't; the freeholder insisted on total confidentiality until all the legalities were finalised, which only happened last night. Literally.' She shakes her head. 'We managed it just in time, before everything closes down for Christmas.'

'And then Georgie, when I saw you on TV, saying what you did on that stage, I bombed down here as quickly as I could,' Nathan interjects, 'Sam had wanted to reveal all tomorrow over lunch, but I knew right away she wouldn't last that long.'

'Now that's been cleared up – Georgie, will you please come with me? We need to talk.' Tom holds out his hand. I glance at Sam. She nods in approval before whispering in my ear.

'Hear him out.' I squeeze her hand and she adds, 'and then think of the incredible sex you'll have making up ... '

'Trust you,' I whisper back and laugh. Typical Sam.

'Now go.' She shoos me away with her hand.

'Where are we going?'

'You'll see,' Tom grins.

I put my hand in his, relishing the warmth of his fingers as they grip tightly around mine, my stomach flipping over and over. He leads me through a door, out into the night, and soon we're running as fast as we can across the lawn towards another section of the hotel. And as the freezing air whips my cheeks and furls around my legs, heightening every one of my senses, I feel so alive. Exhilarated. And it's utterly glorious.

25

We've arrived at a service area in the basement of the hotel. Enormous metal cage laundry trollies line the walls of the long corridor in front of us.

'This way.' Tom looks charged as he strides towards a door at the far end and I have to jog to keep up with him. He pushes the door open and leads me down a flight of stairs to a narrow underground tunnel of exposed brick. It's dimly lit and smells damp. I hesitate, fear and excitement surging through me. 'It's OK. I know the way.' He looks back over his shoulder, his eyes locking with mine. He grips my hand tighter. I nod and follow behind as he navigates us through the junctions and around the corners, running along lengths of tunnel until eventually we come to a steel door. My heart pounds as he taps a number into the security pad before pushing hard with his shoulder, forcing the door open. We step though into a carpeted lift with a metal cage door. A Tiffany wall lamp flickers into life.

Carrington's! We're inside Carrington's. I bet we've just come through one of the tunnels that Dirty Harry used to visit the showgirls – the Mulberry Grand Hotel is almost as old as Carrington's, so it makes sense. Or maybe it was the tunnel that Mrs Grace told me about, where the staff and their families took shelter during the Blitz? Either way, it's magical. It's like being a part of Carrington's history.

As the lift rises, we stand in silence, side by side, with me listening to the drumming beat of my heart and praying that the lift breaks down so we end up having to stay the night in here, together. One last time. Because Tom might not have sent that horrible message, but he still wanted to split up, that day in his office. For all I know he could be seeing Valentina; just because she wasn't at the party tonight doesn't mean they're not together, especially after Zara's antics. It all makes sense now – his white-jodhpured hero moment on the moonlit Corsican beach with her, and then their steamy hot-tub scene in Lapland. I shudder and brace myself. Maybe this is his way of letting me down gently. We're going to his office so he can feel business-like and detached, away from the crowds. Maybe he thinks I'll make a scene and this is his best chance of damage limitation. I saw the way he avoided me earlier; didn't want to be associated with the crazy cow lying in the field.

Eventually the lift judders to a halt and Tom flings back the metal concertina grille. He taps on another security pad and leads me through a door. A sudden gust of invigorating cold air billows all around us as Tom starts climbing up a long narrow flight of steps.

I quickly follow behind. And we're outside. I can see the Christmas lights of Mulberry-On-Sea twinkling all around us and it looks magical. Breathtaking.

'Close your eyes,' Tom says. I do as I'm told, relishing the thrill of this utterly exquisite secret adventure, and I might as well make the most of this time with him – it could be the last we have together. I can feel Tom's hands on my face making sure I don't peep. I shiver with the sensation of his warm body up close against my back. 'Take five steps forward.' He turns me around and whispers into my ear, his breath hot on my cold skin. 'Now you can open them.' And I do. The circular ice rink glistens before me, bathed in a golden glow from the giant neon Carrington's sign high above us. I gasp. It's incredible. Amazing. Like something out of a fairytale.

After pulling off his jacket, Tom swings it around my shoulders and leads me over to the wooden skate-hire booth, deftly flipping the padlock free and opening the door.

'What are you doing? Kelly will go mad if we break in,' I say, the feeling of danger and excitement making my voice sound all breathy.

'Well, it *is* my store. I can do what I like,' he smiles, quickly kicking off his shoes. 'What size?' He glances at my feet. 'Mmm, a five I reckon.' He gestures for my heels. I quickly slip them off and pull on the skates. He flicks a switch and a swingy Rat Pack song starts playing. 'And we need heat, it's freezing up here,' he says, selecting another switch and helping himself to a couple of padded body warmers from a coat stand in the corner behind the till. He puts one on and hands the other to me. 'That should do it.' I leave my clutch on the bench and turn to see. Around the rink's perimeter are a trillion tiny halogen heat lamps studded into the safety wall, twinkling and looking utterly beautiful.

On the ice, and Tom is a pro, or so it seems. He leads me into the centre and twirls me around and around before gliding us to a halt. We're standing opposite each other, with me clinging to his arm, hoping I manage to stay upright.

'Now we can talk,' he says.

'Oh, I see.' I raise an eyebrow and try to ignore the knot forming in my stomach.

'Which is what we should have done, the last time we were together.'

'But you didn't have time,' I say, gripping his arm tighter as my skates wobble on the slippery ice.

'Well, I have time now,' he replies, not missing a beat, and graciously forgetting that I had said the same.

'So what's changed then?' I say, searching his eyes.

'Well, what I really meant that day in my office was that I couldn't talk right then, but before I could explain why, you had gone.' I study his face.

'But you didn't come after me.' I quiz, and my forehead creases.

'I couldn't. I had Kelly herding me towards a car

330

waiting to take me to the airport, and Zara suggesting I let you cool off and ... ' His voice trails off.

'But you must have known Zara had her own agenda, that she was after you. I saw the way she was all over you that day in your office.'

'Not exactly.' He glances away.

'What do you mean, *not exactly?*' I venture, immediately wondering if I really want to know.

'Just that it, well, it happens all the time,' he shrugs, and looks a bit embarrassed.

'What does?' I ask quietly.

'Nothing.' He shakes his head. 'Forget I said anything. Come on, let's look at the stars,' he adds to change the subject.

'But you can't say something like that and then not carry on.' He avoids my gaze by looking up at the sky.

'OK. What I meant is that I'm used to it, I suppose,' he starts, slowly. 'But I've become immune. Women flirt ... ' he says, before quickly adding, 'it doesn't mean anything.'

'Well I don't. I wouldn't dream of pawing a man like Zara does,' I sniff. 'And Kelly, she was just as bad – doing her cougar act all over you.' He smiles softly.

'And that's why you're like no other woman I've ever known before,' he says softly.

'I'm not?' I grin and raise an eyebrow.

'Most definitely not. Look, I don't want to talk about other women, so can we drop this and talk about us?'

331

And the way he says 'us' – so intimately – makes my heart lift and my guard lower. He moves in a little closer.

'Sure. But for the record, when I first saw myself on TV looking ridiculous … well, I felt really betrayed, as if I what we had together meant nothing much at all to you.'

'I understand that now.' He pauses to study my face for a moment. 'Georgie, I'm so sorry I didn't tell you about the show.' He tilts his head to one side. 'I should have put my foot down and explained to the board, or I could have just told you anyway, and then sworn you to secrecy.'

'And I wouldn't have said a word, I really wouldn't have.'

'I guess I just got swept away with it all, trying to do what was best for Carrington's without even thinking about what was best for me, or for us.' He smiles, making his beautiful face look younger, boyish and even more irresistible.

'Well, I'm sorry too. You couldn't tell me – I understand that. I overreacted. I got … ' My voice falters.

'Got what?' he asks, gently lifting my chin.

'Scared I guess.' I look away.

'But why?'

'I don't know, because … ' I clutch onto his elbow with both hands, determined to stay upright, but unable to say the words out loud. That I love him. That I was petrified of getting hurt again, like I have been so many times in the past.

'Please don't be scared. I can't promise that I won't get something wrong or that I'll never hurt you ever again, but I can make a damn good effort to try not to ... if you'll let me?' he says tenderly, his beautiful brown eyes searching mine. 'I really missed you. When I was away from you, it felt like forever at times.' And I know exactly what he means. These last weeks have felt like a lifetime to me. My heart melts and I really want to kiss him, and for everything to be good between us again. To forget everything that's happened. Everything I've seen on the television screen in my shoebox flat.

'But it's not as easy as that,' I say.

'Yes it is. Unless you don't want to ... or perhaps you've moved on. Things are different now, I understand that. You're a celebrity, you're in demand. I saw the magazines. The PR things. The stunning picture of you in that 'girls we'd most like to date' chart in some blokes' magazine.' He smiles wryly. Wow! I didn't know about that. Momentarily, I allow myself to feel really chuffed and ponder on how things have turned around. When I first met Tom, I felt ordinary, and that he was out of my league. Now it seems that's not the case at all.

'But what about Valentina?' I ask, as my mind rakes through all of the emotions I've encountered while he was away. I can't just ignore them and fall back into his arms and ultimately his bed, no matter how much I want him.

'Valentina? What's she got to do with this?' His forehead creases.

'Err, aren't you two ... well, I know she isn't here tonight, but then it is Christmas, so maybe she wanted to stay in Brazil with her family, or maybe she couldn't get a visa or something, I don't know, I just ... ' I shrug awkwardly.

'Georgie. Please stop talking for a moment.' And I do. I stand motionless listening to Dean Martin singing 'Let It Snow' as I wait for the moment of truth.

'Valentina is spending Christmas in Rio.'

'OK.' I swallow hard and focus on the lyrics – 'corn for popping ... and *the fire slowly dying*'. Oh God.

'With her girlfriend!' He shakes his head and gives me a look of sheer exasperation.

'Her ... Oh, I see,' I mutter, feeling like a complete and utter idiot, but as the realisation of what he's saying sinks in, my pulse quickens and my heart soars.

'So it was just a showmance after all,' I say, relief flooding through me.

'That's right, Valentina was only in the show because she happened to be in Corsica at a jewellery convention, and when I took the opportunity of meeting up with her to explain that we wouldn't be stocking her pieces any more, unfortunately they just don't sell well in Carrington's, anyway, KCTV suggested the beach scene – Valentina is a keen horse rider. I thought you knew, I did ask Kelly to mention it, I was conscious of how it might come across, especially after the way things were left between us.'

'Maybe she forgot,' I suggest magnanimously. More likely she deliberately wanted me to think Tom had moved on so she could film me out on dates because it's like Hannah said – 'viewers love all that'. It was all staged, purely to entertain the viewers. And after tonight's performance, it's pretty obvious that Kelly will do anything for the show.

'Maybe. But you really must stop putting two and two together, it's not good for you.' *Hmmm. Ain't that the truth?*

'Well, you can talk. What about ignoring me for weeks, and then not even saying hello when you got here tonight,' I say, sticking my index finger in the air and instantly regretting it when my right leg slip-slides around for a bit and I end up headbutting his chest before flipping backwards with a speed that could induce whiplash.

'Whoa. Don't think you're ready for the Boléro just yet.' He helps me to steady myself. 'You OK?' I nod. 'Good. I'm sorry I didn't call, but like I explained earlier, it was difficult. I was crazy busy all day, and then when I got my phone back and saw that you hadn't called—'

'But I had called.'

'Yes, we know that now. But I didn't at the time. I assumed that you weren't interested any more. I always planned on trying to make things right when I got back home. Anyway, you ignored me too.'

'I did not.'

'Yes you did. When I get back to Mulberry-On-Sea, I couldn't bear it any longer and called you, but you didn't pick up. And then I saw you with another guy, and well ... it made sense. I had let you down and you'd moved on ... ' He called! Oh my God. After all that angst, he actually called! But hang on. 'What call?' I quickly ask, racking my brains. If he did call, then why didn't I know? I definitely would have answered it. Most definitely.

'I can't remember the exact time, but it was the same night I saw you in the street kissing the other guy.' He looks away. There's a short silence. And then I remember. Oh my God. In the bar. The number I didn't recognise ... *because I'd erased him from my phone*. From my life. It was Tom. And to think that I'd longed for him to call me. Yearned even. And then when he did, I ignored him. I mentally kick myself and make a pact to never ever delete his numbers again.

'So I assumed you had moved on? I knew you'd been on dates with a famous singer. You looked really happy together on the bandstand. Zara showed me the magazine pictures of you two together.' *Hmmm, I bet she did.*

'Well, I thought you had moved on too, with Zara. The voiceover guy even said that you might rekindle love with an old flame.'

'Did he really?' Tom says, sounding surprised. 'I didn't bother watching any of the film footage; just felt a bit weird seeing myself on TV.' He shrugs. 'And she was never an old flame. A friend, more like ... or so I thought. We've known each other since childhood.'

'Oh, but I thought you used to be an item,' I say, remembering the Google picture of them kissing.

'No, never. Yes, Zara would often be in the same night-club as me when I did that whole Chelsea scene as a student – not really my thing, and well ... I guess she can be a bit enthusiastic at times when it comes to public displays of affection, she was forever catching me off guard,' he explains modestly. 'Especially if there's a pap hanging around. Zara loves featuring in the society pages of *Hello!* magazine and would often lunge in for a kiss on camera. She's a player, always has been. Everyone in Chelsea knows it.'

'I see,' I say diplomatically.

'Anyway, that's all irrelevant. It's you that I'm interested in ... unless you really have moved on?' he asks, looking straight into my eyes. I shake my head.

'It was nothing. Dan's a nice guy, but not for me. The spark wasn't there – how could it be, when it's only ever been you that I want?' Tom pulls me in tighter.

'Georgie, I'm so sorry. I messed up and let pride take over. I could see that day in my office I'd got it wrong, and you were so annoyed and upset and ... well, I knew I was going to Paris and that would most likely have been the last straw. For some ridiculous reason, I thought you'd be better off without me, that you didn't need the stress, and you know my life can be hectic, and I should never have said what I did. But then when you agreed that you wanted to call it a day too ... '

'Shuuushh.' I place my finger on his lips. 'None of that matters any more.'

'Sooooo,' he starts slowly.

'Go on,' I coax.

'I have two questions...'

'OK.'

'How is Mr Cheeks? I've missed him too.'

'He's fine. And the second?'

'Does this means we can have mind-blowingly incredible make-up sex then?' he grins cheekily, and goes to tickle me, but I'm too quick for him and manage to pull away just in time.

'Well, that depends,' I tease.

'On what?' he says, giving me a quizzical look.

'Your appetite! I don't suppose you fancy having Christmas lunch at my place?' I ask, thinking of the salmon, the supersize turkey that's been thawing in my kitchen sink since Thursday, not to mention the trillion bottles of prosecco, assorted cheese board with cracker selection, two jars of silverskin pickled onions, a honey roast ham joint, four tins of Quality Street (they were 'buy one get one free'), a tub of cheese footballs (they smell gross, but Dad loves them), Twiglets, sprouts, peas, parsnips, carrot batons, red cabbage, bread sauce, cranberry sauce, goose fat roast potatoes, gravy, stuffing, pigs in blankets, Christmas pudding, brandy butter, champagne cream, panettone, Christmas cake, Eat Me dates, After Eights ... I've got the lot and I'm exhausted just thinking about it all. With the best will in the world, there's no way Sam, Nathan, Dad, Nancy and I will get through it all.

Tom laughs and moves in closer. I can't resist him any longer so I slip an arm around his waist and press the palm of my hand up under his jacket. He brings his left hand around the back of my head, drawing my face in to his. His lips feel like fire against my cold cheek as he trails a path to my mouth and it's as if a bumper pack of fireworks have exploded one after the other deep inside me. We kiss for what feels like an eternity until I feel myself falling, sliding down his body. His lips still hot on mine as my hand touches the ice. Tom is lying next to me now, pulling me in closer to his warm embrace.

'I'd love to,' he says, nuzzling his mouth against the side of my neck as we pause for air.

'Phew. That's a relief,' I murmur.

'Pardon?' he says, tilting his head back to look into my eyes.

'Oh nothing. I was just thinking how wonderful it is that we'll be spending Christmas Day together.'

'And I can't think of anywhere I'd rather be,' he says softly, tracing a finger slowly and seductively across my lips.

We turn together to look up at the twinkling, starry

night sky, and as if by magic, fluttery soft snowflakes float silently down upon us. And, right on cue, Bing Crosby is singing 'White Christmas' and I instantly know in my heart that this is going to be the best Christmas ever. Just as we planned. Just as I always dreamed and hoped it would be. With Tom. My one. My happy-ever-after.

Epilogue

Viva Las Vegas babeeee! Nine Months Later ...

A glorious evening breeze cools my sun-baked skin as I fan myself with a copy of the wedding service. Lady Gaga is singing, for real, right in front of us on a little podium as we wait for Eddie and Ciaran to arrive. We're seated in the grounds of the Bellagio Hotel under a white lace canopy that stretches all the way back to the main strip – for privacy, apparently. Claire insisted, having done an exclusive deal with *OK!* magazine for picture rights.

Straight after Christmas Day, having spoken to Claire and deciding that being in the full spotlight really wasn't for me, I gave Eddie her number, so he called Claire, and it turned out that she had left several messages with Zara for him to get in touch after seeing his fabulous presenting skills in the Carrington's pet spa. He really is a natural. Eddie was beside himself with elation, of course, and promptly signed her to be his manager. I also spoke to Claire about Eddie's misgivings over the wedding, 'the fluff', as he called it, and together we managed to scale everything back and make it really heartfelt and much more of a personal event for him and Ciaran. Although they were both ecstatic when their favourite singer agreed to be here ... *weell*, I just couldn't resist organising one little indulgence for him.

Since signing with Claire, Eddie has landed his own reality TV show called, rather aptly, *Eddie: I Do It My Way*, and a chat show that airs on Saturday evening during primetime viewing. He's already become a household name at home, and is rapidly gaining fans here in America too. And he told me in strictest confidence that he's been approached to start talks about being a judge on the next series of *X Factor*. Seems Eddie's dream came true too. We still see each other, despite his declaring Mulberry-On-Sea 'boring'; Eddie still lives there when he's back home. Says it keeps things real. Although he now has a penthouse apartment overlooking the marina with a housekeeper to ensure his walk-in wardrobe is kept pristine at all times.

Annie's life totally changed too – Ryan, the guy she met at the wrap party, wasn't Will's bodyguard at all, no: he owns a string of nightclubs around the world, so Annie spends her time travelling and partying with him in proper VIP style. They got engaged last month and are now planning an extravagant 'Big Fat Gypsy' type wedding that KCTV are going to broadcast as a four-part miniseries. Mrs Grace is now practically running *Good Housekeeping* magazine, or so she would have you think, from the way she talks about it all – she writes a monthly column covering a whole range of topics, and has just been offered a book deal from a major publisher to write her autobiography. She said was particularly made up on hearing that Radio 4 are going to serialise an audio version too, seeing as it's the Queen's channel of choice, or so she's heard.

Whereas, I'm enjoying anonymity again – my YouTube hits eventually petered out, thank God. Although, I did bump into Madison from the bus a while back, and she was excited and asked for my autograph this time, saying she loves reading my weekly fashion and beauty column. I've written about all sorts – international fashion shows, designer dresses at film premieres; I've even interviewed celebrities for my special 'what's in your wardrobe?' feature. I go to their house, flick through their walk-in dressing rooms selecting outfits, and then explain how readers can source the same look by shopping on the high street, preferably in Carrington's. I still work there, just a couple of days per week, though, as the column takes up most of my time and I'm also overseeing the new VIP shopping experience, which went crazy-busy through the summer when all the international customers berthed at Mulberry marina in their super-yachts.

Kelly's kept in touch. I do feel sorry for her, though, as Tom told me that his mother, Isabella, is refusing to have anything to do with her until she enrols on some residential progressive parenting course she's heard about.

It's held on a reservation in Arizona and is specifically for parents who've ruined their children by spoiling them to excess. Last I heard of Zara, she was rumoured to be going into the next series of *Celebrity Big Brother*, with Lawrence in tow. Apparently they got married in a secret ceremony onboard Princess Ameerah's super-yacht, but she's now suing them for seventy-three thousand pounds after Lawrence's sons wrecked three staterooms and 'accidentally' embedded a hammer in the side of the Baccarat crystal champagne bar.

Lady Gaga finishes singing, and is whisked away by her people as Eddie and Ciaran make their way down the little aisle. They're both wearing exquisitely cut white Tom Ford suits with neon blue paisley open-neck shirts. Pussy is bouncing along in front of them in a miniature version of the same outfit, and around her neck is a little satin pouch containing the wedding rings. There's a hushed 'aw, isn't she cute, so adorable' from the crowd. We kept it intimate with just Eddie's parents, beaming with pride in the front row, three of Ciaran's sisters who've flown in from Ireland (his parents gave their blessing eventually, but declined to appear on the show) and forty close friends and other family members.

Tom squeezes my hand.

'Sam would have loved this,' he whispers in my ear, making my neck tingle with desire. I still melt whenever he's close to me. We manage to keep a respectable distance at work; in fact we rarely see each other inside

Carrington's, as I'm not always there and Tom still has to travel occasionally, or go up to London for meetings. The board is thinking about opening another store, which Tom says I'll be fully involved in right from the start if I want to be.

But Tom never travels without me knowing and, to be honest, the Skype calls and late-night text conversations make our relationship utterly thrilling. That old adage of absence making the heart grow fonder is really true – the minute he arrives back in Mulberry-On-Sea we can't get enough of each other. My kitchen table has probably seen more use in the last nine months than in the entire time I've had it, which must be ten years at least.

I smile and nod at Tom, knowing how Sam really wanted to be here. Ever the romantic, she loves a good wedding, but then the twins are due any day, so flying is really out of the question. I spoke to her this morning and she was sorting through a mountain of baby stuff that Jenny from Greggs had passed on to her. Of course Nathan is beyond ecstatic and can't wait to become a dad; he's even considering Sam's suggestion of Holly and Ivy as suitable baby names, which is a relief as at one point, before we knew that the babies were definitely girls, Sam had been pondering Santa and Claus! The babies were conceived over the Christmas period and, from the minute Sam found out, she went straight to the clinic to book her pay-per-view sessions. The clinic manager was so impressed with her daily attendance record that she gave Sam a free belly-casting kit, so now Sam's 'bump' is immortalised in gold spray paint and hangs on the kitchen wall in the Cupcakes At Carrington's café, next to a picture of Alfie.

Eddie and Ciaran look so happy together as they make their commitment to each other, and I think this must be the first time ever that I and both of my best friends, Sam and Eddie, are all blissfully happy and loved-up at the same time. Dad too. I smile at the memory of New Year's Eve, when he asked if I'd mind very much if he proposed to Nancy, I gave him a hug and told him to go for it. I've stopped feeling disloyal to Mum. Sam was right, Mum died a long time ago, I can cherish her memory and still celebrate Dad's new life. One doesn't diminish the other, I know that now.

I run an index finger over the silver locket that Nancy gave me as a Christmas present. It's on a chain around my neck, which I never take off. Inside is a picture of Mum (Nancy got it from Dad) when she was young and vibrant; hair fanned around her smiling face and cornflower-blue bright eyes. In the other side is a picture of me, with a brunette bob and the same blue eyes, taken long before the hair and lash extensions, and a similar image to the one Mum would have seen of me just before she died. I love that Nancy did this; it's as if Mum's memory of me is crystallised forever and ever. Nancy wrapped the locket in tissue paper and put it in a beautiful keepsake box alongside a new bottle of Mum's perfume, YSL Opium (the glorious original one) with a silver embossed card with these words on:

Keep her close to your heart always xxx

Just thinking about it makes me well up. Nancy is such a kind and thoughtful woman, and I'm thrilled that Dad has her in his life. Me too. And I think Mum would have liked her; they might even have been friends had they known each other under different circumstances. Nancy later told me that the necklace she wears with the N on the end had belonged to her daughter, Natalie. She always keeps her close to her heart too. I know Nancy will never replace Mum, and I'll never replace Natalie, but I guess sometimes there are other ways to build a family, and Dad and Nancy are my family now.

And who knows, maybe it will be my turn to celebrate soon – Tom has been very attentive recently, and now that his parents have arrived back from their round-the-world trip, he's invited me to meet them on board their yacht. Meeting the parents – doesn't get more serious than that! I do love a happy ending. And Tom really is my *one* – what we have together is something very much, something special, and something truly amazing after all ...

To be continued ...

Hello everyone. It's me, Sam, Georgie's best friend. Sorry I couldn't make it to Vegas, I'm sure Georgie told you why – well, what she doesn't know yet is that the babies arrived this morning and as soon as Eddie and Ciaran's ceremony is over I shall be on the phone to tell her the wonderful news. And they are so beautiful. Two little cherubs. There's Holly Georgina who weighed in at 7 lb 2 oz, she came first, and then little Ivy Frances (named after my darling Dad – his middle name was Francis) who weighed 5 lb 2 oz. Obviously, Ivy needs feeding up, and that's exactly what I'll be doing. I can't wait to share my passion for baking with the babies, but until then I want to wish you all a cracking Christmas and to share some of my favourite Christmassy recipes to really help get you in the mood.

I hope you like them.

All my love Sam xxx

OK, so to get started, here's a recipe for my vanilla cupcake bottoms with butter cream icing. Mm-mmm. Alternatively, you could just nip down to the superstore on the industrial estate and buy some plain sponge cakes. Decorate them, and voilà! You're a domestic goddess and everyone will love you. Promise.

Vanilla cupcake bottoms with butter cream icing

Makes twelve little beauties.

Ingredients
115 g butter
115 g caster sugar
2 large eggs
½ teaspoon vanilla extract
115 g self-raising flour

Buttercream Icing
Ingredients
125g unsalted butter, softened
400g icing sugar
3–4 tablespoons milk
1 teaspoon vanilla extract

Preheat the oven to 170°C/325°F/gas mark 3.

Line the cupcake tin with paper cases.

In the food processor or a mixing bowl, beat the butter, sugar, eggs and vanilla extract until smooth.

Turn off the motor and add the flour. With the pulse button, or brief bursts of the wooden spoon, mix the flour in, stopping as soon as it is blended.

Divide the mixture between the paper cases, filling them two-thirds full, and bake for 15–20 minutes until golden and springy to the touch.

Cool on a rack.

For the butter cream icing, put the soft butter in a mixing bowl and beat with a wooden spoon or an electric mixer until paler in colour and very creamy.

Sift the icing sugar into the bowl.

Add the milk and vanilla and beat on a low speed until very smooth and thick.

Slather generously over the cupcakes.

Georgie's favourite, the red velvet cupcake, mm-mmm ...

Makes 12 scrumptious cakes.

Ingredients
140 g self-raising flour
2 tablespoons cocoa
½ teaspoon bicarbonate of soda
110 ml buttermilk
1 teaspoon vinegar
½ teaspoon vanilla extract
1 tablespoon red food colouring
60 g butter at room temperature
170 g caster sugar
1 large egg
Pinch of salt

To decorate
Butter cream icing (see recipe above)
Edible silver glitter

Preheat the oven to 170°C/325°F/gas mark 3. Line a 12-hole cupcake tin with cases.

In a large bowl, whisk together the flour, cocoa, bicarbonate of soda and a pinch of salt. In a mug, mix the buttermilk, vinegar, vanilla and red food colouring.

Beat the butter and sugar together until pale and fluffy. Beat in the egg a little at a time. Mix in a third of the flour mixture, followed by half the buttermilk mixture, then another third of the flour, the rest of the buttermilk and finally the last of the flour mixture.

Divide the mixture between the paper cases. Bake for 20 minutes, until risen and springy.

Cool on a rack.

To decorate, pipe on the frosting and sprinkle with edible silver glitter.

Christmas Baileys Biscotti milkshakes

Georgie raved about these after trying them at that cocktail bar in Soho, so I found a recipe. Perfect for Christmas.

Makes four cheeky cocktails.

Ingredients
6 scoops of good-quality vanilla ice cream
10 (25 ml) shots of Baileys gorgeous new Biscotti
   flavour
5 ice cubes (or just a handful)
1 glass of milk
1 can of whipped cream
Good-quality chocolate for grating

Scoop all the ingredients (except the chocolate) into a blender and give it a good blitz.

When it's totally blended, pour the milkshakes into four tall glasses.

Top with whipped cream.

Shave the chocolate over the top, using a grater.

Serve with a straw. And enjoy.

Chocolate orange cupcakes

Another favourite in the café. My customers love them and, although they can be eaten all year round, they remind me of a Terry's Chocolate Orange, which I always have at Christmas. And I know Georgie does too – fifteen to be exact, if I'm not mistaken. She was very keen to offload them on Christmas Day...

Makes 12 cupcakes.

Ingredients
120 g plain flour
140 g caster sugar
1 teaspoon baking power
40 g unsalted butter
50 g dark chocolate, melted
1 free-range egg
125 ml milk
1 orange, juice only
3 tablespoons granulated sugar

For the white chocolate and orange buttercream
125 g unsalted butter, softened
250 g icing sugar
2–3 tablespoons milk
50 g white chocolate, melted
1 orange, zest only

100 g orange chocolate for decoration

Preheat the oven to 170°C/325°F/Gas 3. Line a 12-hole muffin tin with paper cases.

Mix the flour, sugar and baking powder together in a food processor. Add the butter and pulse until combined.

Whisk the melted chocolate, egg and milk together in a jug.

Stir the chocolate mixture into the flour mixture until just combined.

Spoon the mixture into the cases and bake for 15–20 minutes, or until risen and golden-brown and a skewer inserted into the middle comes out clean. Remove from the oven and set aside to cool for 10 minutes.

Meanwhile, mix the orange juice and granulated sugar together in a bowl. Carefully pour the orange juice mixture over the warm cakes and set aside to cool completely.

For the white chocolate and orange buttercream, beat the butter in a bowl until light and fluffy. Carefully stir in the icing sugar and continue to beat for five minutes. Beat in the milk, melted white chocolate and orange zest.

Pipe the buttercream onto the cupcakes. With a sharp knife, make chocolate shavings from the orange chocolate and use them to decorate the cupcakes.

Christmas stollen slice smothered in dusty white icing sugar with an edible sprig of holly on top

Everyone loves a slice of stollen at Christmas, which is handy as this recipe makes about fifteen decent slices. It does take a couple of hours to make, but if you have the time, then it's well worth it.

INGREDIENTS
2 teaspoons dried active baking yeast
175 ml warm milk (45°C/113°F)
1 large egg
75 g caster sugar
1 ½ teaspoons salt
75 g unsalted butter, softened
350 g strong white bread flour
50g currants
50 g sultanas
50 g red glacé cherries, quartered
175 g diced mixed citrus peel
200 g marzipan

TO DECORATE
1 heaped teaspoon icing sugar
½ teaspoon ground cinnamon
Toasted flaked almonds
Edible sprig of holly available online

In a small bowl, dissolve yeast in warm milk. Let stand until creamy, about 10 minutes.

In a large bowl, combine the yeast mixture with the egg, caster sugar, salt, butter, and 260g of the bread flour; beat well. Add the remaining 90g of flour, a little at a time, stirring well after each addition.

When the dough has begun to pull together, turn it out onto a lightly floured surface, and knead in the currants, sultanas, cherries and mixed peel. Continue kneading until smooth, about 8 minutes.

Lightly oil a large bowl, place the dough in the bowl, and turn to coat with oil. Cover with a damp cloth and let rise in a warm place until doubled in volume, about 1 hour.

Lightly grease a baking tray. Deflate the dough and turn it out onto a lightly floured surface. Roll the marzipan into a rope and place it in the centre of the dough. Fold the dough over to cover it; pinch the seams together to seal.

Place the loaf, seam side down, on the prepared baking tray. Cover with a clean, damp tea towel and let rise again until doubled in volume, about 40 minutes.

Meanwhile, preheat oven to 180°C/350°F/gas mark 4.

Bake in the preheated oven for 10 minutes, then reduce the heat to 150°C/300°F/gas mark 2 and bake for a further 30–40 minutes, or until golden brown. Allow loaf to cool on a wire cooling rack. Dust the cooled loaf with icing sugar, sprinkle with cinnamon and finish with toasted flaked almonds and the sprig of edible holly.

Wishing you all a very merry Christmas xxx

Georgie Hart's Guide to a Fabulous Festive Party Season

I *love* the Christmas party season but must confess to having made more than the odd *faux pas* over the years when it comes to fashion, beauty, accessories and plain old-fashioned decorum. And seeing as I have a quiet moment here on the shop floor, I've ducked into the alcove behind my counter to put together a little guide of do's and dont's, so you don't make the same mistakes that I have!

Whether it's the work Christmas party, a romantic meal with your 'one' or Christmas cocktails followed by clubbing with friends, here are my top tips to ensure you dazzle at your do, remain breezy and poised at all times, but most of all upright! Try not to sprawl across the dance floor with Moët splattered in your hair as I did after toppling sideways off one of those slippery Moroccan mini-sofa things at the exact same moment the hottest man on earth, aka Tom, appeared before me. Epic cringe. It happened in the run-up to Valentine's Day and really wasn't the kind of 'first impression' I wanted to make, so take my advice and steer clear of all kinds of soft furnishings when you're out to impress. They're not actually for sitting on – oh *no no no* – they're traps, and best avoided at all costs!

Now, I tend to find the Work Christmas party something of a massive contradiction. I mean, they call it a party, lulling us into a false sense of security and having us believe that it's a chance to let your hair down with colleagues, in a party-like atmosphere. But in my experience, it's the most important event of the year where, no matter what, best behaviour is paramount

– so approach the free booze with moderation as you really don't want to be *that* woman who confesses to her married boss that she has saucy dreams about him every night. Also, steer clear of the random guy in a Superman onesie who latches on and won't leave you alone – who is he anyway? Does he even work in the same place as you? Before I joined Carrington's, I did a week of work experience in an office and got invited to their Christmas party – it turned out that a random guy had wandered in off the street to get stuck into the lukewarm wine and ended up trollied. That didn't stop everyone from thinking I'd allowed my freaky-friend with a superhero obsession to gatecrash, meaning my corporate career ended before it had even begun, which as it turned out was probably a blessing in disguise as I love working at Carrington's. But you may love working in an office, so waiting another year until it's somebody else's turn to make a show of themselves at the office party, is a *loooong* time, especially if you're after a promotion or even just a quiet life.

When it comes to dressing for the occasion, black or navy cigarette pants always look chic and are perfect for your Christmas party. I think they look amazing teamed with a high wedge heel and a glittery vest top or a floaty nude chiffon tunic can add a touch of luxury – there's a huge selection upstairs in Womenswear so you're bound to find one you adore. Accessory-wise, I'd go for an oversize clutch – looking over at the Ted Baker display, I can see a variety of beautiful patent ones which sit nicely under the arm and work well to bring a splash of colour to any outfit.

For make-up, I'd recommend working up your usual day face by adding a bright lipstick and, if you're looking a little jaded after a day at work, then sweeping a small amount of white eye shadow over your eyelids and tear ducts creates a wonderful wide-awake look. Finish with a good lash-extending mascara and remember the dry shampoo; I'd be lost without a can of Batiste, perfect for perking up my hair after a day on the Carrington's shop floor.

Don't forget a generous spritz of your favourite fragrance and perhaps a slick of body glitter gel across the décolletage area (collar bones to the rest of us), depending on how much effort you want to make to truly sparkle at the party, but most of all … enjoy!

PS – if you stumble into a white room, BEWARE. Chances are it isn't actually a snow room at all, and we *aaaall* know what can happen when that mistake is made … hmmm!

*

When it comes to a romantic look for the perfect candlelit Christmas dinner with your lover, think vintage, think Audrey Hepburn! Sophisticated and stylish. Swishy prom-style dresses work brilliantly and there are so many styles and patterns to choose from. Right now, I'm loving the polka-dot full skirt look with matching shrugs in our New Look concession up on the third floor. Kelly introduced it and I'm thrilled she did as it's crammed with divine pieces, trendier than our usual range (available online too). Team your dress with sexy heels or cute flats. I've just treated myself to a gorge pair of rainbow crystal pumps by Pretty Ballerinas, on the pricey side, but they really are an investment with their classic style that won't ever go out of fashion.

To create a sexy evening look I recommend smoky eyes every time, they work well with black flicky eyeliner and flattering false lashes, and teamed with clear lip-gloss, they really will keep your lover's focus firmly on your eyes across the dinner table. Finish the look with super big hair – as you know, I love my giant sleep-in Velcro rollers, but heated rollers or even a blow dry with a huge cylinder brush and plenty of hairspray can work just as well if you're short on time. A flirty handbag like the exquisite polka-dot mini Eva by Lulu Guinness, instore now, is so cute, and will look adorable in the crook of your arm to really make your outfit pop.

Top tip – DO NOT, I repeat, DO NOT drink the water in the little bowl with the slice of lemon … it isn't some kind of special lemon tea! That's all I'm saying …

*

Christmas cocktails followed by clubbing with friends is the ultimate opportunity to get your glam on and I must confess to being a teeny bit in love with the delicious playsuit by Alexander McQueen in a very on-trend seasonal berry colour that I wore on my date with Dan. It's exquisitely cut and the price tag reflects this but there are plenty of high street equivalents that in my opinion look just as good. Top tip – go a size up as a camel toe precaution. In my experience, playsuits have a tendency to cling when you've been peacocking on a bar stool for any length of time.

Team your playsuit with killer shoes; I love my selection of New Look heels, even if Eddie thinks they're trashy. They're reasonably priced and come in such a variety of colours that I can always find a pair to match my mood and outfit. I particularly like this year's festive specials – the raspberry crystal stacked heels are truly spectacular and will certainly make you sparkle on the dance floor.

I *adore* glittery eye shadow and Barry M Dazzle Dust comes in ninety colours so there's bound to be one you'll love too – my favourite is number 78, ~~Kingfisher,~~ which really suits my blue eyes and brunette hair whereas Sam, being blonde, looks fabulous in Electric Blue, number 22. To compliment the look, go for gloss on lips and don't forget the falsies: it's well worth investing in lash extensions, but if you don't want a permanent fixture then take a look inside the Carrington's Beauty Department where you'll find a huge range of false lashes. I promise you, there's a guaranteed no 'blow-up doll danger' unless you're into that, in which case I'd suggest going for neon blue lashes with diamante tips.

Wear your hair in a big high bun – great for reducing the heat when you're getting a groove on out on the dance floor, and a generous-sized coin purse works well for carrying those essentials … Nobody wants to be dragging a handbag around a nightclub. Big mistake. Huge. Sam managed to get the buckle on the long strap of her cross-body bag caught in my hair one time. Yep, that's right – I ended up practically back-flipping my way to the Ladies' room. Double cringe.

So that's all folks. Go dazzle like the star you are, and remember: no soft furnishings, white rooms, special lemon tea or cross-body bags with buckles.

Merry Christmas everyone and see you all in the New Year when I'll be back to share my summer with you!

Lots of love
Georgie xx

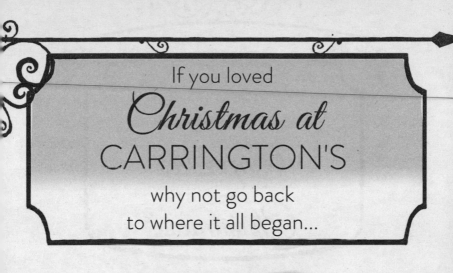

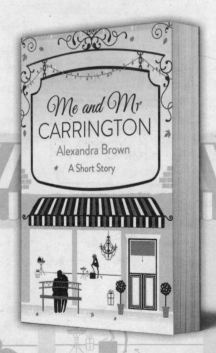

KEEP UP TO DATE WITH ALEXANDRA BROWN

Log on to **www.alexandrabrown.co.uk**
for details of all Alex's books and her latest news.

You can also join Alex on Facebook and Twitter for photos,
competitions and event details. Plus, you'll get to read
exclusive extracts before the books hit the shops.

f /AlexandraBrownAuthor

🐦 @AlexBrownBooks

The W6 Book Café

Do you want to hear more from your **favourite authors**?

Be the first to know about **competitions** and read **exclusive extracts** before the books are even in the shops?

Keep up with HarperFiction's latest releases at **The W6 Book Café!**

 Find us on Facebook **W6BookCafe**

 Follow us on Twitter **@W6BookCafe**